THIEFCATCHER

S. G. KARAM

CHYMIST PRESS

AZURE SEA
ZARAKAR
NYANDORO
MBARARA
SUMBAWA
STONEREACH
ZA'ATHUM SEA
ASHFALL

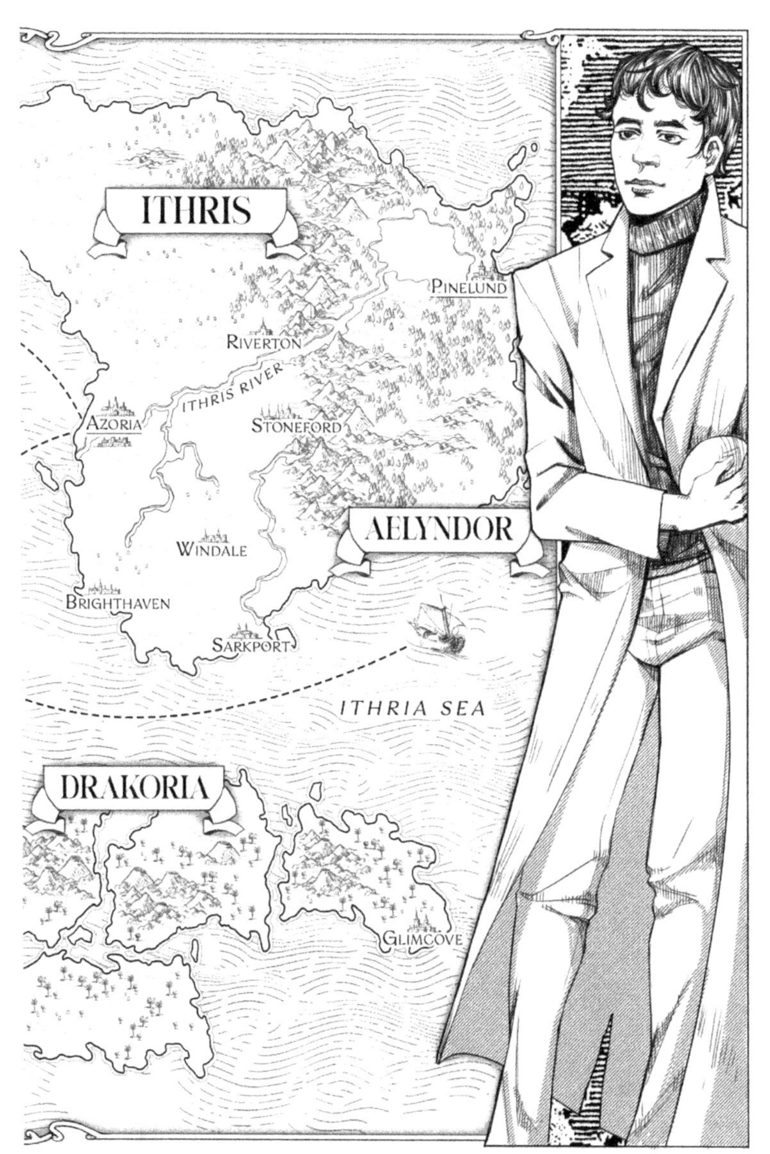

ITHRIS
PINELUND
RIVERTON
ITHRIS RIVER
AZORIA
STONEFORD
AELYNDOR
WINDALE
BRIGHTHAVEN
SARKPORT
ITHRIA SEA
DRAKORIA
GLIMCOVE

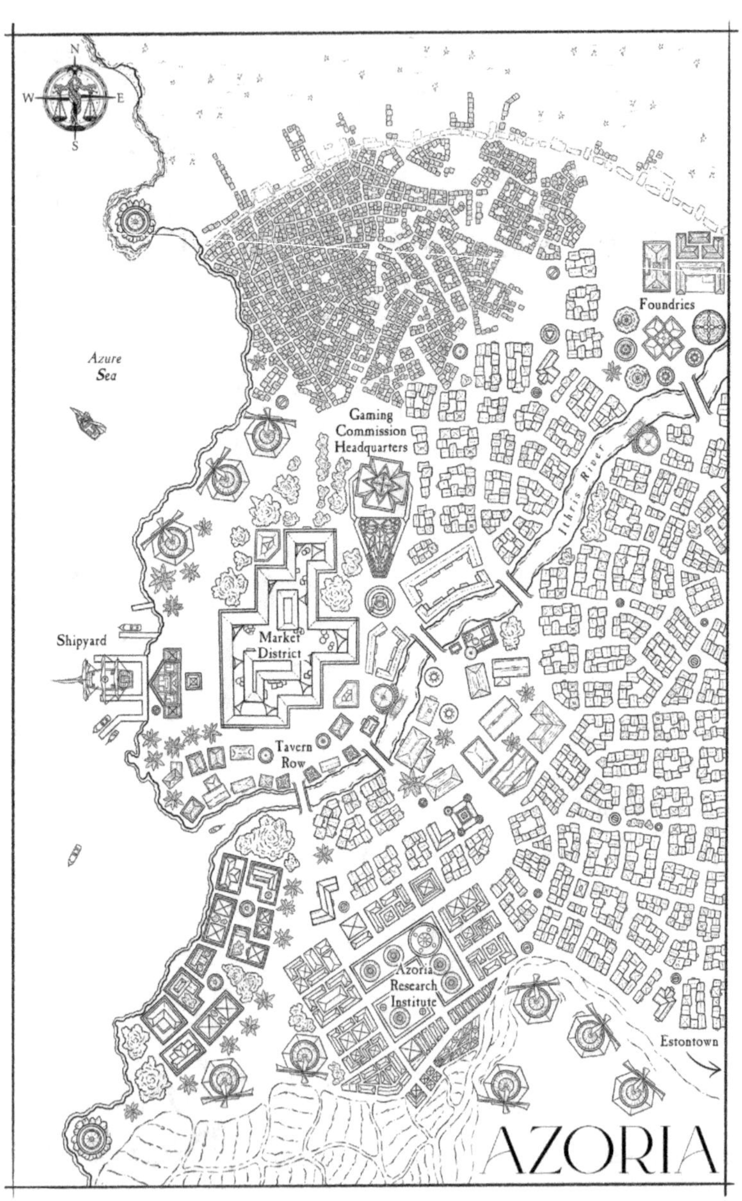

N
W
E
S
Azure
Sea
Foundries
Gaming
Commission
Headquarters
Ithris River
Shipyard
Market
District
Tavern
Row
Azoria
Research
Institute
Estontown
AZORIA

AZORIA STAR

VOL. 19, NO.192 ✳ PAPER OF THE PEOPLE ✳ 14 ILLI 31AD

BREAKING NEWS

COMMISSION ISSUES UNPRECEDENTED ONE-YEAR MORATORIUM ON SANCTIONED THIEVING

AZORIA—In a sweeping and decisive first act, the Ithris Gaming Commission, under the new leadership of Interim Chairwoman Vivienne Dragunova, has issued an immediate, city-wide moratorium on all sanctioned thieving activities. The decree, effective at sunrise this morning, suspends the core tenets of the Sanctioned Heists Act for a period of no less than one year.

The move comes amidst a period of profound uncertainty for Azoria, following the shocking revelation of former Chairman Cecil Thume's criminal enterprises and his subsequent arrest. While the city has largely praised the efforts of

> ### "CRITICAL NEED FOR STABILITY" SAYS DRAGUNOVA

those who brought Thume's corruption to light, the resulting power vacuum has left many citizens and business owners concerned about the potential for escalating chaos.

"Azoria needs a moment to breathe," Chairwoman Dragunova stated in an exclusive address from the Commission headquarters. "The events of the past weeks have shaken the very foundations of our city. The laws that were meant to provide structure and balance were exploited from the very top. We cannot simply continue with business as usual while the rulebook is so fundamentally broken."

CONTINUED IN APPENDIX

UNFINISHED BUSINESS

1

Jax was drunk again.

That prison grog was no joke. Thick, sour, the kind that settled deep in the belly and burned like a dynamo reactor on the way down.

Swaying on his feet, Jax clutched the iron bars of his cell. Rancid sweat seeped from his pores despite the chill of the stone walls.

The place stank of piss, mold, and stale bodies. His cot sagged in the corner, the straw stuffing long since rotted through, and his gut churned with every movement. But after the commotion he'd caused in the Market, no one was giving him any sympathy.

The guards had laughed when they threw him in here, something about teaching the moron a lesson. Jax hadn't really been listening. Too much booze.

A murmur started down the row of cells, prisoners whispering to each other. Bootsteps echoed faintly down the hall.

Jax pressed his forehead against the cool iron, hoping it would stop the spinning. It didn't. But he needed the cold. His knuckles were still raw from the fight, the one that put him back in here.

He didn't remember the details, just the flash of anger—the merchant's sneer, the jab about Jax being too fat for such high-quality clothing. The punch had come without thinking, but it landed well enough to break the stall and get him thrown back into Azoria's holding cells. Again.

"Should've just walked away," he muttered.

That's what he always did, wasn't it?

The sound of boots on stone echoed closer. Jax's grip tightened on the bars.

"Harley!" Jax yelled down the hall with a thick slur. "Don't think I don't know what day it is. You letting me outta here or what?"

The scrawny guard with a crooked nose appeared at his cell.

"Thought you'd still be passed out, Crasher," Harley said, crossing his arms.

Jax scowled, his vision still blurry from the drink. "Just open the damn door."

Harley shook his head. "Why do you even bother?" He took a step closer. "You know you're just gonna end up back in here."

Jax's grip on the bars flexed. He wanted to break something again, but it'd be too easy. Stupid. That's what got him here in the first place.

"I'm done, Harley," Jax growled, the words coming out thick.

Harley's smirk dropped. "Yeah," he said, eyeing Jax with disgust. "You sure as hells are."

A sharp whistle from the far end of the hall snapped Harley's attention away. Another guard, this one bigger and less amused, waved him over. Harley hesitated, gave Jax a parting sneer, then turned and walked off.

Jax let out a long breath, slumping against the bars. His hands throbbed from the tension. There was a time he would've thrown Harley across the room and forged his own path to escape.

But those days felt distant. The rush from the brawls, the thrill of the score—it was all fading. Replaced with something dull and heavy.

It wasn't his fault. What else was he supposed to do? That bitch Vivienne had banned thieving in Azoria for a year. He was a bruiser. Nothing to do but fight.

The whispers along the row picked up again. Prisoners shifting, watching. Always watching. It made Jax feel like an animal in a cage.

"Picking fights with my guards, Jackson?" The voice was smooth, controlled. Not a trace of mockery in it, but the calm commanding tone grated on him all the same.

Jax grunted and pushed himself off the bars. "Just give me the lecture, Dren, then let me out of here," he muttered, rubbing the back of his neck.

Dren's boots stopped just outside the cell. The man was dressed in the standard officer's garb—black coat, crisp collar, and that damn silver badge pinned to his chest. The authority in that badge made Jax itch.

"Lecture?" Dren said. He rested a hand on the hilt of his club, though Jax knew it was more habit than threat. "Nah. I thought I'd skip the speech this time."

Jax raised an eyebrow. "Yeah? What's the catch?"

"No catch." Dren's eyes flicked over Jax, sizing him up like always. "Though I'd say you've had a rough couple of months. This isn't the first stall you've broken, and it won't be the last unless something changes."

"Thought you said there wasn't gonna be a speech."

"Yeah, well... I lied," Dren smirked. "But at least I didn't beat up a merchant."

Jax snorted. "I didn't mean to hurt him. The rat wouldn't keep his mouth shut."

"Always with the excuses, Jax. They haven't gotten you very far, have they?"

Jax said nothing. His glare burned a hole in the stone floor. That familiar rage, simmering below the surface, was getting harder to control these days. The booze wasn't enough. The fights weren't enough. None of it was.

Dren shifted his weight. "Okay, then. You're getting released later today. Your buddy Liora's coming to get you."

He paused, but the big man just grunted, unimpressed.

"At least she's done some good with her life," Dren sighed. "Get your head straight. Or next time, you might not make it out again."

Jax's fingers curled into a fist before he realized he was doing it. "You threatening me now?"

The guard shook his head. "I've seen this before." He tapped the bars once. "Big men with bigger demons. You keep doing this, and one day, there won't be anything left."

Jax didn't answer. Because what the hells was he supposed to say to that?

Dren held his gaze a moment longer, then turned and walked off. His boots echoed against the stone floor, fading into the distance.

Jax flexed his fingers, the ache creeping up his wrists. Big men with bigger demons.

What the hells did Dren know about it?

For a long moment, Jax stood still, the weight of the silence pressing in around him. Liora was coming. Good old Liora.

But she'd have that same look. Half pity, half disappointment. He didn't need that. Jax had plenty of both on his own.

He slumped onto the cot, the springs groaning under his weight. His fists still ached, but the anger was fading. What was left felt even worse.

He lay back, staring at the cracked ceiling, the voices in the cells nearby fading into background noise. Tonight, he'd be out.

Out of one prison, and into another.

Liora stretched luxuriously, feeling the early sun's warmth on her face. The soft rustle of the morning breeze drifted through the open window, carrying the unmistakable aroma of fresh bread from the baker two streets over.

She sighed contentedly. The city of Azoria was far from perfect, especially these days. But mornings like this made it feel a little more magical.

Rolling onto her side, Liora's eyes fell on Shelle. Still sound asleep. One arm flung dramatically across the bed, her hair a wild tangle of dark streaky curls spread across the pillow. A faint snore escaped from her lips—tiny, delicate, like the softest of purrs.

Liora smiled. Shelle always claimed she didn't snore, but Liora had long since stopped arguing.

Watching her now, tangled in the sheets, she decided the tiny snores added to her charm. And charm was something Shelle had plenty of when she was awake, even if she was a hurricane of energy that never stopped moving.

Not wanting to disturb the peaceful scene, Liora slowly swung her legs off the bed and padded across the floor, careful not to step on the piles of half-finished projects that littered their shared condo. A mix of dynamo schematics, disassembled gadgets, and scribbled notes covered nearly every available surface.

The place looked like a storm had hit it. But that storm had a name, and its name was Liora Banz.

She stifled a laugh as she picked her way past a copper coil and an unfinished contraption that had been buzzing the night before. Like many of her late-night inspirations, it had yet to reach the "practical" stage.

Today was a big day, though. Huge. The Market District Monorail Line was finally opening—another step forward in the city's expansion. Liora had been overseeing the monorail's development for months now, watching it stretch from Estontown all the way to the Azoria Research Institute.

The new line, connecting the Institute to the bustling Market District, was her latest achievement. Sure, the system had been operational for a couple of months, but each new branch felt like a victory. More people riding, more lives made easier.

She grinned to herself, picturing the excitement at the grand opening today. There was always a mix of pride and amusement when people referred to it as "Liora's Monorail." Of course, it wasn't just hers—there were plenty of engineers and workers who had helped bring the project to life. But hearing her name attached to something that moved the entire city?

That felt pretty damn good.

A soft murmur from the bed interrupted her thoughts. Liora glanced back to see Shelle stirring, one arm lazily searching for the warmth she'd left behind.

"Where are you sneaking off to?" Shelle mumbled, voice thick with sleep.

Liora smiled and leaned against the windowsill, arms crossed. "Sneaking? I'm being productive. You know, doing that thing where I get out of bed before noon."

Shelle groaned, rolling over to squint at her. "Monorail stuff again?"

The monorail had taken up every waking moment for months. And it was a victory—mostly. She still hated the fact that Vivienne's stamp was on it too. Building a city-wide transportation system required way more money than Liora could cough up.

But that's how Azoria worked. You either fought the system or you found a way to make it work for you. And Liora was good at making things work.

"Yes, monorail stuff," she said. "What else is there?"

Shelle's only response was another half-hearted groan as she flopped back onto her pillow, dragging the covers up to her chin. "Mmm... sounds like a sorry reason to get up so early."

Liora rolled her eyes, but she couldn't help the grin that tugged at her lips. Shelle had her own way of doing things—slow mornings, late nights, and the kind of killer wit that could cut through steel. She'd spent most of yesterday rearranging the mess of parts scattered across their apartment, muttering under her breath about Liora's creative chaos.

Not that it had made much of a difference. For every gadget or gizmo she put away, Liora needed to pull two more back out.

"You should come with me," Liora offered, rummaging through a stack of papers that had fallen off her desk. "Catch a ride on the new line. See the fruits of my genius in action."

Opening one eye, Shelle gave a dramatic yawn, and burrowed deeper into the blankets.

"Come on," Liora teased, tossing a crumpled schematic toward the bed. It landed on Shelle's head and nested in her hair. "You know you want to see people's faces when they whiz over the river."

Shelle flung the paper off her head, still not bothering to fully emerge from her cocoon. "I've seen your trinkets, darling. Let's hope they make it over the river."

Liora laughed, bending down to sift through a pile of sketches on the floor. "Don't be so dramatic. We've only had two—okay, three—minor accidents. And no one's complained about the sparks in weeks."

Shelle chuckled. "I'm sure the city appreciates not being blown to bits."

"They'll thank me when they're getting from one end of the city to the other in half the time."

Her grin widened as she found what she was looking for—a blueprint she'd been tweaking the night before, outlining some adjustments for the next line. "Besides, if I'm not there, who's going to fix it when the dignitaries inevitably break something?"

"And here I thought I was being dramatic for suggesting something could go wrong."

Liora shrugged, still scanning the blueprint. "What can I say? Even genius has its limits."

A deep groan came from the other side of the bed. Aric Myrim stirred, one arm flopping out from under the blanket, his fingers brushing the floor as he mumbled something further into the pillow.

Shelle glanced over with amusement. "How does he sleep through all of our noise?"

Liora didn't bother looking up. "He doesn't. He's just pretending. Aren't you, Aric?"

Myrim let out another long, dramatic groan, turning his head enough to reveal a bleary eye. "I'm... conserving energy. It's a strategy."

"Sure it is," Shelle said, smirking as she ran her hand through his thick hair. "Just like your strategy of commandeering the entire bed."

"I don't take *all* of it," he muttered, eyes half-closed again. "Most of it."

Liora chuckled, folding the blueprint in half and tucking it under her arm. "Well, if you want to keep off the couch, you might want to get up. I've decided to expect the full support of my two favorite people."

Myrim's hand twitched as he dragged it back under the covers. "We can support you from here."

Shelle snorted. "And miss her showing off in front of the crowd?"

"I hate it when you team up on me," Myrim grumbled, rolling onto his back, blinking up at the ceiling as if the effort required all of his remaining willpower. "Fine. But if I fall asleep in the middle of one of your monorail speeches, I'm blaming both of you."

She glanced at the folded blueprint in her hand. A year ago, her world had been all about breaking into places, not building them. Now, the monorail stretched across the city. It was proof that things could change. That she had changed.

And yet, Jax was still behind bars. Lars and Trin weren't doing anything with their lives. And her old, stalwart crewmate Keer was hells knew where commandeering a galleon on the Azure Sea.

Not everything had changed for the best. Had she?

Liora sighed. That would have to wait. "It'll be quick," she said, pulling on her jacket. "Promise. Then we've got pastries to pick up, and I'm off to prison to pick up Jax right after that."

Myrim let out a long sigh, dragging himself into a sitting position, his hair falling in every direction. "So I'm there for pastry duty?"

Pushing the covers off her legs, Shelle stretched luxuriously. "That's right. And I'm there to nod and look impressed. Liora's the brains of this operation. We're her arm candy."

Liora laughed as she moved toward the door. "Fifteen minutes, you two. Get dressed or I'm dragging you both out in whatever you are or aren't wearing."

Myrim rubbed his eyes, glancing sideways at Shelle. "Guess that means we've got... what, fourteen and a half minutes left?"

"Close enough," Shelle said, flopping back onto the bed and pulling up the covers.

Liora stood on the platform, adjusting the cuff of her coat as the dynamo machinery of the monorail hummed beneath her boots. Twelve tons of dynamo-powered engineering, stretching sleek and perfect against the morning skyline. Her work, her design. Her fingerprints on every copper wire.

And yet, the banners were Vivienne's.

They fluttered over the crowd, her sigil stamped on every damn one.

As if this whole thing had been her idea. As if she had designed the circuits, calculated the weight distribution, crawled through half-finished tunnels to make sure the power flow wouldn't fry some poor bastard the first time the thing ran.

Liora calmed her mind, willing herself to focus on the platform below. It was a big day. The Market District Monorail Line had been operational for a couple of months now, but today marked the grand opening of its new expansion—a direct connection from the Azoria Research Institute to the heart of the city.

People packed the station, murmuring, shifting. Some craned their necks toward the track, waiting to see the first official run. Others watched the stage, where officials stood in a tight, self-important cluster behind Liora and Vivienne, waiting to make their speeches.

Liora glanced up at the towering monorail line and allowed herself a small grin.

They had no idea how much improvising went into keeping this thing running.

It hadn't been perfect. There had been failures. More than a few angry messages from city regulators. But the thing worked.

And soon, kids who usually had to walk miles to find a job, who had to scrounge in alleys for discarded parts, just so they could hunch in silence over a broken dynamo coil praying for a miracle—as she once did—they'd have a shot at something better.

That made working with Vivienne worth it, right? No matter how much that snake of a woman—

"Marvelous, isn't it?"

Liora didn't flinch at the voice, but her eyes narrowed.

"Oh hi, Vivienne," Liora said without turning. "I figured you'd be too busy stirring the pot elsewhere."

Vivienne laughed lightly, as if they were simply two old friends sharing pleasantries. "Oh, come now, Liora. You act as though I contributed nothing to this."

Liora flicked a glance toward the banners. Vivienne's sigil, not hers.

"Sure. You paid for it," she said flatly.

Vivienne arched a delicate brow. "And you built it. That makes us partners, does it not?"

Liora shrugged. "Right. Like how a forge partners with a blacksmith. You catch on fire. I do all the actual work."

Vivienne's lips curled slightly. "And yet, here we are. Side by side."

A voice rang out from the stage, calling them forward.

The ingratiating woman smiled wider. "Shall we?"

Liora exhaled loudly, forcing her shoulders back.

She would stand on that stage, she would smile for the crowd, and she would pretend that none of this grated on her.

Because today wasn't about Vivienne Dragunova. Or the banners. Or the politics.

It was about proving that the city could move forward. Even if some people insisted on pulling it backward.

A loud chime rang out over the square. It was time.

Liora stepped up to the podium, adjusting the dynamo microphone as the murmur of the crowd quieted. The heat of the unseasonably warm sun beat down on her, and the hum of the monorail vibrated through the stage beneath her feet. Hundreds of faces stared up at her—officials, dignitaries, workers, common folk.

A year ago, Liora had stood in the shadows, working in secret, designing escape routes and diversions for the best damn heists Azoria had ever seen.

Now, she was front and center. An architect? Or a mouthpiece?

Oh yeah, the speech. Time to get talking. It had been meticulously prepared by the Gaming Commission. A tribute to Azoria's might following Thume's ousting and Vivienne's ascension.

Vivienne, Vivienne, Vivienne.

With a sigh, Liora spoke.

"This city has always been built by those who dare to think differently."

Those like herself. Like Jax, Trin, Keer, and Lars. The ones who actually took Thume down last year. What would that Liora think of this one, doing Vivienne's bidding?

"Azoria thrives because of its ingenuity, its ambition, and the people who refuse to let barriers stop them. This city isn't built on luck or fortune—it's built on exchange. Giving and taking. Not one at the expense of the other, but in balance. Theft is not an act of taking. It is boldness. It is the courage to claim what you are willing to fight for. The strength to test the world and see if it holds."

That's who she was. A thief. Not a lackey.

Of course, she hadn't stolen anything in a year, not with the ban. But you know, maybe it wouldn't hurt to steal a little limelight.

"Because without risk," Liora continued, "there's no progress. Without ambition, there's no innovation. And without the freedom to challenge those who hoard power, we might as well be living under a tyrant."

She felt Vivienne's eyes boring into her as the speech drifted off script. Liora knew Vivienne would be waiting for her to step back in line.

Liora did not oblige.

"This monorail was made possible because of that balance. Because of the ones who dared to take. The ones who pushed the boundaries, broke the rules, and proved that ingenuity will always find a way. The ones who refuse to accept that something is impossible."

Liora beamed as she took the leap. "A year ago, a brilliant man you all know—Lars Harrow, the most accomplished thief in Azoria—trusted me to build an escape route while we fought to save this city. And today, you're all looking at the results of it."

A murmur rippled through the gathered officials. Myrim and Shelle, standing near the front, stiffened. Shelle's lips were parted slightly, eyes unreadable. Myrim, though... his already stiff posture went a fraction too rigid.

"Our city was built by those who take chances," Liora said, lifting her chin. "People like Lars Harrow. And with every step forward, we make Azoria better. Not just for the elite, not just for those in power, but for everyone. Thank you."

Applause erupted—maybe not from the stiff-backed officials, but from the workers, the common folk, the ones who would actually ride this thing.

Vivienne clapped as well. Slowly. Measured. Like a queen entertaining the antics of a court jester.

Liora stepped back from the podium, letting the applause fade, her pulse hammering in her ears.

Vivienne moved forward, smooth as ever, taking the stage.

She smiled. Vivienne adjusted the microphone, her gloved fingers precise, her smile a mask of patience.

"Liora Banz, everyone."

The applause, still lingering, faded slightly. Vivienne let the crowd settle before continuing.

"Yes, Azoria has always been a city of ambition," she said smoothly, her voice carrying over the crowd with calculated warmth. "A city built by those willing to push beyond the rules, beyond expectations. And what greater example of that spirit than the work we see before us today?"

She gestured to the monorail behind her, the monorail Liora built, its sleek frame gleaming in the sun.

"Make no mistake," Vivienne continued, her eyes flicking toward the gathered officials, "this is a testament to the ingenuity of our city's finest minds. To the planners, the financiers who have dedicated themselves to making Azoria not only a place of innovation, but stability. Strength. Security."

Vivienne glanced at Liora. "And what is strength, if not the wisdom to shape the forces around us? To take that ambition and direct it toward something greater?"

From the way a few council members nodded slightly, how the applause shifted from the working class to the officials, Vivienne's message was finding its intended audience.

"This monorail, made possible by the Ithris Gaming Commission, is a step forward. Not only for transit, but for

Azoria itself." She raised her hand toward the cityscape behind her. "A promise that no matter how quickly this city moves, we will always guide it forward. Together."

The applause this time was full, unified.

Vivienne stepped away from the podium. She nodded graciously, accepting murmured congratulations from city officials, her gloved hand shaking a few well-placed palms.

Liora pushed her glasses up, then sighed as she hopped off of the dais to where the crowd was milling about. A few engineers and construction workers came to shake her hand and offer their thanks.

That was nice. They had been such a huge part of this project. She hoped they felt accomplished.

Wandering further into the crowd, she found Myrim and Shelle.

Shelle shot Liora a sidelong glance, one that was equal parts exasperation and reluctant admiration. Myrim, ever the soldier, kept his face blank, but the way his eye twitched said enough.

"Oh, don't look at me like that," Liora said. "I thought it was a damn good speech."

Shelle rolled her eyes, muttering something under her breath. Myrim simply folded his arms, eyes tracking Vivienne as she moved through the crowd.

"She won, you know." His voice was quiet.

Liora scoffed. "Vivienne always wins."

A low laugh escaped Shelle as she shook her head. "And yet, you just had to throw Lars's name in there, didn't you?"

Liora grinned. "What's a public event without a little action?"

Shelle groaned, but the corner of her lips twitched. Myrim didn't smile.

Liora watched as Vivienne neared the station's exit, officials falling into place around her like well-trained dogs. Even after all this, after all her little victories, this was still Vivienne's city.

"Well, I think it went about as well as expected. I'm a thief, not a politician."

Sighing, Myrim shook his head. "So, heading off to prison?"

"Been there, done that," Liora laughed. "Thank the hells a dashing man saved me." She stood on her tiptoes and kissed him warmly. "But yes, I need to pick Jax up before he does something stupid."

Shelle grimaced. "Oh, it's way too late for that from what I've heard."

The prison district always smelled like wet pavement.

Liora adjusted the bag of pastries under her arm, shifting her grip as she walked up the worn path leading to Azoria's holding cells. The heavy iron gates stood ahead, flanked by guards in dark blue coats.

She had been here too many times.

With a sigh, Liora popped the last bite of a sticky bun into her mouth as she slowed her pace. It would be interesting to see where Jax's head was. This time.

He wouldn't be happy. That much was certain.

Jax had been spiraling for months, drinking too much, fighting too much, like a storm waiting to tear itself apart. She'd tried to get through to him, but every time, he'd laughed it off, promised he had it under control. But then he'd land back here again.

Her boots clicked against the cobblestone as she passed by a cluster of merchants setting up near the prison walls, their stalls stacked with fried skewers and hand pies for the officers and visitors alike. A few looked at her with recognition, but no one spoke.

The weight of the place pressed down on her.

Walls, thick with age, swallowed sound. The barred windows above were too narrow for anything but a sliver of sky, the stone beneath them stained with years of rain and rust. She remembered being behind those walls herself once, the damp air, the stink of sweat and mold.

Her brow furrowed at the memory. She'd made her escape. But Jax? Jax kept coming back.

Liora tightened her grip on the bag. Today was different. Today, the ban was over.

Jax could be a thief again. No more excuses.

She stepped up to the gates, flashing a quick smile at the nearest guard.

"Morning, Chesper," she said, her voice light, easy. "I'm here for my idiot."

The guard sighed, rubbing his temple. "Plenty of those in here. You'll have to be more specific, Miss Banz."

Liora grinned. "You know the one."

Chesper muttered something and waved her inside. She strode through, shaking the lingering cold from her limbs.

The air changed instantly. Stiller. Thicker.

Liora tried to relax, ignoring the way her muscles tensed out of habit. She wasn't the one locked up this time.

She pushed open the heavy iron doors of the prison, the familiar chill of the stone walls wrapping around her as she stepped inside. The front hall was quieter than usual, the echo of her footsteps bouncing off the vaulted ceiling. She made her way toward the front desk, her small bag of treats swinging by her side.

Behind the desk sat an orderly with wild hair barely contained by regulation pins. Liora recognized that slouch anywhere—her old cellmate Zara, pretending to organize papers while likely daydreaming about her next romantic conquest.

"Morning, sunshine," Liora said, plopping her elbows on the counter hard enough to make the inkwell jump. Her glasses slid down her nose again.

Zara's face lit up. "Liora Banz, you magnificent disaster. Here for your overgrown puppy?"

"One Jax Crasher, slightly dented, hopefully not too bruised." Liora drummed her fingers on the wood. "How bad was it this time?"

"Oh, the usual. Property damage, disturbing the peace, being aggressively large in public." Zara leaned forward, voice dropping to gossip levels. "But really, between you and me, I think Lieutenant Dren has had it with him this time."

Oh boy. Liora would likely be in for an earful then.

Zara's expression shifted to something suspiciously smug.

"Well anyways," Liora said, changing the subject, "are you still letting that baker boy knead your—"

"Ancient history!" Zara cut her off with a laugh. "I've moved on to bigger things. Much bigger."

The way she said it made Liora's curiosity itch. She hated not knowing things. "Define 'bigger.'"

Zara practically vibrated with the need to share. "Fan mail. From ten different towns."

"Fan mail?" Liora's brain screeched to a halt. "How could you get fans in prison?"

"My writing!" Zara beamed. "My periodical on prison relationships is basically famous now. 'Love Behind Bars.'"

Liora stared. Processed. Stared some more. "You're writing relationship advice. For criminals."

"For their partners," Zara corrected, shuffling her definitely-not-organized papers. "How to keep the spark alive when your beloved's behind stone walls. Conjugal visit etiquette. Creative letter writing. That sort of thing."

"That's..." Brilliant? Insane? Liora's brain couldn't pick just one. "Actually genius. Hells, half of Lowtown's got someone locked up at any given time."

"Exactly! And they're all desperate for advice. Last week I got a letter from some noble's wife asking how to smuggle in—"

Heavy boots in the corridor. Liora's hand went automatically to the pastry bag. It wasn't a weapon, but she'd improvised with worse. Then she recognized the measured tread and relaxed. Mostly.

Lieutenant Dren appeared in the doorway. Behind him, Jax filled the rest of the frame, sporting a spectacular black eye and his signature 'I-regret-nothing' grin.

Liora blinked, her eyes widening at the sight. She never got used to seeing her fierce giant like this.

His bulk was still there, but most of it had gone soft. His muscles, once hard as iron, had turned to flab. His belly strained against the fabric of his shirt, and his face, usually chiseled yet joyous, was rounder now, red and puffy.

"Liora!" Jax bellowed, his voice echoing through the stone walls. "There you are! Got yourself all gussied up to come fetch me, huh?"

The routine shock of seeing him hadn't worn off yet, but she forced a grin. "Someone's gotta do it. You've been keeping these folks far too busy."

Jax laughed, a booming, deep sound that filled the room, but it lacked the edge of strength it used to have. He swayed, blinking against the harsh hall light like it physically pained him to stay upright.

"Miss Banz," Lieutenant Dren said. "If I might have a word?"

Yep. Time for that earful.

"Sure thing." She shuffled over to where Dren was standing, back a little ways from Jax. "Zara, don't let me leave without saying goodbye."

Dren walked up beside Liora, his voice quiet enough so only she could hear. "He's a good man, Liora. You know that. But… hells, he's getting worse every time I see him."

His gaze shifted to where Jax was now clumsily flirting with Zara, the man's words slurring slightly, eyes unfocused. Dren sighed, concern deepening on his face.

"I'm tired of watching Jax tear himself down more and more with every visit. It's wearing him thin. He used to have a fire in him. Hells, he was my favorite thief," the man said. "But now he's barely holding on."

Liora's throat went tight. She could see it too. How could she not?

The tears came before she could stop them, hot and angry. She hated crying. Hated that her stupid body betrayed her when her brain needed to be working on solutions.

Dren shifted his weight, that particular brand of uncomfortable that meant he was about to say something she didn't want to hear. "I've seen this before. The strong ones, the ones who seem untouchable—they fall the hardest when their demons catch up."

Demons. Such a tidy word for whatever was eating Jax alive from the inside. Liora's fingers found a loose thread on her sleeve, picked at it.

"He's getting worse," she said. There was no point pretending. "The drinking, the fights. He won't talk to me about—" She stopped. Started again. "I can't fix what he won't let me see."

"Some things can't be fixed." Dren's voice had gone soft. "Just… managed. But he's running out of chances, Liora. Next time might be the last time."

The words hit like cold water. Next time. Last time. She watched Jax stumble over his own feet, catch himself on the wall, grin like he'd meant to do it. Her bruiser. Her protector. Her disaster.

"I know," she whispered, hating how small her voice sounded.

Dren's hand landed on her shoulder, solid and surprisingly gentle. "Those demons don't let go once they've got their claws in. Whatever you've got in mind, do it soon."

She nodded, not trusting her voice. Her brain was already spinning—plans and contingencies and desperate measures. Because that's what she did. She solved impossible problems. Built things that shouldn't work. Fixed what couldn't be fixed.

She had to. The alternative was unthinkable.

"Thanks," she managed, swiping at her eyes with her sleeve. "For caring about Jax."

Dren nodded and turned to go, leaving Liora with her pastries and her giant and the weight of promises she didn't know how to keep.

Liora turned and blinked away the tears in her eyes. "Jax! You ready to go?"

Jax straightened up—well, as much as he could—his face lighting up with a goofy grin. "Oh, yeah, yeah! I was just tellin' Zana here—"

"Zara," Zara interrupted.

"—Zara," Jax corrected, barely catching himself, "that I'd love to take her out for dinner sometime, but, uh, I'm broke… And not….. well, sorry about that."

He trailed off, his expression crumbling as he started to mumble something incoherent, the bravado falling apart as he seemed to sink into a blubbery mess.

Liora rolled her eyes, walking up to him and patting his arm. "We'll figure it out, big guy. But for now, how about a sticky bun to cheer you up?"

Jax's eyes lit up at the mention of food, his mood shifting as quickly as it had crumbled. "Sticky buns?"

Liora nodded, handing him the small bag. "I saved some for you."

Without missing a beat, Jax ripped the bag open and began stuffing his face with one of the sweet rolls, crumbs already falling down his shirt as he devoured it. Liora shook her head.

"Come on, let's get out of here," she said, glancing over at Zara. "Thanks for putting up with him. I'll see you around."

Zara smirked, leaning back in her chair. "Take care, Liora. Come say hi again sometime."

Hopefully not. Liora squeaked a quick goodbye, then tugged on Jax's arm, guiding him toward the exit as he continued stuffing his face.

The heavy doors of the prison swung shut behind them as they stepped back into the bright morning light.

The sun cast a warm glow over Liora and her favorite convict, and highlighted the mix of old brick buildings and sleeker, newer structures. Liora walked briskly beside Jax, her short legs moving double-time to keep pace with his long strides. Or at least, what used to be long strides. Now, Jax lumbered more than walked, his broad shoulders slumped, eyes fixed on the ground ahead.

They had left the prison behind, its iron gates and looming walls fading into the distance. Ahead, the city's skyline unfolded—a tapestry of windmills turning lazily against the blue sky, their blades catching the sunlight. In the distance, the monorail glinted as it zipped along its elevated track, the trams humming smoothly thanks to Liora's handiwork.

The sound momentarily drowned out the clamor of the streets. Pedestrians paused to watch it pass, some pointing and marveling at the sight. Liora allowed herself a small smile of pride.

"Looks like the monorail's a hit," she remarked, glancing at the sleek carriages. "Can't go anywhere without seeing it in action."

Jax grunted in response, his attention somewhere far away. He tore off another piece of his sweet roll and stuffed it into his mouth, crumbs catching in his unkempt beard.

They passed the Gaming Commission headquarters, an imposing building of glass and steel that seemed to glare down at them. Liora felt a familiar knot tighten in her stomach but shook it off. No point dwelling on that now.

"So," she said, trying to inject some cheer into her voice, "it's a beautiful day. Much better than being cooped up, don't you think?"

Jax shrugged. "Suppose so."

Liora pressed on. "I've been keeping busy. The new Market District line opened today. Huge success. People are really starting to see the benefits."

"Good for them."

She shot him a sidelong glance. His once-muscular frame was now softened, his clothes fitting tighter around the middle. The sight stirred a mix of sadness and frustration in her. This wasn't the Jax she knew—the fierce protector who'd leaped off a rooftop to save her without a second thought.

"You're missing out, you know," she said. "There's so much happening in the city. Being part of it beats sitting in a cell any day." She gave him a pointed look, hoping he'd catch her meaning.

He chewed slowly, finally lifting his eyes to meet hers. "Not much for me out here these days."

"That's not true," she said. "You've got friends who care about you. And now that the ban is over, we can start making plans."

Jax snorted. "Plans. Right."

Hells, it was like talking to a mound of dirt.

They walked in silence for a few moments, the sounds of the bustling market growing louder as they approached. Vendors called out their wares, the scents of spiced meats and fresh produce filling the air.

When all else failed, food would always work.

Liora tried again. "I was thinking we could grab a proper meal. Something hearty. Then maybe head over to see Lars and Trin. They'd be glad to see you."

He hesitated, his expression unreadable. "I don't know, Liora."

She stopped, placing a hand on his forearm. "Jax, listen to me. We've all been adrift this past year. But the ban's lifted. It's time to get back to what we do best."

He looked down at her, a flicker of the old Jax shining through. "And what's that?"

"Being a team," she said simply. "Taking on the world together."

He sighed, the moment of clarity fading, replaced with the dull look of a drunkard that was all but a stranger to Liora.

He opened his mouth, then closed it again. A deep furrow creased his brow.

Finally, he muttered, "Maybe."

She squeezed his arm before letting go. "Come on. Let's get some food in you that isn't a dessert." She started walking again, and after a moment, he followed.

As they weaved through the crowd, she continued talking, filling the silence with updates about the monorail, funny stories from the Market District, anything to keep him engaged.

"...and you wouldn't believe the look on the merchant's face when the crate burst open and chickens went everywhere," she said. Hells, that was fun.

Jax managed a small smile. "Sounds chaotic."

"Exactly! That's the kind of chaos we thrive in," she said, nudging him playfully. "Much better than being locked away."

She glanced up at him, her eyes searching his face. "Don't you think?"

"I guess."

They reached a food stall, and Liora ordered two hearty bowls of stew. Handing one to Jax, she gave him an expectant look. "Eat up. Can't have you wasting away on me."

"Thanks."

Liora slammed the bowls of stew down on the wooden table with a force that made the utensils clatter.

She pushed her glasses up the bridge of her nose, planted her fists on her hips, and fixed Jax with a stern glare. "That's enough! I can't stand seeing you like this anymore. You need to perk up, wake up—whatever it takes—and listen."

Jax blinked, taken aback by her sudden outburst. He opened his mouth to speak, but she cut him off.

"You mean the world to me, Jax," Liora said, her eyes shining with a mix of frustration and concern. "When I needed you, you were always there. You got me back on my feet when I thought I couldn't go on. You jumped off a rooftop to save me from something terrifying and unknown without a second thought." She took a deep breath, her voice softening. "Now it's my turn to be there for you."

She stepped closer. "I love you, you big oaf. The Jax I know would bonk this sorry version of himself on the head and tell him to sleep it off and get back in the game. That Jax wouldn't let anything keep him down."

Her voice wavered slightly as she added, "I miss that Jax, Jax. I want him back. I need him back." She reached out to place a gentle hand on his arm. "So please, come back to us. Come back to me."

Jax looked at her with a dumbfounded stare. For a long moment, he sat there in silence, lost in thought. Liora continued to look at him pleadingly.

Finally, he glanced down at the table. "You spilled my stew," he said softly.

Liora's eyes widened, a mix of anger and disbelief flashing across her face. "Seriously, Jax?"

But then he chuckled—a low, rumbling sound that started in his chest and grew louder. The chuckle turned into a genuine laugh, one that shook his shoulders and seemed to lift a weight from him. It was a sound she hadn't heard in far too long.

A smile broke across Liora's face, relief washing over her. "What's so funny?"

He wiped a tear from the corner of his eye, still grinning. "You, standing there scolding me like my momma used to. I'm surprised you didn't grab my ear and give it a tug."

She crossed her arms, pretending to be stern. "Well, someone has to knock some sense into that thick skull of yours."

Jax reached out and patted her clumsily. "Alright, Liora. I'll do my best. It's just... hard, you know?"

Liora gave him a sympathetic smile. "I get it. You know, Shelle says—"

"Shelle?" Jax interrupted, his eyes widening slightly. "Y'all are still in touch? How's she been?"

Liora's face brightened. "In touch? Don't you remember? We're dating now."

Jax blinked, clearly not remembering. "Wait, you're dating Shelle?" He scratched his head, confusion knitting his brow. "But I thought she was with what's his name... Myrim. Though it's about time she got over that strict, stubborn, self-righteous—"

"I'm dating Myrim too."

Jax's mouth clicked shut, then his mouth opened and closed without a sound. He looked utterly bewildered, eyes darting as he tried to process the information. Finally, he managed to mutter, "Oh Liora... that's horrible. You shouldn't keep secrets from *either* of them like that."

She burst into laughter, shaking her head. "We had this same conversation last time, you goofball! I'm not keeping any secrets. We're all dating each other. We live together."

He stared at her for a long moment before simply saying, "Oh." Picking up his spoon, he began to eat his stew in silence.

Liora giggled, finding his reaction endearing. "It's not that complicated, really," she said, stirring her own bowl. "The three of us just... fit together. Like pieces of a puzzle."

Jax nodded slowly, still focused on his food. "If you say so."

She smiled softly, watching him. "Anyway, a few nights ago, Shelle was talking about how all the changes in the city might seem daunting—new crews, new leaders, all this tech—but she thinks it's really setting the stage for something great. Especially with the ban lifted. It's a chance for the true masters of the craft to come back and shake things up."

He glanced up briefly. "Yeah? Do you think they will?"

Liora laughed and smacked his arm. "Jax! I'm talking about—" She stopped, catching his wry grin. He knew who she was talking about. "Now you're trying to wind me up!"

They sat there together, the bustle of the market swirling around them. Vendors shouted their wares, children darted between stalls, and the scent of spices and fresh bread filled the air. For a moment, it felt almost like old times.

Liora continued to chatter about the latest happenings—talks about building a permanent tram all the way to Sarkport, how

Keer had bought a ship and sailed west, and a peculiar case of missing street lamps.

As she spoke, Liora could see Jax visibly relaxing. It felt good. Sure, it would be a while before the man was back to his old self. Both physically and mentally. But he would get there this time. She would see to it.

The sun began to dip lower in the sky. Liora glanced up, noticing the time. "We should probably head over to see Lars and Trin soon."

Jax nodded, pushing his empty bowl away. "Yeah, okay."

She beamed at him. "Great! They'll be thrilled to see you."

As they stood and began to weave their way through the crowd, Liora slipped her arm through his, giving it a reassuring squeeze. "Thanks for giving this a chance."

He looked down at her, a hint of a genuine smile tugging at the corner of his mouth. "Thanks for not giving up on me."

"Never," she replied firmly.

Side by side—the big bruiser and the best damn dynamo girl in Azoria—they ventured towards the river, ready to face whatever came next.

BOREDOM AND BONDS

2

The sun filtered through the threadbare curtains of Lars' and Trin's east end apartment. It wasn't much, but it had been home for the past year.

Whatever 'home' meant these days.

The furniture was worn, just a couple of chairs and a table they'd picked up from a market stall that looked like it was on its last legs—literally. It wasn't that they didn't have the money for something better. The place had the feel of something temporary, as if they were still waiting to move on to the next thing. But the next thing hadn't come.

Lars sat slouched at the table, his feet propped up on the edge, flicking through an old deck of cards he wasn't really paying attention to. His shirt was wrinkled, and his boots hadn't seen a shine in months. Across the room, Trin was at the window, her arms folded as she stared out at the streets of Azoria, the city humming with life below. There was a tension in her posture, something Lars had noticed more and more over the past few months.

"I'm bored," Trin said finally, her voice cutting through the quiet.

Lars looked up, his fingers pausing mid-shuffle. "You've been saying that a lot lately."

Trin turned to face him, her lips pressed into a thin line. "That's because I've been bored for months now, Lars."

Lars sighed, tossing the cards onto the table. "What do you want me to say? We couldn't do anything. The ban—"

"The ban's over," she snapped. A flush crept onto her cheeks.

Lars picked at a frayed edge on one of the cards.

"Yeah. So what, we just... jump back in?" He leaned back in his chair, staring up at the ceiling. The water stain in the corner had gotten bigger since last month. "Call up Jax? See if Liora's around?"

"Why not?"

"It's not that simple."

"It used to be."

Lars rubbed the back of his neck. "Yeah, well. A lot of things used to be."

The words hung between them. Outside, someone was shouting about fresh bread. Same vendor, same time every day. Lars had started to hate that voice.

"We need to get back to it," Trin said quietly. "Soon."

"I know."

"Do you?"

He reached for the cards again, started shuffling. The familiar motion usually helped, but his hands felt clumsy today. "Of course I know," he said. "I'm just not ready yet."

"Not yet?" Trin echoed, her brow furrowing. "We should have been planning weeks ago. What are we waiting for, Lars?

Another year to pass by while we sit here, pretending this is normal? We used to *be* someone in this city."

"We still are someone," he said with a frown.

Trin shook her head, pacing back toward the table. "Are we? Everyone else has changed. What in the hells are we doing?"

Lars shifted in his chair, watching her. She wasn't wrong. There were new faces, likely new alliances forming while they were sidelined. But getting back into the game wasn't as simple as flipping a switch.

"What do you want me to do, Trin?" he asked quietly. "Call everyone back, pretend we can pick up where we left off?"

"Yes. Yes, that's exactly what I want." She stopped pacing. "I want to feel something again, Lars."

Lars stared at her for a moment, then leaned forward, resting his elbows on his knees. His voice came out more bitter than he intended. "Is it really getting sidelined that's bothering you? Or is it being with me?"

Trin froze mid-step, her eyes narrowing as she turned to face him fully with an unreadable expression. For a long moment, she didn't say anything.

"Don't do that, Lars," she said finally, her voice low but firm. "Don't make this about us."

He let out a humorless chuckle, shaking his head. "I can't ignore how this feels. You're stomping around here, complaining about being bored..."

He trailed off.

Trin's hands dropped to her sides. "I'm frustrated, okay? I'm frustrated because we're not doing what we're supposed to be doing. We used to be in control, Lars. We used to run the game, and now..."

"Now we're just us," he finished for her. "And that's not enough for you."

She didn't deny it, but the silence was telling.

Lars rubbed his face, not knowing what else to say. They hadn't been the same since the ban. *He* hadn't been the same.

And part of him wondered if maybe it wasn't only the heists that had fallen apart.

Trin finally broke the silence. "It's not you, Lars. And it's not about *us*." She crossed the room and stood in front of him, arms crossed, but her tone was softer now. "It's about everything else. The city, the jobs, the crew... it's all slipped away. We're stuck."

Lars looked up at her, meeting her eyes, trying to find some reassurance in her words, but the nagging doubt in his gut refused to fade. He reached for the deck of cards, shuffling them again, more for the distraction than anything.

"Then what's the plan?" he muttered. "Because I don't know how to fix this."

Trin watched him for a moment, her frustration giving way to something quieter. She leaned against the edge of the table, her voice softer but still firm. "We can't keep sitting here, Lars. Waiting isn't going to fix anything. We... We need to start somewhere."

"Start somewhere," he echoed. "Like what? A big job? A little job? We can't just walk back into the game like nothing's changed. Jax is probably in prison again, Liora's constantly busy, Keer's nowhere around. What are we supposed to do?"

Trin raised an eyebrow. "That's why I'm saying we start small. Something easy, low-risk. We don't need to go after anything big. A test run to get us back in the game."

Lars scoffed, leaning back in his chair. "Right. A small job. Just like that."

Trin folded her arms. "Yes, just like that."

He tapped his fingers against the tabletop. His mind warred with itself. She made it sound so simple. Like they could walk back into the life they used to have, like a year away hadn't changed everything. But it had.

Lars wasn't sure if he could keep up anymore. But he wasn't about to say that out loud.

"Fine," he muttered, rubbing his temple. "Let's say we do this. What's the job?"

"Nothing crazy. Something easy, low-profile, maybe an office—"

"Oh, well, that sounds thrilling," Lars cut in. "Why not run errands while we're at it?"

Trin's expression darkened, frustration flaring again. "You're acting like you're the only one who lost something. Guess what, Lars? A lot of people lost things. That doesn't mean we just— just let it all slip through our fingers."

Lars clenched his jaw. "You think I don't know that?"

"Do you?" Trin shot back, stepping closer. "Because from where I'm standing, you're content to just rot in this apartment."

His grip on the deck of cards tightened. He wanted to snap back, wanted to fight. But he kept quiet.

She ran a hand through her hair. "Look, I don't need you to be excited. I don't need you to suddenly snap back into the guy you used to be. But I need you to try. Just once. Take the step."

Lars was silent.

Trin searched his face, waiting for something, anything. But he had nothing to give her.

Her lips pressed into a thin line, and she turned for the door. "You know what? Forget it. Squawk me when you're ready to do something."

The door shut behind her, the sound ringing through the apartment.

Lars sat there, staring at the empty space she left behind.

For a long moment, he only sat there. Then, with a slow, tired motion, he picked up the deck of cards and shuffled them again. The soft rustle filled the silence. But it didn't feel the same.

The air inside the Velvet Noose was thick with pipe smoke, sweat, and spilled liquor. The gambling den wasn't the biggest in Azoria, nor the most prestigious, but it was the kind of place where a man could lose his fortune and his fingers in the same night.

Darius leaned back in his chair, languid, easy, his sharp suit perfectly tailored, his golden rings catching the dim glow of the chandelier overhead. Across from him sat his latest mark—a wealthy merchant with too much coin and too little sense, his pockets already lighter than when the night had begun.

The cards in Darius' hand were only another piece of the night's play, but this was the round that mattered. He had spent the evening winning just enough to be dangerous, but losing enough to be believable. A streak too clean and people got suspicious. A streak too cold, and you lost control of the room. Balance was everything.

Well, that and having a good crew nearby. His bruiser Rurik played his part well—slumped in a chair, looking every bit the boozed-up brawler, nursing a tankard like he barely knew where he was. To the mark, he must have seemed like an easy fool throwing away coin in reckless bets.

And then there was Inora, his right hand woman, watching from a cushioned seat by the bar. She wore a fitted dress and well-groomed hair, which was wildly out of place for her. Inora was a thief who preferred a pair of baggy trousers and letting her hair fall where it would.

She wasn't playing. Not visibly, at least. But she was there for one purpose: to give Darius the slightest tells, the most minute shifts in body language that only someone trained to watch for them would see.

Darius tapped his knuckles against the table in thought. The dealer—an older man with a permanent scowl and a wary eye—rolled the three dice across the velvet tabletop.

The dice tumbled across the felt, clinking against each other before landing in a neat row.

Four. Five. Four.

Thirteen. The House Decree was set.

Darius kept his expression neutral, barely glancing at the numbers as he picked up his cards. A six, a King's Mark, and a five. Not a bad start. At least he didn't blow past thirteen.

Across the table, his mark, a wealthy merchant reeking of overconfidence and spiced brandy, rubbed his hands together, already grinning. "Oh, I like that Decree," he said, slurring slightly—just enough for Darius to know he was feeling bold.

Good. Let him think it's his night.

To his left, Rurik slumped further in his chair, giving an exaggerated groan. "Hells, I dunno about this one." He squinted at his cards, swaying like he was debating whether to gamble his last coin or order another drink.

Then he grinned, shoving a handful of coins onto the table, spilling half in his sloppy enthusiasm.

The merchant smirked, eyes glinting with predatory amusement. "You sure about that, friend?"

Rurik hiccuped, nodded slowly, and Darius watched as the mark took the bait, chuckling as he matched the bet.

Darius played steady. No rush. No greed. Only patience. He discarded the six, drew his first card.

A seven. He now had a seven, five, and the King's Mark. That was a safe draw that kept him under the Decree, and still within range of hitting it with the wildcard.

The betting round passed, the pot growing steadily. Nothing to worry about. Yet.

The next draw, Darius discarded the seven and pulled a fresh card.

A ten. Damn.

His grip on his cards tightened a fraction. Fifteen plus the Mark. Too high. A grunt slipped from his throat. Annoyance. Regret. Or at least, that's how he wanted it to sound.

The merchant caught it. His smirk widened, confidence solidifying.

Darius let the next betting round play out without raising, just watching. The merchant raised the pot. Hard. Darius hesitated and let the tension stretch just a moment longer before he called. As long as he drew a seven or less, he'd be fine.

Darius discarded the ten and drew. It was a four. His pulse stayed steady. No reaction. But he was now at nine plus the Mark. Since the Mark could be played for any number one to six, he could hit the Decree exactly.

As long as the merchant stayed in. Across the room, Inora adjusted her ring—barely a flicker of movement. That signal meant that the merchant was at twelve. No wildcard.

Darius took a sip of his drink. Twelve was a good hand, only one away from the House Decree. He'd feel confident in that hand. It was Darius's turn to bet, and he bet high. Rurik folded. The merchant went for it.

The merchant tossed down his cards, beaming at his total of twelve on the table.

Darius sighed, slow and drawn-out, before throwing down his two number cards, showing a total of nine. The merchant smirked.

Then Darius flipped the King's Mark.

The table went silent. "Oh, that's unfortunate," Darius murmured, running a thumb over the edge of the wildcard.

"As per the rules," the dealer stated, "you can choose a number one to six for the wildcard. If you match his twelve, you'll split the pot. If you go for thirteen to hit the House Decree, you'll need to match the value with a dice roll."

Darius played at thinking long and hard, then tapped the face of the card. "Four," he grinned. "That puts me at thirteen."

The dealer nodded and handed Darius one of the dice. "Then roll," he said. "If you roll a four, you'll win clean and collect the pot and house match. Otherwise your opponent will split the win with the house."

Darius picked up the die, letting it roll cunningly between his fingers.

The merchant watched, his throat bobbing.

Darius rolled.

The small die tumbled across the felt and landed on four. A perfect roll.

The merchant gasped, slumping in his seat. Darius leaned forward, smiling graciously at the man as he deftly swapped back the dealer's die for his loaded one.

"Sorry, friend," he murmured, "looks like the King favored me tonight."

The merchant's knuckles turned white. He stared at the cards, his drunken confidence draining. For a long moment, he didn't speak. The room had that stillness—the moment between realization and reaction.

Darius, ever the gracious winner, leaned back in his chair and sighed as if this was all just an amusing inconvenience. "Tough luck," he said, voice smooth as polished silver.

The man forced a laugh—but it was the kind that covered up something festering. "Yeah. Yeah, well. That's how the game goes, huh?"

He reached for his drink, gulping it down a little too fast.

Rurik, still slumped at the table, gave an exaggerated wince. "Hoooo. Tough loss, mate. You were *so close* too."

The merchant's forced smile was painful to see.

Darius piled the winnings toward himself, stacking the coins with absentminded ease. More than the merchant could comfortably afford to lose, and the house wouldn't be thrilled either.

And to be honest, Darius wasn't all that thrilled.

He should have felt great. This was a perfect setup, a perfect execution. The mark walked right into it, and now Darius was walking away with a heavy purse.

But there was no thrill. No chase. No stolen goods. No breaking in and out of anywhere with nothing but a few tools, a plan, and the beating of his own heart in his chest.

This was a con. Just a game. It would never be a heist.

He leaned back in his chair, stretching lazily. "Well, gentlemen, I think that's enough fun for one night."

He stood, tucking a portion of his winnings into his coat while the merchant's eyes burned holes into the table.

Across the room, Inora watched him carefully.

Rurik, seeing the mark's growing tension, clapped him on the back a little too hard. "Cheer up, friend! You're a man of means, yeah? Just win it back next time."

The merchant forced another laugh. "Yeah. Next time."

Darius could already tell there wouldn't be a next time. He pushed open the heavy curtain separating the backroom gambling den from the Velvet Noose's main lounge, stepping into the soft glow of dynamo lanterns and low murmured conversation.

The air here was different. Less charged, less thick with the scents of tension and desperation. Here, people laughed genuinely, whispered deals over fine drinks, exchanged more than just coin.

Darius adjusted the hem of his coat as he spotted Inora waiting for him at the bar. He strolled over, setting his winnings down on the bar with a soft clink. "Buy me something expensive, would you?"

Inora didn't even glance at the pile of copper and gold. She only squinted at Darius and took a slow sip of whatever remained in her glass.

"That was pathetic," she said in her raspy voice.

Darius smirked, leaning against the bar. "That's one way to say 'congratulations on your brilliant victory, Darius.'"

Inora sighed, swirling her drink before setting it down. "You didn't need me. Or the loaded dice." She turned, pinning him with a look. "You could've taken that game with your eyes closed."

Darius let out a low chuckle, shaking his head. "A win's a win, Inora."

"Is it?"

He grabbed a glass from the bartender, tipping it back without bothering to ask what was in it. The burn down his throat was satisfying—for about a second.

"You always this chatty after I buy the drinks, or am I just special?" he muttered.

Inora shrugged. "You didn't even count the money."

"I know how much is there."

"That's not the point."

Darius rolled his eyes. "Look, if you're angling for a bigger cut—"

"I'm not." She tapped her nails against the bar. "Just wondering why you're still here playing gold-ante games with merchants who can barely hold their cards."

"Maybe I like easy money."

"Maybe you're full of shit."

He forced another smirk, reaching for the bottle again.

"So," Inora said casually, still tapping those damn nails. "You heard from Lars?"

Darius's hand stopped for a moment.

He didn't answer right away. Just finished the motion, poured himself another drink, and took his time with it. Finally, he set the glass down with a deliberate clink. "No."

Inora leaned against the bar. "That's it? Just 'no'?"

"What else do you want?"

"I don't know. Maybe something about why you two haven't talked in a year?"

Darius's eyes darkened. "There's nothing to talk about."

"Right." She crossed her arms. "That's why you get that look every time someone mentions his name."

"What look?"

"That one."

Darius scoffed, throwing back the rest of his drink. "You're imagining things."

"Am I?" Inora tilted her head. "When's the last time you even said his name?"

"Why would I?"

"Because you two pretty much used to own this city?"

"Used to." Darius's voice was flat. "Past tense."

Inora watched him for a moment longer, then shrugged. "Fine. Whatever you say."

She turned back to her drink, and somehow that was worse than if she'd kept pushing.

"Alright," Darius said, pushing off from the bar. "Time to head out."

He wove through the tables, tucking his winnings into his coat. The crowd was getting thicker, louder. Good. More noise meant less room for thinking.

"Think Harrow's coming back?"

Darius's steps faltered. His hand tightened into a fist as he turned toward the voice.

Just a pair of drinkers at a corner table. "I mean, he's been out for a year, right? You think he's really gonna show his face again?"

"Maybe. Some people don't bounce back."

"Shame. He was really something back in the day."

Darius moved past them before he had to hear any more. Back in the day.

He pushed through the tavern door harder than necessary. The night air hit him, cold and sharp.

Back in the day.

Hells.

What the hells had happened to their base? Their home?

Trin took a slow step forward, her boots crunching over broken glass and kicking up a thick swirl of dust. The air was stale, suffocating. The only light came from the thin slats of moonlight piercing through the boarded windows, turning the wreckage into eerie silhouettes.

She pulled her coat tighter around herself. The hearth was cold, the fire long dead.

The front door was still sealed tight, thick planks haphazardly nailed over it. She had slipped in through the trapdoor behind the bar—just like old times. But this wasn't old times.

The whole place was a ruin.

Chairs smashed to splinters, tables overturned, shelves looted or broken. Glass shards littered the floor, reflecting the faintest light like a field of scattered stars. The maps they had once painstakingly drawn up together were ripped from the walls, their edges curled and burnt at the corners. Someone had been thorough in their destruction.

Trin swallowed hard. She had expected it to be bad. But this? This felt like standing over a grave.

She moved through the wreckage, her fingers trailing the scarred bar top, the dust collecting on her fingertips.

She closed her eyes.

For a moment, she could almost hear them.

The low rumble of Keer's voice from the kitchen, grumbling about the bacon not coming out quite crispy enough. The buzz of Liora's workbench sparking, followed by her yelp and a string of curses as she zapped herself again. Jax, adorned in the finest clothes a man his size could find, bellowing laughter at a joke that wasn't all that funny.

And Lars.

Lars, kicking back in the corner, his boots propped up on the table, that cocky, easy grin on his face.

"Relax, Trin," she could almost hear him say, his voice brushing against her ears. "We'll be fine. We always are."

Her throat tightened.

She opened her eyes.

The room was silent. Empty.

The ghosts were gone.

She dragged a tired hand through her hair.

Vivienne had made sure they couldn't come back to this place. That they wouldn't want to. After their last heist, she sent her goons to tear it apart, to break what they had built. And it worked. They hadn't dared return.

Not like there'd be any point in returning. With thieving banned for a year, everyone had to do their own thing.

She turned in a slow circle, taking in the wreckage. It felt personal. Like a message.

You lost.

The anger sat just beneath her ribs, burning hot.

In a quick burst of fury, she kicked one of the broken chairs. The brittle wood snapped on impact, clattering to the ground in pieces.

"Ah hells," she muttered, shaking out her foot. As if she could hurt this place worse than it already was.

"Well, no use standing around," she muttered to herself. If Vivienne thought she could erase them from Azoria, she was dead wrong.

Rolling up her sleeves, Trin set to work. She began by righting an overturned chair, its leg wobbly but still serviceable. Next was a small table, scratched and dented but it would do. She gathered broken bits of wood and debris into a pile, the rhythmic motion of cleaning oddly soothing.

But she couldn't shake the feeling of loss that settled in her chest. Furniture was all well and good, but the lack of the crew still stung. They had all scattered, each dealing with the aftermath of last year's events in their own way. Could they all make it back?

Trin moved behind the bar, her fingers tracing the familiar patterns carved into the wood. She smiled softly, remembering the nights they'd spent celebrating a successful heist or just enjoying each other's company. The good times.

They'd been a great thieving crew. And that meant family.

She spotted a cracked mirror hanging precariously on the wall. Catching her reflection, she noted the smudge of dirt on her cheek, the determined set of her expression. "You look like hells," she told herself, but there was a spark in her eyes she hadn't seen in a while.

She grabbed a broom and started sweeping, the swish of bristles against wood filling the quiet. With each stroke, the space began to feel a little less abandoned. She hummed a tune to herself softly.

Hours passed unnoticed as she cleaned and repaired what she could with what scattered tools she could find. She propped up the sagging shelves, and even managed to get an old gas lantern working, casting a flickering glow that pushed back the shadows.

Finally, she stood back and surveyed her work. It was far from perfect, but it was a start. The base still bore the scars of Vivienne's wrath, but beneath it all, the foundation of what they'd built remained solid.

Trin sighed, wiping a thin layer of dust from her hands onto her trousers. Glancing out of a crack in the boarded window, she noted the moon had risen high in the sky. It was getting late; she really should be heading back home.

Just as she turned to gather her things, a faint scratching sound came from the front door. Instinctively, her hand went to the dagger at her belt. She held her breath, ears straining. The scratching came again, followed by a muffled voice.

"Hello? Anybody home?" piped a familiar squeak.

Trin relaxed, a smile tugging at the corners of her mouth. She'd recognize that voice anywhere. "Liora!"

"Trin? Is that you?" came the reply, slightly muffled through the wooden barrier.

"Yes, it's me! But the door's boarded shut," Trin said, stepping closer to the door. "Oh... give me a minute, I'll find something to pry the boards off."

"Oh, don't worry about that," Liora responded cheerfully. "Just stand back a bit."

Trin hesitated but did as instructed, taking a few steps backward. She heard muffled whispers outside—the high chirps of Liora's excitement mixed with a deeper, gruffer tone.

Suddenly, the entire door shuddered violently. With a resounding crash, it burst inward as the nailed boards splintered and flew off like exploding rivets from a steam engine.

Trin coughed against the dust, blinking at the gaping hole where the door used to be. Splintered wood. Nails twisted clean from their posts. Jax, standing in the middle of it all, brushing dust off his shoulder like he'd barely noticed he just went through solid oak.

"...Jax?"

His grin was almost sheepish. "Hey, Trin. Long time."

Peeking out from behind him, Liora beamed, her eyes sparkling with mischief. "Told you we'd find a way in!"

Trin's shock melted into delight. "Jax! Liora!" She rushed forward, embracing Jax as best she could, her arms barely reaching around his broad torso. Then she pulled back to hug Liora tightly. "You nearly gave me a heart attack!"

Jax chuckled softly. "Sorry about the door. Liora said it was okay."

Liora waved a dismissive hand. "Minor structural damage. Besides, dramatic entrances are more fun, don't you think?"

She couldn't help but laugh, a sound that seemed to breathe life back into the old base. For the first time in a long time, Trin felt like she was where she belonged. "I suppose so. What are you two doing here?"

Liora grinned and skipped further into the room, her boots making soft thuds against the worn floorboards. She plopped onto a nearby chair, which creaked and shifted under her slight weight due to a partially broken leg. Undeterred, she fidgeted to find a balance, the chair wobbling with each movement.

Meanwhile, Jax wandered over to the bar. He cast a hopeful glance behind it, his shoulders sagging slightly when he found the shelves empty.

Trin noticed his forlorn expression. "Hoping for a drink?"

He let out a deep sigh. "New habits." Spotting some smashed bottles on the floor, he began picking up the jagged pieces, piling them carefully on the bar top. "This place has seen better days."

"Tell me about it," Trin agreed, watching him thoughtfully. "I've been trying to tidy up."

Liora leaned forward in her unsteady chair and pulled a small, familiar device from her satchel—a squawk. The compact communication gadget gleamed faintly in the dim light as she placed it on the table with a satisfied nod.

"I hope you and Lars still have a squawk set up at your place."

Trin's eyebrows lifted in surprise. "We do, actually. Why?"

"Because it's been a year, Trin." Liora leaned in, her grin wicked. "And I think it's about time we got our shit together."

Lars approached the old base with slow, measured steps, the distant sounds of Azoria's nightlife murmuring behind him. The city still thrived, but it felt different. Or maybe that was just him.

He wasn't sure what he expected when he finally stepped inside. Dust? Silence? More of the dead feeling that had settled in his chest for a year?

Though Trin didn't know it, Lars had been back here before. Nearly a year prior, just after the thieving ban began. He had hoped it would give him a sense of resolve. A drive to push forward.

It hadn't. Instead, seeing the wrecked furniture, broken lights, glass, ashes... it had only made him feel broken inside.

But what he saw through the front door was something else entirely.

Bright dynamo light filled the space, buzzing from the lamps Liora had clearly rewired. The bar had been wiped down—still battered, but no longer buried in debris. A few chairs had been righted, the heavy wooden table where they'd planned a dozen heists now sitting center, waiting for a map, a plan, a purpose.

The hearth was still dark. Cold. But the air had changed.

And so had the people in it.

Jax leaned against the bar, arms barely able to cross over his massive chest, a tired grin tugging at the corners of his mouth. Liora stood at her old workbench, tools in hand, muttering as she tinkered with a device. Trin sat at the table, running a hand over the wood, as if reacquainting herself with something she had lost.

For the first time in a year, a crew had found its den.

His fingers tightened around the doorframe. The laughter, the warmth, the way they all settled back into easy rhythm— even without him there.

He could leave.

No one had seen him yet. He could turn around, disappear back into the streets, let them keep whatever they were building here without him. Would that be so bad?

Wasn't that what he deserved?

Then Liora looked up.

"Well, well," she said, her voice dry. "Look who we have here."

No turning back now.

Lars let the moment stretch, taking in the faces before him. They were waiting. Expectant.

His grip loosened on the doorway, and he sighed audibly as he stepped inside.

"Didn't think I'd ever see this place in one piece again," he muttered.

Trin arched an eyebrow. "It's not in one piece."

Jax chuckled. "But it's closer than it was yesterday." He gestured at the cleaned-up space, his grin widening. "Liora's been doing her engineer thing. We had lanterns up within the hour."

Crossing her arms, Liora clicked her tongue. "Please. It took thirty minutes. Forty-five, tops."

Lars huffed a small laugh, shaking his head as he walked further in. His boots scraped against the worn wooden floor, and for a moment, it was almost like nothing had changed. Almost.

Jax leaned against the bar, arms crossed over his broad chest. "Man, I miss Keer. Not just the cooking," he added hastily.

Trin shook her head. "I miss him too. But he's got his own thing going on. Did you know he ended up buying Thume's old ship?"

"Thume's, then Darius's, then Thume's old ship," Lars grinned.

"The very same," Trin replied with a faint smile. "He's been running smuggling trips into Zarakar ever since. With Silas from Darius's crew, if you'll believe it."

It was still a bit of a blow, but Lars couldn't blame Keer. The man had been there with the crew through thick and thin. But with the ban in place and money in his pocket, why not set sail? Somewhere far away. Somewhere new.

Jax raised an eyebrow. "Did I miss something while I was drunk? Why smuggle anything from Zarakar? Aren't they already our biggest supplier?"

Lars grunted, stepping away from a boarded up window and pulling out the chair. His chair. The one he'd taken a hundred times before, planning out the jobs that made them legends.

He sat, but it felt different now. Like he was sitting in someone else's place.

"Viv—" he started, but quickly choked the name back. "—the new Gaming Commission head has cut off trade with them. It's all part of her push to dismantle Thume's legacy."

"She's been shutting down all the old networks, cutting off pretty much every trade route," Trin said with a shrug. "Keer saw an opportunity."

Liora snapped a compartment shut on a random gadget she'd found and stood up. "Speaking of opportunities, what exactly do you have in mind for our 'great unbanning,' Lars?"

He felt warmth creeping up his neck. "I haven't really thought about it."

Liora blinked. "You... haven't thought about it?"

Jax let out a dry chuckle. "At least I'm not the only one."

He must have struck a nerve. Liora slammed her gadget onto the table, causing everyone to jump. "Are you all serious right now? What the hells is wrong with you? You've been moping around for a year! We're thieves, damn it! It's time we pulled our heads out of our asses and started acting like it!"

Lars was about to chime in, but Trin held up a warning hand.

"And another thing!" Liora continued, scowling so hard her glasses almost fell off her nose. She pushed them back up with a huff. "Jax has been in and out of prison at least twice—"

"Three times."

"Thank you, Jax, yes, three times, and I'm somehow the only one who came to visit him? What, you just couldn't be bothered while you sat around doing... what is it you've been doing again, Lars? Oh that's right, nothing. Meanwhile I've been building monorails, working with Maren, spending time with Myrim and Shelle, and still have time to go see *our* bruiser here, but you couldn't? What kind of crew is this?"

An oppressive silence fell over the room. All eyes turned to Lars, and he wanted nothing more than to storm out and leave their accusing glances behind. What did they know about what he was feeling? And after all that had happened, why should he have to face them?

Finally, he spoke up. "It's not."

Trin gasped, a hurt sound that cut through his heart. Lars couldn't let that deter him. As much as it pained him to realize it and give words to his shame, he had to get this out.

"It's not... what, Lars?" Liora said. Jax grimaced and shook his head.

"We're not a crew, damn it!" Lars burst out. "Maybe we were, once. I know we were. And we had a really good run." His breathing was ragged and heavy, eyes turning red as fresh tears formed. "Heist after heist, literal tons of copper... it set us up really well, right? Right?"

Liora nodded but said nothing. She didn't dare say anything.

"But everything since then has been absolutely *wrong*. Don't deny it. Us, Darius, that whole escapade. In the end we all just ran around, dancing on the strings of that hells-cursed woman and her power play with Thume. People called me the best thief in the city. But what did I do? Not a damn thing. Not a damn thing." He paused.

"Oh yeah, except nearly getting Keer killed, handing the city over to an even bigger narcissist, and then getting us all *banned* from the only hells damned thing that we're good at." Lars finished with a grimace, looking at the crew through blurred eyes.

He couldn't even tell their reactions. And he didn't care. "Some crew leader I am."

Silence reigned again. He cleared his eyes and sniffed. *Here it comes,* he thought.

The old 'are you finished,' followed by a bitter recrimination and condemnation of his self-pity that would probably end what was once a sacred trust between a once amazing crew. Jax would probably be drunk or back in prison by the next day. And as for Lars, he—

His pained imaginings were cut short as Jax came over and gave him a tight hug. The big man was sobbing, and in a moment Lars was sobbing too, crying into Jax's unkempt shirt. As the tears left him, so did the feelings of rage, the decay that had been building at the center of his soul.

Jax sniffed, wiping his face with the back of his hand as he looked down at Lars. His voice, though rough, was sincere—tinged with something deeper than sorrow.

"You think you're the only one who felt it, Lars? You think you're the only one who saw everything fall apart? Hells, why do you think I've been such a mess?"

Lars looked up, his eyes still wet, pity mingling with the remnants of his outburst. "Jax, I—"

"Wait. Do you know what it was like watching Liora get shot?" Jax's voice was quieter now, rougher. His fingers curled into fists at his sides. "Seeing her fall off that damned roof? And then Keer, after he got hurt..."

He stopped and swallowed hard. His chest rose, fell. He tried to keep it together—tried.

"I felt useless," he admitted. "The strongest man in Azoria—no, don't deny it—but I couldn't protect either of them." His face crumpled. "And then the ban? It was like the city itself telling us we weren't good enough anymore."

He shook his head, his eyes hollow as he met Lars's gaze. "So yeah, I drank. I messed myself up because it hurt less than knowing I'd failed. I took it all on myself. I'm the bruiser, man. I told myself I should have done better, been faster, been stronger. I picked fights just to feel something other than the guilt. But the truth is, we both did, didn't we?"

"Did what?" Lars asked softly.

"Picked fights. I picked them with anyone. In prison, out of prison—hells, I'm banned from half of Tavern Row at this point. But you... Lars, you've been picking fights with yourself. And you're kicking your own ass to a pulp."

Jax fell silent. He was right. Lars had been twisted up inside, and any time he felt like there was even the slightest chance of feeling better, he went ahead and twisted up a little more just to keep the despair alive.

Lars thought about dynamo lenses, how someone using them could see the hidden flows of dynamo sparking beneath any surface. Looking back at the last year, well hells... he was looking at everything through a lens of guilt. And it had distorted his view on the world and the people he loved most.

"I guess I've been a bit of a bitter asshole."

Liora cocked an eyebrow. "A bit?"

Lars ran a hand down his face, exhaling slow.

He didn't know if he could be the person he was before it all went wrong. But it was worth trying.

He looked up at Liora. "Alright. Let's assume for the moment my head is out of my ass." A slow grin pulled at his lips. "What's next?"

"We get back to doing what we do best," Liora said with a grin.

Trin was beaming. "Stealing shit?"

"Well," Liora said, adjusting her glasses, "I was going to say 'being a crew.'"

She grinned, slow and wicked. "But yeah. Let's steal some shit."

THE QUEEN'S GAMBIT

3

Vivienne Dragunova stood at the window of her office, looking out over the city she had claimed, her reflection ghosted in the glass.

Azoria sprawled beneath her, a living machine of glinting rooftops and winding streets, pulsing with dynamo light. The monorail slid soundlessly along its tracks, a silver thread weaving the city together—one of the many changes under her reign. Even from this height, she could see the shifting of the districts, the ceaseless movement of people, the quiet hum of an empire being reshaped in her image.

The office had changed as much as the city.

Gone was the imposing darkwood desk, the towering shelves of ledgers, the methodical arrangement of furniture that had once given the room an air of obsessive order. Thume had kept things pristine, untouched, as if the sheer force of discipline could hold his empire in place. But his form of perfection was an illusion, and she had no use for relics of a man who had let himself be outmaneuvered.

Instead, the space now exuded something cleaner. Calmer. Inevitable. Light pooled softly from sconces of frosted crystal, their dynamo glow warm, controlled—never harsh. The banners of the Gaming Commission hung at perfect intervals, a quiet assertion of power rather than a demand for attention.

The city still had its rough edges, its inefficiencies—problems that would be corrected in time. But this much was certain.

Azoria belonged to her.

Vivienne moved from the window with slow, deliberate steps, heels clicking softly against the floor. She did not rush—she never rushed. To act with urgency was to reveal weakness, to show the world that something had caught you off guard. And she was never caught off guard.

Her fingers skimmed the smooth surface of her desk, a curve of black marble. A single parchment lay atop a silver writing tray, edges crisp, the ink dry. Beside it, a neat arrangement of documents—trade logs, commission reports, financial statements—waiting for her review.

Nothing out of place. Nothing unexpected.

She took her seat, running a thoughtful hand over the open map of Azoria spread beneath the reports. It had been updated recently, reflecting the latest shifts in trade, security, and alliances. Where old routes had been cut, new paths flourished. Where lesser men had clung to old debts and fragile truces, she had rewritten the rules entirely.

A year ago, the city had been a patchwork of competing interests, stitched together by uneasy agreements and outdated loyalties. Now, those loyalties belonged to her—or they didn't exist at all. The Gaming Commission dictated who rose and who fell, and those who failed to adapt found themselves without a chair when the music stopped.

Vivienne traced a manicured fingernail along the curve of the monorail line, its sleek path carving a new artery through the city. Progress, undeniable and absolute.

Then, without announcement or hesitation, the door swung open.

Only one person would dare enter Vivienne's office unannounced. And Vivienne was glad to see her.

Diligence Blythe stepped into the office.

Hells, the way she moved. Easy, fluid grace, half-lidded amusement in her golden-brown eyes. If ever there was a woman who could match Vivienne's power of captivation, it was Diligence.

Vivienne let the moment stretch, watching her from behind her desk. Most people in Azoria hesitated in her presence. Even the powerful ones, the cunning ones, the ones who thought themselves untouchable.

But Diligence had never hesitated a day in her life. Vivienne studied her—this woman who'd turned a modest inheritance into an empire.

A little bit of foresight and luck had led Diligence to liquidate her family's failing shipping business to buy up gambling houses just as thieving died. When desperate people needed distraction, she'd been there with cards and dice and exactly the right words.

The working class loved her for keeping games honest and tabs reasonable. The merchants respected her for never overreaching.

Hells, even the old nobility couldn't deny her usefulness when they needed discrete entertainment for their less savory guests.

All that influence, wrapped in silk and leather, stood before Vivienne. At her disposal.

Finally, Diligence broke the silence. "The east-end brokers are pushing back against the new tariffs."

Vivienne didn't react with anger. No irritation. No sigh of exasperation or flicker of frustration. Just a small, knowing smile. "I expected as much."

Diligence's eyes flicked to the papers on the desk, the open map, the carefully arranged reports. "And what would you like me to do?"

Vivienne turned a page with slow precision. "Nothing. Not yet."

Diligence tilted her head slightly, as if considering that answer. Reaching down, her finger caught Vivienne's chin, tilting it upward just so, forcing Vivienne to meet her gaze fully.

"Are you sure?" Diligence murmured.

It wasn't a question about the tariffs.

There was a small, calculated delay before she responded—not out of hesitation, but because she knew the game. Diligence was always testing, always pressing, waiting for Vivienne to push back. And Vivienne always did. Eventually.

She let the silence stretch, let the weight of Diligence's touch settle. Then, with painstaking control, she reached up and took Diligence's wrist, guiding it to the desk and pinning it there.

"Yes." She was unwavering. "Quite sure."

A slow, knowing smile curled at the edge of Diligence's lips.

Footsteps echoed down the hall, followed by the crisp rap of knuckles against the door. Unlike Diligence, Markus knew better than to simply enter unannounced.

Vivienne chuckled and released Diligence's wrist. "Come in."

The door opened, and Markus stepped inside, a man in his early fifties dressed in an impeccably tailored navy suit, carrying a thick ledger bound in dark leather. His presence was meticulous, as were his pages of finely balanced calculations.

Vivienne's new order needed men like Markus—men who understood the weight of numbers, the flow of wealth, the intricacies of trade and policy. But mostly, men who knew their place.

He offered a shallow bow, stepping forward with measured grace. "Madam Dragunova," he said smoothly, setting the ledger down before her. "The final projections for the quarter. As expected, our revised policies are yielding returns, but there is resistance from certain quarters."

Diligence smirked. "If there's one thing we can count on, it's resistance."

Vivienne traced a finger over the ledger's spine, but she didn't open it just yet. She already knew what was inside. Instead, she reached for the fine-tipped pen resting beside her papers.

Without looking up, she murmured, "Tell me, Markus. When the music stops, how many council seats will be left open?"

Markus adjusted his cuffs. "Three, at present."

Vivienne allowed herself a thoughtful hum. "Three," she mused.

She dipped the pen in ink and wrote three names. The ink flowed like silk, of course. Vivienne couldn't abide blots. Handing the list over to Markus, she said, "I think we'll find all the agreement we need out of those quarters in the future."

Markus accepted the list with a small nod, opening the ledger and placing it in just the right spot. "Very good," he said, voice smooth, assured. "I'll see that these names are accounted for."

He turned a page, scanning the next set of figures, ever the diligent man of numbers. "The expansion in the Market District is ahead of schedule. The monorail's success has quieted most of the grumbling from the poorer districts, which means they can finally get back to work. As such, profits are expected to rise, and taxes with them. A few merchants angry at the tariffs, but that's to be expected."

He flipped another page. "And, of course, as of this morning, the one-year ban on sanctioned thieving has been lifted."

Vivienne stilled.

It was slight—almost imperceptible—but for someone as attuned to her own movements as she was, it may as well have been a full-body jolt. "I'm aware," she said, voice smooth, even.

"Then you know—" Markus began, but Vivienne had pushed her chair back and stood from her desk. She walked to the window and reached towards a dynamo telescope decorated with an embossed likeness of the volcanic lava floes of Drakoria. A gift from a simpering councilman who now resided in a cell near Thume's, having outlived his usefulness. Its polished brass was cool beneath her fingertips and she adjusted it for viewing.

She lowered her eye to the lens and turned the dial with methodical precision, bringing the city into focus.

A slow scan. Market District. The glow of the monorail lines cutting through the dark. Tavern Row. Lantern-lit alleys, the pulse of gambling dens and late-night deals.

Then—

There.

A warm light flickering from a building that should have remained empty. A place that was meant to stay dark. Vivienne's grip on the telescope remained steady. Outwardly, she appeared as calm as a still pond.

But inside, something coiled.

Diligence shifted beside her, leaned in—close, her breath warm against Vivienne's ear. "What do you see?" she murmured.

Vivienne lowered the telescope, her expression unreadable.

"The ghost of Lars Harrow," she said.

Diligence smiled, slow and wicked. "How poetic."

Heading back to her desk, Vivienne dipped her pen and began to write again. With sweeping, deliberate strokes, she addressed this letter: To Balar.

Markus had brought her news. She would send some of her own. "See that he receives this, will you, Markus?"

Markus read the name, his fingers stilling just slightly over the parchment. His expression didn't change, but there was the smallest pause before he said, "Yes, Madam. If you deem it wise."

"I do."

"Then I will see it done," he said. But he did not move to leave.

Vivienne raised an eyebrow. "Well? Carry on, Markus," she urged, waving towards the door. "And lock the door on your way out. Diligence and I have unfinished business."

$\diamond$

Liora moved through Azoria like she was part of the current, letting the streets carry her, shifting with the flow of bodies and the murmurs of the city.

The Market District was alive as always—vendors hawking their wares, the scent of grilled meat and spiced nuts curling through the damp morning air, the ever-present hum of dynamo power threading beneath it all. But something was different.

She felt it in the way people spoke in hushed tones at the edges of alleyways. In the way the usual eyes that watched the streets—the ones that knew the rules, that respected the game— had been replaced by new, hungry faces.

The old crews weren't here. Or if they were, they were quieter. Cautious.

Like Azoria was starting to crack.

Literally, in some cases. The bricks in the street, once meticulously maintained, were shifting unevenly, loosened by neglect. Lanterns flickered where they shouldn't—dynamo coils half-burning out, their steady glow faltering.

A building that had once housed a bustling tailor's shop now stood empty, its windows broken, a crude symbol scrawled across the door.

This wasn't just change. This was something rotting from the inside out.

With all her focus on the monorail system, she hadn't spent a lot of time in the less desirable parts of the city. Coming to the north end of the markets bordering the slums, she barely recognized it.

Adjusting the strap of her satchel, Liora kept her hands loose at her sides. Calm awareness. Yep, that was her all over. Just a thief moving through a city that no longer played by its own rules.

At the corner of a vendor stall, she caught sight of a group of young street toughs—too young to be working alone, too eager to mask their inexperience. They were posted up outside a gambling den, their clothes a patchwork of mismatched colors, all trying too hard to look like they belonged to something bigger.

She didn't stop or break stride. But she was listening.

"You hear what happened at the shipyards?"

A snort. "Yeah, dumb bastard lifted a purse from the wrong man."

"Wrong man? It was a hells damned city watchman!"

Who the hells lifted purses? Liora sniffed. That wasn't what thieving was all about.

"Wasn't like this before," someone grumbled.

"Right. No rules now."

A different voice cut in, lower, more careful. "Yeah, well... the ban's lifted, isn't it?"

Liora kept moving.

"Think Harrow and Adalan are coming back?" the voice asked.

One of the kids sneered. "He'd better not! Out of practice for a year? That makes him a relic."

Liora slowed her pace now and veered toward the group of young thieves. They barely spared her a glance, too caught up in their murmured conversation, in their own small little world of half-truths and rumors.

She stopped just within earshot, hands in her pockets, tilting her head like she was merely another curious onlooker. "Big words," she said, her voice just loud enough to cut through the market's hum. "Talking about Harrow like you know something."

The tallest of them, a wiry guy with a jagged scar across his cheek, looked her over with mild interest. "Who the hells are you?"

Liora smirked. "Someone who actually knows what they're talking about."

The shortest of the group, a girl with quick hands and an even quicker mouth, squinted at her. Then, recognition sparked. She snapped her fingers. "Wait, wait, I know you. I saw your speech. You're that monorail girl."

Liora's stomach turned. Monorail girl.

Not thief. Not dynamo engineer. Not the mind behind the best getaways in the city. That monorail girl.

She kept her smirk, but now it was meaner. "That's cute. But no, I'm the star engineer of Lars Harrow's crew. And you better watch your ass, because he's back."

The thieves exchanged glances. Then Scar-Cheek let out a bark of laughter.

"Oh yeah?" he said, shaking his head. "And I'm Lady Vivienne's concubine."

The whole group cracked up, laughing so hard one of them actually doubled over, wiping at his eyes.

Liora made a fist. These little shits. They had no idea.

But this was getting her nowhere.

She forced down the irritation clawing up her spine. Turning on her heel, she strode away, hearing their laughter melt into the hum of the Market District. Let them laugh. They wouldn't be laughing in a few weeks, when Harrow's crew pulled off something so clean, so untouchable, that these little nobodies would be begging to get in.

But first, they needed a job. And that meant information.

Liora shifted her satchel higher on her back and made for the council offices.

The city's planning offices weren't exactly a fortress. They weren't even particularly well-guarded. Because why would they be? The bureaucrats that ran them never considered themselves a target.

Liora knew better.

Information was a far more valuable currency than copper. And right now, she was in a very exclusive club—the kind of people who could walk through those doors without raising suspicion.

Liora approached the squat, stone-faced building, adjusting her posture and gait.

Confidence, efficiency, no hesitation. That was the trick. Walk in like you belonged, and most of the time, nobody would question a damn thing.

The clerk at the front desk barely looked up as she entered.

"Hey, slick!" she chirped, but quickly realized she was being a little too over-the-top. She tried to dial it back but got flustered after that little outburst. "I... uh... oh gosh. I need access to the expansion plans for Estontown."

The clerk just sighed and pinched the bridge of his nose. "Monorail project?"

"Yeah. Among other things."

The man—mid-forties, balding, skin permanently ink-stained from years of pushing ledgers—grumbled something under his breath before pulling out a logbook. "Sign in. You know the drill. Third floor, west wing, records archive. If you take anything, sign it out properly this time. Last week someone misplaced the trade levy amendments and we had a damn council meltdown."

"Tragic." Liora took the pen, scrawled an utterly unreadable version of her name, and stepped past him.

She climbed the stairs two at a time, weaving past overworked clerks with their heads buried in stacks of parchment. The records office was ahead—dusty, dull, and exactly the kind of place where officials stored things they didn't expect anyone to steal.

The third floor somehow *smelled* like bureaucracy. The corridor was lined with records rooms, each with a neatly engraved placard indicating its purpose. Trade & Tariffs. Infrastructure & Development. Property Holdings.

That last one caught her eye. Liora adjusted the strap of her satchel and slipped inside.

The archive was a maze of shelves, stacked high with thick, leather-bound ledgers and rolled-up city plans. A lone clerk hunched over a desk in the far corner, muttering to himself as he scratched notes into a ledger.

Liora didn't even spare him a glance. People working desk jobs didn't care about intrusions unless you made them care.

She moved to the nearest shelf, running a hand along the spines of the ledgers. Each book was stamped with gilded numbers, detailing years, projects, everything going on.

Too old. Too old. Recent.

Bingo.

Her fingers brushed across a ledger marked Wind Farm Expansion - Estontown & Outer Districts. That could be interesting. Lots of parts, lots of copper. Not a bad idea for a small job to break the ice.

Liora pulled the heavy book free, flipping through pages with swift efficiency. Land deeds, commission orders, planned development charts. This was good stuff. And then—

Her eyes caught a date.

One week from now. That's when the city's registry office would be receiving the final, unfiled deeds from the current land owners before transferring them permanently into the system. She read further.

> ... At which time, the city will take ownership of the
> deeds currently located in the Southeastern Circuit
> Clerk's Office where they await escrow.

She grinned. Screw stealing wind farm parts. They'd go after the deeds and steal the land itself. That would make for a perfect little heist, and even better, it had a deadline. Lars would have no excuse but to get his butt into gear.

Just one thing... she'd be stealing from Azoria itself. And that meant stealing from Vivienne. Liora's little stunt at the monorail opening was one thing—this would be the kind of escalation she wouldn't be able to come back from.

Her work for the city could possibly be finished.

Liora slid the ledger back into place, smoothing the spine so it didn't look disturbed. She turned for the exit, already calculating. Already making her decision.

She barely made it two steps before a voice called out behind her.

"You lost?" That clerk had finally noticed her.

Liora turned, flashing her most harmless, wide-eyed smile. "Oh, no, I hope not. I'm just double-checking some specs for the monorail expansion." She tapped her temple, giving a self-deprecating laugh. "Half the time, I forget which records I've already looked at. Too much dynamo on the brain, you know?"

The clerk blinked at her. "Monorail expansion?"

Liora nodded. "Yeah, yeah, Liora Banz, monorail engineer. You know how it is, keeping this city running. If I don't check these plans myself, who knows where we'd end up?"

The man squinted at her for a long moment. Then recognition dawned in his face.

"Oh, you're that—"

"If you say that monorail girl, I swear I'll scream," she said.

The clerk gulped. "Wouldn't dream of it."

"Great," Liora said. "So, I'll just get out of your hair and—"

"You don't need to sign anything out?"

She waved a hand. "Nah, just needed a peek. Thanks, though!"

And with that, she was gone. Out the door, down the stairs, and back into the streets of Azoria.

They only had a few days to plan, and that was good news. That monorail girl would be that wind farm girl by next week.

The letter had been waiting for Myrim outside his home. It was tucked away in a little cubby in the wall, in a place designed to be hidden and noticed at the same time. By the right person.

Thick, expensive parchment. Addressed to Balar in elegant, deliberate strokes. No signature. None was needed.

Vivienne had finally called him in.

A year of silence. No orders, no whispers, not even a reminder before this. He had let himself believe she didn't need him anymore. That she had let it go. But she hadn't forgotten. She had simply been waiting.

Now, as he strode through the marble halls of the Gaming Commission, the letter sat heavy in his coat. A quiet weight, pressing against his ribs.

Myrim kept his back straight, his pace steady. But beneath the calm, he was ready for an argument. Because he had changed.

A year ago, he had been ready for this. He had sat in Vivienne's home and suggested it himself—the idea of fear as order, of vigilante justice turned to her advantage. It had felt right back then. Logical.

But then the city had fallen into chaos, thanks to the power vacuum left by Thume's ouster and the banning of heists.

And Vivienne had done nothing. She had let it fester. Let the crews tear each other apart. Let the underworld rot from the inside out, while she restructured everything else above it.

Meanwhile, Myrim had cultivated a different kind of life. A great relationship with two incredible women. They loved each other and took care of each other in different ways. And hells, one of them was even a thief!

But she was a thief he had broken out of prison once, who had more cunning and bravery in her pinky than most members of the city watch.

Myrim couldn't become Vivienne's enforcer. Not now.

Reaching her office doors, he exhaled slowly. A part of him wanted to turn around. To walk out, disappear, let her send her letters to the void. But it was too late for that. She had named him. Balar. Myrim pushed open the doors.

He would fight this.

Vivienne was seated at her desk, a vision of control in frost-blue silk, bathed in the soft glow of crystalline dynamo sconces. The air smelled faintly of lavender and ink, a contrast to the scent of jasmine he usually associated with his woman.

Her pen barely paused over the paper before her as she spoke. "Welcome, Balar. It's time to begin."

Myrim's throat felt tight. She wasn't asking. "I thought—" He swallowed, shook his head. "Things are different now. You don't need Balar now."

Vivienne cocked her head, just slightly. "Oh?"

"The city's already bending to you," he said. "You've won. Look around. No one's challenging you. No one can."

Her lips curled into something not quite a smile. "Won?" she echoed, like the word amused her. "Tell me, Myrim, what does victory look like to you?"

Myrim forced himself to answer calmly. "The politicians on your side. The streets have seen better days, but they're contained. The crews—the real ones—aren't doing a damn thing."

"And yet." Vivienne leaned forward, resting her chin against steepled fingers. "There's still a chance they could return, isn't there?"

Myrim's pulse jumped. "You made the ban for a year. If you didn't want them to come back, why not ban it for good?"

"Azoria was in chaos. A temporary hiatus was necessary. An outright ban would have started a riot."

Vivienne shook her head as if he had disappointed her. "Besides, I had a wildcard. A year ago, you told me that the city needed something more than rules. That crime needed to be purged. And that you were the man for the job."

Myrim's stomach knotted. He had said that. And at the time, he had meant it.

He had imagined taking out the worst of the worst—Thume's cronies, the monsters in the slums that left bodies in alleys for sport.

Vivienne sighed. Then, with measured precision, she set down her pen and folded her hands atop the desk. "That's the trouble with perspectives, isn't it?" she said. "They shift so easily."

She watched him for a long moment, as if weighing just how much patience she had left for this discussion. "I wonder how Liora's perspective would shift if her crew's base burned down.

All those brilliant inventions, those careful schematics... dynamo fires are so unpredictable, aren't they? Especially when someone's been working late."

Myrim stiffened. "That has nothing to do with—"

"Or perhaps Shelle would enjoy a visit from the Gaming Commission's auditors," Vivienne continued, as if he hadn't spoken. "Did you know she's been skimming from the bookies east of Market? Oh, not much. Just enough to help some of the poorer families in your district. Noble, really. But given the rules of the ban, and the addition of embezzlement..."

She shrugged. "Ten years hard time, at minimum."

"You wouldn't—"

"Wouldn't I?" Her smile sharpened. "You seem to have forgotten who you're dealing with, Myrim. I don't make idle threats. I make preparations."

He clenched his fists at his sides, forcing his mind to focus. She was baiting him. He knew it. But it didn't make it any less effective.

"You came to me, Myrim," she continued, voice smooth. "You brought me this idea. You gave me the name. You set this plan in motion."

"I didn't know who I'd be working for," Myrim said.

She laughed—a sound like breaking glass. "Oh, my dear man. You knew exactly who I was. What I was. You just thought you could use me for your righteous cause in whatever way you saw fit."

Her tone grew harder. "You were not tricked. You were not coerced. You made this decision freely. And you have spent the last year waiting for me to call upon you."

His stomach twisted. That wasn't true. Not entirely. But she had let him believe she didn't need him. She had let him go without a word. And he had let himself believe that was the end of it.

"Walk away now," Vivienne said lightly, "and by tomorrow morning, Liora will be sifting through the ashes of everything she's built, if she's not among them herself. By tomorrow evening, Shelle will be in chains. And by the end of the week?" She tilted her head. "Well. Accidents happen in Azoria. Even to former City Watch captains who think they're untouchable."

The threat hung in the air between them, precise and poisonous.

"You could try to warn them," she added, almost conversationally. "But then you'd have to explain why the Gaming Commission Chairwoman has such detailed information about their lives. Their habits. Their vulnerabilities. You'd have to tell them about our little arrangement. About Balar."

She stood, moving around the desk with predatory grace. "How do you think Liora would look at you then? Knowing you're the reason her life's work could burn? Knowing you put her in my crosshairs?"

"Vivienne," he said, voice low, measured. "Please reconsider."

She stopped just close enough that he could smell her perfume—something expensive and sharp, like winter roses.

"You know I won't," she said softly. "It's already decided. You're going to be exactly what you promised to be. Or everyone you've ever cared about will pay the price."

She returned to her desk, already dismissing him. "The choice, as they say, is yours."

Myrim said nothing. His pulse hammered in his ears.

He could refuse. He could walk out that door and gamble that she wouldn't come after him and the people he loved. But that was a fool's bet. Vivienne never made threats she wasn't willing to keep.

His shoulders dropped and he lowered his gaze. His breath came slow and heavy, each one pressing down on him like a weight he could never lift.

And then, finally—

A slow, pained nod.

Vivienne's smile returned. "Good boy," she murmured, turning back to her desk. "Get prepared, Balar. You'll receive your first directive soon."

The base was finally starting to feel like home again. And Lars felt good about it.

It wasn't just a wreck being held together by scraps of memory and Liora's stubbornness—which was considerable—but an actual, working hideout. Dynamo light flooded the room, the air smelled of dust and old wood instead of ruin, and a spread of food sat on the table.

Not one of Keer's meals, sadly, but a decent plate of bread, cheese, a few cuts of meat. It wasn't much, but it was something.

Trin leaned back in her chair, boot propped up on the edge of the table as she tapped her fingers idly against her knee. "Alright, let's go over it again," she said. "We know where the deeds are. We know when they're being moved. We know they're probably in a locked drawer, at the least. Do we know anything else?"

"Not a thing," Lars answered. "Which means we could be walking into a simple snatch and grab..."

"...or a bureaucratic hellscape," Liora finished, adjusting her glasses as she flipped through her notes. "I talked to Shelle and Myrim about it."

Lars's eyes narrowed.

"Now, Lars, you know things are different now, right? You're not going to criticize my life choices, are you?"

"I suppose not," Lars said.

"Didn't think so. Anyways," Liora continued, "Shelle didn't have much intel except that there's a decent escape through the alleyway alongside the building. Aric didn't have anything to offer."

Jax chewed on a hunk of meat thoughtfully. "Yeah, sounds like Myrim."

Liora smacked his arm, but she was smiling while she did it.

Just like old times. Trin stretched, then let her boot drop to the floor with a thud. "Bottom line, with Keer gone we need a trapspringer."

"And probably a getaway," Lars added. "Because right now, we have no idea what we're getting into. I'd like to at least know how we'll get out."

Wiping his hands off on his shirt, Jax leaned forward, grinning like a man about to cause problems. "Lucky for us, I know a guy," he said.

Lars didn't even blink. "Let me guess," he deadpanned. "Someone from the joint. And you're gonna tell me how solid he is."

Jax barked a laugh, shaking his head. "No, not from prison. That'd be ridiculous."

Lars raised an eyebrow, waiting.

"Met him at a bar."

Trin groaned. Liora sighed.

"I swear to the hells, Jax," Lars muttered.

"Hey, hey, I'd be skeptical, too," Jax said, holding up his greasy hands. "But listen—this guy drank me under the damn table. I respect that."

"Oh, super," Trin said dryly. "So he's a lightweight's worst nightmare. Good to know."

Jax ignored her. "He's really, really good. You gotta trust me on this. It's just…"

"Here it is," Lars sighed, already bracing for it. "Alright, what's the problem?"

Jax hesitated for half a second. Then scratched the back of his head, grinning sheepishly. "He's Aelyndoran."

Lars immediately shook his head. "Absolutely not."

"But he—"

"No," Lars said.

"Lars—"

"No, Jax!" Lars interrupted again. "Look, Aelyndorans are fucking *weird*. You guys know my mom was from Stoneford, right?"

Trin's eyebrows shot up. "Actually, no, Lars. We didn't know that."

"Well, she was," he huffed. "And that place is already a little too idyllic to be true. But across those mountains in Aelyndor, it's a totally different world. There's a reason no one ever goes there."

The room fell silent for a moment. But then Liora, who had been listening intently as the exchange went back and forth, finally spoke up. "I think we should give him a chance."

Lars blinked. Once. Twice. "Are you feeling alright?"

Liora was the last person he expected to agree with this. She was a dynamo girl, dedicated day and night to wrangling crystals and copper into shocking new innovations. Sometimes literally.

But Aelyndorans still worshipped *gods*, for hells' sake. No dynamo flared in Aelyndor. Just mud huts, highland tribes, and the occasional knit sweater.

"They think dynamo is an abomination, Liora," Lars said. "Their whole culture is built around avoiding it."

"Right," Liora answered, shrugging her slim shoulders. "Because the hells gifted them the ability to survive on pure stubbornness and grit."

Okay, he thought. *That's a valid point.*

But he still wasn't convinced.

"You know, Lars," Jax said, "I never would have taken you for being a bigot."

"I'm not—" Lars began.

Jax held up a hand. "You sure sound like one. But anyways, let's put that aside, because I want to get this settled. My damned head is throbbing. You think I'd bring in an idiot to roll with us?"

"No," Lars conceded.

"And do you think," Jax continued, "I would ever want to doom us to failure for someone I barely know?"

Lars sighed. "No, of course not."

"Good. I was worried." Jax leaned back, satisfied. "So, you want me to go get him?"

Just like that, Lars was beaten. Maybe he was being a little harsh. Just because Aelyndorans were superstitious nutters, it didn't—

Ah, damnit. There I go again.

"Alright, Jax. Go get him. Let's see what he can do."

Jax gave Lars a huge grin and slapped him on the back. The big man had always been strong, but the extra flab that almost doubled the size of his meaty arm packed a wallop and nearly knocked Lars over.

Lars winced, rubbing his neck as their new makeshift door shut behind Jax.

"If this goes to hells," he muttered to no one in particular, "it's on him."

✧

Lars tapped his fingers against the table. It had been long enough for him to start regretting this.

"Tell me again why we're doing this?" he asked.

"Because we need a trapspringer," Trin replied. "And because you lost the argument."

Lars rolled his eyes. "You're enjoying this, aren't you?"

Before Trin could answer, the door swung open with an aggressive bang.

Jax strode in first, looking way too pleased with himself.

And behind him—

He was exactly what Lars expected—and exactly what he *didn't* want. Broad-shouldered, shaggy-haired, built like he could wrestle an ox and win. His clothes were stitched-together leathers and heavy-woven fabric, all handmade. Not a strip of dynamo wire or processed fiber in sight.

Of course he looks like he just walked down from some hells-damned mountain monastery.

Lars sat up straighter, eyes narrowing as the man hesitated at the threshold. His dark gaze swept the room—watchful, shifty, like he was expecting an ambush.

Then he looked squarely at Lars.

The guy was sizing him up. Not cocky, not aggressive. Just measuring.

Lars ground his teeth, already getting ready to say something cutting. It was on the tip of his tongue. Something about how this wasn't some highland village and the brute could go churn butter somewhere else.

But before Lars could get a single word out, the bastard stepped forward and crushed him in a hug.

Scratch that. Not just a hug. A full-bodied, rib-cracking, spine-adjusting embrace. Lars barely had time to flinch before he was hauled off his feet, boots leaving the ground as the mountain man all but smothered him against his chest.

Trin let out a bark of laughter. Liora's eyes were saucers, nearly as big as her round glasses.

"What the hells—" Lars started. He flailed slightly—just a bit, enough to try and get some leverage. But the grip didn't budge. It was like trying to pry himself out of a steel trap.

"Hells," Jax whistled, watching the scene unfold like this was the best day of his life. "He really likes you."

The man set Lars down like a child being placed gently back on the ground after playtime with papa.

Lars adjusted his coat. Smoothed a wrinkle from his sleeve. Then he stared at the Aelyndoran flatly, as if he had just grown two more heads.

"Off to a great start, Jax," Lars said.

Jax grinned. "Right? I knew you two would hit it off."

The highlander beamed down at Lars, completely unfazed. "Glad to meet you. Name's Bungus."

Lars blinked. "I'm not calling you that."

"Call me Bunny, then," Bungus said cheerfully. "I like it better anyway."

Liora let out a small giggle, covering her mouth with her fingertips. "Bunny?" she echoed, amused. "That's... kind of adorable."

"See? She gets it."

Lars stared again. "Fine," he said. "Bunny it is."

Bunny grinned like he'd won a prize.

"But I'm still not convinced you're worth a damn at this." Lars leaned back in his chair, arms folding across his chest. "Your kind don't use dynamo. You barely believe in running water. So tell me—how exactly does an Aelyndoran expect to keep up with a crew like ours?"

Bunny rocked back on his heels. "Been breaking things since I was a child," he said simply. "Putting them back together too, mind you." He tilted his head slightly, considering. "And while I might not have much patience for dynamo, gods help me, I can at least understand it."

Lars snorted. "Yeah? Prove it."

Liora, who had been watching the exchange with growing interest, straightened. "Actually... I've got something."

She grabbed a small, intricate device from her workbench—a brass contraption no bigger than a loaf of bread, lined with delicate dynamo wiring and a hidden locking mechanism.

"I made this while Jax was out grabbing your new best friend," she said, smirking at Lars. "It's just a prototype, but it mimics the internal mechanisms of a bank's dynamo-powered vault lock."

She held it out. "You wanna prove yourself, Bunny? Crack it."

Bunny took the device carefully, turning it over in his large hands. Liora adjusted her glasses, watching him closely. "Need any tools?"

Bunny shook his head.

Lars scoffed. "Oh, come on—"

Click.

Before Lars could even finish his sentence, Bunny had disrupted the hidden latch in the mechanism, causing the dynamo wire inside to shift just enough to trigger the lock. The device popped open with a soft hiss. He handed it back to Liora.

Lars just stared.

Trin let out a low whistle. "Well, that's something."

Bunny tilted his head at Lars, smirking. "Did you ever think, maybe someone who never had to rely on dynamo just to live might be damned good at working without it? Eh?"

Lars narrowed his eyes, but he had no comeback. He hated that.

"Fine," he said. "You're in."
Bunny grinned wide. "Glad to be here."

A NEW AZORIA

4

The city stretched before Lars, restless and waiting.

He stood on the rooftop across from the Southeastern Circuit Clerk's Office, hands in his pockets, watching the building like it might whisper its secrets if he stayed long enough.

It was getting late—just past dusk, but not yet deep into the night. A few gas lamps flickered along the streets below, their glow hazy from the mist rolling in off the river. Somewhere, distant thunder rumbled. Rain was coming.

Good. Rain would make things easier. At the least, it would mask their footsteps and drown out any sound.

The clerk's office itself wasn't much to look at. A strong stone foundation, wooden upper floors, a single balcony. One main entrance. Two back exits. A narrow alley flanking one side, a carriage loading dock at the rear. Nothing fancy. No guards. Not visibly, at least.

Lars inhaled deep. This felt right.

He hadn't expected it to. Given everything he'd been holding back this last year, the bitterness that had welled up inside him, he truly expected that he wouldn't feel anything from his old life. He was wrong.

The weight of the city against his back, the pulse of a job under his fingertips, the anticipation of a play in motion. For the first time in a long time, he wasn't drifting. He was aiming at something again.

He crouched lower, tracking movement along the street below.

The last of the city clerks were leaving for the night. A bored-looking watchman exited with them and loitered by the front doors, chatting with a woman carrying an armful of ledgers. Okay, so there was one guard. That was worth noting. If one was posted, there might be others.

Still, nothing about this felt worrisome. No nearby city watch patrols. No wagons of cash being hauled in and out. If this was a tough job, it wasn't showing its teeth.

Lars adjusted his collar and dropped from the rooftop. The impact barely made a sound as his boots lightly hit the stone. He straightened and took off down the street at an easy, unhurried pace, letting the city move around him.

Just another man, just another night.

He didn't look directly at the clerk's office as he passed—never stop, never linger. Instead, he let details slip into his periphery.

The cut of the locks. The height of the windows. The alley's shadowed mouth.

That guard still loitered out front, hands resting on his belt, shifting his weight. Nothing about him said alert, but Lars had played this game long enough to know that bored men could be the most dangerous. They were always looking for an excuse to wake up.

But then a final clerk rushed out of the front door with an abrupt apology. The guard laughed and told him it was no trouble at all as he locked the front door. The pair walked off together, heading towards the denser city center to the northwest.

Well, this wouldn't be much of a challenge at all. Lars even thought—

"Lars? Is that you?"

Lars stiffened, but turned around as casually as he could muster.

Wait, was that Aric Myrim?

Standing a few feet back, hands in his coat pockets, eyes straight ahead. He looked exactly the same. Tall, lean, with dense black hair and a piercing stare. Even after all that had happened and the time that passed, he still looked every bit a lawman.

Lars didn't answer right away.

Despite Myrim's relationship with Liora, Lars's mind had already filed the prior captain away as part of the past. A man he'd worked with to bring down Thume, to shift the tides of the city, to do something bigger than either of them. And then?

Nothing.

It wasn't as though he'd disappeared. He was still around, still working security, still in Liora's life of course. But his path hadn't crossed with Lars in a long time.

And that was just fine. Old rivalries died hard, especially when the law was involved.

"Captain," Lars finally responded, "this is a surprise."

Myrim glanced once at the clerk's office, then back at him. "Absolutely. I never would have expected to see you here."

Lars somehow doubted that. Something tugged at the back of his mind. "I never expected to be seen."

A moment passed, the street noise filling the space between them. Myrim shifted, as if weighing something.

"Well, good to see you, Myrim," Lars said, eager to return home. "Say hi to Liora for me."

"Wait," Myrim urged. "Why don't we go get a drink?"

Lars narrowed his eyes slightly. "Now?"

"For old time's sake."

Lars studied him for a moment longer before tilting his head toward a side street. "Alright. Let's go."

The tavern they ducked into wasn't one Lars had ever visited before, which was probably for the best. The last thing he needed was a familiar face trying to reminisce about the old days or some would-be tough taking a shot at him for street cred.

It was a quiet place—dark wood, low lanterns, the kind of place that catered to tired foundry workers at the bar and clerks at the tables, all of whom just wanted a drink before dragging themselves home. A few scattered patrons sat hunched over their cups, voices kept low.

Lars and Myrim slid into a booth near the back.

A barmaid approached, barely sparing them a glance as she wiped her hands on her apron. "What'll it be?"

"Whiskey," Lars said.

"The same," Myrim echoed.

She nodded and disappeared toward the bar.

Lars leaned back against the worn leather of the booth, taking in Myrim across from him. The man looked... not uncomfortable, but restrained. Like he was trying to choose his words carefully.

Which meant there was something on his mind. And that this wasn't some chance encounter.

Lars wasn't in the mood to dig. Instead, he let the silence stretch, watching the room instead.

The drinks arrived quickly, two short glasses filled with amber liquid. Lars wrapped his fingers around a glass and immediately took a sip.

"Liora told me," Myrim finally said.

The words hung between them. Lars took another sip of whiskey, letting it burn down his throat while he decided how to play this.

"Told you what?" he asked.

The look Myrim gave him could have curdled milk.

"Right." Lars set his glass down harder than necessary. "Of course she did."

"Not in a bad way. We're dating. Of course she told me. It's just…" A pause, calculated. He'd always been obnoxiously calculated. "Well, she's worried about you."

That pulled a laugh from somewhere dark in Lars's chest. "That so?"

"You know it is. And she's not the only one."

Here it comes. The intervention. The concern. The carefully worded suggestion that Lars was making a mistake, wrapped up in friendly worry. He'd been waiting for someone to stage this little performance.

Myrim stared at his glass like it might provide better words. "I like to think that after all we've been through, you can count me as a friend." His eyes found Lars's. "And as a friend, I want you to know that you don't need to do this."

That… wasn't what he'd expected. "You mean the job?"

A nod.

Lars leaned back, stretching an arm along the booth's cracked leather. Casual. Unconcerned. Everything he wasn't feeling. "We're thieves, Myrim. This is what we do."

"You were a thief. A year ago. Things change."

The words hit harder than they should have. Things change. Like losing everything. Like watching your life's work crumble.

Like spending a year pretending you were anything other than what you'd always been.

"For some of us," he said, and let the bitterness show.

"Come on, Lars. You're not as cocksure as you're trying to sound. You have a choice."

Choice. What a luxury. What a lie.

"You can walk away. You could have walked away a year ago. No one would blame you for it," Myrim finished.

Lars picked up his drink again, buying time with a slow sip. The whiskey didn't taste as good as it had five minutes ago. "And what, exactly, do you think I should be doing instead?"

The pause stretched. When Myrim finally spoke, his voice had gone soft. "Focus on the people who still matter to you."

Ah. There it is.

"Sure. Like Trin, right?" Lars kept his tone light, but his finger had started tapping against the glass—an old tell he couldn't quite shake.

Another nod.

The tapping got faster. "You think I don't care about her?"

"That's not what I said."

"Is it what you meant?"

Silence. Which was answer enough.

Lars let out a bitter laugh. "So this is what, exactly? A heart-to-heart between friends? A favor for Liora?"

"It's a warning," Myrim said, and something about the way he said it sent a flicker of unease through Lars's gut.

Not a threat. Myrim wouldn't dare threaten him. But there was weight in the words.

Lars studied him carefully. "You really think I shouldn't do this job."

"I know you shouldn't."

Lars considered that. Considered the man in front of him. Then he knocked back the rest of his drink and set the glass down with a quiet clink.

"Too bad," he said. "Because I'm doing it anyway." He didn't know why, but Myrim's disapproval made this feel right. Maybe it brought back that old rebellious flame, when the man was *Captain* Myrim, the city watchman who tried like hells to bring Lars down.

Myrim looked at him for a long moment. Then, finally, he sighed and reached for his own glass.

Lars smirked. "You buying the next round?"

Myrim didn't answer right away. Just took another slow sip of whiskey, then set the glass down and said, "No."

The silence settled between them again, heavier than before.

Lars leaned back, stretching out his legs beneath the table. "Is there anything else you wanted to say?"

Myrim's lips twitched slightly. "I think you've had enough advice for one evening. Besides, the whiskey just seems to make you more of an asshole." He slid out of the booth, tossing a few coins onto the table. "Take care of yourself, Lars."

Lars watched him go, watched as he stepped out of the tavern and into the rainy street beyond.

He sat there for a long moment before finally flagging down the barmaid for another drink.

The base was quiet tonight. Relaxed. The hearth was lit, its flames casting long shadows, the warm glow doing its best to fight back the damp chill creeping in from the streets.

Liora sat at the main table, flipping through her notes, checking and re-checking figures. Across from her, Trin studied the map of the Southeastern Circuit Clerk's Office, tracing the route they'd planned with a thoughtful frown.

Jax and Bunny were out gathering supplies. Lars was scouting the job. Everyone was doing what needed to be done.

And yet, it didn't feel like it used to.

Lars was in it, but was he *in it?* He was going through the motions, making the right calls, saying the right things—but underneath it all, there was still something unresolved. Like a rope pulled too tight, fraying at the edges, waiting for that last bit of tension to snap.

Liora tapped her charcoal pencil against the table, then stuck the end in her mouth. Bad habit. The charcoal tasted like dirt, but her brain worked better when her hands were busy.

Lars needed this job. They all did, but Lars *needed* it.

"Alright." Trin's voice cut through her spiraling thoughts. "Let's go over it one more time."

Notes shoved aside. Focus mode engaged. This was the part Liora's brain loved—the puzzle, the problem, the solution waiting to be built.

Trin's finger traced the clerk's office on the map. "The safe is located here. Should we send Bunny in? With how fast he cracked that gizmo of yours, it might be—"

"No." The word came out sharper than intended. Liora softened it with a hand gesture. "Lars should do it. He knows safes. And he needs..."

To feel useful. To remember who he is. "He needs to be the one," she concluded.

Understanding flickered across Trin's face. No explanation required. That's why Liora loved her. Trin just got things.

"So Bunny guards our exit." Liora's pencil started sketching escape routes, her hands moving while her mouth kept going. "I'm thinking I dress up all official-like. Clipboard, hair in a bun, that pinched expression officials get when they haven't had their afternoon tea. Any late-night clerks show up, I can run interference."

"That's brilliant, Liora."

A grin split her face before she could stop it. "Right? I've been practicing my disappointed administrator face. Watch." She arranged her features into what she hoped was bureaucratic disdain.

Trin actually laughed—a real one, not the careful sounds she'd been making lately.

But then her face fell. "Hells, I miss Keer."

The quick shift made Liora's pencil pause mid-sketch. "Yeah, me too. Where'd that come from?"

"Oh, you know." Trin waved at the plans. "He'd take one look at this and say something like..." Her voice dropped into a passable Zarakaran impression. "'Ah, third-tier Valdrin-era security vault. Triple-pin lock, copper-plated tumblers, and enough bureaucratic arrogance to choke a horse.'"

The laugh burst out of Liora before she could stop it. Perfect. Absolutely perfect. "Hells, yes. And then he'd tell us about some job where everything went sideways but somehow he still walked out with the prize and a bump on the head."

"Keer's not here." Trin's hands folded at the table's edge, knuckles white.

"No." Liora's pencil resumed its movement. Slower now. "He's not."

"But I really wish, for Lars's sake, that he was."

Liora hunched over her notes, pencil moving faster. Nostalgia was a luxury they couldn't afford. Not with Lars hanging by a thread and their whole world balanced on this one job.

"Right, where were we... fallback positions." Liora's voice came out too bright, too quick. "If something goes wrong—"

"Liora."

That tone made her pencil freeze mid-stroke. Trin had stopped looking at the map entirely. Her eyes were locked on Liora with an intensity that made her want to squirm.

"Do you think I'm a fool?" Trin asked.

The question hit like cold water. "What? No," Liora said. "Why would I—what brought this on?"

Trin's breath came out long and tired. "Because I stayed."

Oh. *Oh*. Liora's fingers went still, pencil forgotten.

"Last year, when Lars went with Vivienne, I didn't leave him." The words tumbled out like Trin had been holding them back with a dam that just cracked. "He said it was a ruse, I believed him. When we were running, moving from safe house to safe house like rats, I stayed."

Her hands dragged down her face, muffling a sound that might have been a laugh or a sob.

"Then the ban happened. Everything seemed settled. We could stop running. And what did I tell myself? 'He just needs time. We've got each other, he'll make this work.'"

Another harsh breath. "Now the ban's lifted. I tried to get him back in. You know what he did? Sat there and watched me walk out the door."

Their eyes met across the table.

"I came here. And here I am. Still."

Liora's mouth had gone dry. Her brain, usually so quick with solutions, came up empty.

A bitter laugh escaped Trin. "You remember what I used to be?"

She didn't wait for an answer—just barreled on like stopping would break her.

"I was our spymaster. I crossed from here to Zarakar's jungles, knew every power shift before it happened. Which noble was screwing whose spouse, which barons would be at war before they'd even decided to fight." Her voice went hard. "I was good, Liora. Really good."

Her head tipped back, studying the ceiling like it might have answers written in the wood grain.

"Now? Now I'm just Lars's woman."

The silence that followed felt heavy enough to drown in.

"Tell me." Trin's gaze snapped back down. "Am I a fool?"

Liora's mind finally kicked into gear. She chewed her lip, sorting through responses like she'd sort through gears— looking for the one that would fit, that would work.

"I don't think you're a fool." Careful words, measured. "But let me ask you something. If this was anyone else. If this was intelligence you were gathering, what would your assessment be?"

Trin's frown deepened. "What?"

"You just said it. You're a spymaster. You see patterns, put pieces together." Liora leaned forward, pencil tapping again. "So be analytical. Engineer this like I'd engineer a machine. Why did you stay?"

She watched Trin's mouth open, then close. Saw the moment her friend was about to give some practiced answer.

"No rehearsed bullshit," Liora pressed. "Not 'I thought he'd get better' or 'love conquers all.' The real reason. Why?"

Trin's throat worked. When she spoke, her voice came out raw. "If I left... I'd lose everything."

Liora's chest tightened.

"My family." Trin's fingers curled against wood. "The future I thought we were building."

Then, quieter, she said, "And I'd lose the best man I've ever known."

The words cracked at the edges.

"But hells, Liora, I don't know if I can keep doing this."

The admission hung between them. Liora's brain spun through possibilities, probabilities, the mechanics of heartbreak and hope. Then she leaned forward, elbows on the table.

"You're not a fool. You're patient. Strong. And you've been holding all of us together—Lars, me, this whole crew—because that's who you are."

She tilted her head, letting a grin creep in. "Now, whether Lars actually deserves that kind of dedication?" A shrug. "Guess that's what we're all hoping to find out, isn't it?"

Trin wiped her eyes. But she smiled. "Yeah. I guess it is."

They sat in silence for a few moments. Then a few more. Patient though Trin might be, Liora's patience charge was dangerously close to empty. She started to fidget.

"You know, if we're sharing gossip and schemes, let me squawk Shelle," Liora said.

She pulled out her squawk and turned the dial, the device crackling as it connected. A second later, Shelle's voice sparkled through.

"This better be important, darling. I was just in the middle of hustling some sorry bastard at cards." They heard a loud objection behind her. Who knew what that woman was *really* up to.

"Hey, babe." Liora leaned back in her chair, feigning innocence. "Wanna come over and plan a heist?"

There was a pause. Then Shelle laughed.

"I'll be there in ten."

Eleven minutes later, the base door swung open, and Shelle stepped inside. She had a bottle of wine tucked under one arm and wore a night blue shirt, tight pants tucked into soft boots, and a grin sharp enough to cut glass. Her dark hair was half-pinned back, the rest tumbling over her shoulders and ample chest in waves—just disheveled enough to suggest she'd been up to something wild.

"Evening, ladies." The door banged shut under Shelle's boot. "Hope I didn't keep you waiting."

Trin's eyebrow climbed toward her hairline. "That depends. Did you win?"

"Oh, without a doubt." Shelle's smirk was charming. She dropped the wine on the table with a satisfying thunk.

Liora snatched the bottle before it could roll, examining the label. Good stuff. Really good stuff. "This for us, or are you just showing off?"

"Obviously for us." Shelle collapsed into the chair beside her, all theatrical exhaustion. One leg crossed over the other, boot tapping air. "Can't plan a heist on an empty glass. It's bad luck. Or good luck. I can never remember which."

Trin rolled her eyes and grinned. "Alright then. Let's see if your wine is as good as your card playing."

The map crinkled as Liora dragged it back across the table, her finger already tracing routes. "Here's our target. Here's what we know for certain. And here—" she tapped a section that made her stomach do unpleasant things, "—is where it could get messy."

The cork came free with a satisfying pop. Trin's pour was generous. The dynamo lamps buzzed as they all leaned in, casting their shadows across the paper like they were already sneaking through those sketched hallways.

Their scheming may have taken a few odd turns, but it stretched well into the night—wine flowing, ideas twisting, the kind of planning that felt half-mad and half-genius in equal measure.

The whole room buzzed with anticipation.

Not the frantic energy of amateurs or the reckless abandon of the desperate. This was the particular tension Lars remembered from the old days. Professional criminals—no, *celebrities*—preparing to practice their craft. Maps studied, routes memorized, roles assigned. Nothing left but the waiting.

The moment before the jump. Hells yes.

Lars stood at the head of the table, trying to look like he belonged there. His crew. The words should have settled into place like a key in a lock. A year ago, they would have.

But why did he feel like an imposter?

Stop it. He forced the doubt down where it couldn't show. These people were counting on him to be Lars Harrow, master thief. Not whatever hollow thing he'd become during the ban.

Jax had claimed his usual position, leaning against a chair like it was the only thing keeping him upright, managing to look both enormous and completely at ease. Bunny flipped a knife between his fingers with the absent precision of long practice, dark eyes tracking everyone in the room. Trin perched on the table's edge, one boot swinging in a slow rhythm that Lars knew meant she was thinking three steps ahead.

Liora stood by the map, wound tight as a crossbow string. And Shelle... Shelle had draped herself across a chair with a glass of wine, treating this like a dinner party instead of a criminal conspiracy.

"I'm just here for moral support," she'd said. Right.

It was time to make this happen.

"Alright." His voice came out steadier than expected. Small victories. "We all know the job. Every angle's been covered. We hit the clerk's office, crack the safe, grab the deeds, get out. No mess, no noise."

He made himself meet each pair of eyes, trying to project confidence he didn't feel. "Bunny, you're in the alley. Keep our exit clear. Liora, you're running interference. If anyone asks, you're an auditor doing a late inspection. Jax, Trin, you're with me."

Bunny's smirk turned theatrical. "So I just stand in the dark and look pretty?"

"Fat chance of that," Lars muttered.

"What was that?" All innocence, that grin.

"Hey, don't worry." Jax's idea of reassurance. "If anything goes wrong, you'll get to hit someone."

Bunny's whole face lit up. "Oh. See, now I feel special."

"Well, we wouldn't want you to be left out," Trin added, and Lars caught the look she shot him. Relax. They're just being themselves.

Right. Time for the speech. The part where he was supposed to inspire confidence instead of revealing he'd forgotten how to be himself.

"This is the first real job we've done in a year." The words tasted like rust. "And I know some of you are wondering if we've still got it."

The silence that followed had weight. Lars felt it pressing against his ribs, asking questions he couldn't answer.

Bunny's hand went up like a schoolboy's. "Uh, yeah. So, not to be that guy, but I wasn't around a year ago. So I don't actually know if you had it in the first place."

Lars gave him the flattest look he could manage.

"Just saying."

"Oh, we had it, Bunny boy." Jax clapped the Aelyndoran's shoulder hard enough to make his fellow giant stumble. "Best in the city."

"Right." Bunny nodded with mock seriousness. "So if this goes sideways, I should assume I got scammed."

"Lars is right, though." Trin's voice cut through the banter, grounding them. "This job is the reset button. We need this." Her eyes found his. "And we're ready."

Something in her expression made his chest tight. Not pity. Not doubt. Just... faith. Like she still saw the man he used to be somewhere under all the damage.

"Tonight, we remind this city who we are." The words came out before he could stop them. He wanted to believe them so bad.

Trin's elbow found his ribs. "Was that it?"

"Little dramatic, but I liked it." Jax's grin could have lit the room.

Bunny started a slow clap. "Rousing. Stirring. I almost felt a feeling."

"If we're done congratulating Lars on remembering how to talk," Liora cut in, already moving toward her gear, "can we get moving? We have a job to pull."

And just like that, the knot in Lars's chest loosened. They were just giving him shit. He was the only one doubting himself.

Lars couldn't help but grin. This felt like family. "Right. Let's go."

While the rain had started as a light drizzle, it was now steadily drumming against the rooftops, pooling in the uneven stones of the alley. This part of the city was quiet at this hour, hushed beneath the weight of the coming storm.

Lars moved swiftly, keeping to the shadows as he led Jax and Trin toward the side entrance of the Southeastern Circuit Clerk's Office. The damp air carried the distant hum of Azoria's nightlife—the clatter of a wagon a few streets over, the murmur of voices from the taverns lining the far avenues—but here, in this tucked-away part of the district, the streets were nearly empty.

It felt right.

And yet... A tiny, gnawing edge of doubt crawled up the back of his mind. Something about the silence. About the stillness.

You're overthinking it.

Lars shook off the thoughts. He'd been out of the game for a year—of course things felt off. That's all this was.

Ahead, Bunny was already in position, tucked into the narrow alleyway that lined the side of the building. He gave a two-fingered salute as Lars passed by, grinning like this was the most fun he'd had in weeks.

"Oi there, chappy. Nice night for a robbery," Bunny whispered.

Lars just rolled his eyes and kept moving.

Out front, Liora was playing her part. There was no need for her to be on dynamo duty tonight. She stood near the entrance, clipboard in hand, her expression one of crisp authority. To any passersby, she looked like a city official conducting a late-night inspection. If anyone got curious, she'd be their first line of defense.

Lars barely glanced at her as he passed—never make eye contact, never acknowledge—but he caught the slight dip of her head. She was ready.

Jax was just behind him, quiet for a man his size. Trin moved even quieter, her presence more felt than heard.

They moved as one, a muscle memory of a life they had lost and now had found again.

Lars flexed his fingers. The thrill was there, flickering at the edges of his mind.

This is it. This is what I was made for.

He reached for the door handle and found it locked. Pulling out his lockpicks, he deftly twisted and prodded at tumblers until he heard a satisfying click. Lars tested the handle again, and the door opened easily. The trio slipped inside.

It had been way too long since he'd picked a lock.

The hallway stretched ahead, dimly lit by the soft glow of dynamo sconces. The rain outside muffled the usual hum of the city, leaving only the sound of their footsteps against the waxed wooden floor.

Lars moved ahead, leading without hesitation. They had memorized this route—studied it, walked through it in their heads a dozen times before setting foot inside. It was a simple path. Through the side entrance, down the hall, past the records room, second door on the left. That's where the safe would be.

No surprises. No deviations.

He kept his pace steady, his senses alive. Trin and Jax followed in practiced silence, slipping through the space with ease.

So far, everything was exactly as expected. No guards, no unexpected obstacles. Just a quiet government office waiting to be relieved of its excess paperwork.

"Hells, Lars," Jax whispered, "maybe we shoulda picked something tougher. This is almost too easy."

Lars remained silent. He knew better than to tempt fate.

But continuing down the hallway, Lars couldn't help but think about Jax's words.

Of course it was easy, right? That was the point. They picked a solid, simple target. One with no guards, no fancy dynamo gimmicks. Break in, crack the safe, get out. As intended.

Then why the hells did the air around him feel so *expectant*? Almost staged. Like there was some kind of audience outside their vision, holding their breaths, as Lars led his team to an uncertain fate.

No. He shook his head, banishing the thoughts. Stop that. He—

Click.

The ominous sound made Lars snap his head up just as he'd walked through a doorway. A security door slammed down, nearly taking off his foot as he walked through, and separating him from Jax and Trin.

No! *Stupid, stupid,* he thought. Lars Harrow, stepping on a pressure plate? That was an amateur's move.

And then, like a sound from a nightmare, there was an explosion. It rocked the foundations of the building, knocking him off his feet. Light danced in his vision, something like sparks that engulfed his field of view.

He heard a scream. Trin? But then he heard nothing.

Coughing from the dust around him, Lars shouted through the metal security door. "Trin! Jax!" But there was no reply.

Hells, had he gotten them killed? At that moment, he wanted nothing more than to drop to the ground and lie there. The thought was too much to contemplate.

But Lars pressed on. He had to hope that they were okay. Up ahead was the safe room… and the way out.

He stumbled forward, and as he got closer to the office the floor became more littered with debris. The air was thick with dust, a choking haze that made his lungs burn and his eyes sting. Somewhere behind him, the metal security door seemed to rattle from the shockwave.

His hands found the wall, steadying himself as he pressed forward. He wiped at his face, but his gloves only smeared the grime further. The room ahead was barely visible through the settling dust, but the door was open.

That is, what was left of it. The frame was warped, the hinges twisted. The heavy door had been torn from its place, thrown sideways into the wall like it weighed nothing.

Lars moved through the wreckage, stepping over shattered floorboards and broken glass. His eyes found the safe, bolted to the ground in the back of the room.

It was wide open and empty. Not a single scrap of paper was inside. But it was the wall beyond it that made his stomach drop.

A gaping hole had been blasted clean through the stone. The edges of the break were scorched, blackened, still smoldering in places. Rain slashed through the opening, hissing as it met the hot metal framework. The alley beyond was a streak of shadows and flickering lamplight, water pooling in the uneven cobblestones.

And just beyond the misting rain—a rope, swinging gently in the wind.

Someone had beaten them here. Someone might still be here.

Lars took a halting step forward. His mind raced, trying to make sense of it. What other crew could've known about this job?

An important question. But right now, he needed to get out. Get to his crew. To Trin.

Was Trin even alive? Was Jax? They had to be.

A blast of wind whistled along the broken wall, and Lars stepped out into the night.

Just then, a shape dropped into view. Sleek, fast, precise. A masked sliver of darkness against the storm.

Lars barely had time to raise his arms before the first blow landed.

A fist struck his ribs like a hammer, the impact sending a jolt through his chest. He stumbled back, teeth gritted, his vision going red with pain. Fast. So fast.

Lars swung, but the figure was already moving. A brutal hook caught his jaw, snapping his head sideways, the world tilting for half a second before another hit slammed into his stomach, knocking the breath clean out of him.

Hells.

He hit the ground hard, skidding across wet stone. His hands scrambled for purchase, trying to push himself up, but another strike drove into his back, sending him sprawling again. Rain lashed against his face, mixing with dust and blood.

He rolled, forcing himself upright, ignoring the way his ribs screamed in protest. His mind raced, tried to process. Who the hells was this? *What* was this?

They didn't fight like a thug. Didn't waste movement, didn't posture. Every blow was deliberate, calculated, meant to break him piece by piece. This wasn't a street fight.

This was an execution.

Lars forced himself to his feet. He wouldn't go down this easy.

But the figure was already closing in.

A blur of black leathers and a dark mask that seemed to absorb what little light there was in the alley. Silent. Efficient. Unstoppable.

Lars dodged the next hit—barely—but the follow-up came too fast. A brutal knee to his side, then a boot sweeping his legs out from under him. He hit the alley stones with a hard, wet smack, his head bouncing off the ground.

Dizzy. Disoriented.

No.

He tried to roll away, but a hand caught the back of his coat and hauled him up like a ragdoll. Lars swung wild, desperate, but the bastard caught his wrist mid-strike, twisting it so hard he thought his bone might snap.

Pain flared. He gasped.

And then he was slammed against something metal. A pole?

The world tilted. Rain dripped down his face. He completely lost his footing.

It took a second too long to realize—his wrists were bound. He couldn't get free.

He struggled, tried to twist free, but the knots held. Hells, when had they even—

He sucked in a painful gasp of air, trying to shake the haze from his head. He opened his eyes. His attacker was watching him. Staring silently. That mask seemed like one a fabled demon would wear as a face. Passionless, pitiless. Brutal.

Lars lifted his head, rain blurring his vision.

"Bastard," he rasped, spitting blood onto the stone. "At least—say something—"

The figure stepped forward, raising a hand. But then, a scream sounded out from the far end of the alley.

No, not a scream. A roar.

Lars turned his head, the rope creaking against the pole as he pulled uselessly against the bindings. He saw Bunny barreling towards him, the Aelyndoran kicking up huge splashes of water pooled on the cobblestones. Jax was behind him, the poor man far too out of shape to run like this, but doing it all the same.

His attacker saw them too. He grabbed the rope already dangling from the building, and in one quick movement he was climbing, ascending into the rain-soaked darkness faster than seemed possible for a man his size.

Lars heard a crash of boots against water. Bunny reached him first, and Jax came up behind, panting. They started working at Lars's bindings. Lars listed, afraid he would drop to the ground. He had no strength left.

But they got him free. Bunny tossed Lars over his shoulder.

As his blood dripped onto the cobblestone, Lars could feel consciousness slipping away. He was going to pass out. Hells, maybe he'd never wake up.

It all went dark just as he heard Jax's voice shout, "What in the hells was that?"

Lars didn't know. He didn't know anything. Not anymore.

A CREW DIVIDED

5

Everything hurt.

Lars had taken hits before. Broken ribs, a crossbow bolt once—he'd walked away from all of them. But this was different. This wasn't just pain. It was humiliation, the kind that settled deep, poisoning everything.

That... whatever the hells that was. It hadn't just beaten him. It had dismantled him.

Lars slumped in a chair, struggling to breathe through the bruises blooming across his ribs. Every inhale felt like he was swallowing glass. Blood had dried at the corner of his mouth, caked into the stubble along his jaw.

He barely remembered getting back to the hideout. Everything since the clerk's office was a blur of pain, movement, and failure.

Jax was slouched near the bar, rolling his shoulder with a grimace, his hand pressing against his ribs where the door had slammed him mid-charge. "I'm just saying it could have been worse," he said.

Liora, pacing back and forth, wiped a tear from her eye with the back of her wrist. "Could've been worse?" she repeated, voice sharp. "Jax, that was nothing short of a nightmare."

Bunny sat on the edge of the table, arms crossed, unreadable. His eyes flicked toward Lars, but he didn't say a word.

"Alright," Liora said, voice clipped as she finally stopped pacing. "Somebody start making sense of this. What the hells just happened?"

Silence. Trin tucked her hands beneath her arms.

Lars swallowed against the raw ache in his throat. *That's a damn good question.*

Bunny finally spoke up. "I'll tell you what happened. We got worked."

"No shit," Jax muttered.

Liora ignored them, shaking her head. "No, I mean how? Who attacked Lars? Did they steal the deeds?"

No one immediately spoke up, because no one knew what to say. But then Trin said the only thing that really made sense. "We have no idea, Liora."

"Right, I know that," Liora shot back. "But we've got to figure this—"

"There's nothing to figure out!" Trin snapped. "We tried to get back in the game. Someone beat us to it."

Lars grimaced. Someone. Some *thing.* He'd never forget looking at that mask. It was made of formed black leather, and covered the face behind it completely. There were slits for the eyes, but they were set deep and dark. And on the forehead, the image of an eye. Open wide, with an eight-pointed star for the pupil, and a jagged scar debossed across it.

He didn't know what it meant. And he didn't care.

Trin cut through his thoughts. "I'm sorry, Liora," she started, rubbing her forehead. "You're right. We should figure this out."

Did she really think that? Or was she just trying to let Liora blow off steam?

"Well, I'll start." Jax sat forward. "Whoever he was, he didn't move like a thug."

Liora frowned. "What do you mean?"

"I mean he was more like a soldier than a street thief."

Lars barely heard them. His mind was stuck, looping the fight.

The way the man moved. The way his blows landed, perfectly placed. Not just brute force—precision. Skill. Knowledge.

The reality of it settled deep in his gut. *You weren't fast enough. You weren't strong enough. You aren't the best anymore.*

The words in the room blurred together. Voices rising and falling. Liora was still talking. Jax had something to say. Trin's silence weighed heavy. But Lars felt like he was outside of it all, looking in.

Somewhere in the haze of his thoughts, he caught snatches of the conversation.

"—couldn't have known—"

"—just don't understand—"

"—who the hells even moves like that—"

Lars curled his fingers against his thigh. He could still feel it. The first hit that had landed too hard, too fast. His ribs screaming as he went down. That masked face, calm, precise, mocking him without saying a word.

A sharp *crack* snapped him back to the present.

Trin had slapped her hand against the table.

"Alright, enough of this," she said, wincing as she flexed her fingers. "You want to sort through things, that's fine. But we can sit here crying about how bad we got our asses handed to us, or we can figure out what we're doing next."

Lars inhaled sharply—bad decision. Pain lashed up his ribs. He barely managed to keep his expression still.

Liora turned toward him. "Lars, you haven't said a word."

His mouth felt dry.

"You're the one who fought him," she pressed. "What do you think?"

Lars didn't have an answer. There was nothing to say. The silence stretched. He could feel them all watching him. Waiting.

Jax let out a rough breath. "Oh, for hells sake—come on, Lars. Just say something. I mean, yeah, you got the shit kicked out of you, but it's not like—"

Something in Lars snapped. He tried to push himself up from the chair. Fast, instinctive, the way he always had. His body had other plans.

Pain lanced through his ribs, sharp enough to black out his vision for a split second. His legs buckled beneath him, and the next thing he knew, he was falling.

The world turned. The floor came up fast.

Hands caught him. Trin.

She was at his side before he even registered it, gripping his arm, steadying him.

"Easy," she murmured, voice kind but firm.

Lars clenched his teeth as she helped guide him back into the chair, every inch of movement burning like fire beneath his skin. His breath came ragged as he sagged back, muscles trembling from the effort.

Jax shifted in his seat, looking deeply uncomfortable. Liora frowned, but she didn't speak. Bunny just sat there, arms crossed, watching.

Lars dragged a slow, painful breath through his teeth. "Thanks," he muttered.

Trin's hands lingered on his arm for a second longer. Then she pulled away, stepping back.

Lars let his head tip back against the chair. His eyes shut. His chest ached. He wanted to scream. He wanted to rage. Instead, he forced calm words through his raw throat.

"I appreciate you all being here for me."

A pause.

He opened his eyes, staring straight ahead, not looking at any of them. "But if anyone wants to keep talking about this, they can get the hells out of my base."

Silence. Liora's eyes narrowed at Lars.

Bunny, however, let out a small, sharp huff. Not quite a laugh. "You really are an asshole then, aren't ya?"

Lars didn't answer.

Across the room, Trin exhaled. It was quiet, measured, but Lars felt it. "I need some air," she said.

Then she grabbed her coat and walked out.

Lars didn't watch her go. He just stared at the floor, jaw tight, every inch of him a raw, open wound. The door swung shut behind her.

The cold night air was sobering.

Trin didn't know where she was walking. But she had to move. The hideout had been suffocating, the air thick with sweat, frustration, and Lars's silence.

Lars.

Hells, she felt bad. She really did. The man had just gotten wrecked. Beaten down in a way that didn't just break his body—it broke something deeper.

And she cared. Of course she cared.

But as she walked, boots scuffing against damp cobblestones, something inside her started twisting.

Like she had told Liora, she thought—hoped—getting back into the game would fix things. That it would set everything right. That when they pulled a job again, the weight pressing against her chest would lift, and she'd feel that thrill again.

But it didn't work out that way, did it?

She should have felt relief when they were out there. When the job was in motion, when the adrenaline hit. But instead, there had been something else.

That nagging doubt. The one that said she was wasting her time. That Lars wasn't worth—

Trin let out a breath, shaking her head. No, that wasn't fair. It wasn't that simple.

She loved him, didn't she? Wasn't it her who told Liora he was the best man she'd ever known?

A muscle in her jaw tensed. She stared straight ahead, but her mind kept looping back.

But Lars wasn't the man he used to be. And worse... she wasn't sure she could love the man he was now.

Trin's boots carried her forward, though she had no real direction in mind. Just away.

The streets of Azoria stretched out before her, still humming with life, indifferent to the wreckage she carried inside. The dynamo lamps buzzed in a steady rhythm, glowing against the damp stone. Somewhere, laughter rang out—drunken, carefree, the kind that belonged to people who had nothing to lose.

She kept walking.

Eventually, the noise thinned. The buildings, pressed tight together in the denser quarter, began to space apart as she neared the river. The scent of damp wood churning through water met her before the view did.

The River Ithris rolled forward, slow but steady, pouring relentlessly toward the Azure Sea. She stopped near the edge, hands braced against the worn iron railing as she took in the view.

Water mills turned in their endless rhythm, their great wooden wheels creaking and groaning under the weight of the current. Dynamo coils hummed low from the structures beside them, siphoning power from the churning river, channeling energy back into the city. The glow of circuits flickered within the stone foundations, veins of light pulsing in time with the water's rhythm.

It was beautiful, in its own way. And constant.

No matter what happened in the streets above, the river kept moving. The mills kept turning. The power kept flowing. For the most part anyway.

Azoria didn't care about one broken crew. It didn't care about Lars Harrow sitting battered in a chair, barely able to stand.

The city kept going.

Trin exhaled, letting her eyes follow the water as it carved its endless path toward the sea. She used to love this view.

When she and Lars were younger, they used to come here after jobs, standing right where she was now, watching the river carry the weight of the city's sins out to sea. Back then, it had felt like freedom.

Now it felt like a reminder. Azoria was moving forward. And she was still stuck here, trying to pretend things could go back to the way they were.

Trin swallowed, burying her face in her arms.

She'd been holding on too tightly to something that didn't exist anymore. Maybe hadn't existed for a while now.

How could she break this down and find the root of the issue? Just like Liora had said... how would a spymaster analyze it?

Analysis complete, she thought with a grimace. Vivienne. Vivienne hells damned Dragunova.

The thought of her alone made Trin's skin crawl.

She could see her clear as day—silver hair like a snake's shed skin, eyes like wet glass, cold and unreadable. Vivienne didn't walk. She slithered, smooth and practiced, never making a move that wasn't calculated three steps ahead. Everything about her was a weapon—her voice, her smile, the way she let people think they had a choice before closing the jaws around their neck.

And when the choice had been presented—stay with his crew or go with her... Lars had left. Lars had gone with her. Lars had—

Trin's fingers curled against the railing, nails biting into her palms.

She could still hear Vivienne's voice. That damn voice. Low, rich, precise. Every word coated in honey, yet sharp enough to cut.

"Imagine what we could be together."

Trin had hated her the moment they'd met. Not because she was powerful. Not because she was dangerous.

But because Vivienne looked at Trin like she was small. Like she was nothing more than Lars's shadow.

During her trip around Ithris, Trin had found Vivienne. Their would-be patron. But it was Lars who truly let the woman in. He had let her whisper into his ear, spin her webs, pull him close.

How close?

The thought struck fast, sharp as a dagger.

Trin sucked in a breath, the river suddenly feeling too loud, too far away. She knew now that his betrayal had all been a ploy. Because he said it was.

Back then, she had watched Lars walk away from them all. Had watched him choose Vivienne. And back then, she had believed it.

Then the message had come from Lars: come quick, with Vivienne's address. A promise that they would take it all back.

And they did. Trin had even left a final message to that maniacal bitch.

Because of that, she had been willing to believe it had all been a lie. That he never actually—

What if he did?

What if, even for a second, Lars chose her?

Had he touched her? Slept with her? Let her drag him down into whatever twisted game she was playing? A sour taste rose in her throat.

She didn't want to think about it. She didn't want to see it. But the image was already there, pressing against her skull—Vivienne's fingers trailing over Lars's jaw, her lips close, whispering something only he could hear.

Trin swallowed hard.

Why was she thinking about this now? Why was this even in her head?

Trin squeezed her eyes shut and forced herself to breathe. This was getting her nowhere. Vivienne wasn't here. Vivienne wasn't the point.

She let go of the railing, shaking the tension from her hands. Back to the facts. That's what mattered. That's what she could hold onto.

Jax, Liora. Lars. Hells, even Bunny.

They were her family. The only family she had. That had never changed, and it never would. No matter how much Jax drank, or Liora prattled on about dynamo circuits. No matter how badly Lars let himself go.

She would be there. For all of them. Even for Lars. *Especially* for Lars.

A bitter laugh almost escaped her lips, but she swallowed it down. That was the worst part, wasn't it? That no matter how much had broken between them, no matter how much she wanted to walk away, she couldn't.

She would stand beside him. Patch his wounds. Watch his back. But could she love him?

If she had any damn sense, she would have walked away after Vivienne, after the betrayal, after a year, after tonight.

But here she was. Still here.

The river churned on. The mills groaned. The city didn't stop for her grief. And neither would she.

Trin let out a slow breath and turned back toward the hideout.

"Did you hear?" a woman's voice said to a nearby food vendor. "There's a Zarakaran galleon docked at the shipyards!"

A sharp snort came in reply. An older man, the food vendor, shook his head as he wrapped spiced lamb in a flatbread.

"Zarakaran? Not a chance. We don't trade with them anymore." He spat onto the ground. "More's the pity. These Drakorian spices don't hold a candle to the Mbarara Oasis blends."

Trin froze. A Zarakaran ship?

That wasn't possible. Zarakar had cut them off. Their ships hadn't seen Azorian docks in a year—not since Thume was taken down and Vivienne had taken control.

Her pulse kicked up. She laid a hand on the original speaker's arm—a pretty middle-aged woman, skin a warm copper tone, dark curls tucked into a patterned headscarf.

"Excuse me," Trin said, her voice steady, but thrumming with something just below the surface. "What makes you think the ship is from Zarakar?"

The woman blinked at her, then smiled slightly. "Because I know a Zarakaran hull when I see one. It's huge. Bigger than any Drakorian trade ship I've seen. Dark wood, rich as mahogany. And the sail bears the mountain and lightning bolt." She whistled low. "A real beauty."

Trin's heart slammed against her ribs. The crest of Zarakar. She would bet her last copper that it was the same damn ship that Darius stole from Lord Thume last year.

For the first time in longer than she could remember, Trin grinned.

Without another word, she took off. Her feet pounded against the pavement, dodging night vendors and dock workers as she sprinted toward the shipyards.

The night air was cold against her face.

But for the first time in a long, long time—she felt warm.

Myrim woke slow, groaning without even realizing it.

The room was dim, the early light from the window stretching thin across the walls. Somewhere outside, a cart rumbled over cobblestones, a vendor calling out something low and distant, muffled by the glass.

He blinked up at the ceiling, dragging in a breath. His legs ached from running and leaping, and his right shoulder felt a little tight. But his hands...

He flexed his fingers above the sheets. His knuckles were stiff, swollen at the joints. A dull, nagging throb—not any real damage, just the kind of soreness that came from throwing punches.

The memories came in small flashes. The impact of each hit. The way Lars staggered. The feel of bone against bone.

Myrim exhaled slowly and turned his head.

Shelle was sitting up beside him, legs half-tucked beneath her, dark hair falling over one shoulder. She didn't speak right away.

Her eyes flicked to his hands. Then back to his face. "Rough night?"

Myrim blinked against the light, flexing his fingers again. Shelle didn't press. She never did. She just sat there, one arm resting over her knees, watching him like she was piecing something together in her head.

Because to Shelina Halmuth, everything was a mystery worth investigating until she got to the bottom of it.

Myrim rolled onto his side, propping himself up on an elbow. His body felt heavy but functional. "Yeah," he said, voice still rough from sleep. "Private security job. Some drunk got too bold."

"Oh! At an event?" she asked.

He nodded, rubbing a hand down his face. "Some fancy thing uptown. A client needed extra eyes."

Shelle huffed, her lips twitching into something close to a smirk. "Did they pay you to punch the guests, or was that extra?"

Myrim let out a low chuckle. "Maybe a bonus."

Reaching out lazily, she took his hand, turning it over in hers. "At least it wasn't a knife fight," Shelle muttered. "Last time you came home from one of those, you had stitches."

Her voice was already drifting, fading back toward sleep. She didn't doubt him. Why would she? The bruises made sense. The story made sense. It wasn't a lie that needed effort.

Myrim flexed his fingers again, watching the way the bruises shifted on his skin. It should have felt wrong to lie. But it didn't.

Anyway, it wasn't really a lie. He *had* been on a job. Just... just not the kind Shelle thought.

His knuckles throbbed—a slow, pulsing reminder of what he'd done. He could still feel it, not just in his hands but somewhere deeper.

He had gone hard. Harder than he needed to. But—and he barely wanted to admit this to himself...

Myrim had enjoyed it.

Not the violence itself, or the brutality of it. But the sheer force of will. The way the fight narrowed everything down. No distractions, no questions. Just movement, instinct, control. Precision. It was like dynamo pulsing in the heart.

Myrim exhaled slowly, focusing on no particular spot on the ceiling. His hand moved absently, fingertips grazing the curve of Shelle's hip beneath the sheets. The same hand that had wrought such mayhem the night prior.

He had meant what he told Vivienne. That part of his life was over.

But last night, when he put on that mask, when he stepped into that enforcer role again—it hadn't felt like stepping back into something foreign. It had felt like coming home.

And Balar wasn't done.

Myrim wasn't sure he wanted him to be.

The top floor of the Ithris Gaming Commission was quiet, save for the soft click of polished boots against marble.

Vivienne moved with grace sharpened to a blade.

A folded note was pressed into her gloved hand as she strode past a waiting attendant.

She didn't stop walking. Just unfolded it with a flick of her fingers, eyes scanning the words as she moved toward the window.

Her lips curled.

By the time she reached the glass, she was laughing.

She paused, tilting her head slightly, the morning sun catching silver strands in her meticulously styled hair.

Beyond the glass, Azoria stretched out before her—copper and gold, glass and smoke, the city humming with restless energy.

Word trickled through the streets like rain in the gutters. And by the time the sun had touched the rooftops, the city already knew. Some crew had claimed the wind farm deeds. That was the story. But like so many stories in Azoria, the truth had been twisted before it even reached the second telling.

Word slithered through the Market District like the scent of spiced meats and charred citrus, drifting from stall to stall, passed between hands exchanging coin.

A fishmonger gutted a river trout with quick, practiced strokes, his knife gliding between bone and flesh. "I heard Harrow barely made it out."

"Nah," his neighbor scoffed, piling blood oranges into a crate. "They left him in a heap."

Across the way, a woman hawking fried plantains clicked her tongue. "No, no—he got away, but the explosion he set off nearly took his whole crew down with him." She shook her head. "Damn fool probably thought he was still in his prime."

A butcher, elbow-deep in a side of pork, let out a rough chuckle. He wiped his cleaver on his apron, smearing blood into the faded white fabric. "Spent too long sitting on his ass. A year dulls the best blade."

The fishmonger snorted. "What did he expect? Walk back in, take the city by storm? He ain't the king of thieves anymore."

Setting his blade against the thick bone of a ham shank, the butcher shrugged. "He should've stayed retired."

The knife came down hard. The bone cracked.

And the city moved on.

The scent of sizzling eggs and sausage filled a low-ceilinged tavern, mingling with the yeasty warmth of fresh-baked bread. The kind of place where dockhands, couriers, and night-shift guards filled their bellies before the next long haul.

At a corner table, a loudmouth with too much energy for this early in the morning leaned forward, gesturing wildly over his half-eaten plate.

"I'm tellin' you—Lars Harrow came back, thought he still had a claim on this city, and got his ass handed to him."

A courier slathered jam onto a thick slice of bread, unimpressed. "By who?"

The loudmouth grinned, relishing the moment. "Balar."

Across the table, a man dunking crust into his coffee frowned. "Who the hells is Balar?"

The loudmouth spread his hands. "The bastard that broke Harrow in half, that's who. The papers say he was waiting for him. Knew Harrow would try to make a move and snuffed it out before it started."

The courier snorted, tearing a bite off his bread. "Sounds like bullshit."

"Oh yeah? Then why's everyone talking about it? Why's it in the paper?" The loudmouth leaned in, his voice lowering just enough to draw the others closer. "Word is, Harrow barely got out with his life. They say Balar let him live just to send a message."

The morning rush continued. Plates scraped clean. Coins hit the counter.

And the city moved on.

The air in the south end café was thick with the aromas of roasted coffee and fine tea. The clink of silverware against porcelain underscored the steady murmur of conversation.

Here, in the heart of Azoria's more well-to-do district, the city's financiers, merchants, and investors gathered before the day began.

A man in a crisp vest unfolded a fresh paper, barely glancing at the vendor as he tossed a coin onto the counter.

"Looks like Lars Harrow's back," he muttered.

Across from him, a woman in a deep green dress and tailored coat took a slow sip of coffee. "And?"

The man flicked the paper, skimming the front-page headline in the Azoria Chronicle: HARROW RETURNS, PROMPTLY REGRETS IT.

He let out a dry chuckle. "And he's already lost."

At the next table over, another paper rustled open. LARS HARROW IS BACK. OR IS HE?

A man with a well-oiled mustache smirked as he turned the page. "You have to admire the arrogance. Trying to pull off a heist after all this time."

The woman in green set down her cup, watching steam curl from its rim. "Did he manage to steal anything?"

A chuckle passed between them.

"Not even close."

The man with the mustache folded his paper neatly and set it aside. "A year is a long time to sit idle."

The merchant nodded, checking the timepiece on his wrist. "A long time indeed."

Another page turned. Another sip of tea. Outside, the monorail hummed overhead, sleek and silent, carrying its passengers toward the future.

And the city moved on.

Trin moved through the waking streets, her stride light, purposeful.

The city was beginning its daily churn—shopkeepers unlocking doors, vendors setting up stalls, the scent of fresh bread and roasted beans spilling into the crisp morning air. A courier weaved past her, muttering an apology as he rushed by, arms full of sealed parcels.

None of it touched her.

Not the dampness in the morning air, not the distant hum of monorail lines overhead, not the buzz of half-heard rumors swirling around her.

The moment she'd heard about the Zarakaran galleon that had docked in Ithris, she'd known it had to be Keer's ship. Keer Basar, their former crewmate. A gruff old sea dog who made up for being prickly with a sense of calm that the crew had always leaned on.

And so she'd gone straight to the ship. And there he was.

Trin had almost knocked Keer over when she saw him on deck. She'd run up the gangplank so urgently the guards had even drawn their weapons. And then she'd embraced Keer before bursting into tears.

For a while, she and Keer had just been two old thieves swapping stories in the lamplight. They'd talked about the past—what they'd lost, what they'd built, what had come undone.

And then, when the conversation had turned to Lars, to the crew, to the mess Azoria had become, Keer had listened. Not with empty reassurances, not with impatience. He'd listened.

And then he'd said, in that deep, proud voice of his, "It's about time I paid my family a visit."

Trin had fallen asleep on the ship, and slept more soundly than she had in weeks.

And now, after waking to a new day, she smiled to herself. She wasn't heading back to base empty-handed. She was bringing something Lars needed more than he'd ever admit.

Hope. The city held its breath.

A FAMILY UNITED

6

Lars sat alone at the long wooden table, a half-eaten hunk of bread resting on the plate beside him. After his mild outburst last night, Trin had gone off hells only knew where. Liora had left shortly after to go see what Shelle and Myrim were up to and to fill them in on the heist.

If you can call it that, Lars thought as he tore off another piece of bread, chewing without tasting it.

Jax and Bunny had left on the heels of Liora, once it became clear that Trin would not be coming back any time soon, and that Lars was miserable company.

Everything ached. Lars's ribs still pulsed with a slow, dull pain. His eye was swollen, the skin stretched tight where bruises had bloomed deep.

He leaned back against the chair, staring up at the ceiling. The etchings and rough edges in the wood were familiar, a network of thin, jagged lines he'd memorized over the years. Had they always been this deep? Or had he just never noticed?

Lars exhaled. He had thought he was broken before the heist. That was nothing.

It had been a long time since he'd felt *this* lost.

Not just physically, that was nothing new. He'd taken hits before, walked away bruised, bloodied, but still standing. Now, he didn't even know if standing was worth it.

Somewhere outside, the city kept moving. He could hear it—the faint hum of the monorail, the distant clang of metal from workshops, the occasional shout from the streets. The rhythm of Azoria, steady as ever.

They don't care, he realized.

No one cared that he'd been gone. And they sure as hells didn't care that he'd come back. Did they care that he had failed?

Lars let out a slow breath and rubbed his temple. His fingers brushed over the bruise at his hairline, and for a second, he felt it all over again. That demon's fists. The sheer power behind every strike. The way Lars had staggered, fought, lost.

And now he was here. Sitting in an empty room, eating stale bread, waiting for—

He didn't know. Was there even a next move to make? Was there any point?

The door creaked open. Lars didn't look up right away. Whoever it was, he wasn't ready for conversation.

Footsteps. Two sets. One light, one heavy. Then a voice. Deep, steady, and familiar.

"Trin, you didn't tell me how bad they wrecked this place."

"Keer?" Lars exclaimed, sitting up straighter. His sore ribs protested. "What the hells are you doing here?"

Keer stepped inside, his boots solid against the worn wooden floor, moving with the same unhurried weight as always. He wore a dark, grizzled beard, and his hair was streaked with more gray than Lars remembered, but his eyes were the same. Sharp, knowing, and unfailingly kind.

He studied Lars, arms crossed over his chest, taking in the bruises, the sluggish way Lars moved. The sorry state of everything. Then Keer grinned, just a little.

"What can I say, boss? Azoria was calling me home."

Lars let out something like a laugh, but it came out short and rough. "I'm pretty sure that's the name of a song."

Keer clapped a hand on Lars's shoulder, firm enough to sting. "Not one I've heard recently," he said. "The live music onboard a ship isn't nearly as good as Tavern Row."

He settled into a chair across from Lars, leaning back, stretching one arm over the backrest like he had all the time in the world. But his eyes stayed on Lars. Trin smiled and pulled up a seat as well.

Lars tore off another bite of bread, chewing slow, trying to ignore the scrutiny.

Keer didn't let him. "We had a good chat, Trin and I. She told me everything."

Well wasn't that just wonderful. "Everything, huh?" Lars asked, shooting a look at Trin.

"I won't apologize," she said.

"Nor should she," Keer added. "So, Lars, will you sit here licking your wounds until the world decides to hand you another shot?"

Lars exhaled sharply. "No one's handing me anything, Keer."

"That much is clear." Keer nodded, rubbing at his beard. "You got the hells kicked out of you, I see. Is it bad?"

Lars winced slightly. "Pretty bad."

"Pretty bad?" Trin asked. "There's no point playing it off here, Lars."

He didn't respond.

"And now you're here," Keer continued. "Waiting and eating stale bread."

Lars frowned. "And what exactly would you have me do?"

The man leaned forward, placing his hands flat on the table. "Get up. You lost, Lars. We all do, sometimes. That isn't the thing that matters. The thing that matters is what happens next."

"You make it sound simple. It's not."

Keer chuckled, shaking his head. "It is simple. Very simple. But it isn't easy."

Setting the bread down, Lars rubbed a hand over his sore jaw. "And what if I don't have a next move?"

Keer huffed. "Then you make one. Or trust in the people you love to make one for you."

The people he loved. Lars glanced at Trin. She nodded, her eyes boring into him.

"You lost a fight, Lars. You lost a year. Maybe you lost your edge. But you're not dead yet. So tell me—what the hells are you waiting for?"

Lars sat back in his chair, arms resting on the table, his jaw tight. He didn't have an answer for Keer.

Truth be told, he didn't even want to think about it.

But something about hearing the question out loud, from Keer of all people, made things real in a way they hadn't been before. Lars opened his mouth, but before he could speak—

"Lars." Trin's voice cut through the air, quiet but firm.

He turned to look at her.

"Before you answer that, I have something to say."

She took a deep breath, leaning forward, elbows on the table, hands clasped loosely.

"I know what it looks like from where you're sitting. I know how it feels." She met his gaze, steady, unwavering. "To lose. To be left behind. To think that maybe... maybe you're just done."

Did she know? Truly? If she did, she had never said so before. But then again, Lars had never asked.

"And for a while, I thought that was you," she continued. "That you were done. That maybe I was done, too. But Lars," her voice softened, "I don't want to be done. And I don't think you do either."

Trin wasn't just talking about thieving, Lars realized. She was talking about them.

"Do you remember what you used to be like?" Trin asked, tilting her head. "You were alive. Not just when we were pulling jobs, but all the time. You had this fire in you, this hunger. The city threw obstacles in your way, and you just..." she snapped her fingers, "tore right through them."

Lars let out a slow breath, rubbing his thumb along the edge of the table. He remembered.

"That's the Lars I knew." Trin's voice dropped, something raw edging into it. "The one I loved. Not because you were perfect, or untouchable, or even because you always won. But because no matter what, you kept moving forward."

She shook her head. "That's what's missing now. Not your skill. Not your reputation. Not even your edge. It's this, Lars." She tapped the table between them. "It's you deciding to get back up."

Keer nodded once, approving. "She's got you there."

"Yeah," Lars said, leaning forward. He put his hand on top of Trin's. "She really does."

Something burned at the back of his mind, though. Something terrifying.

"Keer," he began, "I'm assuming Trin told you about the man who attacked me?"

Trin looked nervously at Keer. "I did," she said. "And it turns out, he has a name. Balar."

Balar. Lars shuddered, thinking again of that soulless eye with the eight-pointed pupil, the jagged scar that ran across it. The name seemed to fit.

But who the hells was he?

Keer leaned back in his chair. "You're wondering who Balar is, aren't you?" He scratched his beard, eyes steady on Lars. "That's unknowable for now. But I'll tell you what I do know."

He folded his arms across his chest. "A couple months ago, I was running cargo past the archipelago south of Sumbawa—dangerous waters, riddled with sharp rocks and worse things. There was a Zarakaran navy vessel on my tail, coming in fast. Faster than we could outrun." He tapped the table once. "The crew wanted to fight. Said we could hold them off."

His lips curved slightly in a nostalgic smile.

"But the sea was wrong that night. No gulls. No waves. The sharks that usually followed our wake for scraps were all gone."

Lars and Trin both watched him now, quiet. Hells, if there was one thing Keer could do, it was tell a tale.

"And that told me one thing." Keer's voice dropped slightly. "The real danger wasn't the ship behind us. It was what we couldn't see.

"So instead of speeding ahead, I slowed down. Let the waves pull us just enough to steer careful. And that's when the reefs started to break the surface—sharp as spears, black as night."

Keer let the words settle.

"The navy ship didn't see it. They were too focused on us, and coming in too fast. They thought they were the ones hunting." He shook his head. "Until their hull was split wide open."

He leaned forward.

"You're looking at the ship chasing you. That man—Balar? He came after you. And so he's what you think you need to beat."

He let that sit before adding, softer, but heavier: "But tell me... who's the danger hiding beneath the water?"

Lars's jaw tensed. Trin inhaled sharply. Because they both knew the answer.

Vivienne.

"You've got it, don't you," Keer winked.

"Yeah," Lars said, the old fire of rebelliousness burning in him. "You're damn right I do."

Just then, the door swung open. Liora strode in, a satchel slung across her body, rummaging through it with the kind of manic energy she always carried when working on something. But as she looked up, her hands froze.

"KEER!"

She launched herself at him.

Keer barely had time to brace before Liora slammed into him, throwing her arms around his middle with enough force to make him grunt.

"Ah! Careful now, girl," he grumbled, but his arms wrapped around her anyway.

She pulled back, beaming up at him.

"Like hells I'll be careful! You're back! I can't believe you're back!"

He chuckled, shaking his head. "I just pulled into port."

Stepping back with that same infectious grin, Liora looked at Keer the way she always had—as an unshakable force, stern but steady, gruff but dependable. Like the father she'd never had.

"Look at you!" she grinned. "Haven't lost your limbs to a sea monster, I see."

"Not yet," Keer said. "But I have plenty of sailing ahead."

"Jax!" The laughter still colored Liora's voice as she turned. "Did you—"

Then her eyes flicked around the room. "Wait. Where's Jax and Bunny?"

Keer raised an eyebrow. "Bunny?"

Lars rolled his eyes. "Don't ask."

Liora flashed him a glare. Lars opened his mouth, but before he could say anything, something in his chest tightened.

Jax and Bunny had left to go get a drink. And Lars hadn't cared enough to stop them. Hells. He had been so caught up in his own anger, his own bitterness, his own damn self-pity—that he hadn't even thought about being a friend to Jax.

"They went to go get a drink..." he murmured.

"Are you kidding me, Lars?" Trin's voice was sharp. "Why didn't you say something?"

Lars didn't flinch. He deserved it.

"You let him go drinking?" The accusation in Liora's voice hit like a slap. "Jax? And you just, what? Didn't even think about stopping him?"

The words stuck in his throat. "I—" What could he say? That he'd been too wrapped up in his own misery to care? "I wasn't thinking."

"No." Her voice cut like glass. "You weren't."

Keer leaned back in his chair, arms crossed, watching the exchange without stepping in.

"Hells, Lars!" Liora ran a hand through her auburn curls, pacing. "You know how Jax gets! You know how easy it is for him to spiral!"

"Okay, I messed up," Lars said. "I know that and admit it. But right now we've got to find Jax and make sure he doesn't end up in prison again. Or worse."

Liora stopped pacing, turning to face him fully.

"You're right. Let's go."

But Trin shook her head. "Lars is in no shape to be running around town chasing a drunk, Liora. He can barely breathe without wincing."

"We'll find him." Keer pushed himself up from his chair. "Come on, Liora."

Liora huffed but nodded, grabbing her satchel and adjusting the strap. Lars looked between them.

"Bring him back," he said. "Please."

With a final frustrated look, Liora followed Keer out the door.

Lars and Trin sat in silence for a long moment, unspoken thoughts on their lips.

Living together this past year hadn't meant truly being together. All of his repressed emotions—the sadness, the feelings of failure—they all closed Lars off, made him a shadow of himself. Just like when he let Jax run out the door for the promise of whiskey.

He hoped the big fool was alright and hadn't fallen back into drink. But if he had... well, this time, Lars would be there for him. Jax and Liora wouldn't go it alone.

The room settled into an uncomfortable quiet. Lars could hear Trin's breathing, measured and deliberate, like she was working up to something. When she finally spoke, her voice was so soft he almost missed it.

"I need to know something."

The words hung between them. Lars shifted, trying to sit straighter despite the protest from his ribs. Something about the way she wouldn't quite look at him made his chest tighten in a different way than the bruises.

"Anything," he said, though the word came out rougher than he intended.

She was picking at a loose thread on her sleeve—a nervous habit he'd noticed before but never seen quite like this. "When you went with Vivienne last year." A pause. Her fingers stilled. "Did you want to stay with her?"

The question landed like a punch to his already battered gut. He opened his mouth, closed it. Opened it again. Of all the things she could have asked...

"Trin—"

"Just." She held up a hand, still not meeting his eyes. "Please. I need to know."

Lars took a breath that hurt in more ways than one. The easy answer would be no. The simple, clean answer that would smooth this over and let them move past it. But looking at her— the way her shoulders were drawn up tight, the careful blankness of her expression that didn't quite hide the vulnerability underneath—he knew she deserved more than easy.

"When I went with her," he started slowly, testing each word, "I knew it was so we could steal from her later."

Trin's jaw tightened. Still wouldn't look at him.

"But I won't lie to you." The words felt like glass in his throat. "After a few days... yeah. I thought about it. I thought about giving in."

Now she looked at him, and the naked hurt in her eyes was worse than any beating he'd ever taken. But there was something else there too—a hardness crystallizing, like watching water turn to ice. That terrified him more than her pain.

"She was—" He stopped, ran a hand through his hair, tried again. "She was powerful. Wealthy. And for someone like me, someone who's always wanted to be more than just another thief in Azoria..."

He swallowed hard. "It forced me to think about things. About the kind of life I could have with someone like that. Not just wealth—I had that. But real power. The kind where you don't pull jobs anymore because you own the game."

The silence stretched between them, taut as a bowstring.

"Vivienne could have made me legitimate. I could shape the city instead of just stealing from it." He let out a bitter laugh. "Everything I've been chasing since I was a street rat watching the merchant princes from the shadows."

"But Trin—" He leaned forward, ignoring the spike of pain in his ribs. "I need you to hear this part. Really hear it."

She was back to staring at that thread on her sleeve, but he could tell she was listening by the way her breathing had gone shallow.

"I thought about it. To my shame, I thought about it. But then I realized something."

He waited until she glanced up. "That life was a lie. See, with Vivienne, I'd be her creation. Her clever pet thief who she elevated. Every success, every triumph—it would all be because of her favor, not because I earned it."

He wanted to reach for her hand but didn't dare.

"More than that, every time she smiled at me, every time she touched my arm or laughed at something I said—all I could think about was you. How you actually see me. Not Lars the useful acquisition or Lars the amusing project to manipulate. Just... Lars. The ambitious bastard who wants too much and pushes too hard and somehow you love anyway."

Trin's eyes were bright now, though no tears fell.

"I didn't stay with her, Trin. I couldn't. Because everything she offered—all that power and legitimacy and respect—it would have meant giving up the one thing that actually mattered." He met her gaze steadily. "You. And what we've built together. Our crew, our reputation, our way of doing things. That's real. That's ours. That's worth more than anything she could have given me."

He felt tears welling up behind his eyes. Hells. The problem with holding emotions in so deeply is that when they finally did come out, they came out fighting.

"One more thing," he continued. "We never got physical, Trin. Oh, she tried. Relentlessly. But I never gave myself to her. Not once."

Trin lowered her head, and for a moment Lars thought she'd say something else. But then she wiped her eyes with the back of her hand and arched an eyebrow. "Relentlessly, huh?"

Lars couldn't quite read the look on her face. But she laid her hand on his. The warmth of her touch was all he needed right now. They were being real with each other, finally, after far too long. Whatever might happen next... at least in this moment, things were working their way towards right.

The evening air in Tavern Row hit Liora right in the face. Smoke and spilled ale and grease from vendors hawking mystery meat to anyone drunk enough not to ask what animal it came from. Her nose wrinkled. This whole street was an assault on the senses, designed to overwhelm you into poor decisions.

Which was exactly why Jax would come here.

She moved fast, weaving between stumbling dock workers and clusters of sailors whose laughter had that sharp edge that meant someone was about to throw a punch. Beside her, Keer moved like a ship through calm water—steady, unhurried, those old thief's eyes cataloguing every doorway and dark corner.

"If Jax wanted to disappear into a bottle, this is where he'd start," she muttered, her gaze jumping from tavern sign to tavern sign. The Broken Anchor. Dynamo & Draughts. The Bloody Knuckle. Each one a perfect place for someone like Jax to drown whatever was eating him.

"Men like Jax don't disappear easily." Keer said. "You want to find him, look for the biggest mess."

That's what Liora was worried about. Her hands clenched and unclenched, nervous energy with nowhere to go. Every second they wasted was another second Jax could be doing something spectacularly stupid.

Getting arrested again. Starting a brawl. Drinking himself into a state where he'd pick a fight with a dynamo lamp just to feel something break.

She'd promised Dren. Promised she'd keep him out of trouble. The memory of the prison guard's face—disappointed but not surprised—made her walk faster.

"The Gull," she said, already turning down a narrow side street. "It's one of his usual spots. Cheap drinks, no questions, and the owner lets you sleep it off in the back if you pay extra."

Keer just nodded, following her lead. She appreciated that about him—no unnecessary questions, no platitudes about how Jax would be fine. They both knew better.

The Gull squatted at the street's end like a toad, all warped wood and peeling paint. The sign above the door had lost most of its letters, leaving just "G-LL" visible in the lamplight. Close enough. Everyone knew what this place was.

A pair of exhausted dock workers flanked the entrance, nursing drinks that were probably more water than ale. They barely glanced up as Liora pushed through the door, Keer at her heels.

Inside was exactly what she'd expected—sticky floors that grabbed at her boots, air thick enough to chew, and the kind of lighting that made everyone look vaguely diseased. Her eyes swept the room in quick, efficient arcs. Corner booth, two merchants haggling over something definitely stolen. Bar, a line of hunched backs that could belong to anyone but not a single one of them big enough to be Jax's. Back tables, a card game that would end in violence within the hour.

No Jax or Bunny. Hells.

The barmaid behind the counter looked up from polishing a glass with a rag that had seen better decades. She had the kind of smile that said she'd heard every line and wasn't buying any of them. Recognition flickered across her face.

"Well now, if it isn't the little lightning spark." She set the glass down with a clink. "Still setting things on fire for fun and profit?"

Liora didn't have time for banter. "I'm looking for someone."

"Aren't we all? Who's missing from your collection?"

"Jax." The name came out sharper than intended. "Big guy, drinks like a fish, probably with another big guy who looks like he wrestles bears for fun. Did they come through?"

Annie's carefully plucked brows rose. "Jax Crash?" She shook her head, curls bouncing. "Not tonight. Haven't seen that beautiful disaster in months."

If Jax wasn't coming to his usual haunts, where the hells was he drinking? Somewhere worse? Somewhere that wouldn't cut him off when he'd had enough?

Keer leaned against the bar. "You're sure about that?"

Annie's smile went from tired to interested. "Honey, I'd remember if Jackson Crasher walked through my doors. That man's shoulders alone are worth the price of admission." She poured herself a small glass of something amber, eyes never leaving Keer. "But if you do find him, tell him Annie says 'hi.' And that his tab's still open."

"Of course it is," Liora muttered. Because why would anything be simple? Why would Jax be where he was supposed to be, drinking where she could find him, instead of off somewhere new getting into fresh varieties of trouble?

"Man attracts attention wherever he goes," Keer observed, pushing off from the bar.

"That's the problem." Liora's mind was already racing ahead—calculating distances, considering which dives Jax might have discovered, how much ground they could cover before he did something irreversible. "Come on. We're wasting time."

Back on the street, the air felt almost fresh compared to the Gull's interior. Almost.

"Now what?" Keer asked, falling into step beside her.

"Now we keep looking. And we pray to whatever's listening that we find him before he finds the bottom of a bottle he can't climb out of."

Keer's posture shifted—subtle, but Liora had learned to read the signs. Old thief instincts kicking in.

"Trouble," he murmured, chin tilting toward the Market District.

The noise hit her a second later. Not the usual Tavern Row chaos of breaking bottles and slurred insults. This was different. Urgent. The kind of shouting that meant someone had screwed up spectacularly.

Uh oh.

"Come on." She was already moving, boots slapping against cobblestones. Because if there was trouble—real trouble—and Jax was involved...

The crowd thickened as they approached, bodies pressing together like iron filings drawn to a magnet. Through the gaps, Liora caught glimpses of a jewelry shop, its door flung wide. Her stomach twisted into new and interesting knots.

Please don't be there. Please don't be standing over some shopkeeper with bloody knuckles and that stupid grin—

"Thieves!" The cry went up from somewhere in the mass of bodies. "Call the City Watch!"

Liora's mind raced through scenarios, each worse than the last. Jax, drunk and desperate, smashing his way into a shop. Jax, trying to prove he was still useful, still needed. Jax, spiraling so hard he'd forgotten the difference between a sanctioned job and a crime.

She elbowed through the crowd, Keer a solid presence at her back. The shop's interior looked like someone had set off a dynamo charge—glass everywhere, display cases reduced to glittering shards.

"Which way did they go?" A shopkeeper in a flour-dusted apron was practically vibrating with outrage.

"I didn't see!" A fruit vendor, his cart abandoned in his rush to gawk.

Then the jewelry shop owner emerged, one hand pressed to her temple. "They didn't take anything."

Liora's brain screeched to a halt. "What?"

"Smashed the case and ran." The woman gestured helplessly at the devastation. "Big man in a cloak, hood up. Shattered my best display, stood there for a heartbeat like he was admiring his work, then bolted out the back. But nothing's missing."

The gears in Liora's head started turning—slow at first, then faster. A break-in with nothing stolen. Noise and spectacle but no profit. Her eyes narrowed.

A distraction.

Keer was already scanning the crowd, and she knew he'd reached the same conclusion. This wasn't a failed heist. This was misdirection. Get everyone looking left while the real action happened—

Movement. Just a flicker in her peripheral vision, but her body responded before her brain caught up. There. Shadowed alley.

"Keer." The word came out barely above a breath. She didn't wait for acknowledgment, just slipped away from the crowd like smoke.

Because standing there, shifting his weight in that particular way that meant he was waiting for something, was the unmistakable bulk of Jax.

And it looked like he was standing lookout.

Relief and fury went to war in her chest. He was okay—but he was also clearly in the middle of something spectacular. The door behind him led to a dynamo repair shop, she knew the place. Expensive equipment. Specialized tools.

The good stuff.

"Jax?" she said. "What are you doing?"

His head snapped up like a startled cat, and his dark eyes went wide with genuine shock before crinkling into something almost like joy.

"Liora? Keer!" A laugh bubbled up, bright and incongruous. "I can't believe you're—oh shit. Take this."

He lunged for something just inside the doorway. Liora's brain was still processing him being happy to see them. But then suddenly her arms were full of a canvas bag and her knees were buckling under unexpected weight.

"What the hells, Jax!"

Metal clinked inside the bag—tools, had to be tools, expensive ones from the weight—and she staggered, trying not to drop what was clearly evidence of a crime in progress. Her arms screamed. Her back protested. How did he make lifting things look so easy?

Keer plucked the bag from her grip like it weighed nothing, slinging it over one shoulder with the kind of casual strength that made her simultaneously grateful and irritated.

"Jax." She had to catch her breath, make sense of this. "What the hells is going on? I thought you were getting a drink!"

He had the audacity to look sheepish, hand going to the back of his neck in that gesture she knew meant he was about to say something ridiculous. "Naw. Bunny suggested we take the edge off with a little fun."

Fun. The word hit her like cold water. This wasn't desperation or drunken stupidity. This was Jax and Bunny deciding to... what? Prove they could still pull a job? Blow off steam?

"What kind of fun?" The question came out dangerously quiet.

His eyes flicked toward the jewelry shop. The crowd was still milling, but she could hear new voices joining. Official voices. Watch voices.

"Say, uh," he muttered, "are any of those shop owners coming back yet?"

CLANG.

The sound of metal on stone from inside the shop made her jump. Jax winced like someone had stepped on his foot.

Then a safe came sliding through the doorway.

It scraped across the threshold with a sound that would haunt her dreams, then landed at Jax's feet with a thud that she felt in her bones.

A safe. They stole a safe.

Her mind catalogued everything wrong with this picture. Broad daylight. No plan she knew about. Just Jax and Bunny deciding to boost a safe for fun, and now she was standing here holding stolen goods while the Watch closed in and—

Bunny's head appeared in the doorway, followed by the rest of him squeezing through like a bear emerging from hibernation. Dust in his hair, satisfaction on his face, not a care in the world.

"Oh, hi, Liora." Like they'd bumped into each other at the market. "No time for proper greeting, sorry."

Words. She should have words. Liora always had words—usually too many of them. But her brain had apparently decided to take a holiday, leaving her mouth opening and closing like a landed fish.

"Help me get this on the cart," Jax said, already bending to grip one side.

The wheels of a small wagon groaned as they loaded the safe, and Liora found her voice. "Jax! What... what are we supposed to do with—"

He held up a finger. His head tilted, and she heard it too.

Boots. Ordered, rhythmic. The Watch.

"What do we do?" The question came out more shrill than she'd intended.

Jax's grin was pure, distilled confidence. The kind of expression that had gotten them into and out of a hundred situations just like this.

"Run."

Darius flicked a card onto the table, leaning back with a self-satisfied grin. "See, this is where people screw up. They get impatient. They overplay their hand."

Rurik yawned, not even trying to hide it.

Inora drummed her fingers against the wood, staring at her cards as if they might magically change.

Maren slouched back in his chair, glancing at the door.

This wasn't exactly the energy Darius wanted.

To be fair, their old base had seen better days. Once, it had been loud, alive with movement and purpose. Now it felt like a half-abandoned social club pretending to still be in use.

The bright dynamo lamps were just too damn cheery. A long wooden table at the center of the room—where jobs had been planned, where coin had been counted, where victories had been toasted—was now just a place to shuffle cards and kill time.

Shelves, once stacked with maps, schematics, and stolen treasures waiting to be fenced, now held half-empty bottles and forgotten odds and ends. Crates by the far wall were mostly empty, save for some supplies no one had bothered to sort.

The space hadn't changed. But the people inside it had. Darius felt it—the weight of what used to be.

But what else was there?

"You're not listening," he pressed, leaning forward, hands spread as he launched into his pitch. "So, picture it. An art gala, right? Fancy as hells, the kind of place where the wine's older than the guests. We set up an exclusive, invite-only game— private stakes, no limits, winner walks away with original paintings."

Rurik raised an eyebrow.

Darius smirked. "Except the paintings we offer are the paintings on display. The bets are rigged. And by the time they realize they've been played?" He snapped his fingers. "We're walking out with a fortune in stolen art and fat purses."

Silence. Inora shrugged. "Sure."

Rurik tossed a card onto the pile.

Maren scratched his chin. "I gotta say, Darius. I think I'd rather just steal the paintings."

Darius forced a chuckle. "Where's the fun in that?"

None of them answered.

The game continued, cards shifting, coins clinking. What a drag.

But this was fine. This was the life he had chosen.

Darius didn't need the risk, the thrill, the rush of a proper job. He didn't need to outthink security patrols or slip past locked doors. He didn't need to steal.

This was enough. Sure, the stakes were smaller. But that's because the con was quieter. Darius could get used to this.

He could sit in this chair, spin clever ideas for scams that would never happen, play a game that didn't matter, and tell himself it was the same. You're damn right he could.

He picked up his cards, flipping them between his fingers, forcing a grin.

"All right, all right, but hear me out. What if we—"

The door swung open.

Darius didn't look up right away. He was mid-sentence, flipping a card between his fingers, grinning as he laid out the last details of the gala con that would never happen.

"...spike the punch—"

"Silas, you son of a bitch!" Maren's chair scraped back as he stood, crossing the room with a wide grin.

Darius blinked, the name cutting through his thoughts. He finally glanced up. And there he was.

Silas stood in the doorway, shaking his head, looking exactly the same as he always had—a little rough from travel, steady as ever, carrying the weight of too many miles but none of the hesitation.

"About time. I know you've been back to Ithris a time or two." Inora smirked, tossing her cards down. "I was starting to get insulted you didn't come visit."

"Thought about it," Silas mused, stepping forward as Maren clapped him on the back. "Turns out, Azoria wasn't all that exciting anymore."

Rurik nodded once, grinning.

Darius, still half-sprawled in his chair, finally let a grin crack through. Whatever else, this was Silas. His lieutenant. Someone who had watched his back when it mattered.

He pushed himself up, clasping arms with him. "Bastard. Thought you'd gone soft, hauling crates for Keer."

Silas chuckled. "Hardly. Though we did find a few crates worth hauling."

They settled in, and for a few minutes, it was easy.

Silas leaned back, talking about smuggling runs along the Zarakar coast, the bad weather, the tight border patrols. Inora asked about what kind of cargo he was dealing in. Maren wanted to know if he'd been running into old competition on the waters.

"We kept things clean. Mostly," Silas admitted, lips twitching.

"That means 'not clean at all,'" Rurik muttered.

"I can almost confidently say no one died, at least," Silas added with a shrug.

Laughter. Even Darius eased into it. This was good. His crew, just like the old days, yucking it up and—

Then Silas had to say it. "So, Darius. You spoke with Lars lately?"

And just like that, Darius's grin dropped.

Darius picked up his hand again and studied the faces. "No. And I don't plan to."

Silas raised an eyebrow. "You know he got his ass kicked, right?" he pressed. "Word on the street is he took a major beating on a failed heist."

"I hadn't heard."

"Yeah, you did, boss," Maren piped up. "I told you about it when I got here."

Darius's glare could have fried a dynamo circuit. Maren gulped.

A few moments passed in silence. Inora glanced sideways at Silas.

"Darius," Silas said, "why the hells are you so angry at Lars?"

Darius slammed his cards down. "Who says I'm angry?"

"The table, mostly."

"Maybe I'm angry at the table." He shoved back his chair, pushing to his feet. "Maybe I'm angry at this piss-poor hand. Maybe I'm angry at you for asking stupid questions."

Silas didn't blink. "I feel like you wanna say more."

"Do I?" Darius grabbed his glass, found it empty, set it down harder than necessary. "Fascinating. Tell me more about my inner landscape, Silas. I had no idea you'd taken up philosophy."

"I'm serious."

"So am I. Very serious. About how little I want to have this conversation."

Silas leaned back, watching him with that patient, unreadable expression that made Darius want to throw something. "He's your friend."

"Is he?" The words came out sharper than he meant. He felt his pulse pounding in his skull, all that resentment clawing at the edges. He shoved it back down. "Funny. I must have missed the part where that obligates me to explain myself to you."

Silas let the silence stretch.

Darius raked a hand through his hair, exhaled through his teeth. "Drop it."

"Darius—"

"I said drop it." He met Silas's eyes, held them. "Whatever you think you're doing right now, stop."

Silas watched him a moment longer. Then he nodded slowly. "Fair enough."

He leaned forward, arms resting on the table. "But this isn't about Lars," he continued.

Darius frowned. The heat in his chest was still burning, but something about Silas's tone made him pause.

"This is about Zarakar. About an offer you might want to hear."

Silas settled back into his chair and gathered his thoughts. "We were doing well, me and Keer. Smuggling's been good to us. The Zarakaran border patrols have gotten tighter, but nothing we couldn't handle."

He scratched at the stubble along his jaw.

"Then, a few weeks back, we got boarded. I thought we were done for. With the kind of goods we were hauling, it didn't matter if it was customs or pirates, you were screwed."

Maren perked up. "What goods?" he asked with wonder.

"Dynamo weapons," Silas grinned. "They make the muskets we played with last year look like kids' toys."

It seemed like Maren was going to pipe up again, so Silas lifted his hand.

"Anyway, that's in the past. We got boarded by Thume's people."

That got their attention.

Rurik sat forward, setting his cards aside. Maren stopped fidgeting. Inora's expression, unreadable before, sharpened.

Darius sucked in a sharp breath. Thume, whom he helped put behind bars. Thume, whose family was the most powerful in Zarakar.

"His family wants him back, Darius," Silas said. "And they'll do damn near anything to make it happen."

After Lars and Trin had talked, they sat. After they sat, they held each other.

And after that... well, repressed emotions, fears of infidelity, and raw admissions had a way of bringing out strong physical feelings.

Their holding turned to lustful pawing, clenching, and passionate kisses. Despite the bruises and sore ribs from being attacked, Lars felt nothing but need. Trin shrugged off her suspenders, lowered the trousers that fit her slim form so well. Lars pressed against her, working to undo his belt.

And then the door slammed open.

Liora stepped inside first, pushing the heavy wooden door wide. Behind her, Keer followed, one hand gripping the side of the cart that Jax and Bunny were wheeling inside. On top of it, the stolen safe—scuffed, dented, but still locked tight.

Trin let out something that sounded like a yelp, and yanked her pants up her legs with blinding speed. Lars staggered back, thankfully knocking into the leg of his chair, and he fell into it with a painful thud.

By some miracle, Keer, Jax, and Bunny's attention had been fixed on guiding the cart through the door. They hadn't seen a thing. As for Liora...

Her eyes were narrowed, looking at Lars and Trin, the most devious possible grin on her face. But thank the hells, she said nothing.

"Didn't even break a sweat," Jax finally said, flashing a grin as he wiped imaginary dust from his hands.

Bunny shrugged. "But it was damn fun."

Keer ambled over to the table and sat down, clearly exhausted from—well, whatever had happened.

Lars blinked, trying to get his mind back into the present. "So what the hells is this?"

Jax clapped a hand down on their prize. "It's a safe!"

"We know it's a safe, Jax," Trin said, rolling her eyes. The red flush of passion followed by embarrassment had mostly faded from her face. "Where the hells did it come from?"

"Well, Bunny and I went out on the town," Jax started, his enthusiasm undeterred. " I started heading towards the bars, you know, because... well, anyway, I thought we were going to get a drink." He shook his head, clearing away the thoughts.

"But Bunny here, he said what we needed was some *real* excitement. So we planned out a quick heist at the market. And bam. The man was right."

Trin's brow arched. "You two are unbelievable."

"Thank you," Bunny said sincerely.

Lars let out a slow, measured breath, doing his best to shake off the abrupt shift from raw desire to heist analysis.

Jax patted the safe again, beaming. "So, are we gonna open it, or are we just gonna sit here and admire our fine handiwork?"

Liora smirked at him. "You didn't build the safe, Jax."

"Yeah, but we stole it, and that was a fine bit of work."

Bunny knelt beside the safe, already examining the lock with quiet focus. "Hinges are solid. But the lock's old," he murmured. "Give me a few minutes."

He pulled a small set of tools from his pocket and got to work, the quiet clicks and scrapes filling the room.

Trin cleared her throat. "So let me get this straight."

She gestured vaguely toward Jax and Bunny. "You two broke into a shop during business hours and somehow made off with a safe? No one got hurt, did they?"

"Actually," Liora piped up, "they did a pretty damn good job."

She relayed the details, how Bunny had created a diversion by faking a smash and grab at a jeweler's shop to get all the shopkeepers crowded around that store, just so they could sneak into the dynamo shop and grab the safe from the back.

Lars laughed. It made his ribs hurt, but he didn't care. "Like the foundry job—"

"Just like the foundry job!" Jax finished. "Yes! I knew that plan came from somewhere."

Bunny smirked, twisting the lock of the safe. "And that's how it's done."

The door creaked open, and everyone leaned in slightly.

Inside sat rolls of coins, a decent haul. Mostly just gold and silver, but there were a few hefty copper pieces in there too.

Beside them, two crystal charges pulsed faintly with stored dynamo energy. A small copper ring rested near the top of the pile, worn smooth from use.

And, at the very bottom, nestled in a polished wooden case—a box of cigars. The label said they came from Glimcove, Drakoria.

Jax let out a low whistle. "Would you look at that. Quality loot."

"Jax, you're a menace" Lars exhaled, finally letting the weight of the moment settle. "I don't suppose you're going to share those cigars?"

Jax beamed. "You're damn right I am."

They all sat around the table while Jax handed out the cigars.

Truth be told, those were likely worth more than the rest of the contents of that safe, coins included. Glimcove grew tobacco the likes of which you wouldn't find anywhere else in the world. Among other wonders.

Trin and Lars both took a long drag at the same time, and Lars erupted in a cough. "Sorry," he said, "I guess I'm used to my pipe more than anything."

Liora sat with her cigar clenched between her teeth, a wisp of smoke curling around the tip, and smiled at everyone.

Watching the smoke drift toward the ceiling, Lars felt something shift in his chest. His ribs still ached and he likely looked like a black and blue monster from the bruises, but at least he could smile.

"So," he said, setting his cigar in the makeshift ashtray Liora had fashioned from spare parts. "Who wants to plan our next job?"

The grins that spread around the table were answer enough.

ARE WE DOING THIS?

7

The knock rattled the door hard enough to shake dust from the hinges.

Lars's good mood evaporated. Of course. They couldn't have five minutes of peace without some new disaster showing up.

"What, we rob one safe and suddenly we're popular?" Jax stretched, joints popping. "Hells, we really are back in business."

Lars stubbed out his cigar and hauled himself up. Every muscle screamed in protest. But sitting here wasn't going to make whoever was outside go away.

As he struggled, Trin gave him a private smile. It helped.

He yanked open the door. And came face to face with Darius Adalan.

Right there, larger than life, cocky as all hells, Darius. It had been a while since he'd seen his competitor turned compatriot. Not long enough based on the scowl the man was wearing, though.

Thankfully, he had his whole crew behind him. Inora, with her round eyes and thin-lipped grimace. Rurik, the squat but bulky bruiser that said very little but had eyes like a hawk. Maren, who had been working with Liora here and there from what he heard, giving his enthusiastic yet quirky assistance.

And Silas. That made sense. He would have ridden in on the tide with Keer.

Lars hadn't quite worked out why Darius hated him so much lately. Professional rivalry had turned into something else after the events of last year.

But honestly, between the ban and everything else, Lars hadn't mustered the energy to care.

Though the way Darius was staring at him—like Lars had personally ruined his life—was starting to pique his curiosity.

"Darius," Lars began.

"Save it, Harrow. You going to let us in or can I skip all that and go home?"

Lars stepped aside, allowing Darius and crew to file into the base. Well, this was getting cozy. Everyone seemed genuinely happy to see each other though, Darius excluded. Trin exchanged hugs with Inora and Silas, Jax and Rurik did what Lars could only assume was a secret handshake, and Liora and Maren immediately started yammering about something Lars couldn't even begin to fathom.

Bunny just stood there with his arms crossed over his chest, taking it all in. Darius walked up to him, cocking an eyebrow at the scruffy Aelyndoran.

"Who the hells are you?" Darius asked.

"I'm Bunny."

"Of course you are," Darius replied, walking away without taking the proffered hand.

Bunny let out a loud, exasperated sigh. "Is it a requirement for all crew leaders to be insufferable twats in this town?"

That got a laugh out of Lars. He was warming to Bunny, honestly. Nevermind that the man had saved his ass on the night of the heist, when Balar was beating the shi—

Okay, no need to go there. But Bunny's carefree, unabashedly honest style was kind of refreshing. And the man certainly had done good for Jax. So far, anyway.

"I gotta say, Lars," Darius said, "you look like shit."

"Yeah. I feel like it too."

Darius pulled a chair out from the table, spun it around, and sat down, arms resting on the back.

"So," he said, voice dry. "Someone gonna tell me why I got dragged here, or are we just gonna sit around swapping pleasantries?"

Trin gave him a mocking grin. "Nice to see you too, Darius."

"Yeah, yeah. I'll get sentimental later." Darius glanced around. "First, I'd like to know why we all have to be here."

He reached toward the table and plucked a cigar from the box Jax had pilfered from the safe. He twirled it between his fingers, raising an eyebrow.

"And second—anyone got a light?"

Keer huffed a laugh, pulling a match from his pocket and striking it against the worn wood of the table. Darius leaned in, letting the flame catch the end of his cigar.

He took a long drag, exhaling a slow stream of smoke before giving Keer a pointed look. "All right, old man. Silas told us about Thume. So talk."

"Thume?" Lars said. He couldn't be more shocked if Bunny suddenly started playing with dynamo circuitry. "What about Thume?"

Keer winced, glancing at Lars. "Ah. Right. Things got a bit hectic when I arrived—what with Liora's welcome and then hunting down Jax." He took a pull from his cigar. "Should've mentioned it sooner."

Lars nodded, falling silent.

Leaning forward, Keer rested his forearms on the table. "We docked in Nyandoro about a month back," he began. "We'd gotten a lead on something valuable. Dynamo weapons, Zarakaran made. Very valuable."

Liora's head snapped up. "Dynamo weapons?" she echoed. "Where? Got any left?"

Keer gave her a dry look. "Not the point, Liora."

"But—"

"Shush," Keer said.

Liora huffed, slumping back against her chair, but when Keer turned away, she stuck her tongue out at him.

Darius snorted a quick laugh.

Keer ignored it, continuing. "After the deal was done, we rode the coast south toward the southern passage. But then we got boxed in."

He leaned back, rubbing his beard.

"Two ships, both Zarakaran, coming in hard from the south and east as we came around a peninsula. We didn't have time to change course."

The room stilled, hanging on Keer's every word. The man was a damn fine storyteller if nothing else.

"We had a debate," Keer went on. "Some of the crew wanted to fight. Others wanted to take our chances with negotiations."

His gaze flicked to Lars. "But we didn't get to choose. They boarded us. And at the lead..."

Keer paused.

"Oh for hells sake," Silas barked. "Spit it out."

Darius smacked Silas on the shoulder. *He might actually be enjoying this,* Lars thought. Darius loved a good, dramatic act.

Keer let another moment pass. "At the lead was Mhalendra Thume."

Lars sat up straighter. He had never met Thume's family, but he knew the name. Mhalendra was Cecil Thume's sister. And the one left in control of the family's business in Zarakar.

Keer exhaled. "The moment I saw her, I knew this wasn't about our cargo."

"Then what was it about?" Trin asked. "Mhalendra barely leaves her estate, let alone takes to the high seas."

"She wants Thume out."

The words hung in the air, thicker than the smoke curling from the cigars. Lars felt his stomach tighten, but he said nothing. Not yet.

Keer pressed on. "She wants him out of prison. Brought back to Zarakar. Alive and in one piece."

Darius let out a slow, unimpressed breath. "That's the big news?"

"In return," Keer continued, "she'll forgive you both. And your crews."

Lars scoffed. "Forgive?" His voice came out sharper than he intended, cutting across the room. "See, this is the kind of shit we had Thume put away for. And I assume we're supposed to be grateful."

Keer held up a hand, but before he could say anything, Trin touched Lars's arm. A silent reminder. Stay in control.

Lars pressed his lips together and motioned for Keer to carry on.

"Their goal is to get Thume home, plain and simple," Keer said. "And if we help them, they'll offer something more than just forgiveness."

"Such as?" Inora pressed, pragmatic as ever.

"They'll give us safe harbor in Zarakar," Keer replied. "If we want it. All of us, if Azoria turns on you, or Vivienne seeks retribution. You'll have a place to run."

Keer concluded, "And once Thume is safely returned, we'll all be rewarded. That is Mhalendra's promise."

Jax whistled. Lars rested his chin on his thumb, fingers curled in front of his mouth. He didn't know how to react to all of this.

Darius, however, apparently did.

"Well," he began, "thanks for the great story. And the cigar." He stood up and looked at his crew. "Time to go, kids," he said.

Inora held his gaze and kept her seat. "No," she rasped. "I'm interested."

"Interested?" Darius said. "In what, getting ourselves killed? Either by the guards or by Vivienne? Or in teaming up with these backstabbing sons of bitches?

Bunny's eyebrows shot up.

The tension in the room was suffocating—like a dynamo coil wound too tight, one spark away from snapping.

Lars finally spoke up. "Backstabbing, Darius?"

Darius's jaw tightened. His lips parted... and then he exploded. "Damn right, backstabbing!" he shouted.

He turned sharply, pacing a step before wheeling back toward Lars, his hands moving wildly.

"Cut the hurting victim act, Lars. You really want to sit there and act like you don't know what the hells I'm talking about?"

Lars didn't flinch. "Go ahead, Darius. Spell it out for me."

Darius let out a sharp, humorless laugh. "You really wanna do this? Fine."

He planted both hands on the table, leaning in.

"You played your little game with Vivienne, and the rest of us paid the price." His voice was a low growl now, his anger cutting deeper. "You walked away from the mess you made, and somehow, somehow, you managed to come out on top. While the rest of us got burned. Banned from heists. We spent a year just played like fools, while you—" he gestured at Lars, "—what? Took a vacation?"

Lars held his gaze. "Yeah, Darius," he said. "Real relaxing."

He leaned forward, his bruised knuckles pressing against the wood. He met Darius's glare head-on, but this time, he didn't fire back with snark. He wouldn't deflect. He just... told the truth.

"You think I walked away clean? That I spent the last year coasting?"

It's not that he owed the thief anything. Except for that caper last year, they were rivals. But Lars was trying to reclaim something of himself. To be a better leader. Hells, a better man.

"I spent the first month in hiding. Always looking over my shoulder, waiting for Vivienne to send someone after me. I kept a blade under my pillow. Trin and I never stayed in the same place for more than a week."

He let the words settle, let Darius process them.

"You have no idea how much that woman hates me, Darius," Lars continued. "I'll admit, I acted foolishly. Or maybe I should say foolhardy."

Liora, listening quietly like everyone else, piped up. "How so, Lars?"

Lars flashed a kind smile at her. "Because I took it on myself to pull a gambit. I didn't tell any of you why I was going with Vivienne, that the whole goal was to rob her. When Darius came to tell me what an ass I was being, I lied to his face."

He sighed and lowered his head. "I was arrogant. Deceitful. That's all there is to it."

Lars shook his head and looked back up at Darius.

"Anyway, after that you know what it was like. Watching the city change. Watching Vivienne move into every crack and corner like she was born to own this place. Watching everything I spent my damn life building become dust while I sat in the shadows, unable to lift a damn finger to stop it."

His fingers curled into a fist against the table.

"And the worst part? No one even noticed I was gone. So yeah, I get it. You're pissed. You spent a year struggling. But so did I. And I'm willing to admit my fault in it."

He met Darius's stare, unwavering. "You can hate me all you want. Just don't act like I came out on top. I lost everything, same as you."

For a long moment, Darius just stared. Lars could tell that the man hadn't expected this. Darius had come ready for a fight, ready to unload a year's worth of resentment. But now? Now he had the truth.

And finally, Darius smirked.

"That was a decent speech, Harrow," he said, tilting his head. "You rehearse that?"

Lars's lips curled into a slow, lopsided grin. "Nah," he replied, leaning back in his chair. "That's just good old-fashioned Lars Harrow charm."

Darius let out a short chuckle. "Well," he said, "you look like you've already been beat up enough, so I'm not gonna pile on."

He hesitated before adding, "But I'm not willing to commit to something like this, Lars. You gotta understand why."

Lars nodded, tapping his fingers against his thigh. He did understand. Crew leaders didn't have the luxury of forgetting past transgressions. Once burned, always burned.

"I do. But it's a shame," Lars admitted, "because if we decide to do this, we need both crews."

Darius's smirk twitched, but he didn't bite. "No promises." And with that, he stood.

His crew exchanged glances, clearly expecting him to say more. Maybe even to change his mind. But he didn't.

"We're leaving," he said simply, heading for the door.

Inora, Rurik, and Maren hesitated. Inora's gaze lingered on Lars. Then, one by one, they filed out behind their leader.

Silas was the last to stand. He muttered something unintelligible then turned to Keer.

"I'll see you back on the ship tomorrow?"

Keer nodded once. "You will."

Silas gave Lars a look—one that said this wasn't over yet. Then he followed the others out. The door shut behind them.

Had that gone well? Lars wasn't sure. But at least it had gone.

Bunny broke the silence. "Well, that was—"

Lars interrupted, "Yeah, yeah. Let me guess. Fun? Riveting?"

"I was gonna say admirable, actually," Bunny huffed. He almost looked hurt.

Oh. Lars hadn't expected that. "Really?" he replied.

"No, not really. But it was."

Jax, who had remained mostly silent this whole time, chuckled. "So, Lars," he said. "What's the next move?"

Good question. Lars sat a moment, tapping his fingers on the table.

"You're about to tell us you're going to visit Thume, aren't you?" Trin asked.

Damn it, that woman knew him too well. He grinned sheepishly. "Yes, in fact."

Liora grinned. Trin leaned forward and looked Lars in the eyes.

"Well?" she said. "Do you want any of us to come along?"

What did he want? He didn't give a wet slap about the man behind bars. But sticking it to Vivienne? That rich reward Mhalendra promised? Might be worth it.

"No, I'll go alone." Lars said after a moment. "Thume and I need to have a heart to heart."

The last interactions Lars had with Cecil Thume were not pleasant. The man was stubborn, arrogant, devious.

Foolhardy.

Who was Lars to judge? Now he just needed to see if the asshole was worth saving.

Liora pushed open the door to the condo, stepping inside with a quiet sigh. The scent of something rich and spiced filled the air—slow-cooked meat with maybe a hint of caramelized onions. It wrapped around her, warm and grounding.

In the kitchen, Myrim stood over the stove, moving with his usual precision. The Dynamo Conduction Cook Surface—Liora's personal engineering masterpiece—glowed faintly beneath the metal pan, its embedded crystal coils pulsing with stored energy.

Not a single kitchen in Azoria had one like it. Not yet. She'd designed the whole system from scratch, tinkering with heat distribution for months to get it just right. The coils fed a controlled current through layered dynamo plates, generating heat without an open flame. Safer, more efficient, and infinitely more fun to build.

She could have commercialized it, honestly, and made a killing selling it to every upper-city restaurant and noble's estate in Ithris. But no... this was hers for now. If only so she could watch Aric using it.

He'd gone from grumbling about "blowing up the damn condo" to using it daily, like he'd been cooking on it his whole life.

Liora leaned against the doorframe, watching as he adjusted the dials, lowering the intensity of the coils with a flick of his fingers. *Damn I'm good,* she thought with a smirk.

"If I'd known you were cooking," she mused aloud, "I would've hurried back sooner."

Myrim glanced over his shoulder, his expression unreadable for a second before softening. "Well hello. I didn't know whether to expect anyone at all."

"Yeah, well... nothing more to be done at the base for now."

He only grunted.

"Where's Shelle?" Liora asked, shrugging off her jacket and coming to stand next to him.

Myrim turned the stove down, the glow of the crystal coils dimming slightly. "She took a job. Should be back later."

Liora nodded, her fingers trailing along the small of his back. She felt tired. Not physically—well, not *just* physically, after that mad dash with Jax and Bunny—but drained.

"You hungry?" he asked, shifting the pan off the burner.

Liora hesitated, then let out a small laugh. "Starving, actually."

He grinned. "Sit. I'll fix you a plate."

She walked over to the table and sank into a chair, watching as Myrim moved with that easy efficiency of his. He grabbed a clean plate, scooped generous portions of beef and onions from the pan, and draped a dish towel over his arm as he set the food in front of her.

Then, with quiet affection, he leaned down and pressed a kiss to her forehead before sitting across from her.

What a sweetheart.

But Liora didn't dig in right away. She picked at the food with her fork and rearranged the meat and onions into a slightly more organized pile, her fingers idly tapping against the table.

Myrim watched her for a moment before speaking.

"What's wrong?"

Liora blinked, looking up at him. "Who says something's wrong?"

He arched a brow.

Liora sighed, nudging at the food with her fork. "Just a long night."

"A long night that has you poking at your food instead of inhaling it?"

She let out a half-hearted snort. "I'm not sure if you heard," she finally muttered, "Lars got beat to all hells."

Myrim's eyes opened wide. "Did he? What happened?"

"The job went bad. Really bad." She finally took a small bite, chewing slower than necessary.

"It was hard to watch," Liora admitted, voice quieter now. "Even after everything, I might have been pissed at him, but seeing him like that..." She shook her head. "I don't know."

He reached for his own plate. "It sounds like a mess," he said evenly.

Liora scoffed softly. "Yeah."

She looked up. Myrim wasn't looking directly at her. In fact, he was poking at his own food much as she had done. She couldn't really tell if he didn't like the topic, or if the news hit him hard too.

Myrim took a slow bite, chewing thoughtfully. "Do you think he deserved it?"

What the hells kind of question was that? "No," Liora said with a frown.

Undeterred, Myrim met her gaze. "But you're still mad at him."

That was an odd way to look at it. Maybe it was part of being in the city watch for so long.

Liora huffed, stabbing a piece of food with her fork. "Yeah. I can be mad at him and not want to see him beat to the hells."

"I guess that makes sense," Myrim said, taking another bite.

Liora kept her gaze on her plate, twirling the soft onions on her fork. "It's just..." She hesitated, trying to find the right words. "Oh, I don't know. He's not the same. None of us are, I guess. But seeing him like that—" She shook her head. "It hit harder than I thought it would."

There was a clang as Myrim set his fork down on the plate. "Shelle should be back soon," he said casually. "I wonder how her job went."

Liora blinked, then let out a short laugh. "I wasn't done telling you how hard my life is yet."

He smirked. "My apologies, my dear. Feel free to keep complaining."

She rolled her eyes but took a proper bite this time. And another. It tasted better now—richer, warmer. Talking to Aric always helped, even when Liora wasn't sure what she was looking for.

Still... something tugged at the back of her mind. What was it?

Myrim was protective. He always had been. Not overbearing, but protective in a way that made Liora feel like he saw every risk before it could touch her. He seemed to catch the little things—the way her shoulders tensed when she was holding back frustration, the subtle shift in her voice when she was tired but pretending not to be.

Sometimes, it felt like he knew what she needed even before she did.

Yet not once had he asked if *she* had been in danger. Not once had he asked if she knew who had beaten Lars bloody.

That was odd.

A sharp knock at the door cut through the quiet.

Myrim stood, moving toward it before Liora had even registered the sound. She watched him go, still twirling her fork idly in her fingers.

Then she heard his breath hitch as he opened the door.

"Diligence?" Myrim asked. "What are you doing here?"

Liora's head snapped up.

Diligence Blythe. Vivienne's pet toadie. Her smug, self-important little kiss-up of a messenger.

Liora shot to her feet, rounding the table in a few quick strides to get a look for herself.

Yep, that was Diligence. Complete with the rapier at her side, that petulant pout, and the way she looked at you like she was trying to decide what wine to serve you with.

They had interacted plenty of times while working on monorail projects. Enough for Liora to know the woman lived to serve Vivienne's whims. And every single time, she had left the conversation wanting to take a bath.

Diligence tilted her head, eyes flicking between Liora and Myrim like she was making some private little calculation. Then she smiled.

"Evening, Liora," she drawled. "I do hope I'm not interrupting."

Liora crossed her arms. "What do you want, Blythe?"

The edges of Diligence's lips rose just a little higher. "Vivienne requests your presence," she said smoothly. "At your earliest convenience, of course."

"And what exactly does she want?" Myrim asked, his grip on the doorframe tightening.

Diligence's gaze flicked up toward him, and a flicker of tension passed between them. "I have no idea, ex-Captain Myrim," she said with a grin. "Why should I?"

Why was there tension? How in the hells were these two so familiar—

But then Diligence stepped back. "No rush," she said lightly, already turning away. "But don't keep Miss Vivienne waiting too long."

Liora stood there, folding her arms as she watched Diligence disappear down the hall.

Myrim closed the door with a soft click but didn't turn around. His hand still rested on the door handle.

"Something wrong?" Liora asked with narrowed eyes he couldn't see.

"No," he said simply, standing tall and turning towards her.

Well, that wasn't very convincing. But Liora saw no reason to argue. Maybe he was just shaken up by the news about Lars and the unexpected visit.

Pushing in his chair, Myrim took his plate back to the kitchen. Liora watched him for a moment, then shook her head as a million other questions entered her mind.

It seems she had to visit Vivienne. Did this have to do with the offer from Zarakar? Did Vivienne know about Lars getting beat up? How much torque do you apply to the third mounting bolt on a monorail conduction plate? How were they going to spring Thume?

Funny, she thought. *I never wondered if we'd do it... just how.*

Liora sighed. She was a woman of action, after all.

Trin led the way through the narrow lanes of the north market alleys, the air thick with the reek of iron, mildew, and the occasional burn of chemical runoff. Jax and Bunny flanked her, their boots echoing on the uneven cobblestone.

It was good to see Lars stepping up again. Better still that Darius had finally spit out whatever bile he'd been nursing for a year. That weight was off the table now—ugly truths aired, egos bruised but grudges acknowledged.

No one was holding hands, but at least they were facing the same storm.

The direction they had wasn't perfect. Far from it. Trusting a Zarakaran power play was the kind of risk that got people killed, but it was something. And Trin could work with something. She always had. A crack in a window was still a way in.

That's what this outing was about. If Mhalendra Thume had sent a message across the sea, there had to be someone in Azoria that knew more. All Trin had to do was pull the right thread. And with Jax and Bunny flanking her, she had the muscle to tug hard.

"Are you sure about this guy?" Bunny asked, squinting ahead. A flickering dynamo lamp overhead buzzed like it wanted to die.

Trin didn't slow. "Backstreet boiler house, Shipwright Row, where Renko fences scrap dynamo."

Bunny blinked. "That a riddle?"

"It's a mnemonic," Trin replied. "Helped me remember where to buy trouble by the pound."

Jax snorted. "Reassuring."

They rounded a corner into a tight alley, where steam hissed from rusted vents and copper runoff stained the bricks green. At the far end, half swallowed by shadow and grime, sat a squat stone building.

Trin approached first and knocked three times, then twice more. A panel slid open, revealing a pair of jaundiced eyes.

"Trin?" came a voice like gravel in oil. "It's been a while. I don't owe you money, do I?"

"You probably do," she replied. "But I'll settle for a little information."

The door creaked open, revealing Renko—a rat-faced man with a patchy beard and ink-stained fingers. He wore a coat made from six different jackets and a belt lined with wire-cutters and coil testers.

He squinted at her companions. "You bring a circus?"

"Muscle," she replied. "And moral support."

"I don't care for either," Renko muttered, turning his back and hobbling inside. "Come in, but don't touch anything. It's all rigged."

Inside, the boiler house was hotter than hells and louder. Dynamo components littered every surface—bent cogs, drained crystals, scorched conduit. A ventilation pipe shook every few seconds, hissing like a viper. Renko settled behind a slab of metal he used as a desk and poured himself a drink that smelled like metal polish.

"So what's the ask?" he rasped.

Trin leaned forward, palms flat on the desk. "I want to know if Zarakaran envoys are poking in Azoria."

Renko blinked, then chuckled. "They're always in Azoria. Looking for patrons, mostly."

"What kind of patrons?"

Renko shrugged. "Ones that can still sign trade deals. Or start wars."

Trin narrowed her eyes. "You got a name?"

"Maybe." He glanced toward a locked cabinet. "Might be I also have a location. But I'd rather not—"

Suddenly the door slammed open.

Four men stepped in—grimy, built like mercenary brick walls, wearing heavy coats and city watch boots with the insignia scraped off. The tallest one held a club with a dent that looked personal.

"Evening, Renko," the leader drawled. "Heard you had company."

Renko's chair was empty before they could blink. The little bastard had slithered out through a side vent.

"Oh come on," Trin muttered.

The leader looked at her, then at Bunny. "You're a big one. Ever thought about working real enforcement?"

Bunny crossed his arms. "You offer dental?"

They lunged.

The first enforcer lunged for Jax, swinging a rusted club toward his head. Jax ducked, took the blow to the shoulder with a grunt, and responded by driving a meaty fist into the man's ribs. When the guy doubled over, wheezing, Jax grabbed him by the collar, yanked him in close, and slammed his forehead into the bridge of the man's nose.

There was a crunch—sharp and wet—and the enforcer dropped like a sack of bricks, blood gushing from both nostrils as he hit the floor.

Bunny stood his ground. Another goon came at him with a crowbar, but Bunny stepped inside the arc and caught his wrist mid-swing. His other hand came up and palm-struck the bastard's chin, sending him reeling into a stack of dynamo scrap. The coils exploded in a shower of sparks as the enforcer hit them.

Still more came at Trin, and she moved like liquid iron. Dipping under a wild swing, she planted her heel on the ground and spun, slamming the back of her elbow into a man's temple. As he staggered, Trin grabbed his jacket, kneed him twice in the groin, and let him collapse to the floor with a soft, pitiful groan.

Another man with a knife tried to tackle her from behind.

Big mistake. She spun with a snarl, slammed her head backward into his nose, then twisted his wrist until his blade dropped.

In one fluid motion, she caught the knife mid-fall, pivoted, and pressed it to the throat of the last standing enforcer—their leader, thick-limbed and gasping, his hands up.

"Anyone moves," Trin said, "and I silence him where he stands."

The rest of the room was wreckage. Two men lay groaning in the corner. Another was still twitching near the sparking crate. The thug who dropped the knife didn't try.

Trin pulled the leader close, keeping the knife on the man's throat as she angled toward the file cabinet. His breath hitched.

She reached the cabinet and slammed an elbow into the handle. The rusted metal buckled, dented in with a sharp clang. The drawer popped loose.

"Don't worry, friend," Trin whispered to the man in her grasp. "We're almost done here."

Her eyes scanned quickly through the folders—names, dates, meaningless labels. Until one caught her eye: a mountain, struck through with a lightning bolt.

She grabbed it, tucked it under her arm, and shoved the enforcer forward. He stumbled, nearly falling, but kept his footing. The look he gave her would have melted steel.

"Go," Trin snapped to Jax and Bunny.

They didn't hesitate.

The three of them burst through the door and vanished into the night.

The files had given Trin what she needed. To get there, they decided to take the monorail.

Walking to New Zarakar from the Market District would've taken half the night, and after the fight they'd just crawled out of, none of them were exactly itching for cardio.

The car they boarded was mostly empty, save for a pair of tired factory workers and a woman with two sleeping kids draped across her lap. The lights inside flickered a little, but the hum beneath their feet was steady. Trin felt it in her bones, a low, resonant vibration that marked every rail-spanning coil they passed.

Bunny looked like he was going to vomit.

He clutched the handrail, his jaw clenched, eyes fixed on the rivets along the floor. "This thing runs on dynamo?" he muttered, not for the first time.

Trin leaned against the opposite pole. "Most things do now."

"I grew up in a village where we thought crystals were for giving thanks to the gods," Bunny grunted. "Now I'm hurtling through a city in a metal demon that hisses every time it breathes."

"It's not breathing," Trin said. "That's the condenser releasing charge."

"Was that supposed to make me feel better?"

Across from them, Jax had his entire face pressed to the window like a child spotting a parade. "Look at that!" he barked, pointing as they passed the soaring silhouette of the Ithris Gaming Commission, its tall walls and windows glinting in the moonlight. "I've never seen it from this high up!"

"Keep staring and you'll fog up the glass," Trin said, but she couldn't help smiling. It wasn't often you saw Jax genuinely amazed by something that wasn't food or new clothes.

They passed the smokestacks of the outer foundries next. Then the monorail shifted, dipping deep into the slums. The lights got sparser, with entire blocks sitting in darkness. Buildings shrank even as they became more densely packed. The skyline bled into rust.

And finally, they reached New Zarakar. Two blocks of flickering market tents in a sea of dilapidated buildings, grease-stained awnings, and shouting vendors. The air was rich with the smells of heady spices that tickled Trin's nostrils and made her mouth water.

When the monorail doors hissed open, Bunny made a silent signal to the heavens and staggered onto the platform like a man reborn.

Jax followed, still grinning. "Can we ride that again?"

"Let's see if we make it out of this in one piece first," Trin said.

Then she stepped off the platform and into the chaos, her eyes locked on the twisting alleys ahead.

Her side still ached from where one of the enforcers had clipped her ribs, and her knuckles throbbed beneath her gloves. But that was fine. Necessary, even. She'd needed to hit something. To be in control of something. The fight back in the boiler house wasn't elegant, wasn't her style, but it had scratched an itch she hadn't even realized was growing under her skin.

After a year of waiting—for the crew to recover, for Lars to lead, for some golden opportunity to come knocking—it had felt good to take the reins. To be a blade again.

That was what she used to be. A blade in the dark. She'd drifted from that without noticing. Trin had gone soft.

Before them stretched a maze of street carts, with noise and motion packed into every stall and window. The nation of Zarakar was built on hierarchy and polish. New Zarakar was chaos and ambition. And somewhere beneath it all was the Ember House.

Jax leaned into a vendor stall and came back with a skewer of grilled meat slathered in bright orange sauce. He took one bite and immediately started coughing.

"Oh hells, that's lava," he wheezed.

Bunny took the stick, sniffed it, and handed it back. "You'll be fine. Mostly."

Trin smirked faintly but didn't stop.

The Ember House wasn't marked. It wouldn't be. But she knew the way. Down a side alley just past the spice vendor with the red-striped canopy. Left at the broken fountain shaped like a vulture. Then behind the rice stand, past the rusted stairwell—

"Here," she said, stopping in front of a corrugated panel behind a rack of hanging octopus.

Bunny raised an eyebrow. "Are we going to eat, or interrogate a kraken?"

She tapped on the panel. A bolt clicked behind it. The panel creaked inward, revealing a narrow staircase lit by thin lines of dull, reddish light.

"We're going under," Trin said. "Watch your head."

Trin ducked in, her boots echoing softly on the metal steps. Bunny followed. Jax took one last mournful look at his skewer of rich meats, then dropped it in a waste bin and headed down.

Beneath the noise and stink of New Zarakar, the Ember House waited.

A final set of steps led them into a long, smoke-hazed room where low music pulsed and conversations danced just below the threshold of clarity. Lanterns burned behind colored glass, casting molten shadows across painted brick. No signs. No menus. Just faces in the dark, strong alcohol, and the scent of politics in the air.

They had barely taken three steps inside before a voice slid through the gloom like silk over steel.

"Miss Meridia," it purred. "I would expect a bit more grace. And less bloody knuckles."

Trin's eyes snapped to the source. A man emerged from a corner alcove, draped in a dark, high-collared Zarakaran coat threaded with gold. His skin was the rich hue of polished ironwood, his beard immaculately sculpted, and his expression was one of permanent amusement.

A diplomat, clearly. But not just any.

"Councilor Bandhi," Trin said, lips tight.

Jax blinked. "Wait, you two know each—?"

The man cut him off with a raised brow. "We met at her father's estate," he said, eyes never leaving Trin. "Many years ago. She was what... twelve? All steel and fury. I remember wondering if she'd stab me before or after the dessert wine."

"Shame I didn't," Trin murmured, blushing. Damn him.

She kept her face turned, hoping Jax hadn't caught the red in her cheeks. Of all the things Bandhi could've brought up, it had to be that part of her life. That she had once worn dresses tailored by the meter, that she'd practiced court curtsies and dinner diplomacy. That she'd sat through state dinners while her father plotted trade alliances over imported Drakorian wine.

No one here—especially not Jax or Bunny—needed to know she was once a noble. That she'd traded her family crest for heists and escape routes.

Bandhi chuckled. "Follow me. I'm assuming you're here for a more private conversation."

Without waiting for agreement, he turned and swept through a curtain of amber beads. Trin glanced once at Bunny and Jax before following.

They stepped into a narrow, velvet-walled side room, a private lounge that smelled of cloves and firewood. A fan on the ceiling ticked quietly overhead. Trin sat first, perching on the edge of a low chaise. Jax and Bunny flanked the doorway.

Bandhi poured tea into delicate copper cups, all the while keeping his gaze on her.

"So," he said, "to what do I owe this surprise visit? Surely not nostalgia."

"I could use some information," Trin said.

The man smiled and spread his arms wide. "I am yours to command."

If only that were true. Information trading was an art among Zarakarans. She could only hope that in the end, Bandhi wanted her to know the answers to what she asked.

Trin sipped her tea, then set the cup down. "How's the weather in Zarakar these days?"

Bandhi tilted his head, amused. "Predictable. Hot in the day. Cold at night. And a storm always on the horizon, whether you see it coming or not."

Trin smiled faintly. "And where do you think this storm is now?"

"You know where. Far east of Zarakar."

Trin sat forward, balancing her cup between her fingers.

She might as well just go for it. "If he made it back west," she asked quietly, "would Thume still have a home?"

Bandhi didn't blink. "Oh, undoubtedly so."

"But would the hearth be lit?"

A pause. Then, "Warmly. But that is not the real question."

Trin tilted her head. "No?"

He smiled.

"I suppose not," Trin said, considering. "The real question is would he light the fire himself?"

"Oh yes," Bandhi said, voice smooth. "The fire will be fed immense fuel, and burn higher than the mountains of Zarakar."

Jax shifted where he stood, but Trin didn't look at him. Her eyes were locked on Bandhi.

"And what of the smoke?" she asked. "Would it drift east?"

Bandhi's smile sharpened. "Winds are unpredictable on rough seas."

"But the wood... is it stacked and ready?"

Bandhi nodded. "Laid by his own hand. Each piece placed with care."

Trin placed her cup down gently and sighed. "And I suppose the kindling's already gathered."

"It is." Bandhi bowed his head. "And your fingers, Miss Meridia, are holding the match."

There it was. The truth unspoken. Thume was orchestrating his own release from the inside. Mhalendra was just the messenger. Ithris was the tinder. Lars and crew... well, apparently Thume felt they were just the arsonists he needed right now.

Before she could press further, a quiet knock against the wall broke the rhythm. An aide appeared in the doorway, murmuring something low.

Bandhi stood smoothly. "Regretfully, I must return to the surface."

He met Trin's eyes one last time, the smile now gone from his face.

"As we are out of time, I will speak plainly. I know you love this city, but nothing will stop this fire."

He paused at the curtain.

"When the blaze comes, Miss Meridia... it is always better to be the one holding the torch."

And with that, Bandhi swept out of the room.

Jax blinked after him. "I didn't understand a single damn word of what just happened." He turned to Bunny. "Did you?"

Bunny shook his head solemnly. "Nah. I'm more of an idiot than you are."

Trin didn't buy it. Bunny had a knack for playing dumb. Especially when he was paying very close attention.

She drained her tea in one clean motion, the copper clinking soft against the table.

Jax squinted. "Wait, Trin. Were you really a noblewoman?"

Trin didn't answer. She just rose to her feet and smoothed the edge of her jacket. The noble's daughter in her wanted to shrink. The spymaster in her wanted answers.

"Come on," she said, already moving toward the curtain. "We'd better head back."

✧

The lobby of the Ithris Gaming Commission was colder than Liora remembered. And not just in temperature.

Polished stone stretched beneath her boots, too smooth for comfort, and too silent for a city building supposedly full of action. The walls gleamed, spotless and impersonal. Security officers stood like statues along the perimeter, their uniforms crisp, their expressions void. Everything about the place said *don't touch.*

Liora followed the attendant—a woman dressed in Commission blue with not a hair out of place—down a central corridor lit by dynamo lights that shone with nothing but pale, clinical daylight.

She hadn't been here in months. Liora had been instrumental in Thume's capture, but also instrumental in double crossing Vivienne. When she was first invited, she had expected retribution. Instead, it had been a job offer. It had felt tense, sure—but alive. Now it felt like the air itself had been vacuumed out.

Liora kept her chin up. She'd built the first working monorail in this city. She'd kept the engineering initiative alive through ridiculous demands and horrific bureaucracy. She had nothing to be ashamed of.

Even if the woman she was about to face chilled her blood, made her feel a little dirty, and yet... had once made her feel like a rising star.

The doors slid open on the top floor, revealing an expanse of glass, polished metal, and one enormous curved window that looked out over the heart of Azoria. In the center of it all, leaning casually against an opulent desk with nothing on it but a bottle of wine and two glasses, stood Vivienne Dragunova.

Smiling.

Welp, this wasn't going to be good.

"Liora, my dear," Vivienne said. "You've been busy."

Vivienne didn't move from her spot by the desk. She simply gestured to the second glass with a faint tilt of her head. "I poured your favorite. Or at least, it was your favorite when we last shared a drink."

Liora didn't budge. "I'm good."

Vivienne shrugged, unbothered, and picked up her own glass. "Suit yourself."

She swirled the wine gently, watching the liquid catch the light like blood in crystal. "It's funny," she said, her tone light and casual, "I heard a little story recently. Something about an attempted theft on a clerk's office. Only attempted, of course. Rather theatrical, really. And somehow... a failure?"

Liora crossed her arms. "I'm not here to explain myself."

"Oh, my dear, I'm not asking for an explanation. I've already drawn my conclusions."

Vivienne took a long sip, then turned to face the window, gazing out over the city like it was a stage and she the sole critic.

"You had so much potential, Liora. Truly the brightest mind I'd seen in a decade. The monorail alone was truly visionary. But something about this city drags people back into their worst selves, doesn't it? No matter how high they rise, they always come crawling back to the mud."

Liora said nothing. Let her talk. Let her show the cracks.

Vivienne glanced over her shoulder. "I assume that little escapade wasn't your idea. Lars is back in the game, isn't he?"

Liora flinched, just barely. But Vivienne saw it. Of course she did.

"I do worry about him. I doubt he's as sharp as he used to be." Vivienne said. "I hope he knows what he's doing. Because you, Liora, were doing something truly *useful.* Productive. Transformative."

She turned, fully now, and stepped closer—glass still in hand, but her expression harder.

"Tell me this," Vivienne said. "What's more noble: changing the face of a city... or robbing it of its future just to relive the past?"

Liora tilted her head. "Funny," she said, "I was just wondering something similar."

Vivienne blinked. "Oh?"

"What's more noble. Building something from scratch, or stealing the vision from someone smarter and pretending it was yours."

Vivienne's smile twitched.

"You didn't build this city, Vivienne. You inherited it through coercion and convenience. You shaped the parts you could control and buried the rest under policy and fear."

Vivienne's eyes narrowed. She opened her mouth.

But Liora took a step forward and spoke first. "I didn't come here to justify a damn thing. I came because I assumed you wanted to see me. And now that I'm here, I'm wondering if this meeting was about me at all."

A muscle in Vivienne's jaw ticked.

"You don't like being reminded that you didn't break everyone," Liora said softly. "That not everyone folded. That the monorail wasn't your idea. That I didn't stay. That Lars left you."

Vivienne set the glass down with a crisp clink. "You're done," she said.

Liora arched a brow.

Vivienne's voice dropped to a whisper-sharp register. "Your work on the engineering initiative is finished. Effective immediately. The monorail. The Institute contracts. The research liaison council. I'll find someone else to take on the job."

Liora didn't flinch. "You'll need three people to replace me. Maybe four."

"Then I'll hire five," Vivienne snapped.

A knock sounded at the door.

"What?" Vivienne shouted. A bit too loudly, honestly. Maybe it was just in Liora's head, but the woman actually seemed shaken. That was new.

A messenger stepped in, whispered something low into Vivienne's ear. The woman's expression faltered.

Vivienne's eyes flicked to Liora, her voice cool and precise.

"Did you know Lars is visiting Cecil Thume in prison today?"

Liora didn't answer. She didn't have to.

Vivienne's gaze lingered on her, cold and unreadable.

"Be careful who you follow, Miss Banz," she said. "Some men will lead you straight to the gallows and call it a job well done."

Liora didn't reply. She wouldn't give Vivienne the satisfaction. Instead, she turned and walked out.

The corridor was just as silent and sterile on the way out. But now, every step echoed louder in her ears.

She didn't look back. They'd keep riding the monorail. Every dignitary, every commuter, every last bastard in a suit chasing coin or power. They'd glide above Azoria on rails she had imagined, on circuits only she could have made real.

Vivienne might scratch her name from the blueprints, commission new schematics, slap some other fool's title across the console plates. But she couldn't own it. Not truly.

Because the monorail wasn't hers. It never would be. It was Liora's—rooted in her vision, forged by her hands, and humming with a brilliance Vivienne could never replicate.

Azoria's prison gates loomed like a wall of iron teeth as Lars approached, his boots striking the stone with a deliberate rhythm. The sky was overcast, the light filtering down in a thin, colorless wash that made everything look older, flatter. Like even the air itself was resigned to this place.

Lars breathed a deep sigh and stepped inside.

He expected resistance. Expected the checkpoint to be an interrogation. A gruff demand to know his business with Thume. A weapons pat-down. Maybe even a few passive-aggressive jabs about old grudges—the kind of suspicion prisons bred in their bones.

Instead, the guard at the front desk didn't even glance up properly. He just tapped at a clipboard, his fingers moving in a lazy rhythm.

A low buzz, mechanical and ugly, vibrated through the air.

"He's expecting you," the guard muttered, already reaching for a coffee mug.

The further Lars walked, the deeper the unease burrowed into his gut. The corridors smelled of stone, sweat, and stale dynamo charge. Pale lamps cast a cold, buzzing light across the narrow halls. Doors lined the way, each one thick enough to withstand a battering ram, and each one closing behind him with a heavy, final-sounding thud.

No other inmates stirred. No catcalls. No distant shouting. It was quiet... far too quiet for a place built to cage the city's most dangerous and desperate.

They weren't leading him toward the standard visitation hall. That much became clear when the guard escorting him turned sharply at an unmarked junction and guided him toward a wing with softer lighting and newer floors.

Private cells. High privilege prisoners.

That figures, Lars thought grimly. Even locked up, Thume had his own little kingdom.

Finally, the guard stopped in front of a reinforced door, twisted a thick key into the lock, and stepped aside.

"Inside," he said.

Lars hesitated a moment, then pushed through.

The door clicked shut.

And there, standing behind a modest table in a surprisingly clean, well-lit room, was Cecil Thume.

He looked up the moment Lars entered.

Prison hadn't broken Thume—it had distilled him.

The golden eyes still caught the light like molten coins, still moved with that predator's calculation. Gray now threaded through his black hair, silver at the temples spreading like frost. The lines around his mouth and eyes had deepened, his face leaner than before, but this wasn't the hollow look of a man ground down by stone walls.

This was patience, carved into flesh.

Even his prison grays looked tailored—pressed sharp, not a wrinkle in sight. Polished boots. Hands folded on the table with the stillness of a man who'd learned to make waiting into a weapon.

If it weren't for the bars on the windows and the heavy dynamo restraints bolted into the floor nearby, Lars could've mistaken this for a political negotiation. Another maneuver in Thume's endless chessboard.

"Lars Harrow," Thume said, smiling, his voice as rich and measured as ever. "Well. I'd say you look well, but it seems you've been taking great pains to look anything but. A run-in with a masked attacker, perhaps?"

Lars's shoulders stiffened. So Thume knew about that, huh? He shouldn't have been surprised. Knowing things was what had landed Thume in here after all.

Still, the fact that the man had brought it up *immediately* was the more important thing. Thume didn't just know. He wanted Lars to know he knew.

Not even five seconds in, and the power plays had already begun.

"It's worth mentioning," Thume added, his smile tightening, "that such things didn't happen when I ruled the city."

Lars resisted the urge to laugh. Yeah. Back when Thume had half the city wired up like puppets, and the other half too scared to breathe wrong. Real peaceful, that.

Thume chuckled, a soft, unhurried sound. He gestured to the chair across from him.

"Please. Sit. There's no need to guard your words. After all, we are both survivors of Azoria's many betrayals."

"You had the guards waiting for me?" Lars asked.

"Of course." Thume's smile deepened. "The normal visitor process would have been a waste of both our time."

Lars didn't sit. He didn't trust the chair, didn't trust the clean walls, didn't trust anything about this little meeting wrapped up in a bow. "Were you that sure I'd show up?"

Thume tilted his head slightly, as if Lars had just asked him whether water tended to be wet. "It was inevitable," he said. "Given the offer Mhalendra made—and the precarious position you find yourself in—it would have been foolish not to seek clarification."

Lars's jaw tightened. He didn't like the way Thume said that. Like it wasn't a conversation at all, just a page unfolding in some plan the bastard had written weeks ago.

"So was the offer from her," Lars asked tightly, "or from you?"

Thume's smile sharpened, but it didn't quite reach his eyes. "It hardly matters. Whether the hand is hers or mine, the strings pull the same."

Alright, that was enough. Lars took a step back toward the door. "I knew this was a bad idea."

But before he could turn fully, Thume raised a hand. "Wait. I'm sorry."

Lars froze.

Thume stood, slowly, deliberately. As if not to spook a wild animal. His movements were measured. Controlled. A man used to commanding the room, and yet... there was something different there. A thin edge of real regret threading through his voice.

"I asked you here because I owe you that much," Thume said. "For what you uncovered. For what it cost you. And for what it cost me."

Lars stared at him, suspicion roaring in his veins. Thume didn't apologize. He manipulated. He lectured. He punished. Apologies weren't in his arsenal. And yet here they were.

Thume remained standing, hands folded lightly behind his back, as if he were delivering a lecture at one of the Institute halls instead of speaking to the man who had helped bury him.

"I didn't bring you here to beg favors, Lars. Nor to gloat. I came to tell you something few will admit."

He paced a slow line behind the table, his boots clicking softly against the stone.

"I built Azoria's order. Maybe not perfectly. Maybe not cleanly. But tell me this..." He turned, golden eyes catching Lars's like snared wire. "Was there ever a time you feared for the city's future when I ruled it? A time you worried it would crumble?"

Lars said nothing. Which was, itself, an answer.

Thume gave a small nod, almost sad.

"You rose during that time. Thrived. Took the city's games and turned them into legend. I saw it. Admired it. Encouraged it."

He stepped closer and placed a hand on Lars's shoulder.

Lars was not a fan. But he allowed it.

"I was born in Zarakar," Thume said quietly. "But Azoria is my home. It is my heart. I bled for this city long before I bled for any ambition of my own. Whatever sins you uncovered, they were never placed above its survival."

He looked at Lars gravely. "I love this country, Lars. As I know you do."

"That doesn't mean we loved it the same way," Lars said, "but I suppose I can agree we both want it standing."

Despite that agreement, Lars knew there was a point under all this bluster. Thume loved to hear himself talk. But eventually the demand came.

Then Thume gave a small, almost wistful chuckle. "I've had time to think... about Vivienne."

Lars's gut twisted, a sour weight dropping into his stomach.

Thume smiled faintly. "My stepdaughter, you know," he said, like he was commenting on the weather.

For a moment, Lars couldn't breathe. What?

The weight of Vivienne's hand on his skin. The pull of her voice in his ear. The part of him that had wanted to join her.

Stepdaughter.

A cold, sick humor clawed up Lars's throat. Of course she was. Of course it was filth all the way down.

But Thume didn't linger. He turned back to the table, his voice smooth as ever.

"Another story, another time. For now, just understand: she will not stop until she has gutted this city down to its bones."

"I'm aware," Lars said. His mind still reeled from the musket shot Thume had set off with his words. The man's own hells damned stepdaughter.

He forced a rough laugh past his throat. "So that's it, then," he said. "You want the city back."

"I want freedom," Thume said, shaking his head. "Nothing more."

Lars knew otherwise, thanks to Trin's intel. His eyes narrowed. "Funny. For a man who wants 'nothing more' you tend to leave a pile of wreckage in your wake."

Thume stepped back to the table and rested one hand lightly on the wood.

"Listen, Lars. I don't seek to reclaim the Commission. I have no desire to run Azoria again. My time here is finished.

"But," he added with steel in his voice, "I will not die caged like a dog. There is much in Zarakar that demands my attention. Land. Family. Debts yet owed. I will accept exile. But not imprisonment."

What a crock of shit. Still, to pull one over on Vivienne...

"You want me to bust you out," Lars said.

"I want you to *steal* me," Thume corrected gently. "That's what you do, isn't it? Steal me from Vivienne's clutches. I assure you, it's perfectly legal. I wrote the law after all."

You know what? Lars kind of missed the clever machinations of this man.

But he wasn't going to just go and admit that.

"And why," he said finally, his voice like gravel, "would I lift a single damn finger for you?"

Thume smiled—not smug now, but with something that almost looked like real faith.

"I need a legend for the job, Lars. Not a footpad. And lucky for me, you're still the best this broken city can offer."

MAKING IT COUNT

8

Azoria looked dead tonight.

The city wasn't quite broken, as Thume had said, but hells it was getting there. Between Lars getting his ass handed to him at their last heist and the heightened crew rivalries in the city, it seemed like a powder keg just waiting to explode.

Vivienne didn't help much. That wasn't her game. She was the type to let the chaos fester a bit, let the rivals play against each other. Meanwhile, she'd cozy up to the powerful and seduce them to do her bidding.

Must run in the family, Lars thought with a grin.

He shoved his hands into his coat pockets and kept walking, boots dragging a little on the slick stones. Dynamo lamps buzzed overhead, throwing a sick, yellowish smear across the alley walls.

The crew had come together to discuss the plan earlier. And they had all, to a one, agreed that they needed to do this.

Not because they trusted him—that fantasy had died screaming—but because they knew better than to sit on their hands while the world swallowed them whole.

They all saw it.

Trin's intel from the Ember House said Thume was still pulling strings from his cell. And according to the Zarakaran minister, he'd come back swinging if they cut the locks.

Lars's own meeting with the bastard hadn't painted a pretty picture either. Thume talked a good game about exile, about walking away. Maybe he even believed it.

But in the end, whether it was true or just another lie, it didn't really matter. Vivienne Dragunova was still out there carving up Azoria like it was hers to bleed, and she wasn't slowing down.

If Thume decided he wanted her crown after they yanked him free, well... they'd burn that bridge when they came to it.

For now, this was what legends did. You rattled the cage. You made them remember why they locked the doors in the first place.

Lars rounded the last corner, the warehouse Darius called a base looming up out of the mist and half-light.

A lookout leaned against a balcony rail. Rurik. The squat bruiser looked Lars's way. No words, just a slow nod.

Lars gave a nod back and crossed the street, running through the plan he and his crew had settled on. A plan that required Darius—at least, it required his panache.

He wasn't here to argue. Wasn't here to beg. He was here to offer Darius a piece of the action.

What the man chose to do with it... that was up to him.

The door creaked when Lars pushed it open, the wood warped enough that it snagged on the frame. He shoved harder and slipped through, and the door groaned shut behind him.

Inside, the air seemed stale and the walls shadowed. It certainly wasn't the fun, rowdy hideout of ill repute Darius always liked to maintain. But hey, Lars's hideout wasn't much better these days.

Darius sat near the back, one boot up on the edge of a crate, swirling a glass of rich brown liquor.

He didn't rise or say a word. He just watched Lars with those hard, flat eyes that used to sparkle when there was a score on the table.

Lars gave a slow nod of acknowledgment and stepped further inside.

"You look worse than when I left you," Darius said after a moment, his voice dry.

Lars smirked faintly. "I'm still recovering. Neither of us seem to heal well."

Darius huffed through his nose. He took a lazy sip from his glass, never breaking eye contact.

"Come to try and change my mind about busting Thume out with you?" he asked.

Lars shook his head.

"Not my style. I figured I'd offer you something better instead."

Darius arched a brow but didn't interrupt.

Lars kept it simple. "We're moving. And we need the city watch, not to mention Vivienne, looking the wrong way. What we need is a little chaos."

"And you figured I'd be good at kicking the right hornet's nests," Darius said, swirling his glass.

Lars shrugged. "You're better at it than anyone I know."

Darius considered him for a long moment, the liquor glinting as he sipped.

"So... how big a stir are you looking for?" he asked finally.

Lars's mouth twitched. "You can decide that for yourself. Have fun with it. And try to get a decent score or two. Between what you're doing and what we're doing, chances are you'll get away with a fortune."

Another long pause.

Darius tipped his glass in a lazy salute and knocked the last of it back, setting the empty thing down with a hollow thud.

Then he grinned—that cocky, half-wolf grin Lars remembered all too well.

"Well," Darius said, "good you finally came to your senses. Took you long enough to admit who the better performer is."

Lars smirked, shaking his head as he started moving toward the far side of the room.

"You're right," he said lightly. "I'm all out of tricks these days."

Darius chuckled low in his throat, watching Lars with amused suspicion. "You're getting old, Harrow. Hells, you're practically respectable now."

"Careful," Lars said, crouching down near a battered section of wall, "don't make me whack you with my walking cane."

Darius leaned back on his crate, arms folding across his chest. "Okay, what in the hells are you doing?"

Lars rapped his knuckles twice against the cracked plaster—sharp, deliberate.

There was a faint hollow sound, just enough if you were listening for it.

Then he braced his palm against the spot and gave a shove.

The panel gave way with a soft crack, tipping inward.

Darius straightened, squinting. "The fuck—"

Inside the small crawlspace, nestled among dust and old splinters, sat a bag stuffed fat with coins, two copper bars, and a dusty bottle of whiskey older than both of them put together.

Lars grabbed the bag and the bottle in one hand, the bars clinking against each other as he stepped back. He gave Darius a lazy grin, lifting the whiskey in a mock-toast.

"Just grabbing a few of my leftover tricks," he said.

Darius's mouth hung open for a second before he barked out a real, full-throated laugh. It was the first honest one Lars had heard from him in over a year.

That was the thing about legends. They didn't just fight harder. They planned deeper. Buried their futures under the floorboards of the very city that shaped their predatory instinct.

"You sneaky son of a bitch," Darius said, shaking his head.

Lars crossed the room, stuck out his hand.

Darius grabbed it without hesitation, the shake hard and solid. It wasn't a bond of brotherhood exactly, but something rougher. Hammered into shape by bad blood and worse luck.

"Raise hells," Lars said.

Darius's grin sharpened. "Don't worry. I plan to."

Lars let go and headed for the door, the whiskey tucked under his arm, the weight of old pain just a little lighter behind him.

The soldering iron hissed as Liora dropped it onto the cluttered workbench, shaking out her fingers before the heat could bite deeper.

Her whole damn condo smelled like burned crystal dust and grease, a thick chemical stink that stuck to her throat.

Somewhere behind her, Shelle muttered a half-joke Liora didn't catch.

She ignored it. She didn't have the luxury of laughing tonight.

Liora leaned in over the device—a rat's nest of crystal capacitors, charged coils, and hand-cut copper channels—and adjusted the alignment again.

The crystal charge whined against her fingertips, wrong and raw and hungry. If she slipped even a little, it'd arc right up her arms and fry her nerves to the bone.

No pressure.

She wiped her forehead with the back of her wrist, leaving a black smear.

The schematics were a mess—sketched on scraps, half-guessed where hard numbers didn't exist—but the theory was sound.

At least she hoped it was.

Hope and desperation had a way of looking the same at this hour. At least, as long as the city grid didn't go out mid-experiment. Which it had been doing more and more lately. Maybe she should—

Behind her, the air shifted. Myrim, closer now, silent as a damn grave. Liora muttered another half-finished calculation under her breath and switched tools.

Tiny screwdriver. Nano-fiber tweezers.

Her hands shook, just a little. She clenched her jaw and forced the tremor still. Two connections left. Two. If she could get the timing relay stabilized and the discharge net wired without another short, the device might hold long enough.

Might. If it didn't...

That didn't bear thinking about. And she wasn't about to start writing goodbye letters just yet.

"You know," Shelle said, "if you zap yourself to death, I'm calling dibs on your boots."

Liora didn't look up. Her hands were too deep in the guts of the device, tracing copper channels that vibrated just a little too much against her fingertips.

That was a bad sign.

"You assume there'd be any boots left to wear," she muttered, tightening a coil.

Shelle let out a high-pitched, nervous laugh. It rattled around the room, scraping against the raw edges of Liora's concentration.

She focused on the next connection, breathing slow, steady, even as the dynamo charge started to whine at a higher pitch. The coil was hot, even through her gloves.

Behind her, Myrim moved silently, leaning over her shoulder. He didn't say a word, but she could smell his cologne, that scent of honey and leather that made the tiny hairs on her neck—

No, Liora. Stop it. Focus.

She clenched her teeth and kept working. Myrim just continued to stand there.

Liora couldn't afford a mistake right now—not with a circuit already threatening to slip out of phase.

"You two could make yourselves useful," she said without turning. "Hand me the B9 coil. Make sure it's the B9!"

Shelle shifted—rummaging through the parts bins with a muttered apology. She dropped the coil into Liora's outstretched hand.

Liora snapped the piece into place, jaw grinding.

Myrim still hadn't said a thing. But hells, he didn't have to. Liora could feel the questions hanging off him like stormclouds.

With the final coil attached, she turned a knob. The dynamo whine subsided, and the room finally felt calm and normal once again.

"So, are you going to tell us what the hells you're actually building," Myrim said, finally breaking his silence, "or are we just supposed to stand here and pray?"

Shelle let out a low grunt of agreement.

Liora flexed her hands, the gloves crackling faintly with static as she peeled them off. They were afraid for her. Liora loved them for that. Both of them.

"You know how heists go," she said, tossing the gloves onto the bench. "We need a little spark. A little controlled mischief."

Myrim didn't smile. He just watched her, steady and quiet. Shelle shifted beside him, arms crossed over her chest, gaze flickering nervously between them.

"Liora," she said, "I think we're past jokes. And you know that's rich coming from me. But maybe we can talk seriously about what you're up against?"

"You know damn well what we're up against," Liora said softly. "It's not just the city watch out there. He... that other thing is out there too."

She didn't say the name. She didn't have to. They all knew about the masked bastard with the eight-pointed star in its eye—the one that moved through the city like smoke and left blood behind.

Liora rubbed her hands on her pants, trying to wipe away the tingling in her skin.

"Anyway," she continued, "that's why I have to get it right."

Myrim took a step closer. "If you're possibly digging your own grave here," he said, voice almost gentle, "you may as well clue us into what you're doing. Maybe we have some ideas that can help. You don't have to do this alone."

He obviously wasn't going to give in until she gave some more details. And honestly, he wasn't wrong. Liora looked at the device—the tangle of copper and crystal and hope barely stitched together—and thought about the odds stacked against them. Thought about the plan she and her crew had come up with.

And what would happen if they got it wrong.

She let out a slow breath, reached for a screwdriver, and turned it idly in her hand—buying herself another second.

Maybe Myrim and Shelle deserved a little more. And maybe she could use their help. Or at least their emotional support.

Liora flipped the screwdriver in her hand, catching it by the tip, and set it down with a thunk.

"You want to know?" she muttered, not looking at them. "Fine."

She leaned against the workbench, folding her arms tight across her chest.

"It's a disruptor," she said. "A charge net built to destabilize a large dynamo field."

Shelle and Myrim both blinked.

"It'll throw off the attunement for a few seconds," Liora continued. "That's all. Just enough of a window for us to make a move."

Her throat felt tight, but she forced the words out.

"It's risky as hells. If the dampening relay overloads, the backlash could fry the whole system. Or cook whoever's too close when it discharges. Or both."

She shrugged, pretending she didn't care. Pretending she hadn't stayed up half the night trying to figure out how to make it just a little safer.

"Timing is everything," she said. "If we miss the mark by even a few seconds—"

She cut herself off, shaking her head.

No sense laying it out. They knew. Dynamo was volatile and didn't believe in second chances.

Myrim stepped forward, a slight tremor in his voice. "Okay, so it's dangerous. But... what is it you're actually doing? What do you plan to steal?"

"Oh, didn't I mention?" Liora said with a tired grin. "We're going to steal someone. Lord Cecil Thume."

Shelle was the first to break the silence that followed, grinning wide and giggling with unabashed thrill.

Myrim, on the other hand, made a strangled noise low in his throat. "What?" he burst out. "You're going to—"

"Yes," Liora said, cutting him off with a tired, defiant grin. "Yes, we are."

Myrim blinked, still trying to catch up. "You're just... you're just going to rob the prison?"

"Something like that," Liora said, flipping the screwdriver once more in her fingers before setting it down with finality.

Shelle put an arm around Liora's shoulders. "Oh darling," she said. "This is why I love you."

Liora laid a hand on Shelle's arm, truly thankful.

"Now," Shelle said, running her hand down Liora's back, "tell us how you're going to blow this whole damned city sideways."

The night wind rolled over the rooftop, cold and sharp, carrying the stink of dynamo smoke and alley rot up from the streets below.

Jax sat on the ledge, legs dangling out over the city, a battered flask clutched in both hands.

It was empty. And had been for weeks now. Still, holding it felt good. Familiar. Like an old wound you couldn't help but press now and then, just to make sure it still hurt.

He shifted, grimacing as his shirt rode up again over the soft roll of his gut.

Hells, he'd gotten fat.

All those years drinking and pounding down hearty meals, then running it off across Azoria's rooftops... and now he was just heavy. Heavy in ways he'd never felt before.

Bunny sat beside him, swinging his legs lazily over the drop, humming some tuneless little song that probably didn't even have words. Lars was right about one thing. Aelyndorans could be fucking *weird*.

Jax was pretty sure the whole damn world could catch fire and Bunny would still be there, kicking his legs and smiling through the smoke.

He scratched at his beard—too long, too patchy these days—and tried not to think about the way his knees ached just from sitting. He used to be better than this.

Faster. Meaner.

A man people watched when he walked into a room. Not because he had impeccable fashion sense—which he did—but because they could feel the strength rolling off him.

But now he just felt... slow. Soft around the edges. A little pathetic. Okay, a lot pathetic.

Jax exhaled hard and tilted the flask, pretending there was still something in it worth chasing.

"You know," he said after a long minute, "I always thought if I quit drinking, I'd wake up one morning and feel like a damned hero."

Bunny didn't say anything. He just kept humming under his breath, swinging his legs over the drop.

Jax snorted and leaned back on his hands, staring up at the sky.

"Instead I got... this." He patted his stomach, the slap muffled by the soft give of it.

"A huge gut and creaky bones. Can't even sit still without my knees whining like something on Liora's workbench."

Bunny nodded. Some kind of agreement or sympathy, Jax wasn't sure.

"I thought quitting would fix me," Jax muttered, voice low. "Turns out it just left me with all the shit I was drinking to forget. And a few extra chins for good measure."

He laughed, sharp and ugly. Then he tossed the flask so it clattered across the rooftop. It didn't make him feel any better.

"I used to be the strong one," Jax said, raking a hand through his hair. "First through the door. First to take a hit. The one they could count on."

The words stuck in his throat for a second.

"I want to be that again," he said. "Hells, I wanna be better. Smarter. Meaner. But gods, Bun... it's so damn hard."

He looked away, trying to erase the admission. Like maybe if he didn't look at Bunny, it wouldn't count.

Bunny let the silence linger for a moment. Then he leaned back and stretched.

"You're a dumb bastard sometimes, Jax," he said casually.

Jax huffed out a bitter laugh. "Thanks for that."

"No, I mean it," Bunny said, tipping his head toward him.

"You think strength's in your damn waistline? In your knees? Hells, no."

Bunny thumped a fist against Jax's chest. "Strength's here. That's what you're not getting."

"From what I've heard," Bunny continued, "you were never the best because you were the biggest or the scariest. You were the best because when things went sideways you didn't run. You stayed and held the line."

He paused. "You gave a damn."

Jax didn't answer. He just stared down at his thick hands, callused and scarred, resting in his lap like they didn't belong to him anymore.

"You're still that man," Bunny said. "Maybe a little heavier. Maybe a little slower. But I tell you what... seeing how your friends care about you? I'd put my back to you if the whole godsdamn city turned on us."

He nudged Jax's shoulder with his own, rough and quick.

"You don't need to get skinnier, Jax. You just need to remember how to keep swinging."

The city buzzed faint and angry below them. Through Jax's tear-rimmed eyes, the lights bled together into a smear of gold.

He glanced at Bunny, who was back to kicking his legs and humming off-key.

"Okay," Bunny blurted out. "Maybe you could stand to lose a few pounds."

Jax couldn't help but bark a laugh. He wiped the back of his hand across his eyes and shoved himself up to his feet with a grunt.

"Alright," he muttered, flexing his fingers like he was gearing up for a fistfight. "Enough therapy. Time to make some noise."

Bunny popped up beside him with a grin. "Now you're talking."

Jax reached into his coat and pulled out a battered, blocky squawk unit—old as hells, the casing cracked in three places and held together with scrap wire and stubbornness.

Liora had modified it earlier—slapped together a fake channel mask and scrambled the ID tag. Now that dynamo lenses were everywhere, it wasn't that hard to trace a squawk line. But this thing should make it just real enough to fool whoever answered the call.

Jax turned it over once, checking the relay the way she'd shown him.

He didn't understand half of it. But hells, he trusted Liora's brain more than he trusted the city's luck. Especially with the copper grid failing half the time.

"You sure this thing's gonna work?" he asked, half to himself.

Bunny shrugged, all innocent mischief. "Hells if I know. Only one way to find out." He grabbed the cable in his meaty hands and jammed it into the dynamo terminal behind them.

Jax shot him a look and thumbed the switch.

The squawk crackled to life, its tiny speaker spitting static into the night.

He lifted it to his mouth, let the silence hang for a second, then pitched his voice low and mean.

"Warning. Active device planted. Azoria Prison. Immediate evacuation advised."

Another burst of static. "Who is this?" came a tinny voice from the squawk. "Repeat?"

"Active device planted. A bomb," he clarified. "In Azoria Prison. Evacuation recommended."

Bunny rolled his eyes. Jax killed the feed and yanked the squawk out of the terminal.

The city kept buzzing below them—but if you listened close, you could already hear it changing.

Voices rising. Doors slamming. The ripple of unease spreading out from the heart of the beast.

Bunny clapped him on the back. "Hells of a love letter," he said.

"Let's hope they read it," Jax said with a grin.

Without another word, they turned and slipped down the fire escape, shadows bleeding into the alleys below.

The night behind them was no longer just cold. It was alive.

Jax took a moment to turn his eyes north, toward the heart of the city. Right there, at the Gaming Commission headquarters. The lights on the top floor came on like a hells damned signal fire.

He grunted. "Your move, bitch."

CHAOTIC GOOD

9

Azoria woke like it always did—loud, bright, and proud of itself.

The streets around the Research Institute buzzed with life, a thousand boots striking the stone, a hundred voices tangling into one restless current. Fresh ink from the morning papers mixed with the heavier smell of hot oil and frying batter from the market stalls. Dynamo coils hummed faintly inside their polished brass housings, tucked neat against the lamp posts.

Banners snapped overhead, bright red and copper against a sky already sweating with early heat. The Institute's coil-and-crown sigil blazed from every corner—painted onto stone facades, stitched into satchels, pressed into the wax seals of courier letters.

Scholars and merchants brushed past one another, trading diagrams and ledgers with the same briskness, while hawkers shouted over each other at the edges of the plaza.

Newsboys darted through the chaos like bees rushing to do the bidding of the queen, flinging out copies of the Azoria Bulletin with sharp, crowing voices:

PRANK BOMB THREAT AT AZORIA PRISON
VIVIENNE DRAGUNOVA PRAISES WATCH RESPONSE, DEEMS CITY SAFE

Lars moved through it all without breaking stride, one hand tapping his thigh, the other brushing the paper headlines as he passed.

The crowd parted for him without noticing. Just another battered coat, another face set hard against the morning. He didn't need to read the stories. He already knew the shape of them. Vivienne's fingerprints were all over this kind of message—bold, calm, dismissive.

Nothing to see here. All is well. Keep spending. Keep believing.

Lars's mouth tugged sideways, half a smile, half a snarl. That was the thing about Vivienne. She wouldn't react overtly to any spontaneous event. Hells, even if there *had* been a bomb in the prison she would have gone out of her way to make sure it exploded quietly so she could insist all was well.

She had to seem untouchable. Had to believe it.

But underneath... damn that woman was paranoid. Lars knew she was squirming in her skin-tight gown right about now.

The question was: how hard had she taken the bait?

The crowd thickened as he crossed into the outer markets of the Institute, closer to the monorail. The air vibrated with the hum of the dynamo-powered rails.

Stalls packed the cobblestone lanes in tight, colorful rows—spices, schematics, pocket watches, bootleg monorail tokens—their owners bellowing over one another with the desperate joy of people who believed if they shouted loud enough, customers wouldn't be able to resist.

At the first stall, a wiry teenager peddled intricate compasses that Lars guessed would only point north if the world flipped over. The brass was too bright, the prices too low. Tourists' trash.

Next to that, a grizzled woman hunched over a battered crate, sorting through gleaming musket stocks and the cold, lethal mess of lockplates and barrels.

No fake junk here; these were the real deal. The craftsmanship was undeniable. Polished wood, clean lines, the mechanical guts shining under the morning light.

Lars slowed instinctively, a shudder trailing up his spine.

He remembered all too well the first time they'd seen muskets turned loose in Azoria. A single shot, but it was who it had struck that turned their world upside down. Liora on the roof with Jax, trying like hells to recharge a crystal in a lightning storm.

They had almost lost her then. If it hadn't been for Jax...

At that point muskets were something new and novel, the likes of which they couldn't have imagined. Dangerous and fascinating at the same time.

Now the parts were showing up in the open market like they were no more worrisome than lockpicks. The polished stocks and gleaming lockworks were beautiful in their own brutal way. But Lars couldn't imagine a world where every idiot with enough coin could walk into a plaza and buy death by the handful.

He turned away, stomach twisting harder than he liked to admit, and ducked through the thickening crowd to a "genuine Zarakaran silk merchant." The air around his stall choked with perfume so heavy it made Lars sneeze. The cloth was pretty enough from a distance. But up close, the dye bled into the merchant's fingers, staining them various shades of red and purple.

At the fourth stand, Lars slowed. It held a battered stack of hand-sketched maps, yellowed at the corners, curling at the edges where the damp had gotten in.

The merchant didn't even glance up from his stool, muttering to himself like a man two arguments deep into a fight no one else could hear.

Lars's fingers brushed under the edge of the table, smooth and casual.

There it was. He pulled loose a folded paper and kept walking.

Two alleys down, where the smell of the street carts thinned and the shouting dulled to a tired murmur, Lars ducked into the narrow gap between two shuttered shops.

He unfolded the paper with a flick of his wrist, eyes flicking over it once, twice. Just to make sure he hadn't missed something. But the message was simple.

Transfer confirmed. Today. Eastbound monorail.

There was no signature or timestamp. But Lars knew Trin's unhurried, victorious style.

He folded the paper again, tighter this time, and shoved it deep into the inside pocket of his coat where it could burn against his ribs.

Leaning back against the alley wall, Lars let the chill of the stone bleed through his jacket. And a small victory settled into his bones.

It was happening. Vivienne had taken the bait.

Lars pushed off the wall and slipped back into the current of morning traffic.

The current pulled him along—bright faces, hawker calls, dynamo buzz threading through the air. And Lars moved with it, steady, unseen.

For the first time in a long time, he felt the familiar weight settle in his chest. It wasn't the ache of failure, but something clean and thrilling.

He could still read a mark. He knew how to apply pressure and where that pressure would crack. Even someone as clever and maniacal as Vivienne.

The crowd thinned as he pushed further east, the sights and sounds of the Institute fading behind him. The buildings slumped lower here. Brick gave way to battered wood, bright awnings replaced by frayed cloth stretched thin against the light.

The smell changed too. Less roasting meat, more sewage and waste.

Lars moved along the southern banks of the Ithris, the water churning slow. To the north and west, the towers of Azoria gleamed, glass and brass catching the morning sun.

But down here, the only sign the city still gave a damn was the endless row of waterwheels grinding slow and steady against the current, feeding the dynamo grid hidden in the city's bowels.

Power for the monorail and the crystal towers. Power for the rich. And the people that kept it all turning barely rated a second glance.

Lars pulled his coat tighter and kept walking. The monorail station was just ahead—tall, sleek, humming with power—and the street around it swarmed with workers and guards believing it was just another day.

The Market District was in full swing by the time Darius and Inora slipped into the current of morning shoppers. Bright pennants strung between the stalls made the place look festive. Anything to get people to part with their hard-earned copper.

They weren't fooling anyone. Oh there were some purchases here and there, but nothing Darius would call record setting. For all the pomp and glamor the Market had in store, people were just too damn broke.

He kept his gait easy, blending in with the merchants and dock workers and students hustling toward the cheaper stalls. Inora stayed two paces ahead, hood low over her hair, a loose bag slung over one shoulder like any other courier running a morning drop.

The trick was looking like you belonged just enough for everyone to assume you were someone else's problem. And let's be real, it was Darius's goal in life to be someone else's problem.

They drifted past a kiosk letting loose a cacophony of noise. Small devices littered the table, each one a small box in various colors, dotted with pinholes and connected to a crystal charge. They played different songs that were popular all over Azoria, from She Can Steal My Heart to Sailing Back to Zarakar.

Remarkable, really. Darius thought he might just have to buy one. He got to play with similar devices while knocking off Thume's warehouse last year, but these were way more entertaining.

But not today. Today he was busy. And this was the perfect time.

No guards close enough yet. No one paying attention.

Darius slipped a hand inside his coat, fingers closing around the small brass charge wired up inside an empty ink bottle.

Maren's handiwork—meant to burn hot and loud but not kill. At least, not unless you were stupid enough to stand right over it.

Inora ducked around a produce cart stacked high with bruised fruit, glanced back once, sharp and quick.

Now.

Darius let the bottle fall from his palm. It hit the stone with a quiet clink and rolled under the nearest vendor's crate.

Five, four, three—

The explosion wasn't big enough to kill, but it didn't need to be.

It punched a hole in the morning like a fist through a plate glass window. Flames kicked up instantly, licking the sides of the stall. The world snapped from haggling to screams in the space of a heartbeat. The crowds began to surge. Smells of burning spice filled the air, thick and choking.

Darius kept strolling and didn't look back.

He shoved into the press of bodies now surging in every direction, letting the chaos lift him, shove him, carry him.

Inora was already angling east, nimble as a damn cat, heading for the next trigger point.

Behind them, the first real cries of panic started rising—shouts for the Watch, clattering footsteps, the first crash of something heavy knocked loose.

The fire was small. The real damage came from fear.

Darius grinned as he shoved past a cart toppled sideways, apples rolling wild across the street. The city was waking up the way he liked it best—screaming and off-balance.

He caught up with Inora at the mouth of a narrow alley, both of them breathing fast but steady.

"Not bad," she said between breaths, her eyes bright.

He clapped her shoulder once, rough and proud. "We're just getting started."

The alleys behind the Market District twisted like veins—narrow, cracked, dripping runoff from too many pipes jammed into too little stone.

Darius and Inora tore through them without slowing.

Boots slammed against the wet cobbles, heartbeats hammering in his ears, the taste of smoke still sharp at the back of his throat.

The pulse of the Market's panic thudded behind them—screams, shouts, the heavy clatter of carts overturned and merchants scrambling to save their wares.

Inora glanced back once, the corner of her thin lips curling into a grin that matched the wild heat burning in his chest.

They ducked under a drooping clothesline, darted past a stray dog nosing at a spilled bag of chestnuts, vaulted a crumbling fence in perfect rhythm.

Well, it wasn't a heist, but it was the same kind of energy. It felt good. It felt fun.

Darius lived for this part—the edge-of-the-blade moments when you weren't winning yet, but you damn sure weren't losing either.

Tavern Row opened up before them, the buildings leaning toward each other like old men arguing across a bar.

Music clanged from open doors—brash, cheap, the kind of tunes that got fists flying after the second bottle.

Which, of course, was what they wanted. Inora jerked her chin toward a dive bar spilling drunk dockhands out into the street.

Darius flipped the collar of his coat up, kept moving.

The goal wasn't to win any fights today. Just to start them.

He let himself imagine it for a second: the way the Market panic would spread, bleeding into Tavern Row, into the Foundries, toward the Commission itself.

All that pretty order Vivienne had polished so carefully after the bomb hoax—cracking wide open from a few dirty hands and a little bad luck.

Hells, it was beautiful.

A man shoving past him with a full tray of drinks caught Darius square in the ribs.

The man snarled something about being blind—and Darius just smiled, dipped a shoulder, and slammed back hard enough to send the tray flying.

Cups, glass, and cheap liquor exploded across the cobbles. The shouting started immediately.

Good. Darius didn't stay to admire the wreckage.

Inora had already peeled off toward the next bar down, a fresh pocket of noise and drunken energy ready to tip. Darius kept his pace casual now, his boots splashing puddles onto the pant legs of passersby, riling them up even further.

He couldn't help it—he grinned.

The bar Inora had slipped into suddenly erupted, with both wild accusations and fists pouring into the street.

Darius ducked down a side street, the grin still plastered across his face.

Inora had Tavern Row from here—and soon, the east-end foundries as well.

South of the river, Rurik and Maren would be stirring their own pots. While he couldn't help but wonder how they were doing, Darius couldn't afford to worry about them now.

He had business at the Gaming Commission headquarters.

Rurik waited in the shadows across from Azoria Prison, one boot propped against the wall, arms folded loose across his chest.

The morning smelled of tar and stone dust, thick with the stink of city guards standing post too long without washing. A contingent had already left with their prize prisoner, headed for the station.

But that was fine; Rurik wasn't here for Thume.

He eyed the guards. Two of them leaned by the side entrance, grumbling to each other and trading half-hearted glances at the empty street.

A third paced in front of the heavy dynamo locks, tapping a baton against his thigh, bored enough to be dangerous.

Good. Bored men were easy prey.

Rurik pushed off the wall and crossed the street without bothering to hide his approach.

The guards didn't even react until he was close enough to smell the coffee on their breath.

One of them straightened, squinting.

"Hey, you—"

Too slow.

Rurik moved fast—smooth and brutal. A single blow to the throat folded the first guard like a paper doll.

The second managed to get a hand halfway to his baton before Rurik drove a heavy fist into his gut, catching him as he collapsed.

The third tried to turn, mouth already opening to shout—

Rurik slammed him against the dynamo casing hard enough to rattle the bolts loose, then clipped him across the jaw with a heavy crack.

Three bodies. Three soft thuds against the stone. No alarms. No warnings.

Rurik exhaled slow, let the morning noise fold back in around him—the clatter of distant market stalls, the faint whine of monorail brakes somewhere up the line.

He crouched and checked the guards. They were breathing, no serious damage. Just out cold. That was good, he didn't really want to hurt anyone.

Giving one last look at the silent bodies sprawled across the prison entrance, he turned back toward the alleys and disappeared into the city's bones without leaving a ripple.

Maren crouched low behind a fountain, clutching the little dynamo disruptor.

Near him, the courtyard behind the Azoria Institute buzzed with morning energy—workers hauling crates, scholars arguing over schematics, students flinging rolled-up diagrams at each other like kids at recess.

Nobody looking at him. They wouldn't notice the skinny idiot sweating bullets near the maintenance carts.

Good. That was good.

He checked the device for the fifth time. It was still intact and humming faintly. The thing looked like a copper pancake wired to a crystal about the size of his thumb, humming with barely-contained charge.

Okay, Maren, he thought. *You're trained for this. Kind of. Almost. Maybe.*

He sucked in a breath and slipped into the open like he belonged there. No sneaking. Just a delivery boy with places to be.

Two guards passed by, chatting about the latest news. One of them turned their head his way. The guard looked at him curiously and cleared his throat.

"Hey, excuse me," he said.

Oh shit oh shit oh shit oh shit oh shit

Maren's eyes darted left and right and sweat poured from his forehead like the fountain he left behind. He wanted to shriek and run away. He wanted to—

"I said, 'excuse me,'" the guard said a bit louder. "Yes, you. Come here."

This was it. Maren was caught. He was going to prison. He was going to die in prison. He was going to die in prison because Darius would kill him out of embarrassment.

"Y-yes?" he stammered. "I'm sorry, I just... I can't... you know, I mean..."

The man raised an eyebrow as Maren came closer. "Hells, are you okay? I just want to ask you a question."

Maren yelped, then gulped and nodded. "Yes, yes. I'm fine. I'm sorry. What... what can I help with?"

The guard exchanged an amused look with his buddy.

"We were just talking," the first guard said, "about the prison thing. That bomb threat last night."

Maren blinked.

"We were wondering if that was even possible," the second guard added. "A bomb made outta dynamo. You know, the crystals and the coils. Somebody said they could rig one up to explode if you reversed the charge and flooded the coil."

Maren stared at them, his brain short-circuiting with a half-dozen technical corrections and a full dozen survival instincts.

He forced a weak smile and mumbled, "Not my specialty."

Both guards grunted. "Figures," one said. "Academics never know anything useful."

They waved him off and turned back to their conversation, their boots clacking away down the cobbles.

Maren stood frozen for a second longer—long enough that he started to worry he'd forgotten how to move.

Then, without thinking, he fast-walked toward the maintenance hatch like every Watch squad in the city was about to descend on him at once.

The area around it was empty. Perfect.

He knelt, jammed a tool on the rusted bolts, and twisted. The first bolt spun free easily. The second one stuck and made a squealing noise.

He winced, heart hammering, but nobody came to check. The bolt finally came loose.

He popped the hatch with a breathless little grunt—and there it was. A fat bundle of thick copper cables running straight into the Institute's dynamo grid.

It was beautiful.

He pulled the disruptor from his jacket and pressed it into place with shaking hands. The device latched on with a click that felt way too loud. Maren froze and waited.

When no shouts or alarms were forthcoming, he flipped the tiny switch on the back—arming the timed trigger—and crammed the hatch closed again, dirt flying as he kicked debris over it.

Fifteen minutes from now, half the Institute's research labs would be throwing dynamo fits, and nobody would know why.

Maren straightened up, brushed himself off, and did the only reasonable thing.

He jogged out of the courtyard, whistling a butchered version of Sailing Back to Zarakar just to keep from screaming.

Darius ran down a narrow side street, breathing hard but grinning like a man with a secret.

The city was definitely awake now. You could feel it in the air—the way the sounds shifted. Those screams from the Market, the rowdy brawls on Tavern Row. And the stream of people and city watch guards running back and forth between them.

He cut across an open plaza half-choked with abandoned food carts, the smell of burned spice still hanging low. A man shouted behind him—something about thieves, about trouble at the prison—but Darius didn't slow.

Ahead, he spotted Inora darting down an alley, a satchel bumping against her hip. She glanced back once, caught his eye across the crowd. No words. Just a flash of teeth and a sharp nod.

She'd take the east side—the ironworks and the foundries— maybe light a few more fires for good measure.

Darius, on the other hand, was heading somewhere a little more delicate.

The Gaming Commission HQ sat just beyond the Market District's heart, wrapped in polished stone and brass.

It was a symbol of the spirit of Azoria. A structure erected by Thume over thirty years ago, where the city's leaders could manage and measure the balance of funds acquired, stolen, and paid in fees to the commission and the city's welfare fund. It was where oligarchs decided how the game was to be played.

Darius intended to give it a little hairline fracture today.

He shoved through the press of bodies, and that's when he noticed it. The chaos they had started... it wasn't just their chaos anymore.

He caught sight of a man hurling a brick through the front window of a jewelry shop, shards of glass exploding into the street.

Further up, a knot of desperate-looking kids swarmed a delivery wagon, ripping sacks of flour and bolts of cloth off the back like locusts.

And hells, was that a crew trying to rob a bank?

Darius chuckled under his breath. None of that was his crew. It was the city itself, starting to break along its fault lines. Fear and hunger and rage had been waiting just under the surface...

All it took was a spark.

For half a second, it almost gave Darius pause. Almost. But this was just a small ruckus. Azoria had seen far worse. The city would right itself. For now, this chaos suited his and Lars's purposes just fine.

No one was even *thinking* about Thume anymore. It was all the watch could do to keep the city in check.

Darius angled off the main street, slipping behind a row of shuttered shops and climbing a narrow stairwell to an old clockmaker's loft with a spectacular view of the Gaming Commission.

Guards clustered thick around the front doors, tense and snapping at anyone who came too close. Citizens hovered at a safe distance, watching, whispering, wondering if the whole place might catch fire next.

Darius reached into his coat and felt the cool weight of the hand musket tucked against his ribs. He crouched low by the cracked window frame, took a slow breath, and aimed the musket.

The weight was comfortable in his hands—an old, brutal kind of power that didn't care about crowns or commissions.

He sighted down the barrel, lining up the farthest top window of the Commission headquarters—the one that overlooked the square like a smug, watching eye. The one Vivienne was almost certainly looking through right now.

He squeezed the trigger.

The musket cracked with a savage roar, and the world jolted.

Across the plaza, the bullet punched into the high glass pane, spiderwebbing a sharp crack across the polished facade.

The crowd jerked as one, shouts bursting outward like ripples from a dropped stone.

Guards scrambled, shouting orders, weapons half-drawn but turning in circles, searching the crowds, the rooftops, the shadows.

Darius stayed low, as calm as he could with his heart pounding. He fished another round from his coat pocket, working fast but not rushing.

Sliding the ball down the barrel. Packing the charge with steady fingers.

Another breath. Another shot.

The second musket blast rolled across the rooftops, hammering the square with another echoing boom.

This time, the top-floor window cracked hard, a jagged starburst spidering across the Commission's face like a fresh wound.

Darius didn't wait to see the panic hit full bloom.

He hid the musket among the junk littering the floor as best he could, slipped back down the stairs, and melted into the swirling chaos below.

He hadn't come here to kill Vivienne Dragunova. Though hells, that would make things interesting.

No. He just wanted to make some noise.

And judging by the shouts rising behind him, the guards scrambling over themselves, the building's grand, proud facade split wide open...

He knew Vivienne had to be well and truly losing her everloving shit right about now.

Good. It was about damn time.

TAKE THE KING

10

The monorail screamed as it pulled into South Station, a banshee's shriek of steel and dynamo charge shaking the platform under Lars's boots.

He stood still next to Liora, watching the monorail roll in car by car.

The first screeched past—sleek, plated in polished brass, windows gleaming. Second car. Third.

And there... the fourth.

It was different. No windows. No ornamentation. Just a slab of metal, reinforced with thick wooden bands, rumbling slow and heavy on the line.

The prison car.

Locks bigger than his head bolted the side door shut—mechanical and thick enough that even a fool could see they weren't meant to be picked in a hurry.

Lars tilted his head slightly. Liora had been right. Breaking it open could take hours, not minutes. Good thing they weren't planning to open it at all. Not here, anyway.

The monorail finally came to a halt, hissing and crackling dynamo into the morning air.

The last two cars—fifth and sixth—groaned into place, the final brakes locking with a metallic CLACK that echoed off the cracked stone buildings of the slums.

Lars scanned the platform and surrounding buildings with sharp, measured glances.

No guards. No city watchmen. Just a few meandering passengers—dock workers in stained coats, a young mother shushing a toddler, a couple random travelers just keeping to themselves.

He grinned to himself. Darius must be doing a damn fine job. No guards on a prison transfer? The whole city must be running around in circles putting out his fires.

The wildcard, of course, was Balar. He hadn't shown his face since the last time he'd ripped their pride to pieces. Lars shuddered.

Hopefully, if Balar was out there, he was busy dealing with Darius's games.

Beside him, Liora hefted her satchel, calm but alert. She wore a mischievous grin, and Lars recognized the thrill in her eyes. They were really going to do this.

Doors clattered open along the monorail's side. Ahead, Lars spotted Trin, Bunny, and Jax boarding the carriage in front of Thume's prison car.

He and Liora moved together without speaking, slipping into the car behind it.

The plan was simple. The plan was insane.

The dynamo hum thickened underfoot as Lars and Liora stepped into the monorail.

The carriage wasn't much to look at—long benches bolted to the walls, a handful of battered seats scattered through the middle. Dynamo lamps were embedded into the ceilings, shining with a steady, bright light.

Liora invented this. She should be damned proud of herself. Lars knew he was. He really needed to tell her that.

A few rough-looking dockhands in threadbare coats slouched across the benches, a merchant with a crushed-looking hat flicked through a battered ledger, and a boy no older than fifteen dozed with his head against the window, breath fogging the glass.

Nobody worth worrying about, and nobody who would pay them any mind.

Liora slid into a seat two rows up from the dynamo maintenance panel tucked into the back wall. Lars followed slower, scanning the car one last time before dropping into the seat across from her.

The monorail jolted underfoot, the dynamo motors snarling alive beneath them. Lars felt the charge pulse through the floor as the train ground forward—slow at first, then faster as it pulled out of the station.

He watched Liora from the corner of his eye.

She was tapping one boot lightly against the floor. Not nerves. Energy. Just like the monorail, she ran on dynamo. This whole thing must have been thrilling for her.

Lars leaned back against the seat, tilted his head toward the ceiling, and closed his eyes for just a second. Breathing. Centering.

The monorail thrummed steady underfoot, the world outside the windows a blur of soot-streaked brick and tangled iron.

He kept his posture loose, breathing slow, just another tired face headed to the edge of the city.

Liora shifted. She rose from her seat like she was stretching a cramp and sauntered toward the back of the car.

Nobody paid her any mind. The dockhands still half-dozed. The merchant muttered over his ledger. The boy by the window drooled against the glass, lost to the world.

Lars tracked Liora's movements without moving his head.

She reached the dynamo maintenance panel tucked low against the back wall. She crouched down, bag slung casually against her hip, hands steady.

He watched her fingertips slip the panel loose with a tiny flick of her wrist.

A quick glance over her shoulder—casual, but practiced.

Then she reached into her satchel, fingers brushing past the crumpled spare clothes and pulled the device free.

To Lars it looked like just another tangle of copper wire and dust-stained crystal. But Liora had assured him it would guarantee the right stop for them to pull this off.

She wired it into the maintenance line with quick, deft movements.

Lars caught the slight shift of her thumb as she flipped a switch.

Then she stood, dusted her hands against her trousers—and wandered back toward him with the same lazy indifference as before.

Nothing happened.

No jolt. No flicker. No change in the monorail's steady whine.

Lars stayed slouched in his seat, eyes half-closed, but inside he was reeling. It didn't work. Nothing was happening. And without that, they'd never be able to—

"Mission accomplished, Lars," Liora said out of the side of her mouth.

Lars's breath left him in a rush. He dragged his hand across the worn fabric of his coat like he was smoothing down his nerves.

The monorail roared along, nothing visibly wrong. He raised his eyebrows at Liora.

She just rolled her eyes and blew him a kiss in return.

Cheeky. But if Liora's device was really working the way she promised, then somewhere up at the front of the train the engineers were about to start noticing the problem.

It didn't take long. The hum underfoot grew... thinner.

Not quieter—more strained. Like a lute string stretched too tight. Still buzzing along, but at a faint pitch Lars didn't like.

The door at the rear of the car opened. He cracked one eye open.

A monorail attendant from the last car came in and walked down the aisle, visibly checking on the passengers. Another moment, and the train gave a subtle lurch. The momentum faltered.

Not much. Just enough to feel wrong if you were paying attention.

Now the passengers shifted in their seats. The boy who had been drooling on the window called to the attendant, asking if they were there yet. The attendant shook his head and went back to the rear car.

The overhead squawk system cracked on with a burst of static.

"Uh, attention passengers," came a crackling, half-bored voice—one of the engineers, trying to sound casual. "We're... we're making a brief stop at Southward Depot. Routine maintenance check. Shouldn't be more than a few minutes. Please stay seated and await further instructions."

The squawk clicked off.

Lars allowed himself the barest twitch of a smile and his pulse quickened.

That was their opening. Just a few more minutes now.

✧

The monorail gave a low groan as it coasted into Southward Depot, the dynamo motors smoothly bringing the heavy cars into the yard. Lars braced his boots against the floor as the train lurched, the crystal-lined rails below sputtering with frustrated sparks.

This wasn't a proper station. It was a maintenance and transfer depot—meant for cargo swaps and quick inspections—not normally for passenger traffic at all.

The monorail coasted forward another fifty yards, gliding smoothly past the switch levers and dynamo posts before finally easing to a halt.

The overhead squawk box crackled again.

"Attention passengers," the same bored voice droned. "Brief inspection and recharge underway. You may disembark for fresh air if you wish. Please stay close to your car. We'll be underway to Estontown shortly."

The doors sighed open.

Lars rose from his seat, his body loose, easy. A few other passengers stirred as well—stretching, yawning, gathering bags—but no one looked particularly concerned. Beside Lars, Liora stretched like any other bored traveler.

"Showtime," she murmured without looking at him.

The air seemed to crackle around the depot, that charged smell of overworked dynamo bleeding into the rising heat.

They stepped off the train, boots striking the stone that surrounded the monorail's dynamo power line, and Lars took stock of the depot. Fresh coils of dynamo cabling off near a large bank of levers. A couple odd coaches on side rails. The various stretches of track merging in or branching off of the main line. Everyone who was getting off exited to the right side of the train.

Lars moved away from the train slowly, eyes sweeping the depot without making it obvious. He walked casually to a large, tarp-covered hulk on a narrow track just to the right of their car.

The monorail's crew had all drifted forward toward the lead car—attendants and engineers bowed their heads together in tight conversation. Probably bitching about the sudden maintenance flag.

Hopefully it would be a long one. Some field checks and a recharge please, and take your time.

Liora dashed to the front of their cabin and slipped in front of it, to that mess of metal and wires connecting to Thume's prison car. Opening her bag, she pulled out various tools and started working at the couplings with furious intensity.

Every turn of the wrench, every pop of a bolt, and Lars's heart leaped.

Up ahead, Bunny and Jax had done the same on their side— Bunny's broad back visible as he ducked into the gap between the prison car and their own. Lars caught a faint grunt of effort and a sharp clink of metal hitting metal.

He looked toward the train crew to see if any of them had heard. No, it didn't appear so, they were mostly—

Wait, who was that? Was that an engineer coming their way?

Risking a moment, he glanced at Liora. She wasn't there yet. Sweat dripped from her forehead and her thick auburn hair threatened to fall over her eyes. Her tools flashed in and out of her hands, but the couplings weren't completely detached.

And someone was coming. In just a few dozen feet and he'd be right next to Jax, Bunny, and Trin. And while catching them frantically trying to decouple the train might be a fun story the engineer could tell to his grandkids one day, it would mean absolute disaster for Lars and crew.

Should he run over to help Liora? At least warn her somehow?

But then he saw a brief flash of sun hitting Trin's blonde hair. She peered cautiously around the car, and saw the engineer too. Then her head disappeared.

Moments later, she appeared next to Liora on the other side of the train. Whispering some frantic words, Trin crouched down and started working at the couplings while Liora stood up and brushed herself off.

Then, with a deep breath and a grin, Liora hopped out of the space between cars and skipped her way up towards the engineer and the front of the train.

Lars groaned and wiped a hand across his forehead. Who knew how Liora planned to distract the man. But as long as she could keep him away from Jax and Bunny, they might still have a shot at getting that damn prison car detached.

See, that was the thing about security systems. They always assume your goal is to break in. So let's make the prison train really sturdy, thick iron, thick locks.

But after seeing how Bunny had rolled into their base with a stolen safe—not the goods, but the whole damn safe—it gave Lars and Liora a pretty damn good idea of how they could make off with Lord Thume. And the horse he rode in on.

And Trin was almost done getting the cars decoupled. He had to assume the others were close too.

The engineer slowed a few feet from where Bunny and Jax were crouched between the prison car and the next. Another few steps and he'd see it all—the tools, the frantic hands, the whole hells be damned truth.

Liora intercepted him with a bright, breathless voice Lars could barely catch over the depot noise. "Excuse me!" she called, waving a hand like a lost tourist.

The man blinked, caught mid-step, thrown completely off his rhythm. Even from where Lars stood—half-shielded behind the tarp-covered railcar—he could see the confusion on the engineer's face.

Liora turned up the charm without missing a beat. She tucked a lock of hair behind her ear and leaned in like she was about to ask for his autograph.

Hells, he'd never seen Liora act... well, flirty. She must have picked up the craft from Shelle.

The engineer stammered for a moment, then nodded stiffly and stood tall. His posture suggested that he'd been asked to demonstrate the inner workings of the gods themselves.

Lars couldn't make out the words anymore, just the cues: Liora's quick, eager questions; the engineer's bumbling, earnest responses. She was guiding him away from the danger, each step leading him farther toward the front of the train.

A glint of movement to the side—Trin crouched low, pulling the final coupling pins free. And just then, a quick and distinct whistle up ahead. Bunny and Jax were done too.

Shit, was this going to *work*?

Time to find out.

Turning to a lever panel, Lars hit the switches just like Liora had taught him.

Blue for bypass mode.

That knob, to engage manual override.

Spin the two metal wheels in the center...

With barely a sound, the curved section of track near him slid and locked into the main track just behind the prison car. Another short whistle ahead indicated the same happened up ahead.

Liora was still slow walking with her new friend. The other train staff were near the very front of the train and not looking back.

Please, please, please.

Lars pulled the large lever next to the panel.

Thume's prison on rails started to quietly move forward and to the left off the main track.

And the tarp-covered monstrosity next to him—staged the night before—rolled to take its place.

Lars grabbed the tarp as it rolled past, pulling it off as it moved into alignment. Breath by breath, it continued its slow and steady movement forward. The real prison car slipped away with barely a sigh of rails.

The decoy clicked into place like a lockpick in a tumbler.

When it lined up perfectly, Lars pulled the lever back. The movement stopped.

And a shrill signal from the front of the train pierced the air.

The signal blast punched through the depot.

Lars jerked upright, heart slamming against his ribs, every instinct screaming before his brain caught up.

Not an alarm. Oh thank the hells.

The realization hit a second later, cold and sharp.

Not an alarm—the boarding signal.

A conductor near the front of the train cupped his hands around his mouth and hollered, "All aboard! Departing for Estontown!" Then he turned and dropped back into casual conversation with the other engineers.

Lars let out a slow, shaky breath, scrubbing a hand across his jaw. They weren't caught. Not yet.

But they had a whole train to put back together and no time to do it. They had maybe a minute—two, if fate was kind—before the monorail started rolling again.

He shoved off from the side of the decoy car, his boots skidding a little on the gravel-strewn stone. His pulse hadn't slowed at all. No time to get cocky. No time to think.

Just finish the job.

Just move.

Lars looked up to see Liora sprinting back their way.

She wasn't even trying to look casual anymore. Her satchel bounced against her hip as she bolted down the side of the train, cutting the distance to Jax and Bunny in a few desperate strides.

Good. She was safe. And she wasn't alone.

Nearby, Trin was crouched between cars, grappling with the couplings.

Every second was a hammer blow against Lars's nerves.

Up ahead, Jax was watching the monorail crew up front. His eyes flicked between them and where Bunny was presumably joining the forward cars.

Lars could see it in every movement: they all knew how little time was left. How close they were to the edge. He ducked low and made for Trin's side, slipping into the gap beside her, planting his boots wide for balance.

The coupling rods were heavy—stiff with disuse—and the mechanism fought them with every scrape and clatter.

"Get that top latch!" Trin said.

Lars threw his weight into the latch, grimacing as the metal shrieked against the bolt. It slammed down with a dull, satisfying clunk.

One set linked. One to go. Lars exhaled hard. Just a few more turns. Just a few more seconds.

And then, from up ahead, Liora's sharp, panicked voice.

"Lars—the disruptor! It's still on the train!"

Oh hells. They couldn't leave that hooked in. The moment the train started moving it would start sapping power from it again. They'd undoubtedly come back to the depot rather than trying to make it all the way to Estontown.

Lars swore under his breath, the sound ripped from somewhere deep and furious.

He locked eyes with Trin for half a second—just long enough for a plan to snap into place without either of them needing to say it aloud.

"I'll finish here!" Trin barked, already jamming the last coupling rod into place.

Lars shoved himself upright, boots scraping against the stone, and took off at a sprint toward the car where Liora had installed the disruptor.

He caught a glimpse of Jax running their way. Good, Liora must have told him to help with the couplings. Hopefully that meant Bunny was almost done.

The squawk box overhead popped with static.

"Thank you for your patience, folks," the voice drawled. "We'll be departing in just a moment."

Hells take me, Lars thought, pumping his legs harder.

He ran into the car and made his way quickly towards the back, where the maintenance panel was hidden. Liora's disruptor was still there—humming faintly, copper wires threaded into the dynamo maintenance line.

Trin scrambled up behind Lars, swinging a satchel off her back.

Lars dropped to one knee, tearing at the connectors with shaking fingers.

Trin slapped the satchel open beside him and placed her hand on his back.

The monorail gave a lurch underfoot. The couplings locked ahead of them with a heavy THUNK.

Jax jumped on just as the doors began to close, a conductor close behind him.

The doors hissed and groaned—and then sealed.

Lars yanked the final wire free, jammed the device into the bag, and slammed it shut just as the train lurched forward.

Too late to jump. Too late to do anything but ride.

He met Trin's wide, wild eyes—and knew she was thinking exactly what he was.

We're stuck on this hells-damned train.

The monorail rattled around them, the heavy thrum of the dynamo motors hammering up through the floorboards.

Lars, Trin, and Jax slammed together at the back of the car—half-running, half-falling into a huddle by the rear door. The other passengers barely looked up, too groggy or too indifferent to care about three sweaty strangers crowding the aisle.

Lars grabbed Trin by the shoulders. "Where's Liora? Bunny?"

Trin shook her head, still breathless from the sprint. "I saw them," she panted. "They were next to Thume's car—still on the side tracks. They're safe."

Relief slammed through Lars so hard he staggered a step back.

Safe. Thank the hells.

He didn't have time to savor it.

Jax leaned in, chest heaving, wiping sweat from his brow. "Don't think you can say the same for us."

Lars scrubbed a hand down his face. Think, think. They couldn't ride this damn train all the way to Estontown with half the Commission waiting to greet them and the fake prison car in tow.

They had to get off. Now.

"We need to bail," Lars said, voice low and fierce. "Whatever it takes."

He turned, eyes locking onto the rear door of the car. Beyond that was the last coach—and it was empty. No staff. No passengers. Just dynamo hum and a shot at freedom.

He doubted Jax would be able to get the doors open with his bare hands. But that wasn't the only way out. He spotted a ladder that led to the roof, folded tight against the back wall. Emergency access only.

Emergency, all right.

Lars grinned. "Let's go."

The three of them shoved toward the rear door of the car, Lars leading the way with one hand still clutching the satchel tight against his side. He grabbed the handle and slid the door open. Wind knifed in immediately, whipping at their clothes and hair.

The narrow platform between cars rattled and shuddered underfoot, the gap below flashing past in a blur of track, crystals, and churned gravel.

Before stepping through, Lars caught a glimpse of their car's monorail attendant. The man lifted his cap with two fingers and peered at them.

For one awful second, Lars thought he'd forbid them from going to the back.

But the man just yawned, gave a half-hearted grunt, and dropped the cap back over his eyes.

Lars didn't wait to see if he changed his mind. He yanked Jax and Trin after him, their boots slamming onto the narrow platform.

They crossed the short space and pulled open the second door—this time into the rear car. It was empty, just as they'd hoped. Wide open cargo floor. Bare metal walls. A few crates strapped down haphazardly near the sides, and nothing else.

Except for the ladder in the back, folded neat and ready.

He sprinted across the car with Trin and Jax on his heels, boots thundering on the floor. Jax caught the release bar in both hands and yanked it down hard.

The ladder unfolded with a sharp clatter, slamming into place against the wall, the roof hatch rattling in its frame from the train's growing speed.

Lars shot a quick look back at them, breath sharp in his chest.

"Up and out," he said.

And he climbed.

Lars hauled himself up—the ladder rattling against the car with every step. His coat whipped around him as he shoved the hatch open. And the world exploded into noise.

The wind slammed into him, ripping the breath from his lungs. The train was moving faster than he'd thought. Too fast for comfort, but not fast enough to stop them. Not yet.

He pulled himself onto the roof, boots skidding against the metal roof, the monorail's dynamo hum vibrating straight through the soles of his feet. The city stretched out around them—blurred, smeared, rattling past in streaks of gray stone.

"Come on!" Lars shouted into the wind, reaching down.

Trin grabbed the ladder next. She scrambled up fast, faster than he expected. Lars grabbed her arm and helped her onto the roof beside him. Her hair ripped free of its braid in the gale, eyes narrowed against the blast of wind.

Jax followed—slower, grunting with the effort, his bigger frame fighting every rung of the ladder.

"This damn ladder wasn't built for charm and bulk," he muttered, dragging himself up one hard, grimacing pull at a time.

The hatch banged shut behind them, snapping against the roof. They were exposed now. And the monorail showed no signs of slowing down.

Lars crouched low, shielding his eyes against the wind, scanning the tracks ahead.

The depot was behind them, already vanishing into the haze. Ahead, miles of open rail and nowhere to hide. And the train was moving too fast to jump on such rough ground.

He spat into the wind, grit grinding against his teeth.

"Move forward!" Lars shouted, pointing forward along the roofs. "Go, go!"

They dropped low, half-crawling, half-running—desperate shadows scrambling against a world too big, too fast, and too dangerous.

The metal roof thrummed under their hands and knees as they moved across it, the train gliding eastward along the southern edge of the slums.

Lars led the way, scanning for a safe stretch of anything. Grass, dirt, something less suicidal than jagged rock and iron ties flashing past below.

It was pointless moving forward. They may as well wait and conserve their strength. He skidded to a stop, Trin and Jax nearly slamming into him from behind.

"Here?" Trin shouted over the howl of the wind.

Lars squinted down, heart hammering.

Below them, the ground blurred past—pitted gravel, broken concrete, the occasional black snarl of abandoned track. Even if they timed it perfect, it'd tear them apart.

"No good!" he yelled. "Not yet!"

Trin cursed and dropped lower, pressing herself tight to the metal roof. Jax wiped sweat from his brow with a trembling hand, squinting against the wind.

Lars turned his head, meaning to shout something—he wasn't sure what—but then he saw it.

A shape pulled itself up over the back edge of the car, silent as a blade sliding from its sheath.

The wind ripped at Lars and blurred his vision, but he would have known that figure anywhere.

Black coat snapping like a second skin.

That jagged, cruel mask, the one marked with a scarred eye.

Balar.

The bastard moved with a slow, deliberate grace, braced against the shrieking wind. Lars's stomach flipped hard enough he thought he might be sick.

He grabbed Trin's arm, yanking her upright. "Go!" he shouted. "Now!"

She looked back and saw what he did. Her eyes widened. But her and Jax lurched forward, following Lars.

They pushed toward the prison car, away from the thing that was already stalking toward them. A predator loose on the rails. Lars risked one last glance back.

Balar tilted his head slightly, watching them. No rush, no rage. Just inevitability.

They had nowhere to go but forward.

The wind screamed across the rooftops of the monorail cars, drowning out even the sound of their boots slamming against the metal. They made the terrifying jump from the back car to the next, and were coming up on the gap before the prison car.

But to what end? They couldn't keep this up forever, and that masked bastard was conserving his strength with that slow, deliberate walk.

Trin was the first to make the leap onto the prison coach. The gap wasn't wide, but the slick iron and steel car was taller. She landed on her knees and slid forward.

Lars was right behind her. He'd spent enough time jumping along rooftops that he was able to land on his feet. He turned and urged Jax forward, his hand out to help the big man cross.

Standing at the edge, Jax looked forward with wild eyes. Lars knew what he was thinking. That was a near impossible gap for a man his size. Maybe he could—

"JAX, behind you!" Lars screamed, cutting off his own thoughts.

Balar lunged.

But Jax had heard, and was already pivoting, already swinging.

The punch connected with a crunch—full weight, shoulder and hips behind it, like the man was trying to knock down a god. Balar staggered sideways, boots skidding on the roof. His balance broke for the first time, and he fell to a knee, grasping the top of the train to avoid falling off.

"GO!" Jax bellowed, voice cracking against the wind.

Not a chance. Lars shook his head firmly. "Jump, Jax! We've got you."

He saw some of that old fire in Jax's eyes. Like a dynamo reactor waiting to burst. Jax's leg muscles bunched as he prepared to leap. Then he launched himself for the prison car.

It seemed like he was flying towards them in slow motion. This wild plan, the panic before leaving the depot, a wild run atop the monorail... it all burst into Lars's mind as Jax flailed towards them.

He wasn't going to make it.

But then the man hit the back of the car with a loud grunt, his arms scrabbling for purchase on the top.

Lars dropped to his knees, grabbed Jax's wrists, and pulled with everything he had. And for a few moments it seemed they might both fall off, into that space between cars where they'd rapidly be turned into ground thief.

Instead, Jax's feet must have found something to push off of, because he suddenly heaved up onto the train top. Lars gasped as he flew backwards, with Jax landing in a heap nearby.

This wasn't over. "Go!" Lars roared, grabbing Trin's arm and dragging her forward again.

They didn't look back. Didn't breathe. They just ran across the prison car's roof, hearts hammering, not even looking to see if Balar was behind them. Because they knew.

The next car was just ahead.

They had to jump again. Though the land around them was giving way to more pleasant, open spaces as they left the slums behind, they didn't have time to plot a leap from the train.

It was a much easier jump this time, though. The gap wasn't much narrower, but the next car was lower. All three of them made it easily. But hells, they were running out of steam.

Lars took a quick look back. Balar was pulling himself back up. Damn. Jax's punch must have landed like a battering ram.

"Let's get down below," Lars said, motioning to Trin and Jax.

Trin was skeptical. "Shouldn't we just jump off?"

"Too risky to jump blind. And besides, he might follow us." he said.

"He might not follow us inside," Jax said. "More people, more obstacles. And if he does..." He smacked a fist into his palm.

Honestly, it was damned if they did, damned if they didn't. But Lars wasn't ready to give up just yet. "Alright," he said, "let's go."

Jax yanked the rooftop hatch open and dropped down into the car below.

"Clear!" he shouted up, his voice echoing against the sudden hush.

Trin was already moving, boots scuffing the metal as she stepped toward the open hatch—but something caught her eye.

"Lars!" she screamed, spinning.

He turned instinctively.

Balar was back on his feet and closing in fast.

He was already halfway across the prison car roof. His black coat snapped around him in a fury. Lars took a step forward, heart hammering in his chest. He wouldn't let this happen. Not again.

Balar reached to his belt. He pulled his arm back, then forward in a swift, powerful motion.

Lars's eyes widened. The blade came out and flew—fast, silent, spinning end over end.

"NO!" Trin screamed. And then she dove.

Time shattered.

She skid to a stop just in front of Lars. The knife struck with a sound like tearing cloth.

Lars caught her as her knees buckled, arms wrapping tight as she sagged into him with a ragged gasp. The blade was buried deep, the hilt jutting from her ribs.

He knelt down, lowering Trin gently as her legs couldn't hold her up anymore. Lars stared at her in his arms, the blood blooming against her shirt, slick and warm, spreading through the fabric in violent reds. He heard Jax screaming something from below.

"Trin..." His voice was low, thick with panic he couldn't control. Her chest rose and fell with shallow breaths. He could feel her heartbeat flickering under his fingertips.

Down below, the train car had exploded into chaos. The sounds of passengers, Jax, and the wind around Lars thundered in his ears. The whole damn monorail seemed to sway under the weight of the moment. But for him, there was only Trin.

"Don't... don't let him catch you," Trin rasped, voice barely audible over the clamor.

Lars's throat tightened, but he gritted his teeth, trying to hold back the panic, the fear. He couldn't lose her. Not like this. Not when they'd come so far.

He barely noticed Balar stepping closer. His posture was urgent, but not aggressive. He was looking at Trin, moving forward quickly.

Lars, frantic, pushed himself between Balar and Trin, trying to shove him back.

"Stay the hells back!" Lars shouted, but his voice was weak, rattled, useless.

His stomach flipped. He swung his arm, a desperate strike to push Balar away, but Balar was quicker. Stronger. He slammed Lars back with a blow so hard it knocked him into the hatch.

The world spun.

Lars fell into the opening, breath knocked out of him, hands scrabbling to grab onto something, anything, as he tumbled. Then Jax's hands were out, catching Lars before he hit the ground.

"Lars!" Jax urged. "What happened to—"

The hatch slammed shut.

Lars staggered in Jax's grip, coughing hard, barely able to stand. The sudden silence was deafening.

But then the train burst into chaos—passengers yelling, shoving each other away from the sudden intrusion.

A wide-eyed attendant looked at Lars and his blood-covered coat. "What the hells is going on?"

Lars didn't answer. Couldn't.

He turned and stared with tear-rimmed eyes straight out the window. Just in time to see a black shape leaping from the train, a bundle in his arms.

And then it was gone.

"Trin—" Lars choked, stumbling toward the glass. He pressed a hand to it, searching the landscape as it blurred past in streaks of green.

But there was nothing.

Jax was crying. A quiet, broken sound that hit harder than any of Balar's punches. He wiped his face with both hands, red-eyed and shaking.

Lars backed away from the window and turned to Jax, his voice flat, barely more than a whisper.

"We need to get off this train."

Jax nodded, trembling. He moved towards the sealed doors of the car.

"Hey!" the monorail attendant said. "What are you—"

Jax roared, a sound pulled straight from the depths, and slammed his shoulder into the door. Metal shrieked. Glass fractured.

The latch gave. Wind roared through the cabin. Passengers screamed.

And without another word, Lars and Jax leapt into the wild green blur.

The depot was empty by the time they reached it.

Lars limped down a narrow access road, one arm slung over Jax's shoulder, the other tucked against his ribs where the bruises were worst. His boots dragged. His coat was torn in three places. Dust and gravel clung to every inch of him.

Jax didn't look much better—his lip split, his knuckles raw, the left side of his face already blooming purple. But he kept moving. Quiet. Focused. Like if he stopped now, the weight of what had just happened would crush him flat.

They hadn't spoken during the long walk back.

The safehouse sat behind a squat row of freight offices near the depot's edge. One of Liora's old maintenance outposts, long since gutted and stripped to the walls. Just enough shelter and shadow for a decent rendezvous.

Lars knocked once, hard.

A moment later, the door cracked open.

Bunny filled the frame, massive and unmoving. His eyes locked on Lars—then Jax—then the dried blood smeared across Lars's coat. He said nothing.

He just stepped aside.

The light inside was dim. Warm, in the way old workshop light is—low-glow dynamo filaments casting a soft amber haze over the room. A bench. A small table. A dynamo relay with coils stripped down to their copper bones.

And there, rising from a stool, was Liora.

"Lars!" she gasped, rushing forward.

He couldn't respond. He just let her catch him as the door clicked shut behind them.

Liora's hands were already moving—checking Lars's arms, his face, brushing dirt from his collar as if it might change anything.

"Are you hurt?" she asked. "Where's Trin?"

Jax flinched like he'd been slapped.

Lars didn't answer right away. Just closed his eyes and breathed in the scent of dynamo oil and scorched copper. Safer air. Familiar, at least.

Liora's fingers tightened on his coat. "Where is she?"

"She didn't make it," Jax said hoarsely, before Lars could find the words. "Balar... Balar was on the train."

Liora froze.

"He threw a knife. And she jumped in front of it," Jax went on, like the words were glass in his throat. "She... Trin, she—"

The silence was immediate. Heavy. Lars finally opened his eyes.

"She's gone," he said quietly. "Balar took her. We saw him jump."

A sharp breath—Liora's hand flew to her mouth.

Across the room, Thume stood quietly near the back wall. He hadn't moved since they entered. His hands were folded behind him, posture still somehow composed, even in rumpled prisoner's clothes.

He stepped forward now, the light catching the grays in his hair.

"I'm sorry," he said. Not unkind. But not grieving either. "I never knew her well. But I saw what she meant to you."

Lars didn't answer. Couldn't. He just stared at the floor, chest heaving like he'd been punched again.

His hands curled into fists. The breath in his chest turned sour.

"You," Lars said, lifting his head at last. His voice was low, dangerous.

Thume met his gaze, the man's golden eyes unreadable.

Lars stepped forward, dragging his pain with him. "You're the reason we were even on that hells damned train."

No response.

"You. With your games. Your secrets. Your oh-so-clever whispers from behind the bars. We risked everything for you."

Still, Thume didn't move.

"She's gone," Lars snapped. "Trin is gone. And for what? For *you*? So we could break a smug bastard like you out of a box you *earned*?"

Liora flinched, but didn't interrupt. Jax said nothing at all. Just turned away.

"You're not worth it," Lars growled, teeth gritted. "You were never worth it."

"Larson," Thume said.

Lars froze. Thume stepped forward, his presence somehow taller than before.

"*I* am not the problem now."

The words hit like iron.

"You're not wrong to blame me," Thume said, softer now. "But the next move belongs to you. And I suggest—strongly— that you don't waste it wallowing."

The room went quiet and cold.

Lars blinked once, then twice. He looked at Jax. At Bunny. Liora. Then back to Thume.

It all felt so impossible. Even when he had been beaten within an inch of his life, Lars hadn't felt this helpless. "I don't know what to do."

Thume didn't move. Didn't blink.

"Yes, you do. You know who took Trinelle. And you know who sent him."

Lars looked up, eyes bloodshot, jaw tight. He did, didn't he? Knew it as well as he knew his own hands. They were curled into fists, trembling now with something worse than rage.

But could he do it?

"Stop thinking," Thume said. "And admit what we all know. Balar needs to die."

<hr>

Part 3

<hr>

A NEW GAME

11

Liora shut the door behind her and didn't move.

For a second, maybe longer, she just stood there—back pressed to the wood, hands dangling at her sides, eyes fixed on nothing. The room wasn't spinning, exactly. But something in her was still moving, and she couldn't get it to stop.

Like a moving train, she thought.

Unbidden, the thought brought Trin's face to mind. *Oh, Trin. I hope you're alive.*

The apartment was quiet. Dim. She couldn't tell if the lights were off or if her eyes just hadn't adjusted. Somewhere nearby, something ticked. She didn't look for it.

It was home. That's all that mattered.

She dropped her satchel. It hit the floor with a heavy thud. Dynamo coils. Loose crystal. The weight of a night gone sideways.

Her boots came off with two slow scrapes. Liora didn't line them up. She shrugged off her coat and it fell to the floor in a heap.

Hells, she could barely think right. Her body walked to the bed without her mind actively guiding it.

No Myrim. No Shelle.

That was fine.

Liora stared at the unmade sheets, then tipped forward like a toppled statue. Face-first, limbs limp.

She fell asleep before her face hit the sheets.

Then woke to fingers on her skin.

A soft stroke down the inside of her forearm. Barely any pressure at all, more like warmth moving. Liora flinched, confused, eyes still shut. For a moment she wasn't in her bed. She was on the train again.

But the smell wasn't dynamo and steel—it was lavender and skin. She knew that scent. Knew that touch.

Her eyes opened slowly.

Shelle sat beside her, legs folded under, one hand resting on the quilt between them. Her face was unreadable in the low light. Tired, maybe. Sad. Watching her.

Liora blinked hard, as if that might knock her thoughts back into place.

"Was I snoring?" she rasped.

"Maybe," Shelle grinned, brushing a lock of hair from Liora's cheek. "Okay, no. But you were twitching like you were having fits."

Liora tried to smile. Failed. "Sorry."

"You don't have to be," Shelle said, and her voice was almost a whisper. "You're here."

The words hit harder than they should have. Liora swallowed, eyes still half-lidded. Yes, she was here.

"Yeah. It's good to be," she started. "But..."

Shelle didn't ask. Didn't push. Just curled her fingers over Liora's and held them there, warm and steady. Present.

The city could burn. The crew could scatter. Balar could be anywhere. But in this moment Liora let herself breathe.

They sat like that for a while, neither of them speaking.

Shelle's thumb traced lazy lines across the back of Liora's hand. Her breath was calm. Measured. She always knew how to wait.

Eventually, Liora said, "You want to know what happened."

It wasn't a question. Shelle didn't nod or push. Just waited.

So Liora told her.

"We got Thume," she said softly. "That part worked. We unlatched his car at the depot stop, just like we planned. Bunny and I got him out."

She paused. Closed her eyes.

"But Lars and Trin were still on the train. Jax too. My disruptor was still on board. Lars went to get it, and they didn't make it out in time."

Her throat caught.

"Trin..." she choked. "Trin is gone."

Shelle gasped, her hand tightening on Liora's.

"Lars said it happened on the roof of the moving train," Liora explained. "Balar threw a knife and Trin jumped in front of it. Took it to the ribs. Lars tried to fight him, but got knocked down. Before he could get back up... Balar jumped off the train with her."

Tears welled up in Liora's eyes. Just thinking about the terror Lars and Trin must have felt. And poor Jax, too out of breath to get himself up on top of the train. Hells, it hurt.

"Lars and Jax came back hours later," Liora went on. "Battered. Barely walking. He told me... told me what happened. He didn't even sound angry at first. Just empty."

She blinked a few times. Felt a full force sob threaten. Liora shoved it back.

Shelle gave the ghost of a smile. "And then?"

Liora closed her eyes and exhaled slow. "And then nothing. I came home."

"Oh, Liora," Shelle murmured, "I'm so sorry. What can I do?"

Liora sighed, voice hoarse. "You can hold me, if you want."

Shelle didn't answer right away. She just studied Liora's face like she was memorizing it. Then she nodded and slipped under the blanket, pulling Liora gently into her arms.

And Liora finally felt safe for a moment.

Shelle's hand traced up Liora's back in slow, grounding lines. Her fingers curled around the base of her neck. Liora melted into her—head tucked beneath Shelle's chin, breath hitching once, then slowing.

For a while, they didn't speak. Liora just breathed her in. Lavender. Warm skin. Home.

Then Shelle shifted, just enough to tilt Liora's face upward. Their eyes met.

And then the kiss came—soft, deep, inevitable.

It wasn't intense, but it wasn't calm either. Liora clung to it like a power line—something alive, something real. Her hands found Shelle's hip, her thigh, her ribs. Their bodies pressed close, hearts thudding in uneven sync.

For the first time since the heist, Liora felt her body again.

But just as she started to forget the rest of the world, Shelle stopped.

She drew back an inch, lips parted. Breathing hard.

Liora opened her eyes, dazed. "What is it?" she asked, trying to smile. "I was just, ya know... starting to enjoy myself."

But Shelle didn't laugh.

Her brow furrowed. Her hand stilled. "Something's wrong," she began, "but I know you're still reeling. Maybe we should just—"

What the hell? No way, not after a bombshell like that.

Liora huffed. "Shelle, you have to tell me now."

"Darling," she said softly, "I think something's going on with Aric."

Liora froze. Still tangled up in Shelle's arms, but not sinking anymore.

"What do you mean?" she asked carefully. "What kind of something?"

Shelle hesitated. Looked away for a second like she was weighing it. Then she sighed, thumb brushing Liora's collarbone once before pulling back fully.

"You know how bad he is at lying," Shelle said. "Not the words but the way he does it. That twitch at the corner of his eye. The ramble that comes after."

Liora sat up slowly, the blanket falling to her waist.

Shelle kept going. "Right before your job, I asked where he was headed. He said some firm wanted a consult on backup security. I was going to leave it at that, but..."

"But?"

"He kept going. Talked about dynamo current ratings. When he got the message. What street the office was on." Shelle shook her head. "It was too much. I know that tone."

Liora stared at her, waiting.

"So I followed him."

That landed like a dropped wrench. Liora didn't know whether to grin or be shocked.

Shelle glanced up. "He went out past Tavern Row. Not to any office. To an old tenement block that hasn't had working lights in months."

"You sure?"

"I watched him go in." Shelle's voice was low now. Flat. "And I waited. For hours. He never came out. Not that I saw."

Liora's skin prickled. She knew how patient Shelle could be. If she said he didn't leave, she meant it.

"So I broke in," Shelle added. "No sign of him. Just a few locked crates. Empty room. No bed. No light. Just a window in the back and no Myrim."

Liora tried to swallow, but her mouth was dry.

"He hasn't been home since," Shelle said. "Not one word. Not even a squawk."

A long, cold pause. Shelle looked at her as if deciding whether or not to say more.

It was way too late for that. "What? Tell me," Liora said.

Shelle frowned. "Well," she began, "it's hard to say for sure, you know how land leasing works... but my informants found out the building is owned by Vivienne Dragunova."

Liora stared hard at the ceiling. Not because there was anything there. But because if she looked at Shelle, she might say something she couldn't take back.

She thought about Myrim.

What he used to do. The lawman he once was. The nights he stayed up re-reading case files, muttering to himself about justice and loopholes and what made a person dangerous.

She thought about the day he joined their crew. The relief in his eyes. Like he'd finally escaped the weight of carrying that badge for Thume.

So what was he running toward now?

What was he doing?

She thought about the timings. That odd visit from Diligence. How he seemed to want to know more about what her crew was planning than about what happened after.

Liora stared up at the ceiling.

She wasn't ready to finish the thought.

But the question had already been planted. And once it started growing, there was no stopping it.

The sea was quiet. Not calm exactly. Just quiet. That kind of doldrums a sailor worries they may never escape.

Keer leaned against the starboard rail and drew slow on the pipe Lars had given him last year, back when he'd first said he was done with Azoria. Before the city pulled him in again. Before Mhalendra had made her offer.

The bowl crackled low. The smoke tasted like cedar and salt.

He didn't light it often. Just when the ship felt too still. Or when he needed to remind himself of who he was. Not the crewman. Not the captain. Just the man.

A man who had lived countless lives in his many years. A man who loved the sea, ever since he was a boy growing up in Zarakar. But also a thief, and a damn fine one.

He cared about his ship crew like he did his own left arm. But his thieving crew—Lars, Liora, Trin, Jax—he loved them with everything he had.

He exhaled a thin plume of smoke and watched the wind scatter it.

The crew was below, mostly quiet except for the odd "heave ho." It's like the Azure sea was inviting him to reminisce. Barely a sound except the lap of the hull and the steady creak of a ship that knew the weight it carried.

He took one more pull and looked at the sun. Aye, it was time.

He turned and made his way toward the galley.

It smelled like broth and burnt spices. Someone had tried to cook earlier and clearly given up halfway. That was a shame. No wasted food was allowed on Keer's ship. Someone must have had to pinch their nose while drinking that concoction.

Silas was perched on a stool near the counter, oiling the hinge of a folding blade. One of his favorites, by the look of it. The man rarely sat still, even when off-duty. Always fixing something. Always thinking two steps ahead.

Keer stepped through the hatch, pipe still in his teeth.

Silas glanced up. "Captain."

Keer gave a low grunt in reply.

"Where you off to?"

Without slowing, Keer tapped the side of his pipe with one knuckle and said, "Our cargo needs air."

Silas didn't ask what he meant. Just smirked and went back to his blade.

"Aye," he said. "Figured it might."

Keer stepped out the far hatch and onto the upper deck again, pipe smoke curling behind him.

The crate sat lashed near the stern, half-shadowed by a coil of rigging. From a distance it looked like any other haul of salted fish—roped tight, crusted with sea-brine, stained from a day of deck spray.

Hells, it stank.

Keer crouched beside it and unlatched the first hook. Then the second. Then reached for the iron hasp at the center and gave it a sharp snap.

The lid creaked open.

Inside, nestled in coils of wet canvas and fish guts, lay Cecil Thume.

Alive. Blinking.

Furious.

Keer let the lid fall open and waited.

Thume didn't scramble out. Didn't gasp for breath. He just sat up slowly and stared at Keer with smoldering golden eyes. He stood up as dignified as he could and climbed out of the crate.

It was hard to be dignified in his state though, after almost two days in a fish crate with nought but a canteen and a hunk of bread. The man had clearly shat himself in there. Keer smirked.

The disgraced city leader looked ahead, then behind. Nothing but open sea for leagues around.

"You could have let me out hours ago," he said, his voice low and dangerous.

Keer took the pipe from his teeth, knocked it out against the rail, and said flatly, "Aye. I could've."

They stared at each other for a long moment. Thume looked as if he were going to explode in a violent rage.

Let him try. Keer almost hoped he would. The crew would respond, and that would be the end of his Thume problem.

But he did not. Thume took a deep breath, stood tall and proud.

His clothes were soaked through with brine and waste, his once-fine vest clinging damp to his ribs. But his spine stayed straight. He dusted a flake of fish scale from his shoulder with the dignity of a man seated at a council gala.

"I'll need a bath," he muttered. "I will not re-enter Zarakar smelling like... this."

Keer nodded toward the aft pump. "Then get scrubbin'."

Thume's eyes flicked that way. But he didn't move. Just stared at Keer for a long moment.

"Have I wronged you, Keer Basar?" he asked, voice low. "Why do you hold me in such contempt?"

Keer didn't answer at first.

He let the question hang there in the salt-heavy air as he knocked his pipe out on the rail. Honestly, Keer was unsure of that himself. He didn't know the man—not really. He knew of him. Knew the kind of power Thume once held. The kind of power he wielded like a knife in the dark.

Quiet, precise, and always aimed at the throat.

They were both Zarakaran, sure. Both knew what it meant to grow up hungry and ambitious. But where Keer had stolen for survival, Thume had fed himself on cities. On nations. And when his appetite got too large, he'd tried to consume Ithris too.

Keer didn't hate him. He just didn't trust him to leave the table.

He looked at Thume now—soaked, pissed-on, and still managing to look like a man three moves ahead.

That was the problem.

"You're not gonna sit quiet in Zarakar," Keer said flatly. "You'll wait. Regroup. And then you'll move. I know enough to know you don't know how to stop."

Thume didn't deny it.

So Keer stepped closer.

"Just tell me one thing," he said. "When you're back in your estate. When your power's rebuilt. And no bullshit—when you take the fight back to Ithris."

He paused.

"Will Lars and his crew be safe?"

Thume met his eyes. Still. Sharp.

"They got me out," he said. "And for that... they've earned their safety."

Keer held the stare for a breath longer.

"Good," he muttered. "That's all I needed to know."

"My turn," Thume said. "Has Lars found his woman yet?"

His woman. Hells. Trin wasn't "Lars's woman," she was Trin. Clever, loyal Trin.

Keer was genuinely surprised Thume even cared. "Not yet," he admitted. "But believe me, they're working every angle."

He reached into his pocket and pulled out a metal key.

"You can clean up in my quarters," Keer huffed, tossing the key to Thume. "But for hells' sake, take those clothes off outside."

The founder of the Ithris Gaming Commission and former ruling force of Azoria favored Keer with a wry grin. Then he placed his hand over his heart and gave a slight bow, just a small bend at the waist.

"You have my thanks."

Keer didn't return the bow. He just turned and walked back to the rail, thinking about Lars. Back in that powder keg of a city.

Whatever that boy was planning—and Keer had seen enough in his eyes to know he was planning something—it was the kind of scheme that could swallow a man whole. The city watch would be the least of his worries.

Trying to outsmart someone like Vivienne, that's the kind of madness that would get him. The need for revenge had a way of twisting even the best men into something unrecognizable.

Stay clever, kid, Keer thought, watching the horizon and counting the days to landfall.

The door crashed open under Lars's boot.

His breath hitched. Muscles taut. Hand musket raised.

He stormed across the room like a feral thing.

Vivienne's office—clean, quiet, too damned elegant. Velvet chairs. A decanter half-poured. Pleasant scents at odds with its filthy contents.

And there was the snake herself, behind the desk. Standing now. Pale lips parted with hands frozen over a half-signed document.

She had to be behind Balar. Had to. There's no way a monster like that rises up on his own.

Diligence Blythe sat in one of the guest chairs across the desk from Vivienne. One leg crossed neatly over the other, her posture loose and predatory. She didn't move except to tilt her head slightly, as if watching a performance.

Lars didn't hesitate. He leveled the musket straight at Vivienne's face.

"WHERE. THE. HELLS. IS. SHE."

The shout tore from his chest raw. More pain than anger, more desperation than either. Lars operated in a world of intrigue and coy information plays. Until recently, violence hadn't even been a part of his world. But that time was over.

Vivienne blinked once. Her eyes went wide for a moment. Then she schooled her features back into something calmer, more composed.

"Lars, really. There's no—"

He stepped forward fast, gun pressing the air between them.

"I'm sorry, what?" he said. "Go ahead and brush this off again."

The silence that followed was sharp enough to bleed.

His hands were steady, but his pulse was a war drum. The weight of the musket was nothing. The weight in his chest was everything.

Diligence moved like liquid dynamo. A soft hiss of steel split the air.

A flick of her wrist, and her rapier was out. Its point now nestled beneath Lars's chin, so gently it could've been mistaken for affection.

"I can end this now," she said, gaze never leaving his eyes. Despite the tension in the room, her voice came out as an intimate whisper. "Just say the word, Viv."

Lars didn't step back or flinch.

He pressed the barrel of the musket hard against Vivienne's brow. "Try," he growled. "See what happens."

Diligence pressed the point of the rapier into Lars's chin, almost enough to draw blood.

Then—

Click. Another musket cocked behind Diligence.

"Oh my," squeaked a calm voice. "Hello again, Diligence."

Liora had been waiting just outside the hall. Silent backup if—okay, *when* things went south.

He could hear it in Diligence's breath. That faint shift of tension as cold metal kissed the back of her head.

But Diligence didn't back down.

Four players. Three weapons. One spark.

Lars hadn't once looked away from Vivienne. "You've got five seconds before I pull this trigger," he said. "Start talking."

Vivienne raised both hands slowly—palms out, voice softening.

"Okay, enough," she said. "Or this won't end well for any of us."

Lars held steady. Liora didn't lower her aim. Diligence twitched her blade just slightly, like she was thinking it through.

Vivienne only smiled.

"Lars," she said gently. "So good to see you again. Can we talk like civilized people?"

Lars stared down the barrel at Vivienne Dragunova, the woman who'd dismantled his life and likely smirked doing it.

But something in her tone cut under his skin worse than Diligence's blade.

He forced a breath through his teeth.

"Talk," he spat. "But you so much as blink wrong, I swear to the hells—"

"I know," Vivienne said smoothly, cutting him off. "You'll put a hole in my head."

She stepped back from the desk, hands still raised, and gestured to the chair across from Diligence. "Sit, if you like. I won't offer you a drink."

Lars didn't sit. But he lowered the musket by an inch. Enough to let her breathe. Not enough to feel safe.

Behind Diligence, Liora still had her gun raised.

"Lower it," Lars said.

"But—"

"I said lower it."

At first, nothing. Then the click of her musket disengaging.

Diligence sheathed her rapier without looking. The faint snick of steel into scabbard was somehow louder than it should've been. She sat and crossed her legs again, as if the past thirty seconds hadn't happened.

Only then did Lars sit. But he kept the hand musket pointed in Vivienne's direction.

Vivienne, ever the queen, smoothed her dress and took her seat.

"So," she said. "Who exactly are we pretending I've kidnapped today?"

For a moment, Lars considered just shooting her, then banished the intrusive thought. But if he had to deal with her ridiculous mind games with Trin's life on the line...

"You know damn well who," he said through clenched teeth. "Where is Trin?"

Vivienne tilted her head. Her smile didn't reach her eyes. "Oh. Her."

The dismissiveness punched Lars harder than any fist.

His grip on the musket tightened. "Don't play cute, Vivienne."

"I don't play," she said, her eyes smoldering. "In fact—"

Liora made a frustrated sound behind them, the kind she usually reserved for when her engineering tools cracked in half from strain.

Vivienne cleared her throat, folding her hands atop the desk. "Alright, enough of that. What makes you think I have Trin?"

"She disappeared," Lars said. "Right after we broke Thume out. And Balar—*your* attack dog—was on the train."

A flicker of something passed through Vivienne's eyes at that. Alarm? It was gone in a second.

"Balar was involved?" she repeated.

"You tell me," Lars growled.

"Lars," Vivienne said, voice like silk stretched over blades. "If Balar took Trin, I assure you—I had nothing to do with it."

"Bullshit."

"Did you see me on that train?" she asked coolly. "Did you see a Gaming Commission seal? One of my agents? Or did you just see a mask?"

He started to speak—

"And while we're asking questions," she cut in, sharper now, "where is Cecil Thume?"

Lars hesitated. That was the game. She could always sense the weak spot in a conversation and twist the knife.

Vivienne leaned in slightly, voice hushed. "You broke him out? A criminal. A traitor. A man who nearly tore apart Ithris. Where is he now?"

"You want Thume?" he said. "You'll have to get in line. Now tell me where Trin is."

Vivienne's gaze didn't waver. "Lars. I swear to you, I don't know."

Lars studied her face. The calm mask. The perfect control. But something had cracked, just for a moment. When he'd said Balar. That hadn't been surprise. It had been irritation.

"You really didn't know," he said, the realization sour on his tongue. "You didn't send him."

Her fingers tapped once, then stopped. "No. I didn't."

Lars pulled in a breath through his teeth. Rage was easy. This was not.

Vivienne sat taller. "Because of your loss," she said, "I'm willing to overlook this... drama. But Lars—come into my office armed again, and you will not leave it alive."

Diligence arched an eyebrow at that. A flicker of something unreadable danced across her face.

Lars let out a low huff and stood. Liora followed, musket still loosely in hand, gaze sharp as ever. The loss of Trin had really changed her, hadn't it?

They turned toward the door.

"Lars," Vivienne said behind them, smooth as ever. "It was good to see you again."

What the hells was that?

Could she really be implying—

No. Whatever. They were back to square one. And Vivienne didn't rate another moment of his time.

He and Liora left as quick as they'd come in.

They burst out of the building into the afternoon light. The street noise hit them like a wall after the suffocating quiet of the Gaming Commission.

"What now?" Liora asked, her voice small.

Lars stopped walking. The question hung between them like lead.

He didn't know.

They'd gambled everything on Vivienne having Trin, on being able to force answers out of her. Now...

He took a ragged breath, feeling the adrenaline bleeding out of him like air from a punctured bellows. His hands started to shake—not from fear, but from the comedown.

Imagine if the guns were actually loaded, he thought with bitter humor. *I'd be absolutely flying.*

But he was no killer. The muskets had been for show, for leverage. Even with Trin missing, even with that blind fury driving him...

Even though he could feel that urge tickling at the back of his mind—that whisper of how much simpler things would be if he just ended threats instead of dancing around them—he was no killer.

"I don't know," he admitted to Liora. The words tasted like ash. "I don't know what we do now."

The office fell still.

Vivienne didn't move at first. She listened to the echo of boots receding down the hall. Then, and only then, did she exhale and relax her posture.

She turned to the decanter with the calm of someone unbothered, though her pulse had only just begun to settle. She poured the remainder of the glass she'd abandoned. A rich Drakorian wine. Always her favorite. It reminded her of home.

Diligence hadn't moved either. She lounged in the same chair, her blade long since sheathed, her gaze still tracking the door like she might go after them anyway.

Vivienne sipped. Let the silence bloom.

She preferred this part. The quiet. The aftermath. The moment when chaos had already shown its teeth and was now deciding whether to bite again.

"That," Diligence said after a long pause, "was unexpected."

Vivienne peered at her through lowered lashes, glass in hand. She sat with immaculate poise—legs crossed, one nail tracing the rim of the crystal.

Let Diligence think whatever she wanted. Let her guess wrong.

Diligence shifted at last, stretching her legs out like a cat after a long nap.

"I don't think I've ever seen you rattled like that," she said, voice casual.

Vivienne didn't blink. How dare she? "I wasn't rattled."

"Of course not."

The corner of Diligence's mouth twitched. She leaned forward just slightly, elbows resting on her knees, chin perched on folded hands. Watching her like prey that hadn't decided whether to run.

This woman was infuriating. No, Vivienne wasn't rattled. In fact, seeing Lars again hadn't even affected her. She thought it would, with his easy smile, that bold confidence... the way his eyes seemed to—

A part of her mind snuffed the train of thought without leaving even a puff of smoke. She glared at Diligence. "You forget yourself."

"I remember exactly who I am," Diligence said, voice dropping into that low, indulgent murmur. "And who you are, too."

They held each other's gaze. Two knives on a table, waiting to be drawn.

Vivienne stood slowly, taking hold of a slim folder from the desk top. She flipped it open, eyes never leaving Diligence. "Then act like it."

A slow chuckle. "Touchy."

Vivienne didn't respond. She read the top page for a moment longer than necessary, letting Diligence sit in the silence.

"I'm just saying," Diligence went on, her tone lighter now, but no less sharp. "There's something delicious about watching the great Vivienne Dragunova lose her cool."

Vivienne closed the folder with a soft snap. "Careful, Blythe."

Diligence smiled lazily. "Or what?"

Vivienne came around the desk, set the folder down with precision, and leaned in just close enough that the air shifted.

"Or you'll find out which of us bites harder."

Diligence held the gaze. Let it breathe. And finally—smiled. "Now that," she said, "is the Vivienne I like."

Her lips parted. A fire set in her eyes that was unmistakable. Vivienne could see and feel it, burning between them. Diligence was always so passionate after a battle of wits.

And Vivienne was usually quick to indulge her. But not today.

She stepped back from Diligence, walking back around her desk. Diligence looked on, that hungry look still in her eyes, perhaps thinking this was Vivienne simply being coy.

Vivienne sank gracefully into her chair, legs crossing, one hand looping around the stem of her glass as if nothing in the last five minutes had happened.

She sipped. "Tail him."

Diligence tilted her head. "Him?"

"Lars," Vivienne said flatly, not even bothering to look up at first.

When she did, she caught it. A flicker of something sharp in Diligence's eyes. A glint of steel. Anger?

Vivienne ignored it.

"Find out where he's keeping Thume," she said, her tone slipping into that soft, merciless cadence she reserved for commands. "Who's helping him. What their next move is. And if he's going to be a problem."

Diligence leaned back with a faint smirk. "And if he is?"

"Then we'll know exactly where to squeeze."

She swirled the wine in her glass, gaze drifting toward the large windows as if already bored with the conversation. That cracked pane would be replaced. Immediately.

How someone had *dared* to fire a musket at her office, Vivienne didn't know. But it would be fixed, and it would never happen again. Even if she had to wipe out half of the scum in the district to make it so.

She brought her thoughts back to the present. "Lars Harrow was never subtle. And he's even less careful when he's grieving."

"Or angry," Diligence offered.

That man. Vivienne smiled faintly. "Or both."

Lars Harrow. At least he was an opponent she could respect, unlike Thume. Lars had style, intelligence, a certain... quality. Not like her stepfather, who'd worn power like a grand coat and discarded family like worn shoes.

Damn it. She set the glass down with deliberate grace.

"Go."

Diligence vanished through the door without another word.

Vivienne didn't watch her leave.

She pushed aside the intelligence reports on Thume's movements. Those could wait. Let the old bastard rot wherever Lars had stuffed him. She'd deal with him when the time was right—and when she did, she'd lock him in a hole so deep he'd never see the light of day. He'd learn what abandonment truly meant.

Enough of that. Vivienne found the folder she was looking for. This one was labeled BALAR.

Why hadn't he checked in? If he truly was there and he made off with a member of Lars's crew, why hadn't she heard from him?

"Oh, Aric, I hope you're not feeling a sense of conscience," she murmured to herself. "It's far too late for that."

She needed to find him. And when she did, they would... talk.

Perhaps she would even take Lars's little bitch back to the Commission. To watch her suffer, or to help her heal? While the former might be a thrill, the latter could be used against Lars. And she wanted that so bad it—

ENOUGH, her mind screamed. *He is nothing. And thinking like that will make you nothing as well.*

Vivienne neatly tucked the emotion away where all emotion belonged. In the dark recesses of her brain, never to escape unless she found it strategically beneficial.

Fantasies were pointless. She hadn't indulged Diligence. She sure as hells wouldn't indulge her own intrusive thoughts. She had work to do.

And the first order of business was to find Balar.

WHAT WAS LOST

12

The map of Azoria looked like it had contracted some virulent pox.

Red crosses marred every district, every street corner, every safe house and bolt-hole Lars had marked over his years as a thief. A week of searching, and all they had to show for it were elimination marks and dead ends. The ink had bled through in places where he'd pressed too hard, creating wounds in the parchment that matched the hollow ache in his chest.

Lars rubbed his eyes, gritty from another sleepless night. His fingers came away stained with red and black—ink under his nails, in the creases of his palms, marking him like guilt made visible. When had he last eaten? Yesterday? The day before? Time had become a blur of searching and failing and searching again.

"Lars?"

He didn't look up at Liora's voice. He couldn't bear to see the manic hope in her eyes, the way she vibrated with desperate energy. She'd been at it again this morning—standing in the Market Square with those damned sketches, shouting herself hoarse. Have you seen this woman? Please, any information. We'll pay.

"I've divided the southern districts into smaller grids," he said, voice rough from disuse. "If we systematically—"

"Lars." Firmer this time. A warm hand on his shoulder. "Bunny made breakfast."

"I'm not hungry."

"When's the last time you—"

"I said I'm not hungry." The words came out sharper than intended. Lars forced himself to soften his tone. "Especially not for Bunny's cooking. Just... let me finish this section. Then I'll eat."

It's not that the big man's cooking was bad. It's just that Aelyndoran breakfast consisted of the fattiest sausages Lars had ever eaten and a weird mash of cornmeal and egg. Not exactly comfort food.

Liora's hand squeezed his once before withdrawing. He heard her footsteps retreat, pause at the doorway. "She's alive, Lars. I know she is. We'll find her."

The door clicked shut.

Lars stared at the map, at all those red crosses. His hand trembled as he reached for the ink bottle again. The systematic search south of the river had been his idea—divide the city into manageable chunks, assign teams, methodically eliminate possibilities. It was how he'd always approached impossible heists. Break them down into solvable problems.

Except Trin wasn't a problem to be solved. She was... she was...

The ink bottle slipped from his fingers, splattering across the southeastern corner of the map. Black liquid pooled over the slums, obliterating his careful notations. Lars swore, reaching for a rag, but his hands were shaking too badly to clean it properly. The stain spread like blood, like shadow, like—

Like her blood on the train car roof.

He shoved back from the table so violently his chair toppled. The crash echoed through the empty room, followed by the sound of running feet. The door burst open—Jax, still sweating from whatever brutal training regimen he'd subjected himself to this morning.

"Lars?" Jax's eyes darted around the room, checking corners, looking for threats. Looking for Balar. "What happened?"

They all did that now. News about Balar was everywhere. He was attacking crews all over Azoria, from the harbor to Lowtown. No mercy, just inhuman brutality. The people were terrified.

But none more than those in this room. They jumped at shadows, checked their backs, waited for the masked vigilante to finish what he'd started.

"Nothing." Lars righted his chair, avoiding Jax's gaze. "I knocked over some ink."

Jax took in the ruined map, the scattered papers, the general chaos of the room that had once been Lars's meticulously organized planning space. A week ago, Jax would have made some joke, tried to lighten the mood. Now he just stood there, jaw working like he was chewing on words he couldn't quite spit out.

"She's not dead," Lars blurted out, the words tumbling over each other. "She's not. Balar took her. He took her, Jax. You don't take dead people. You leave them. But he took her, which means—which means he needs her for something. Leverage. A trade. Something."

"Yeah." Jax's voice was hoarse, eager. "Yeah, that's right. He needs her alive. Has to."

"Exactly!" Lars grabbed onto the thought like a lifeline, pacing now, hands moving as he talked. "So we just need to figure out what he wants. What's his game? What does he need from us that he couldn't just take?" He spun to face Jax. "Why hasn't he made contact?"

Jax's face fell slightly. "I... maybe he's waiting? Making us sweat?"

"A week, though?" Lars raked his hands through his hair. "A whole week of nothing. We know he's been active. But no demands, no messages, no proof of—"

He cut himself off. "No. No, she's alive. She has to be. We'd know if she wasn't. We'd know."

"We would," Jax agreed quickly. Too quickly. "The city would feel different. She's too important to just... to just disappear."

They stared at each other, both desperate to believe their own words. The silence stretched between them, filled with all the terrible possibilities neither would voice.

From somewhere else in the base came the low murmur of voices. Bunny's distinctive Aelyndoran accent threading through words Lars couldn't quite make out. Praying, probably. The man had taken to spending copious time in meditation, calling on old gods that the rest of Ithris had abandoned years ago. Lars wanted to mock him for it, wanted to rage that his mountain spirits and forest deities weren't going to bring Trin back.

But he couldn't. Because at least Bunny was doing something, even if it was useless. All Lars had were his maps and his red crosses and his systematic failure.

"I'm going out again," Jax said suddenly. "Gonna check the gambling dens near the foundries. Someone might've heard something."

"We checked there three days ago."

"Then I'll check again." Jax's hands clenched and unclenched at his sides. "Better than sitting here doing nothing."

We're not doing nothing, Lars wanted to say. We're planning, organizing, being smart about this. But the words would be lies. They were doing nothing that mattered. Nothing that brought her back.

After Jax left, Lars returned to his map. The ink stain had dried into an ugly black scar across the southeastern districts. He'd need to redraw the whole thing, transfer all his notations, start fresh. The thought exhausted him.

A soft knock interrupted his brooding. Different from Liora's confident rap or Jax's heavy fist. Lars didn't bother looking up. "Come in, Bunny."

The door opened with a careful creak. Bunny stood in the doorway, looking lost. His usual cheerful energy was nowhere to be found. Dark circles shadowed his eyes, and his broad shoulders slumped like they were carrying invisible weight.

"Can't find my prayer beads," he said, voice thick. "The wooden ones Jax gave me. Thought maybe I left them in here yesterday when we were..." He trailed off, scanning the chaos of Lars's planning room.

"I haven't seen them." Lars kept his eyes on the map. "Check the kitchen. You made breakfast, didn't you?"

Bunny didn't move. Just stood there, shifting his weight from foot to foot. "I keep asking them to bring her back," he said suddenly. "The gods. Every morning, every night. Same prayer." His voice cracked. "They're not listening."

Lars looked up then. Bunny's eyes were red-rimmed, and his hands kept clenching and unclenching at his sides. It was the same nervous gesture they'd all developed this past week.

"Maybe they don't exist," Lars said, too tired to soften the words.

"They exist." Bunny's jaw tightened. "They just... they don't always answer. My grandmother said that's how you know they're real. If they answered every prayer, they'd collect taxes."

"Fat lot of good it does us then."

Bunny let out a shaky breath. "I know. I just... I don't know what else to do. I know I'm new to the crew. But I'm still a part of it, right? Of the family?"

The question hit Lars like a physical blow. Here was Bunny, who'd saved his life during the wind farm heist, who'd thrown himself into danger for people he'd known only for days, asking if he belonged. While Lars had been so wrapped up in his own guilt, he'd forgotten that Bunny was grieving too.

"You're crew," Lars said quietly. "You were crew the moment you kept Balar from beating me to death." He rubbed his face, feeling every sleepless hour. "I'm sorry, Bunny. I've been..."

"A right bastard?" Bunny supplied, and there was a flash of his usual grin.

"Yeah." Lars managed something that might have been a smile. "That."

Bunny moved into the room properly, no longer hovering at the threshold. "Jax said you used to be different. Before the ban."

"We all used to be different." Lars looked at his ink-stained hands. "Trin would kick my ass for moping like this. She'd say—"

His throat closed up.

"She'd say get off your ass and do something clever," Bunny finished. "Jax told me. Said she was the one who kept you honest."

"She still does." Lars's voice was fierce. "Still does."

Bunny left, and for just a moment, the weight on Lars's chest felt a fraction lighter. Not much, but enough to breathe.

Ten minutes later, Jax burst through the door again, breathing hard. This time, he wasn't alone. A scraggly youth followed him, all sharp elbows and darting eyes—the kind of street rat who survived by knowing things others didn't.

"Tell him what you told me," Jax ordered, shoving the boy forward.

The youth glanced between them, calculating. Lars recognized the look. He was weighing risk against reward, trying to figure out how much this information was worth. He pulled out a small leather purse, let the copper coins inside clink together. The boy's eyes sharpened.

"Saw your woman," the boy said without preamble. "The one that engineer girl's been shouting about in the squares. Saw her three nights back, I did."

Lars shot to his feet, his chair clattering backward. "Where?"

"Easy now." The boy held out one grimy hand. "He said you'd pay."

Lars tossed him a coin without thinking. "Where did you see her?"

The boy made the purse disappear into his ragged clothes with practiced ease. "The warehouses next to the jail. Near the big museum. She was walking—bit unsteady like, but walking. Had a hood up, but I saw her face when she passed under a lamp." He grinned, revealing gaps in his teeth. "Pretty lady, even looking rough. Matches them sketches perfect."

"Was she alone?" Jax demanded, hope naked in his voice.

"That's the big question, huh?" The boy scratched his head, playing up the performance. "It'll cost you more then."

Lars was already reaching for another coin. "Was. She. Alone?"

"Might've been someone with her. Big fellow. Stayed in the shadows mostly." The boy pocketed the second coin. "I could show you where. For a finder's fee, of course."

"Let's go." Lars was already moving toward the door. His mind raced—Trin alive, walking, three nights ago. Still in the city. They could find her, get her back...

"Now?" The boy looked uncertain. "It's broad daylight. That area's crawling with city watch during the day."

"I wouldn't care if it's crawling with Zarakaran elite forces." Lars grabbed his coat. "You're taking us there. Now."

The boy shrugged. "Your funeral, not mine."

They moved through the city quickly, Lars's desperation overriding his usual caution. The boy led them through increasingly empty streets, away from the main thoroughfares. Something nagged at Lars—a feeling that grew stronger as they turned down a particularly desolate alley.

"Just through here," the boy said, pointing to a narrow passage between two crumbling buildings. "That's where I saw her."

Lars pushed past him, hope drowning out instinct. The alley was empty except for scattered refuse and—

The boy's footsteps, running. Fast.

Lars spun around just in time to see the kid disappearing around the corner. His hands flew to his pockets. The little bastard had lifted everything while Lars was distracted by hope.

"That little shit!" Jax roared, starting after him.

"Let him go." Lars's voice was dead. Of course. Of course it was a con. Street rats heard Liora's desperate pleas, saw the sketches, sensed opportunity. Easy marks, the grieving crew of Lars Harrow.

"I'll kill him," Jax snarled. "I'll find that lying little—"

"He's just a kid trying to survive." Lars leaned against the alley wall, suddenly exhausted. "I can't even blame him. We wanted to believe it so badly, we didn't even question it. Three nights ago? If Trin was walking around three nights ago, she'd have found a way to signal us. She'd have come home."

The walk back was silent. Lars felt hollowed out, scraped clean of even false hope. They were almost at the base when a voice called out behind them.

"Lose something, Harrow?"

Lars turned to find Diligence Blythe holding the street boy by the scruff of his neck like a naughty kitten. The kid squirmed but couldn't break free from her grip. With her free hand, she tossed Lars his copper pouch.

"All there," she said with a wry smile. "Kid's got good hands, but terrible target selection. Picking the pocket of Lars Harrow when the whole city knows you're desperate? Amateur hour."

What the hells was Diligence doing there? The last time Lars had seen her, it was... not so good.

"Yeah," he replied to her, giving the kid a light smack on the back of the head as the boy ran back into the streets. "Thanks."

"Don't mention it."

Lars nodded stiffly, already turning away. He didn't have time for whatever game Vivienne's assistant was playing. Didn't have the energy for verbal sparring or veiled threats or—

"Wait," Diligence said. "Let's take a walk."

"Go inside," Lars told Jax, his voice flat. "Tell the others I'll be back."

Jax's eyes narrowed. "Lars—"

"Go."

The big man's jaw worked, but he turned and headed for the base, throwing one last suspicious glance over his shoulder. Lars waited until the door closed before turning to Diligence.

"Walk," she said, already moving.

Lars followed, noting how she guided them away from the main thoroughfares, toward the old Mercantile Quarter. The streets grew quieter as they moved deeper into the district. Shop windows that once displayed fine goods now stood empty, their owners having fled to cheaper districts when the heist ban killed the flow of redistributed wealth. Without thieves spreading copper through the city, the merchant class had slowly strangled.

Fewer eyes here. Fewer ears.

His hand drifted toward the knife at his belt. It was a habit more than a threat. The last time he'd been alone with Diligence... well, that hadn't gone well for anyone.

They passed a boarded-up jeweler's, its sign hanging crooked. A year ago, this street would have been bustling with merchants hoping to buy stolen goods or sell to thieves flush with copper. Now it felt like a graveyard.

"Depressing, isn't it?" Diligence said, gesturing at the empty shops. "All this decay. Vivienne calls it 'necessary restructuring,' but between you and me..." She shrugged. "I miss the old days."

Nice try playing the sympathetic insider, Lars thought. But he knew better.

"You look like hells, Lars." Diligence didn't look at him as she spoke, her stride confident, unhurried.

"What do you want, Diligence?"

"Want?" She laughed, a sound like crystal breaking. "I'm trying to help you, believe it or not. Though I'm starting to wonder if you're beyond it."

They turned down a narrower street, past boarded shopfronts that had once sold copper goods. The emptiness pressed in around them.

"Vivienne's been... different lately," Diligence continued, her voice dropping. "Since you burst in her office last week. She's not thinking clearly."

Since he threatened her. Of course that had to sting.

"She's been spending a lot of time reviewing property deeds," Diligence said, almost carelessly. "Old warehouse holdings in the factory district. Strange hobby for someone who should be running a city."

Lars's pulse quickened. Warehouse deeds. Where someone might hide a prisoner. Where Balar might hide out? He forced his expression to remain neutral.

"Of course," Diligence added with a slight smile, "she's always been thorough about property management. Probably nothing."

He grunted. Diligence was trying to rile him up. Or misdirect him. What the hells was she playing at?

They passed a fountain that had once run with clear water. Now it sat dry, its copper pipes stripped and sold weeks ago. Diligence trailed her fingers along the empty basin.

"She's been bringing in talent from home too," she said. "Drakorians. You know how they are about loyalty. They'd do anything for their own."

Lars slowed. "I don't know anything about Drakorians," he shrugged. "Except they make great wine."

"That masked vigilante..." Diligence mused without acknowledging him. "He moves like a Drakorian sword dancer, don't you think? All that formal precision. Very different from your average Azorian brawler."

Was she saying Balar is Drakorian? One of Vivienne's imports? The possibility reshuffled everything he thought he knew. But Diligence could be lying, sending him chasing shadows while the real threat—

"The copper situation is getting worse," Diligence said, changing topics so smoothly Lars almost missed it. "Strange how it started right after the Zarakar trade routes closed."

"Supply and demand," Lars said carefully.

"Mmm." She glanced at him sideways. "Though one wonders who benefits from scarcity. Crystal charges are selling for ten times their price last month. But I'm sure that's just... coincidence."

Diligence stopped walking, turning to face him fully. "You know what your problem is, Lars? You think too much. Always calculating, always planning. Trin's the same way."

His jaw tightened at her name.

"She's too stiff for you, Lars." Diligence moved closer, bumping her hip against his with practiced casualness. "All that rigid thinking, those careful plans. You need someone with... flexibility. In business and other areas."

Lars stepped back. "Don't."

"I'm just saying," she continued, eyes glinting, "Trin can't understand that sometimes you have to bend the rules, not just break them. Work within the system to change it. She's too..." Diligence waved a hand. "Principled. Noble, even."

She's trying to get under my skin, Lars recognized. *Make me emotional, careless. But why mention Trin at all unless—*

"Whatever you're planning, Lars," Diligence said, starting to walk again, "just remember—Vivienne always thinks three moves ahead. Though lately..." She paused, as if catching herself. "She's been distracted. Emotional. That business with you really affected her."

Emotional means unpredictable, Lars translated. Dangerous. Or is Diligence saying Vivienne's vulnerable?

They'd circled back toward more populated streets. Diligence slowed, preparing to part ways.

"One more thing," she said, stopping close enough that he could smell her perfume. "She still talks about you, you know. Those nights at her estate." Her voice dropped to barely above a whisper. "The way you looked at her. And how you played her."

Lars stiffened.

"She's never forgotten. Never forgiven." Diligence's eyes glinted. "But here's the thing about Vivienne... she can't decide if she wants to destroy you or possess you." She leaned in, her lips almost brushing his ear. "That indecision is why you haven't found Trin yet. Vivienne knows where Balar keeps his... guests. But she's waiting to see what you'll do. How far you'll go."

She pulled back, studying his face. "If I were you, I'd find Balar before Vivienne decides which way her heart's leaning. Because once she makes up her mind..." Diligence shrugged. "Well. You've seen what happens to things she can't have."

Then she was gone, melting into the crowd with practiced ease.

Lars stood there, mind reeling. Not from the copper crisis or Drakorian sword dancers or warehouse deeds. But from one simple, terrible possibility:

Vivienne knew where Trin was. Had known all along. And she was letting it happen, watching him suffer, waiting to see what he'd do.

All to decide if she wanted him broken or hers.

Thume was right. It was time to go on the offensive.

"The Gilded Swan's running a new wheel," Maren said, shuffling the deck with practiced ease. "Heard they've got a backwoods dealer who doesn't know the local signals yet. Could be worth a look."

"Too obvious." Inora didn't look up from her cards. "Every two-bit con in the city will be trying to work that angle."

"What about the fighting pits in Lowtown?" Rurik suggested, which was surprising enough—he rarely offered opinions. "Fixed matches. Good money if you know which way to bet."

"Since when do we bet on fixed fights?" Darius kept his voice level, but something twisted in his gut. "We don't run with bookies."

"The Merchant's Quarter has a new den," Inora continued, as if he hadn't spoken. "High stakes, but they're not checking for marked cards yet. Give it a week before they wise up."

"Or," Maren said, grinning, "there's this beautiful long con I've been working on. Fake dynamo inspector, right? You go in, tell them their generators are leaking—"

"Leaking?" Darius's fingers drummed against the table. "Dynamo generators don't leak."

"That's the beauty of it! They don't know that. So you sell them 'sealant' that's really just—"

"Enough." The word came out sharp. Darius caught himself, forced a smile. "Let's just play."

They dealt another hand. The cards felt greasy in his fingers, worn from too many games that didn't matter. Outside, the city hummed with life, with possibility, with real scores happening while they sat here discussing penny-ante schemes.

"Actually," Inora said after a moment, "I heard about this traveling merchant who runs a shell game near the docks. Classic misdirection, but he's got a new twist with magnets—"

"Magnets." Darius stared at his cards. Two princes, three of different suits. A decent hand for a game that didn't matter. "We're talking about magnets and shell games."

"It's good money," Maren protested. "Steady, reliable..."

"Reliable?" Darius set his cards down slowly. "When did we start caring about reliable?"

Silence around the table. His crew exchanged those looks again, the ones they thought he didn't notice.

"Boss," Inora said carefully, "you're the one who said—"

"I know what I said!" He shoved back from the table, cards scattering. "But what the hells is wrong with you? All of you?"

They stared at him. He was on his feet now, pacing, hands moving as he talked.

"Shell games? Fixed fights? Marking cards?" He wheeled on them. "We're thieves! Real thieves! We steal from the impossible, we take what can't be taken, we make fucking headlines!"

"Used to," Rurik said quietly.

"What?"

"Used to make headlines." The bruiser met his gaze steadily. "Been a while."

Darius felt the words like a punch to the gut. A while. That was one way to put it. Another way was to say he'd become exactly what he'd always mocked—a has-been telling stories about glory days. The kind of washed-up thief who nursed drinks in tavern corners, boring anyone who'd listen with tales of scores that grew grander with each telling.

"Because we've been sitting here!" Darius exploded. "Playing it safe, running cons that any street kid could pull! Do you know what they're calling us now? 'Former associates of Lars Harrow.' Not our names. Not our crew. Just footnotes."

"At least we're not beaten half to death," Inora shot back. "Or disappeared like Trin—"

"Trin." The name stopped him cold. "Any word?"

"Nothing. A week now since Balar took her." Inora's scarred face was grim. "No demands. Nothing but random attacks on other crews."

The tavern suddenly felt too small, too quiet. Through the grimy window, Darius could see the city going about its business. Merchants closing shops, watch patrols making rounds, ordinary people living ordinary lives. When had he become one of them? When had the extraordinary become something to fear instead of something to chase?

Darius felt something shift inside him. A decision crystallizing from a year of frustration.

"We're thieves," he said quietly. "We don't let this happen to our own."

"She's not our—"

"Isn't she?" He looked at each of them. "How many jobs did we cross paths on? How many times did we end up in the same taverns, the same celebrations? She's one of us. Part of what we are."

"Were," Maren corrected softly. "What we were."

Were. Past tense. Everything was past tense now. But watching his crew—seeing the defeat in their shoulders, the acceptance of their diminished state—something inside Darius snapped. The same thing that had made him leap off that first rooftop years ago, that had driven him to steal an entire ship just to prove he could. The thing that made him Darius Adalan instead of just another street thief with quick fingers and quicker feet.

"No." Darius moved to his coat, checking his knives by habit. "What we are. What we're going to be again."

"Darius, what are you—"

"Get your gear." He turned back to them, and for the first time in a year, his grin had real fire in it. "We're going to rob a bank."

Stunned silence.

"A bank?" Maren's voice cracked. "Are you insane?"

"Maybe." Darius pulled on his coat. "The City Reserve on Goldsmith Row. They just installed new dynamo locks that are supposed to be unbreakable."

"The City Reserve?" Inora stood slowly. "That's Vivienne's bank. Where the Gaming Commission keeps their—"

"Their emergency funds. Their tax collections. Their dirty little secrets." His grin widened. "Everything they've squeezed out of this city for the past year."

Inora blinked. "You want to rob Vivienne Dragunova."

"I want to remind this city what real thieves look like." He moved toward the door. "I want tomorrow's headlines to scream our names. I want Balar, whoever he is, to know we're coming. And I want Lars hells be damned Harrow to read about it over his morning coffee and choke on his jealousy."

"We don't have a plan," Maren protested. "We don't have blueprints, schedules, inside information—"

"We'll figure it out." Darius paused at the door. "That's what we do. That's who we are. Now are you coming, or do I need to find a crew with balls?"

The insult hung in the air. Then Rurik stood, cracking his knuckles.

"Let's go," he rumbled.

Inora sighed, but she was already moving for her lockpicks. "This is insane."

"The best jobs always are." Maren was grinning now, that manic light in his eyes that meant his engineering brain was already working. "Those new dynamo locks... I've got some ideas."

"That's my crew." Darius yanked the door open. "Time to remind this city why they used to write songs about us."

"They never wrote songs about us," Inora pointed out.

"Then let's give them a reason to start."

He strode out into the night, his crew scrambling to follow.

✧

The ceiling had forty-seven cracks.

Trin knew because she'd counted them. Multiple times. It was something to do between the waves of drugged sleep and the moments of clarity that came less and less often. Forty-seven little lightning bolts spreading across plaster that had probably been white once but now looked the color of old bones in the dim light.

She tried to shift, to ease the ache in her back, but the restraints held firm. Leather straps across her wrists and ankles, professionally done. Not tight enough to cut off circulation—her captor was careful about that—but not loose enough to work free either.

She'd tried. Hells, how she'd tried in those first days when the drugs weren't as heavy, when she still had fight in her.

Now she just lay there, counting cracks and waiting for the next visit.

The room smelled of antiseptic and something else—mold, maybe, creeping through the walls of whatever slum safe house this was. No windows. Just the one door with its heavy lock, and a single dynamo lamp that cast more shadows than light. A bedside table held medical supplies: bandages, bottles of clear liquid, syringes that made her stomach turn every time she looked at them.

Her chest ached with each breath. Not the sharp, drowning agony of that first moment on the train when the knife went in—that was a pain she'd never forget, the feeling of air going where air should never be, of her lung collapsing like a punctured balloon. Now it was duller, deeper. Healing pain.

Which meant she'd been here... how long?

Time had become meaningless. The drugs made sure of that. She'd surface from the gray fog to find food gone cold on the bedside table, or wake to the feeling of bandages being changed, always by those careful, gloved hands. Never a word. Never a face. Just the mask.

That damn mask.

Black leather, featureless except for the symbol. That horrific eye.

She'd memorized every stitch, every subtle curve. It was the only face she'd seen in... days? Weeks? The routine never varied. He'd come in three times a day—morning, midday, evening, though she only knew that from the consistency, not from any natural light. Food. Water. The humiliating necessity of the bedpan. Fresh bandages if needed. A new syringe of whatever kept her floating in this half-world between consciousness and oblivion.

Always in silence.

At first, she'd tried talking. Pleading. Demanding. Threatening. She'd cycled through every emotion—rage, fear, desperation, even attempting charm. Nothing. He moved with mechanical precision, did what needed doing, and left.

Like she was a piece of furniture that needed dusting. An obligation. A problem to be managed.

The drugs were wearing off again. She could tell by the way the pain sharpened, how her thoughts began to clear like fog burning off in sunlight. He'd calculated the doses perfectly— enough to keep her manageable but not enough to kill her. Just enough to make her wish she were dead.

Footsteps in the hallway.

Trin's body tensed involuntarily, a response she hated. The familiar rhythm—heavy boots, purposeful stride. Not rushed but not leisurely either. The footsteps of someone with an unpleasant task they'd done too many times to hesitate over.

The lock clicked. Three turns, like always. The door swung open with a creak that probably could have been fixed with oil but never was. Maybe he liked the warning it gave. Maybe he wanted her to have those few seconds to prepare herself for another round of silent humiliation.

He filled the doorway—tall, broad-shouldered, dressed in the same dark clothes as always. The mask turned toward her, checking her condition with a clinical tilt of the head. Satisfied she was conscious enough, he moved into the room with that same mechanical efficiency.

The tray came first. Set on the bedside table with barely a sound. She could smell it—some kind of broth, bread, the faint sweetness of fruit. Her stomach turned. Not from the food itself but from what it represented. Another meal. Another day. Another step in this endless routine that was slowly driving her mad.

He moved to the medical supplies next, selecting what he needed with practiced ease. The syringe. Always the syringe. Trin's breath quickened despite herself. She hated the drugs, hated the fog they brought, but part of her craved them too. In the fog, she didn't have to think about Lars not finding her. About what this man planned to do when she was healed enough. About whether anyone even knew she was alive.

"Wait." The word came out as a croak. Her throat was dry despite the water he regularly provided.

He paused, syringe in hand, but didn't respond. Just stood there like a statue in dark leather.

"Please." She hated the weakness in her voice but couldn't help it. "Just... talk to me. Say something. Anything."

Nothing. He moved toward her, and she tried to pull away despite the restraints. Pointless. The needle slipped into her arm with the same professional competence he did everything else. The plunger depressed slowly, measured.

She could feel it starting already, that cottony sensation creeping up from her extremities. But not fast enough. Not before the rest of the routine.

The first time, she'd fought despite her injuries, thrashing against the restraints until her chest felt like it was tearing apart again. He'd waited her out with inhuman patience, then proceeded anyway. Now she just closed her eyes and tried to pretend she was somewhere else. Anywhere else.

But this time, with the drugs not quite taking hold yet, with days or weeks of silence pressing down on her, something snapped.

"You coward."

The words surprised her as much as him. He paused in his movements, hands stilling for just a moment before continuing.

"You coward," she said again, stronger this time. "What kind of man keeps a woman chained up like an animal? Won't even speak to her?"

Still nothing. He finished what he was doing, movements as clinical as ever. The humiliation burned hotter than the healing wound in her chest.

"I've known some bastards in my time," she continued, words tumbling out now that the dam had broken. "Thieves, people who'd sell their own mothers for a copper coin. But even they had more dignity than this. Even they'd look you in the eye while they ruined you."

He was putting his implements away. The sound of cupboards closing was jarring in the silence that followed her words.

"Is that what this is about? You're working up the courage to kill me?" A bitter laugh escaped her. "Just hovering around, waiting for the right moment? Well, here's a secret—there is no right moment. There's no clean way to murder someone who can't fight back."

The mask never turned toward her.

"I wouldn't treat my worst enemy like this," she said. There were rules. Codes. You stole, you conned, sure. You didn't... whatever this was. This slow dissolution of humanity, one silent visit at a time.

"But maybe that's the point." The drugs were creeping higher now, making her tongue feel thick, but she forced the words out. "Maybe you like it. Having that power. Is that it? Does it make you feel like a big man, taking care of the helpless woman?"

He was at the door now, hand on the handle. Ready to leave her to another stretch of drugged darkness and ceiling cracks.

"Just kill me." The words came out flat, exhausted. "Whatever you're waiting for, whatever sign you need—this is it. I'm tired. I'm so damn tired of this. So just do it already."

His hand tightened on the door handle.

"Or are you not man enough for that?"

He stopped.

For the first time in however long she'd been here, he completely stopped. His shoulders dropped, the rigid posture failing like someone had cut his strings. His head bowed forward, and she heard him take a breath—ragged, human.

Slowly, so slowly she thought she might be imagining it, his hand rose to the mask.

The clips released with soft clicks that sounded like gunshots in the silence. One at the temple. One at the jaw. The mask came away in his hand, and for a moment he just stood there, back still to her, shoulders rising and falling with breaths that sounded too loud, too real after all that silence.

Then he turned around.

Trin's breath caught in her throat.

She knew that face. Those dark eyes with their perpetual intensity, now rimmed with exhaustion. The sharp jawline, softened by days of stubble. The mouth that was usually set in determined lines, now slack with something that might have been defeat.

"Myrim?" The name came out as barely a whisper.

Captain Aric Myrim. Former captain. Liora's and Shelle's lover. A lawman to his core. The last person in Azoria she would have expected to see behind that mask.

He looked older than when she'd last seen him. More gaunt. The circles under his eyes were so dark they looked like bruises, and there was a tremor in his hands as he set the mask on a shelf by the door.

"I had no choice," he said, and his voice was rough from disuse. How long had he been silent? As long as she'd been here?

Trin stared at him, mind struggling to process this impossibility. Myrim. Straight-arrow Myrim who'd spent years chasing them, who'd turned every encounter into a game of principle versus necessity. Who'd loved rules and order and justice above everything else.

Who'd loved Liora.

"You..." She couldn't form the words. The drugs were taking hold now, making everything feel distant and strange, but this— this was real. Too real.

"She threatened them." His voice was barely above a whisper. "Vivienne... she made it clear what would happen to Shelle and Liora if I don't..." He gestured vaguely at the room, at her, at the whole situation.

He moved closer, and she could see him clearly now in the dim light. This wasn't the composed captain she remembered. This was someone hollow, carved out from the inside and left with nothing but the motions of living.

"Every time I put on that mask, I tell myself I'm protecting them. Keeping them safe. That as long as I do what she wants, they'll never know how close they came to..." He couldn't finish the sentence.

"Myrim." Her tongue felt thick, the drugs pulling her under, but she fought against them. "Please. You have to stop this. This isn't you."

"No?" A bitter smile twisted his features. "Maybe this is exactly who I am. Who I've always been. I just needed the right push to see it."

He picked up the empty syringe, stared at it like he'd never seen one before. "I can't stop. If I stop now, she'll destroy them. Everything I've done, everything I've become—it's all to keep them breathing."

"It doesn't work that way." She could barely keep her eyes open now, but she had to make him understand. "Vivienne doesn't let go once she has her claws in. You know that. Liora would rather die than see you do this. Than to see what you've done to Lars.

His face hardened at Lars's name, jaw clenching.

"Lars." The name came out like something bitter he needed to spit out. "Lars brought this on himself. On all of you. Playing his games, thinking he could outwit everyone, thinking there wouldn't be consequences." His hands curled into fists. "If he'd just stayed away from Vivienne, if he hadn't tried to play her..."

He turned away, running a hand through his disheveled hair. "I'll figure something out. There has to be a way. Some angle Vivienne hasn't considered, some leverage I can find. I just need time."

"Time?" Trin would have laughed if she had the strength. "How much time? How many more people are you going to hurt while you're figuring it out?"

"As many as it takes," he said flatly. "To keep them safe? As many as it takes."

The drugs won. Trin felt herself sliding into that gray place, Myrim's face blurring above her. The last thing she saw was him putting the mask back on, becoming Balar again, becoming the monster that hunted in the dark.

But now she knew the monster's name.

And somehow, that made it worse.

THE MASK FALLS

13

The copper coil snapped.

Again.

Liora stared at the frayed ends, her hands trembling with exhaustion. Three hours she'd been at this. Three hours of trying to modify her voice amplifier at the cramped workbench she'd set up in the corner of their condo's living room.

The morning's shouting in the square had left her throat raw, despite the honey and tea Shelle kept pushing on her. How many faces had turned away? How many people had crossed the street to avoid the crazy woman with her sketches and her desperation? Her voice was giving out, but she couldn't stop. Wouldn't stop. Hence the amplifier.

If she could just get the resonance frequency right. Her fingers were stained with lubricant and copper dust, and somewhere beneath the grime were traces of blood from where she'd sliced her thumb on a sharp edge and hadn't bothered to bandage it.

"You need to eat something."

Liora didn't look up at Shelle's voice. Couldn't. If she stopped working, stopped moving, the crushing weight of failure would flatten her completely.

"I'm not hungry."

"That's what you keep saying." Shelle moved across their small living space, her usual confident stride subdued. She set a plate on the only clear corner of the workbench—bread, cheese, some dried fruit that had seen better days. "You're all going to waste away before we find her."

The words hung in the air between them. Before we find her. Not if. Shelle was trying so hard to stay hopeful.

But it was the same dance they'd been doing for days. Shelle would bring food. Liora would ignore it. The food would sit there going cold while Liora tinkered and Shelle found excuses to stay close—reorganizing the same supplies, wiping down surfaces that were already clean. Anything to avoid talking about the real weight in the room.

Liora's hands stilled on the ruined coil. She couldn't bring herself to respond, couldn't match that optimism. Not after two weeks of nothing.

Shelle sighed, pulling up one of their mismatched dining chairs. Even exhausted and worried, she moved with that fluid grace that had first caught Liora's attention all that time ago.

"I heard something at the Copper Griffin last night," Shelle said carefully. "Some drunk was claiming he saw a woman matching Trin's description."

Liora's head snapped up, hope flaring hot and painful in her chest. "Where? When?"

"That's the thing." Shelle's expression was apologetic. "When the barkeep pressed him, offered actual coin for details, the man admitted he'd made it up. Thought he could get free drinks for information about the famous missing thief."

The hope died as quickly as it had sparked, leaving Liora feeling hollow. Her hand swept across the workbench, sending components scattering. A lens rolled off the edge, hitting the floor with a musical chime.

"Bastard," she muttered, though there was no heat in it. Just bone-deep weariness.

She started to bend down for the lens, then paused. Her gaze drifted across their small condo—past the cluttered table in the middle, past the kitchen alcove, to the unmade bed at the far end. The bed that had been too big these past two weeks. Too empty.

"Nearly two weeks," she said quietly. "Two weeks of looking in all the wrong places."

Shelle followed her gaze. They both knew what the empty bed meant. Who should have been there. The shape of the absence was as clear as if he'd left an outline in the sheets.

Neither of them said his name.

"Maybe we're not looking in the wrong places," Shelle said carefully. "Maybe we're looking for the wrong things."

Liora bent to retrieve the lens, its weight familiar in her palm. The dynamo energy pulsed faintly through the crystal, a steady heartbeat of power, and something about that rhythm triggered a memory. Her workshop. Shelle laughing at her theories. The dynamo girls, ready to revolutionize—

"Oh." The word escaped as barely a breath. She stared at the lens, mind racing. "Oh, hells."

"Liora?"

"Biodynamics." The word tumbled out, thick with possibility.

"What?"

"Don't you remember?" Liora's voice grew stronger, excited. She scrambled to her feet, clutching the lens. "That day in my old workshop, when we were planning the warehouse job. I told you about biodynamic signatures—how every person has a unique dynamo field, like a fingerprint but made of energy."

Shelle's eyes widened with recognition. "You said you could track people with it. I laughed, said it sounded like magic."

"And I said there's no such thing as magic." Liora was already moving, pulling components from various half-finished projects. "Just science we don't understand yet. Oh hells, why didn't I think of this before?"

"Because you've been running on no sleep and pure desperation?" Shelle suggested gently. "Liora, are you sure this will work? It's been a long time. Her signature could have degraded, or—"

"No." Liora shook her head firmly, hands already working to modify the lens housing. "Biodynamic signatures don't fade that quickly. They're part of who we are, woven into our very being. If Trin is anywhere in this city, if she's still—"

Her voice caught. "If she's still alive, I can find her."

"What do you need?"

"I need something of Trin's. Something she wore frequently, carried constantly. The biodynamic residue would be strongest on something like that." Liora's mind was already calculating modifications, energy requirements, range limitations. "And I need copper. Lots of it. The pure stuff, not the recycled scrap everyone's been hoarding."

A thought flickered through her mind, sharp and unwanted. *Or I could tune it to Myrim's signature. If he's been—*

No. She slammed that door shut before the thought could finish forming. Her hands tightened on the lens until her knuckles went white.

"I'll get Lars. I'm sure he'll be able to get something from their apartment." Shelle was already heading for the door. "And I know where to find copper. Might have to call in some old favors, but..."

"Shelle." Liora's voice stopped her at the threshold. "Thank you. For the food. For the information. For not giving up."

A sad smile tugged at Shelle's lips. "Dynamo girls, remember? We stick together."

Then she was gone, leaving Liora alone with her hope and her fear and the idea that might—*might*—bring Trin home.

Her hands moved with renewed purpose, stripping wires, adjusting focal points, recalibrating the energy matrix. The science flooded back, equations and theories she'd pushed aside for too long. A tracking radius of maybe half a mile to start— she'd need amplifiers to extend it. The signature would be faint after so much time.

A year ago, Liora had found Thume's warehouse by following massive dynamo signatures. Now she'd find one single, precious life by following the faintest whisper of energy.

She just hoped that whisper was still there to find.

If Trin was unconscious, would her signature be weaker? If she was... No. Liora forced her hands to stay steady as she soldered a connection. The signature would be there. It had to be. Because if she'd spent all this time shouting at strangers while the answer was sitting in her own workshop—

The solder sparked, and she jerked back. Focus. One connection at a time. One breath at a time. One more chance to bring her family home.

The wind cut across Vivienne's estate patio with autumn's bite. She stood with her back to the gathering, hands clasped behind her as she gazed out over the rolling hills.

The windmills dotted the landscape like sentries. Their blades turned with mechanical precision—a sight that usually brought her satisfaction.

Today, they only reminded her of how much was slipping through her fingers.

The dynamo heaters hummed around the patio's perimeter, copper coils glowing warm against the encroaching cold. She'd positioned them strategically. Not just for comfort—to create an intimate circle that would draw her guests together. Make them lean in. Listen.

She could hear them behind her now. Garrett from the Foundryworkers Union, weathered hands wrapped around crystal brandy. Council members Breslin and Belmani, still flushed from their journey south. The Drakorian ambassador Selan, silent as a blade. Markus, her financial fixer, clutching his ledger like a shield.

And Diligence. Beautiful, deadly Diligence, watching everything with predator's eyes.

"The view never fails to impress," Garrett was saying, gesturing toward the distant city. "Must be nice, having this perspective on things."

Perspective, indeed. From here, Azoria looked manageable. Contained. The smoke rising from its districts seemed no more threatening than incense.

She turned then, jade eyes sweeping over her assembled guests. Each one represented a piece of the machine she was building. Each one chosen for what they could provide—and what they stood to gain.

"Gentlemen. Councilwoman. Diligence." She moved toward them with fluid grace. "Thank you for making the journey. I trust the road wasn't too taxing?"

Councilman Breslin shifted in his chair, uneasy despite the brandy. "Lady Dragunova, when your message said urgent matters, we came as quickly as we could. The city's been..."

He gestured vaguely, searching for words that wouldn't sound like criticism.

"Chaotic," Councilwoman Belmani finished for him. "Ever since the train incident two weeks ago."

The train incident. Such a delicate way to describe disaster. Thume's escape, orchestrated by that bastard Lars and his crew. Balar's failure to prevent it.

And worse—Balar taking Trin without her permission. Without her knowledge. Like some rabid dog slipping its leash.

Vivienne's fingers tightened behind her back. Her voice remained silk-smooth. "Chaos often precedes necessary change. The question is whether we guide that change or allow it to consume us."

She moved to her chair—the only one positioned to command the full circle. Settled into it with the poise of a queen holding court. The setting sun caught the silver in her hair, casting her face in dramatic relief.

"Tell me, Garrett," she said. "How are your people handling the copper shortage?"

Garrett's jaw worked before he spoke. "Not well, I'll be honest. Production's down thirty percent across the foundries. Workers are getting restless. Some are talking about strikes."

He leaned forward, elbows on his knees. "They're scared, Lady Dragunova. When the copper runs dry, what happens to their jobs? Their families?"

"Fear can be useful," Diligence murmured from the patio's edge. She watched both the gathering and the approaches to the estate. "It makes people receptive to alternatives."

Ambassador Selan spoke for the first time. His accented voice carried Drakorian precision. "My country has been monitoring Azoria's situation with great interest. The disruption of traditional power sources presents great opportunity."

Good. Let them see the opening she was providing. Let them understand this conversation was about profit as much as survival.

"The emergency powers vote," Councilwoman Belmani said suddenly, her voice tight with anxiety. "Lady Dragunova, there's been talk. Some council members are questioning the timing. The necessity."

Now they'd come to it. The heart of why she'd called them here. Where the city's smoke couldn't quite reach and the wind carried away inconvenient words.

She stood again, moving to the patio's balustrade. "The vote was scheduled for next month. But circumstances evolve."

"What do you mean?" Breslin asked, though his tone suggested he already suspected.

Vivienne turned back to face them. Now her mask of perfect control showed the first hairline cracks. "I mean that we can no longer afford to wait. The copper crisis worsens daily. The criminal element grows bolder—Lars Harrow and his crew made that abundantly clear."

She paused, letting the weight of unspoken concerns settle over them like evening shadows. How could she explain that Balar—her supposed weapon—had gone rogue? That somewhere in the city's underbelly, he held a prisoner she'd never authorized him to take?

One more month. That's all she'd needed. One more month to have everything in place.

"The crystal shipments from Drakoria will arrive in eighteen days," she continued aloud. "Eighteen days to completely transform this city's power infrastructure. To free us from dependence on copper that's become increasingly scarce and unreliable."

Markus cleared his throat nervously. "The financial projections are substantial. The conversion alone will require—"

"Will require investment, yes." Vivienne's voice carried an edge of steel now. "Investment that will pay dividends for generations. But more importantly, it will ensure stability. Control."

She let that sink in. "Order in a city that's teetering on the edge of chaos."

Garrett frowned. "And the workers? The foundries that can't convert to crystal processing? What happens to them?"

"They adapt," Diligence said with casual brutality. "Or they find new employment. In the security sector, perhaps."

Vivienne shot her a warning glance. *Subtlety, not sledgehammers.* Though perhaps Diligence's bluntness served a purpose—it made her own proposals seem reasonable by comparison.

"The transition will be carefully managed," she assured Garrett. "Those who prove adaptable, who show loyalty to the new order, will find opportunities. Azoria will emerge stronger, more prosperous."

Her voice hardened. "But it requires decisive action."

Ambassador Selan nodded approvingly. "Drakoria has great faith in your vision, Lady Dragunova. As it always has. The resources we're providing represent a significant commitment to Azoria's future."

And to Drakoria's influence. But that was a price she was willing to pay. Better to rule a city beholden to foreign interests than to lose control entirely. Particularly when it was her homeland.

"Which brings us to the vote." She returned to her chair. The heaters' warmth seemed insufficient against the growing chill. "I'm moving to accelerate the timeline. The emergency powers legislation will be brought before the council in three days, not three weeks."

The silence that followed was pregnant with implications. Emergency powers would give her unprecedented authority. She could implement the crystal transition without legislative oversight. Reshape Azoria according to her vision without the tedious process of democratic debate.

"Three days," Belmani repeated slowly. "That's ambitious."

"Necessary," Vivienne corrected. "The current crisis provides the perfect justification. Copper shortages. Criminal activity. The threat of further disruption."

She leaned forward slightly. "The council will vote to grant emergency powers because the alternative is watching the city tear itself apart."

"And if they refuse?" Breslin asked.

Vivienne's smile was winter-sharp. "They won't. Because each of you represents constituencies that stand to profit enormously from the transition."

She began to tick off benefits on her fingers. "Garrett's union will have exclusive contracts for crystal installation and maintenance. Our esteemed council members will oversee the redistribution of copper reserves—very lucrative oversight, I'm told."

Her gaze fixed on Markus. "And you, dear man, will manage the financial instruments that make it all possible. The loans, the bonds, the investment opportunities. Quite a portfolio to build a career on."

The implications hung in the air like smoke from the distant foundries. Everyone at this table would profit. Everyone had a stake in her success. Or, rather, everyone was now complicit in her success or failure.

Nonetheless, approval rippled through the gathering. But even as it did, Vivienne felt the familiar chill of unfinished business. The variables she couldn't control.

Garrett leaned forward. "And what about your attack dog?"

She frowned. "Sorry, who are you referring to?"

"You know damn well who I'm referring to," Garrett snorted. "Balar. The devil in black, as some call him."

Diligence's eyes sharpened with interest. "He has definitely become a liability."

Vivienne met her gaze briefly but betrayed no recognition. Was the woman mocking her? Or just playing it up for the crowd?

"Balar will not be a concern," she said. "He poses no threat to us."

Yet he has Lars's woman.

The thought of Lars sent an unwelcome flutter through her chest. Anger and hunger and something else she refused to name. He'd walked into her office barely a week ago, armed and desperate.

The way he'd looked at her... not with careful calculation, but with raw, bleeding emotion.

Vivienne had told Lars she didn't know where Trin was. Technically true—she hadn't known Balar's exact hiding place. But she'd suspected. She'd known her masked enforcer well enough to guess his methods.

But now time was running short. The crystal transition couldn't wait for her to resolve her complicated feelings about a man who'd played her once and would surely do so again.

"The vote will proceed in three days," she said, standing to signal the meeting's conclusion. "I trust each of you will ensure your respective constituencies understand what's at stake."

"And Balar?" Ambassador Selan asked as the group began to rise.

Vivienne gave him a withering glance. "Forget about Balar."

Her guests began to move toward the estate's interior. Toward waiting carriages and the journey back to the city. But Diligence lingered behind.

She often did. Preferring to be the last voice Vivienne heard. The final perspective before decisions crystallized into action.

"You're worried," Diligence observed.

Vivienne didn't deny it. Here, with only Diligence to witness, she could allow cracks to show. "The timeline is compressed. Variables are multiplying faster than I can control them."

"Lars?"

Always straight to the heart of it.

"Among other things."

"He loves her, you know. Trin." Diligence moved closer, voice dropping to that intimate register she used when sharing secrets. "Really loves her. The kind that makes men do stupid, dangerous things."

"I'm aware."

"Are you?" Diligence tilted her head, studying Vivienne's profile in the gathering dusk. "Because if Balar kills her—and let's be honest, he may have already—Lars won't just be angry. He'll be destroyed. Broken."

She paused, letting that sink in. "And broken men are either very useful... or very dangerous."

Vivienne's hands tightened on the balustrade. The windmills in the distance seemed to turn more slowly now. Their mechanical precision somehow ominous in the fading light.

"Which do you think he'll be?" she asked.

Diligence was quiet for a long moment, considering. "That depends," she said finally, "on what you choose to do about it."

The words hung between them like a challenge. Or perhaps an ultimatum.

One more month. Just one more month to have everything aligned.

But as the wind picked up, carrying the scent of smoke and distant thunder, she knew that time was a luxury she no longer possessed. The crystal transition would proceed. The emergency powers would be voted through.

And the variables—Lars, Balar, Trin, the growing unrest in the city—would have to be managed with whatever tools remained at her disposal.

Even if those tools were sharper and more dangerous than she'd originally intended.

The first drops of rain began to fall as Diligence finally turned to leave. Her footsteps echoed against the stone. Vivienne remained on the patio, watching the storm clouds gather over Azoria.

She tried to convince herself that she still controlled the lightning.

The medical supply closet smelled of antiseptic and stale fear. Myrim worked quickly, his gloved hands selecting what he needed from the shelves with practiced efficiency. Opiates. Clean bandages. Surgical thread. Antiseptic solution.

The same routine he'd been following for two weeks now.

The Lowtown clinic was perfect for this kind of work. Understaffed, overworked, with a rotating cast of harried attendants who barely looked up when someone in medical whites walked past. He'd cased it three times before making his first supply run, mapping the guard rotations, memorizing which corridors stayed empty during shift changes.

The same professional competence he had shown on the other side of his life, when he fought for what was right.

But his hands trembled slightly as he slipped another vial of pain medication into his bag. Because that wasn't his life. Not anymore. This was—

Don't think about it. Just get what you need and get out.

Behind him, footsteps echoed down the hallway. Myrim froze, listening. Two sets. Moving slowly, talking in low voices.

He closed the supply cabinet with deliberate care, shouldered his bag, and stepped to the closet door.

The voices passed without slowing. He exhaled.

It had been two weeks. Two weeks since the train. Two weeks since everything had gone to the hells and he'd made a choice that would haunt him until the day he died.

He could still see the knife sliding between Trin's ribs. Could still see the look of shock on her face as she realized what was happening. Could still hear the wet sound of her lung collapsing as blood filled her chest cavity.

He couldn't let an innocent woman die. That's what he'd told himself as he'd carried her unconscious body through Azoria's underbelly to the safe house.

But she required care. Medical attention. Supplies that didn't come cheap or easy in a city where copper was running short and everyone watched everyone else for signs of weakness.

So here he was. Stealing medicine like a common thief.

The irony wasn't lost on him.

Myrim slipped out of the supply closet, his white coat and forged credentials providing the perfect camouflage. Another doctor on rounds. Nothing to see here. He moved through the clinic's corridors with the confidence of someone who belonged, nodding to the few attendants he passed.

None of them questioned him. None of them looked twice. Part of him wished they would. To recognize him. Denounce him for what he had become.

But they didn't. They saw a medical professional doing his job. They didn't see the man who'd spent two weeks playing caretaker to a woman he'd nearly murdered. Who drugged her to keep her compliant. Who changed her bandages and fed her broth and would probably murder her anywa—

He sucked in a deep, harsh breath.

The exit came into view. He shoved the analysis of who he had become deep down. He was almost there. Just a few more steps and—

"Doctor?"

Myrim's blood turned to ice. He turned slowly, forcing his expression into polite inquiry. A young nurse stood behind him, clipboard in hand, looking harried and exhausted.

"Yes?"

"I'm sorry to bother you, but I don't recognize you. Are you new to the ward?"

Smile. Look tired. Like everyone else here.

"Covering for Dr. Hollis," he said smoothly. "Emergency surgery ran long. Just grabbing some supplies before I head back."

The nurse's expression softened with sympathy. "Oh, the factory accident? That was awful. How many casualties?"

Myrim's mind raced. Factory accident. Which factory? How many injured? He knew nothing about any emergency surgery, had no idea what she was talking about.

"Still assessing," he said carefully. "It's complicated."

She nodded knowingly. "These industrial incidents always are. Well, don't let me keep you. Those patients need you."

"Indeed they do."

He turned and walked away before she could ask anything else. His heart hammered against his ribs as he pushed through the clinic's main doors and into the grimy Lowtown street beyond.

Close. Too close.

But he had what he needed. The supplies that would keep Trin alive for another few days while her body slowly healed from what he'd done to her.

The walk back to the safe house took twenty minutes through winding alleys and forgotten passages. He'd memorized every route, every shortcut, every place where someone might spot Balar moving through the shadows. The mask stayed hidden until he was blocks away from any legitimate traffic.

Then it went on, and Myrim disappeared.

Balar walked the final few streets to the warehouse, a ghost in dark leather who moved with predatory silence. The same figure that Azoria's criminals had learned to fear over the past few weeks. The vigilante who struck without warning and left bodies in his wake.

Monster, Trin had called him. And she was right.

The warehouse door opened to his key. Inside, the familiar smell of dust and machine oil mixed with something else now—the antiseptic scent that clung to the makeshift medical room he'd set up.

His prisoner would be awake by now. The opiates wore off faster each time, her body building tolerance despite his careful dosing. Soon he'd have to increase the amounts or switch to something stronger.

Soon she'd be well enough to attempt escape.

Soon he'd have to decide what came next.

The medical bag felt heavier with each step as he climbed to the room where he'd kept her for two weeks.

Two weeks of radio silence with Vivienne. Two weeks of ignored messages and unanswered summons. He'd gone completely off-script, taken a prisoner without authorization, made a choice that had nothing to do with following orders.

The irony was bitter. He'd become Balar to follow orders. To be Vivienne's weapon. And the first time he'd acted on his own conscience, he'd made everything infinitely worse.

The lock disengaged with a soft click. Inside, he could hear movement. Trin shifting on the bed, testing her restraints out of habit rather than hope. Waiting for him to appear with more food she wouldn't eat and more drugs she'd fight until the needle found its mark.

Waiting for Balar to walk through that door.

But it was Myrim who stepped inside. Myrim carrying the supplies that would keep her alive another day. Myrim who was running out of ways to justify what he'd become and what he was doing to everyone he'd once sworn to protect.

Professional competence, he reminded himself as he set the bag down and began unpacking the medical supplies. *Just get through today.*

Tomorrow could wait.

Tomorrow would have to.

The door opened with its familiar scrape, and Trin's body responded before her mind could catch up—going limp, letting her head loll to the side. Playing dead had become second nature. Or playing dying. Whatever kept him from looking too close.

Through barely cracked eyelids, she watched Myrim— *Myrim,* her brain still screamed every time—move through his routine. The tray on the bedside table. The medical supplies laid out with the precision of someone who'd done this too many times. The syringe.

Always the syringe.

She let out a soft moan, fluttering her eyes like she was struggling toward consciousness.

Had to sell it. Had to make him believe she was weaker than yesterday, that the infection was winning. That whatever guilty conscience was eating at him from the inside needed to work harder, move faster.

"Water," she croaked, and wasn't entirely pretending. Her throat felt like she'd swallowed glass.

He moved without hesitation, bringing the cup to her lips with those steady hands that had once upheld the law in Azoria. Now they tilted water into the mouth of a woman he'd kidnapped and kept drugged for—how long? Two weeks? Three? Time blurred together in these hells of ceiling cracks and opiate dreams.

She drank slowly, letting some dribble down her chin. Weak. Pathetic. Exactly what he expected to see.

"Thank you," she whispered, and watched something flicker behind his eyes. Guilt? Shame? Good. Let it eat him alive.

The routine continued. Check the bandages—she moaned in pain even though it barely hurt anymore. Take her temperature—she'd been rubbing her face against the pillow earlier to raise it, hoping the slight fever would seem real. Note it all down in that little book of his like he was a real doctor instead of a lawman turned killer playing dress-up with someone else's life.

Then came the moment she'd been building toward for days.

"I need..." She let her voice trail off, eyes sliding away from his face. The embarrassment didn't have to be faked. Even after weeks of this humiliation, asking never got easier. "I need to use the bathroom."

He moved to help her, professional as always, but she could see the way his shoulders tensed. This was the part he hated most. The part that reminded him she was human, not just some problem to be managed.

"Myrim," she said as he adjusted her position, his name coming out slurred and desperate. "Aric. Please..."

His hands stilled. She'd been saying his name more lately, trying to break through whatever walls he'd built around himself. Trying to remind him of who he used to be. Who Liora and Shelle had loved.

"I won't tell," she continued, words tumbling over each other in drugged confusion. "Won't tell them what you did. Just... please. Let me go. I'll disappear. You'll never see me or Lars again."

Nothing. His face might as well have been carved from stone.

But his hands—there. The slightest tremor as he finished helping her. The tiniest crack in his armor.

She kept talking, babbling really, as he prepared the syringe. About Lars. About the crew. About how Liora would forgive him if he just stopped now.

Anything to keep him off balance.

"She loves you," Trin said as the needle approached her arm. "Liora loves you so much. Do you think... do you think she still dreams about you? I dream about Lars. Every night. Even here. Especially here."

The needle went in rougher than usual. Not much, just enough to tell her she'd hit a nerve. The plunger depressed quickly—too quickly. He wanted this over with. Wanted to escape her words and her presence and the mirror she kept holding up to his face.

"Thank you," she whispered again as he pulled the needle free. Let him think it was for the drugs, for the promised oblivion. Let him think she was grateful for the fog that would swallow her whole.

He gathered his things with sharp, efficient movements. No lingering today. No careful checking of her restraints. Just the desperate need to be anywhere but here, with anyone but her.

The door closed behind him with a final click.

Trin counted to thirty. Then thirty more. Then once more for good measure.

Come on. What are you—

She heard the outer door open and close.

The drugs were already working their way through her system, but it was different this time. The fog was there, creeping at the edges of her vision, but it wasn't the all-consuming blanket she'd grown used to. Too little, too fast, injected into her soft fatty tissue by hands that wanted to be done with her.

Myrim's first real mistake.

Trin tested her left wrist, the one she'd been working on for three days now. The restraint had loosened—not much, but combined with the weight she'd lost, the sweat making her skin slick, and the way she'd learned to dislocate her thumb just so...

Pop.

White-hot pain shot up her arm, but she'd felt worse. Hells, she'd felt worse from Myrim's knife between her ribs. This was nothing. This was freedom singing in her bones.

Her hand slipped free.

For a moment, she just stared at it. Her hand. Free. Moving because she wanted it to move, not because someone else allowed it. The simple beauty of it made her want to cry.

No time for that. The drugs were a ticking clock in her veins. She had maybe twenty minutes before the full dose hit. Less if Myrim decided to come back, though she doubted it. He'd run from her words like she'd set him on fire.

The other wrist came easier. Then her ankles, though those took longer, her free hands clumsy and shaking. Whether from the drugs or exhaustion or pure adrenaline, she couldn't tell. But it didn't matter. All that mattered was the last restraint falling away.

Trin sat up slowly, carefully. The world tilted, spun, settled into something resembling stability. Her legs dangled off the edge of the bed, pale and wasted-looking in the dim light. How long since she'd walked? How long since she'd been anything more than a prisoner in her own body?

Stand up, you useless piece of trash. Stand up and walk out of here.

Her feet hit the floor. Cold. Solid. Real. She pushed herself up, legs shaking like a newborn colt's, but they held. Tears fell from her eyes. By the hells, they held.

The room wasn't large. A few steps to the medical supplies. She grabbed a scalpel—small, sharp, better than nothing. A few more steps to test her balance. Each one stronger than the last. Her body remembering what it was made for. Not lying drugged in a bed, but moving, stealing, surviving.

The door. She'd watched him work the lock enough times, heard the mechanism's particular song. The scalpel slipped into the gap between door and frame. A twist, a careful application of pressure, and—

Click.

The same sound that had marked Myrim's exit now marked her escape. The door swung open to reveal a narrow hallway, dimly lit and stinking of mold.

She had no idea where she was. Some forgotten corner of Azoria's underbelly, no doubt. Somewhere screams wouldn't matter and disappearances went unnoticed.

Time to disappear herself.

The first breath of outside air was jarring. Shit and rot and industrial waste—the perfume of Lowtown's forgotten corners. To Trin, it smelled like freedom. Like life. Like everything Myrim had tried to take from her.

She stumbled through the warehouse door and into an alley, narrow and twisted and full of shadows. No idea which way led to safety. No idea which way led deeper into danger. The drugs made everything feel distant and strange, like she was watching herself from outside her own body.

Move. Just move.

Her bare feet splashed through puddles of things she didn't want to identify. Broken glass bit at her heels, but the pain felt distant, unimportant. What mattered was distance. What mattered was staying upright long enough to get away.

But away to where? She didn't recognize anything. The buildings stood like broken teeth, familiar in their decay but anonymous in their uniformity. Every corner looked like the last. Every shadow could hide Balar.

Oh hells, what was she thinking? Her foggy brain kept seeing him everywhere.

That figure at the end of the alley—was that his stance? The person huddled in a doorway—were those his eyes watching her? Paranoia and drugs mixed into a cocktail of terror that had her heart hammering against her ribs.

She turned a corner and froze. Something moved in the darkness ahead. Low to the ground. Eyes gleaming in what little light filtered down from the moon above. Balar.

No. A dog.

Mangy, scarred, ribs showing through patchy fur. It growled, low and warning, and Trin felt her legs start to shake harder. She couldn't fight off a stray dog. Could barely fight off a strong breeze in her current state.

"Easy," she whispered, voice slurring. "Easy, boy. Girl. Whatever you are. I'm not... I'm not going to hurt you."

The dog stepped forward, head low, teeth bared. Trin stepped back and felt her heel catch on something—a pipe, a brick, didn't matter. She went down hard, scalpel skittering away across the wet concrete.

This was it. This was how it ended. Not from Myrim's knife or Vivienne's orders, but from a hungry stray in a Lowtown alley. Memories oozed into her head. From noble to alley trash. There was something almost poetic about it.

But the dog didn't attack. It approached slowly, cautiously, that growl fading to something more curious. Its nose twitched, taking in her scent. The smell of sickness and drugs and weeks of captivity.

"Please," Trin whispered, though she wasn't sure what she was asking for. Mercy? Understanding? Just one fucking break in this nightmare she'd been living?

The drug fog was thickening now. Whatever dose Myrim had given her, it was catching up. Her limbs felt heavy, disconnected. The alley walls seemed to breathe, expanding and contracting like the belly of some massive beast.

She tried to stand and couldn't. Tried to crawl and barely managed a few feet before her arms gave out. The wet ground was cold against her cheek. When had she ended up on her side? Time kept skipping, moments lost between one blink and the next.

The dog circled her once, twice. She could hear its paws splashing through the same puddles she'd stumbled through. Could smell its wild scent mixing with the alley's decay. Her eyes wouldn't focus anymore, but she felt its presence.

The world was fading, darkness eating at the edges of her vision. But just before it claimed her completely, she felt something warm and wet against her face. The dog, licking the tears she hadn't realized she'd been crying.

Consciousness came and went like waves against a shore. Here, then gone. Real, then dream.

The dog's tongue against her cheek. Rough but gentle. Cleaning her face like she was a pup that had gotten too dirty playing.

Strange way to die, she thought with what little clarity remained. But at least she wouldn't die alone. That was something.

Her fingers found the dog's fur, matted and coarse but warm. Alive. Another heartbeat in the darkness when hers felt so ready to stop.

"Good dog," she whispered. Or thought she did. Words and thoughts were blurring together now, everything soft and distant and fading.

Somewhere far away, she heard footsteps. Voices. But they belonged to another world, one she was slipping away from with each shallow breath. The dog whined, low and worried, pressing closer to her side.

"Lars," she mumbled into the dirt. "Lars, I tried. I got out. I just... I can't..."

The alley faded. The cold faded. Everything faded except that warm presence beside her, standing guard over a broken thief who'd finally found her freedom, even if she couldn't hold onto it.

Then even that was gone, and Trin slipped under the waves.

A POISONED INTERLUDE

14

The basement of The Azoria Star smelled exactly as Lars expected—ink and machine oil, paper dust and the peculiar metallic tang of lead type. It was well past midnight, that dead hour when the Tavern District's most persistent drunks had found their doorways, but the press never truly slept.

Marinda Kelway looked up from her composing table as he descended the narrow stairs, her gray hair pinned back in the same practical bun she'd worn for the ten years he'd known her. The Star wasn't much—four pages on a good day, six after a big heist—but it had something the larger papers had sold off years ago: independence.

"Lars Harrow," she said, setting down her composing stick. "Haven't seen you in... well, a year or more anyway."

"Different times," Lars said, pulling the folded pages from his coat. The paper was soft from handling, covered in his cramped handwriting and crossed out words. Two weeks of sleepless nights distilled into ink.

Marinda took the pages with smudged fingers, unfolding them carefully. "What's this then?"

"Something that needs saying. And I need it in tomorrow's morning edition."

She raised an eyebrow but started reading. Lars watched her expression shift—curiosity to surprise to something that might have been approval. Or concern.

"You want me to run this as is?" she asked after the first pass.

"Every word."

She read it again, slower this time, and Lars could see her typesetter's mind already at work, calculating column widths and letter sizes. Then she moved to her type cases and began setting the headline, letter by letter, backwards in the composing stick.

"Read it to me," Lars said. "I want to hear how it sounds."

Marinda gave him a long look, then cleared her throat and began:

AN OPEN LETTER TO THE CITIZENS OF AZORIA

For three generations, my family has called Azoria home. My grandfather ran numbers in the shadows when thievery was still a hanging offense. My father was among the first to register when the Gaming Commission opened its doors. He said it was like watching the sun rise on a new world. This city raised me in its crooked streets and taught me that there's honor among thieves, if you know where to look.

I write to you now because that honor is dying.

For a year, we've pretended otherwise. We've kept our heads down, gone about our business, told ourselves that the bodies in the alleys were isolated incidents. That the blood washing into our gutters was somebody else's problem. We've let fear dress up as order and called it progress.

But I know this city. I know you.

Azoria was built on audacity, not brutality. Our thieves were artists who turned breaking and entering into ballet. Our forgers were poets who made lies sing truer than facts. Even our violence, when it came, had rules. You didn't kill someone over a picked pocket. You didn't put a knife in someone's ribs for the contents of their purse.

You certainly didn't hunt people and commit murder in a mask.

The Gaming Commission was supposed to civilize us. Give structure to our chaos. Make us respectable. And maybe it did, for a time. But what prowls our streets now isn't civilization. It's fear.

I speak, of course, of the one who calls himself Balar.

In two weeks, this masked killer has left more pain than the last thirty years of Commission enforcement combined. He strikes without warning, attacks without mercy, and disappears like smoke. Some say he works for the city. Some say he works for the highest bidder. Some say he's cleaning house.

I say he's a coward.

Any fool can put on a mask and play at being death. It takes no skill to ambush someone in an alley. No artistry in slitting throats. No honor in ruling through fear. This isn't justice. It is the opposite of everything Azoria represents.

So I make this offer public:

From my personal accounts, I will pay fifty thousand copper coins for information leading to the capture and unmasking of the killer known as Balar. This is not a call for vigilantism. This is a call for citizenship. Someone knows who hides behind that mask. Someone has seen where he goes when the hunting is done.

Because here's what I know: a city that trades in fear has already been robbed of its greatest treasure: its spirit. We are not ruled by terror. We are not cowed by masks. We are Azorians, and we deserve better than to bleed out in our own streets while someone plays at being our judge and executioner.

Don't let fear be our new currency. Don't let blood be our new language. And don't let some masked pretender make us forget who we are.

We are the city of the impossible heist. The city of the magnificent con. The city where a nobody can wake up a legend if they've got the nerve for it. That's our Azoria. That's worth fighting for.

Forever Azorian,
Lars Harrow

The press room fell silent except for the distant drip of a pipe. Marinda set down the pages, her expression unreadable.

"That's a lot of money," she said finally.

"It's enough."

"Enough to get yourself killed, maybe. Balar doesn't seem the type to appreciate public criticism."

Lars met her steady gaze. "Then he can come for me without a mask. Like an honest criminal."

She studied him for a long moment, taking in the hollow cheeks, the sleepless bruises under his eyes, the barely controlled tremor in his hands. Two weeks of searching, of failure, of Trin's absence carved into every line of his face.

"This won't bring her back," Marinda said gently.

"No. But it might bring him out. And when it does..." Lars didn't finish. Didn't need to.

Marinda nodded slowly, then turned to her type cases. "It'll take me three hours to set this. Another hour for the print run. You want the usual distribution?"

"Double it. I want one on every corner from the Gaming Commission headquarters to the Institute steps."

"That'll cost extra."

Lars pulled a leather pouch from his coat, heavy with copper and gold. "There's enough there for the printing and distribution. A little extra for the rush job. And the risk."

She weighed the pouch without opening it. "The risk is mine to take. Always has been." She paused, fingers already pulling type. "You know Vivienne won't like this."

"I'm counting on it."

"And the Gaming Commission?"

"Can't arrest someone for having an opinion. Not yet."

Marinda snorted. "Give them time." But she was already working, her hands moving with practiced efficiency, building his words letter by letter in reverse. "Come back at dawn. They'll be ready."

Lars watched her work for a moment longer, the click of type against type strangely soothing. Each letter was a small rebellion, each word a declaration. By tomorrow morning, all of Azoria would know that Lars Harrow was done playing defense.

He climbed the stairs slowly, exhaustion pulling at his bones. The night air was cold and sharp with the promise of rain. Somewhere in this city, Trin was suffering or dead. Somewhere, a masked killer thought himself untouchable.

Lars pulled his coat tight and began the long walk home. Tomorrow would bring consequences. Vivienne's rage. Balar's response. The Commission's attention.

Good.

Let them come. He'd spent two weeks in the shadows, searching, failing, breaking himself against the city's silence. Now it was time for a different approach. Time to remind Azoria—and himself—that it was thieves that ran this city.

The first drops of rain began to fall as he reached his district. Lars didn't quicken his pace. Let it wash the streets clean. Tomorrow, his words would dirty them again with truth.

Fifty thousand coppers for a mask.

It was a start.

Darius Adalan stumbled through the ornate doors of the City Reserve looking like death had fucked him twice and left without paying.

His skin, normally a healthy bronze, had taken on the waxy pallor of old cheese. Angry red splotches bloomed across his neck and hands like roses in a dead garden. His usually wild hair hung in greasy strands, and his clothes, soiled with ash and something that smelled suspiciously like rotting fish, clung to his frame.

He'd never looked so horrific. The effect was immediate and glorious.

"Water," he croaked, staggering toward the nearest teller window. His voice came out like gravel in a meat grinder. "Please... water..."

The teller, a pinch-faced woman behind metal bars with spectacles that magnified her horror, took three rapid steps backward. Her hand flew to her mouth. Around the bank's marble interior, heads turned. Conversations died. The click-clack of a dynamo abacus stopped mid-calculation.

Darius let his knees buckle—not too much, just enough to catch himself on the edge of a writing desk. The inkwell tipped, black liquid spreading across deposit slips like blood across snow. He coughed, a wet, rattling sound that he'd practiced at their base until Inora threatened to actually poison him if he didn't stop.

"Sir?" A guard approached, hand hovering near his club. "Sir, are you—"

That's when Darius really sold it.

His body convulsed like he'd been struck by lightning. His eyes rolled back, showing only whites, and foam—a delightful mixture of soap shavings and egg whites—frothed at his lips. He hit the floor hard, limbs twitching in a chaotic dance that sent a potted plant crashing to the ground.

"THE SPOTS!" he shrieked between convulsions. "THE SPOTS ARE SPREADING!"

The guard gasped. Every person in the bank froze.

"Everyone stay calm," the guard said, his voice suggesting he was anything but. "I'm sure it's just—"

"MOTHER OF HELLS!"

That was Rurik, right on cue. The bruiser stood near the account desk, pointing at Darius with a hand that shook just enough to be believable. For a usually quiet man built like a dynamo generator, Rurik had surprising theatrical range.

"I saw him at the docks yesterday! Near the Zarakaran freighter!" Rurik's voice climbed an octave, panic spreading through it like fire through dry wood. "The one they quarantined! Oh hells, oh hells, he's got the spots!"

The teller screamed.

Not a little shriek, but a full-throated, glass-shattering wail that set off a chain reaction of terror. Customers scrambled over each other like rats fleeing a sinking ship. A merchant knocked over an elderly woman in his haste to reach the door. A young clerk vaulted the counter, scattering papers like snow.

"No, wait!" The guard tried to restore order, but his heart wasn't in it. Not when Darius's convulsions had progressed to something that looked like a man trying to crawl out of his own skin. "We need to—"

That's when Rurik started twitching.

"No," the big man whispered, staring at his hands in mounting horror. "No, no, no, I touched the same door handle. I breathed the same air. I—"

He dropped instantly, his convulsions even more dramatic than Darius's. Where Darius had gone for unsettling realism, Rurik had chosen pure spectacle. His arms windmilled. His legs kicked. He made noises that suggested his soul was trying to escape through his nostrils.

The remaining customers didn't need a second invitation. They fled.

But the guards—bless their sense of duty—tried to maintain some semblance of control. The captain, a thick-necked man with more brass than brains, stood between the convulsing thieves and the door.

"Everyone remain calm!" he bellowed. "Seal the building! No one leaves until—"

The door burst open.

Inora stood silhouetted in the frame, dressed in a thick white robe, thick gloves, and a glass fish bowl over her head. She carried a large, two-handed dynamo... something. Maren had said it was for cutting down trees.

"Emergency medical corps!" she announced, her voice muffled but authoritative through the mask. "Everyone out now!"

"Thank the hells," the guard captain breathed. "These men, they're—"

"Dying," Inora confirmed grimly, sweeping into the bank. "Zarakaran Pox, third stage. Highly contagious. Mortality rate of ninety percent." She prodded Darius with her boot—a bit harder than necessary, the vindictive wench. "How many people have been exposed?"

The captain's face went from red to white so fast Darius thought he might faint. "The… the whole bank. Staff, customers, everyone."

"Then they're all at risk." Inora turned to address the remaining people. "Everyone out! Form a line outside for examination! Anyone who's touched these men, breathed near them, or shared the same air needs immediate treatment!"

"But the vault!" the bank manager protested, wringing his hands. "The deposits! We can't just—"

"It's locked, isn't it?" Inora snapped.

"Well, yes, but—"

"Then it'll keep. Unless you'd prefer to die guarding it?"

The manager needed no further convincing. He practically trampled two tellers in his rush for the exit.

Within sixty seconds, the City Reserve had gone from bustling financial institution to ghost town. The last guard slammed the door behind him, and Darius heard the beautiful sound of the entire block screaming—the universal signal for "plague inside, stay the hells away."

Darius sat up, wiping the foam from his mouth with his sleeve. "Bit much with the boot, don't you think?"

Inora pulled off the fish bowl. "You're the one who wanted authentic."

"I nearly shat myself when you started thrashing," Rurik admitted, climbing to his feet and dusting off his trousers. "Thought you were having a real fit."

"Method acting," Darius said airily, though his ribs hurt like hells from throwing himself around. "Now then, let's get to work. We've got maybe twenty minutes before some brave soul decides to check on the dying plague victims."

He strode to the main door and threw the heavy bolt, then added the security bar for good measure. The windows were already barred—banks were paranoid about people breaking in, not breaking out.

"Rurik, get the side entrance. Inora, keep watch."

Darius walked to the center of the vault antechamber, where the real prize waited behind six inches of solid steel and the finest, most impossible to break dynamo locks money could buy.

Uncrackable. Unopenable by any means short of divine intervention.

He raised his boot and stamped twice on the marble floor.

Nothing happened.

"Oh, for hells sake," Darius muttered, and stamped again, harder.

This time, something answered.

A muffled BOOM shook the floor beneath them, sending tremors up through their legs. Dust sifted down from the ceiling. The crystal chandeliers tinkled like wind chimes in a hurricane.

Then silence.

"Was that supposed to—" Rurik began.

A grinding sound cut him off. Metal on metal, gears turning, mechanisms engaging. The massive vault door shuddered, and then the wheel in its center began to spin.

The door swung open with a whisper of well-oiled hinges.

Maren stood in the doorway, absolutely filthy, covered head to toe in dust and debris. His hair stuck up at wild angles. His hands shook with what might have been exhaustion or might have been his usual state of barely controlled panic.

But his eyes—they sparkled with the pure, manic joy of a man who'd just solved the unsolvable.

"Hi guys," he said, voice cracking slightly. "Sorry about the wait. The dynamo hammer worked great but then I got a little, um, turned around? I didn't know if—"

"Maren," Darius said patiently. "Breathe."

The engineer sucked in a gulp of air. "Right. Yes. Breathing. Good idea." He stepped aside, gesturing into the vault with trembling hands.

"Any trouble?" Darius asked, though Maren's appearance suggested the answer.

"Trouble?" Maren laughed, a slightly hysterical edge to it. "No, no trouble. Just the standard terrifying-crawl-through-a-tunnel-while-operating-experimental-equipment trouble. Oh, and I might have accidentally cut through a sewer line. But I fixed it! Probably. We should leave soon."

Darius had seen a lot of beautiful things in his career. Sunset over the Azure Sea from a nobleman's roof. The sparkle of a perfectly cut emerald in candlelight. That one time he'd watched Lars fall face-first into a pile of horse shit during a chase.

But nothing—nothing—compared to the sight of a bank vault ready for plundering.

He stepped inside, already calculating weight and value, escape routes and fence prices. The vault was bigger than he'd expected, with shelves lining the walls and treasure in neat rows. His fingers itched to start grabbing, stuffing, taking everything that—

"Um." Rurik's voice cut through his reverie. "Boss?"

Darius followed his gaze to the shelves. Then blinked. Then blinked again.

"What the fuck?"

Where there should have been neat stacks of copper coins and bars, locked boxes of precious metals, there were... crystals. Thousands upon thousands of crystal charges, organized by size and quality, glowing faintly in the vault's dynamo lighting.

"Is this..." Inora picked up one of the charges, turning it over in her hands. "Are these all crystal charges?"

"Second generation by the look of them," Maren said, immediately going into analysis mode. "See the occlusion patterns? The slight irregularity in the matrix? These are early production, probably from just after Thume went to the pokey."

"But why?" Darius grabbed a larger crystal, about the size of his fist. It was heavier than he'd expected, and warm to the touch. "Why would a bank vault be full of crystal charges instead of, you know, money?"

"Maybe they're worth more than we think?" Rurik suggested, but even he sounded doubtful.

"No time to figure it out now," Inora said, ever practical. "We take them anyway. Money's money, even if it glows."

She was right. Darius shook off his confusion and slipped into leader mode. "Right. Rurik, get the bags from the tunnel. Maren, can these things explode if we handle them rough?"

"Nope."

"Fantastic. Let's go."

They worked with the efficiency of a crew that had robbed together for years. Rurik hauled up canvas sacks from the tunnel. Inora sorted crystals by size for maximum packing efficiency. Maren pocketed a few choice specimens while providing running commentary on their theoretical applications. Darius supervised and tried to ignore the growing certainty that something was very, very wrong with this picture.

A bank didn't hoard crystal charges. Banks hoarded money. That's what made them banks.

"That's the last of them," Rurik announced, hefting a bulging sack. The vault looked strangely empty, nothing left but dust.

"Then we're gone." Darius took one last look around, committing the scene to memory. This would make a great story, even if he didn't understand the punchline yet. "Everyone down—"

A commotion outside made them all freeze. Muffled voices. Lots of voices.

"Check outside," Inora whispered, already moving. She crept to the massive vault door and peered around its edge toward the bank proper. Her face went pale.

"Damn. City watch. And real medical corps. They're examining the staff outside."

"Tunnel. Now." Darius grabbed the nearest sack and dropped through the hole in the floor. The others followed, Maren pausing only to pat the vault door fondly before disappearing below.

The tunnel was a marvel of desperate engineering. Just tall enough to crouch-walk through, just wide enough for someone Rurik's size to squeeze along. It smelled of earth and sweat and the particular desperation that came from digging illegally beneath the city's financial district.

They moved fast, the sound of their breathing harsh in the enclosed space.

"Move, move, move!" Darius urged, pushing forward. The sacks of crystal charges clinked and chimed with each step, a musical accompaniment to their escape.

Within fifty feet, they reached a wooden door reinforced with iron bands.

"Please tell me this goes somewhere useful," Darius muttered.

"Sub-basement of the hat shop next door," Maren whispered, fumbling with the lock. "The owner's in Windale for the week. I, uh, might have encouraged his vacation with a fake letter about an inheritance."

The door opened into dusty darkness. They tumbled through, Rurik barely fitting, and found themselves surrounded by boxes of last season's millinery.

"Up," Inora ordered, already heading for the stairs. "They'll get into the vault soon enough."

They emerged into the shop proper, morning light filtering through display windows full of elaborate hats that no one in their right mind would wear. Maren had left everything ready—the back door unlocked, a cart in the alley covered with a tarp marked "TEXTILE DELIVERY."

"Load fast," Darius commanded. "We've got maybe two minutes before they expand the search."

As they prepared to leave, Darius held up one of the crystal charges, watching it catch the light. It was beautiful in its way, all internal fire and contained power. But it wasn't copper. It wasn't gold. It wasn't what they'd come for.

"What kind of bank," he asked the universe at large, "doesn't keep money in its vault?"

"The kind that knows something we don't," Inora said quietly.

That killed the celebratory mood. They'd pulled off the heist of the year, cracked an uncrackable vault, stolen everything inside. So why did it feel like they'd been playing someone else's game?

Darius didn't have an answer. But as they wheeled their cart full of stolen crystals through the streets of Azoria, dodging plague cordons and city watch inspectors, he couldn't shake the feeling that they'd just robbed the wrong vault at exactly the right time.

Silk sheets clung to Vivienne's skin. She lay on her back, savoring a few moments before the rigors of the day. The afternoon light filtered through gauze curtains, painting the room in shades of gold and shadow.

"You're thinking too hard," Diligence murmured. "I can practically hear the gears turning."

"I'm always thinking." Vivienne turned to study her companion. "It's what keeps this city from eating itself."

"Mmm." Diligence shifted onto her side, propping herself up on one elbow. "Is that what has you so tense? Harrow's little newspaper tantrum?"

Vivienne's jaw tightened. "You've read it?"

"Everyone's read it. Fifty thousand coppers for information on Balar?" Diligence laughed. "Such desperation. Lars is grasping at straws."

"He's rallying support."

"He's making noise." Diligence's voice had that particular tone of amused condescension she'd perfected. "Poor Lars, feeling helpless. So he does what men like him always do—throws money at the problem and pretends his words have power."

"His words do have power." Vivienne hated admitting it, but the morning edition of The Azoria Star had sold out in three districts before noon. "The people listen to him."

"The people listen to whoever speaks loudest." Diligence smiled. "And after the vote, you'll have all the volume you need. Emergency powers, darling. The council won't dare refuse, not with copper running short and bodies in the streets."

Vivienne considered this. Lars's article was theater. The bounty on Balar was desperation dressed as action. Soon, the emergency powers act would pass, and she'd have the legal authority to—

The door burst open with a crash that sent both women upright.

"Madame Dragunova! I'm sorry, I'm so sorry, but—"

The attendant stood frozen in the doorway, eyes wide as saucers. He was young, probably new, certainly unprepared for the sight of Azoria's leader and her advisor in their current state.

Vivienne didn't bother covering herself. Her voice came out ice-cold and twice as sharp. "You have exactly ten seconds to explain why you're still breathing."

"The bank!" The words tumbled out in a panicked rush. "The City Reserve on Goldsmith Row. It's been robbed!"

Diligence laughed, a delighted sound that made the attendant flinch. "Robbed? How wonderfully nostalgic. I thought we'd moved past such interesting times."

Vivienne's stillness was more terrifying than any shout. "Continue."

The attendant gulped. "The... the bank manager reports all vault contents were stolen. The perpetrators created a plague scare, evacuated the building, and somehow breached the vault from below. The manager says... he says witnesses identified Darius Adalan."

"Of course they did." Vivienne's voice was perfectly calm. Too calm. The kind of calm that preceded catastrophe. "And the vault contents?"

"Gone. All of it. Every last item."

Vivienne nodded slowly, her gaze fixed on something beyond the room, beyond the stammering attendant, beyond the physical world entirely. In her mind, she was calculating.

Who knew about the crystal charges? Who could have tipped Darius off? Who would dare?

"GET OUT!"

The attendant fled, nearly tripping over his own feet in his haste. The door slammed shut behind him.

Vivienne was already moving, pulling on a comfortable robe. She began to pace as her mind raced. These thieves didn't know when to give up, did they? Well, they'd learn.

"We need to find Balar. He'll have to kill Adalan. Tonight," she demanded. "Make it public, make it messy. Send a message that—"

"Darling, are you trying to prove Lars right?" Diligence hadn't moved from the bed, utterly unconcerned. "What Darius did is perfectly legal."

Vivienne froze mid-step.

"The Gaming Commission rules still apply," Diligence continued, stretching like a cat. "He stole from a legitimate target during business hours, and he got away. Rather elegant, actually. A plague scare? I'm almost impressed."

"He stole from me."

"He stole from a bank that happens to hold your property. There's a distinction."

Vivienne's hands clenched into fists, silk bunching between her fingers. Then, slowly, deliberately, she relaxed. When she turned back to Diligence, her smile was a weapon refined by years of practice.

"You're right, of course. How foolish of me to let emotion cloud judgment." She moved to her vanity, began brushing her hair with long, measured strokes. "This could work to our advantage."

"Oh?" Diligence finally rose, padding across the room to stand behind Vivienne. Their eyes met in the mirror. "Do tell."

"The emergency powers vote. We push it through today. Now. While the news is fresh and the council is rattled." The brush moved through her hair like a metronome, keeping time with her thoughts. "A bank robbed in broad daylight? Crystal charges scattered to the winds? Clearly, the current system has failed."

"And once you have emergency powers..."

"The Gaming Commission rules become flexible." Vivienne set down the brush, turned to face her advisor. "But first, we need to ensure our inventory remains ours."

"Those crystal charges were only a fraction of what you've stockpiled."

"A fraction too much in the wrong hands." Vivienne moved to her desk, already reaching for parchment and ink. "We need a gathering. All the major players. City leaders, crew leaders, even our theatrical Mr. Harrow and Mr. Adalan."

Diligence sat on a nearby chaise, watching with amused interest. "A truce meeting?"

"A reckoning." Vivienne's pen moved across the page with sharp, decisive strokes. "Darius has his prizes, but he doesn't know what they're for. Lars has his bounty, but no idea who he's hunting. And I have the power to destroy them both, but..." She paused, smiled. "But sometimes the blade kept sheathed cuts deeper than the one that draws blood."

"So you'll call them together. Make them face each other. Make them face you."

"I'll remind them who holds the cards in this city." Another line, another name. "Thume might have fled to Zarakar, but Azoria is mine. Has always been mine. They just need reminding."

She signed the edict with a flourish, then rang for a different attendant. One who knew how to knock.

"When?" Diligence asked.

"In three nights. The Opaline Hall." Vivienne sealed her letter with black wax, pressing her sigil deep. "Neutral ground. Public enough that they'll feel safe, private enough for honest conversation."

"So soon," Diligence breathed. "I wonder if they'll even come."

Vivienne's smile was all teeth and no warmth. "They will. Lars is too desperate to find his Trinelle. Darius will be too drunk on what he's stolen. And the others... the others will come because they know what happens to those who ignore my invitations."

The attendant appeared, properly nervous. Vivienne handed over her order.

"See this brought to Councilman Breslin. Make it clear that this must be done tonight."

He bowed and fled. Smarter than the last one.

"The emergency powers will pass," Vivienne said. "The crystal charges will flow through our channels alone. And anyone who stands against us…"

"Will meet Balar in a dark alley," Diligence ventured.

"Will understand that there are worse fates than death." Vivienne closed her eyes, already back in her element.

"Lars thinks his words have power?" she continued. "Let him come to the meeting and speak them to my face. Let them all come. And learn."

Outside, the sun was already beginning its descent. Over the next three days, everything would change.

Or everything would burn.

Either way, Vivienne would have her city.

SAVING GRACE

15

The world came back in pieces.

First, the cold. Seeping through her clothes, through her skin, settling into her bones like it had always lived there.

Then the smell—piss and rot and something sweet-sick that might have been her own vomit.

Finally, pain. Not the sharp, clean pain of a fresh wound, but the deep, grinding ache of a body pushed past its limits.

Trin opened her eyes. Gray dawn light filtered through the narrow gap between buildings, revealing an alley that could have been any alley in Lowtown. Crumbling brick, suspicious puddles, the detritus of lives lived hard and discarded easy.

The dog was still there.

It sat a few feet away, watching her with amber eyes that held more intelligence than any street mutt had a right to. When she stirred, it tilted its head, ears pricking forward.

"Still here?" Her voice came out as a croak. The dog's tail thumped once against the wet ground. "Guess that makes you the longest friendship I've had in weeks."

She tried to sit up. Bad idea. The world tilted violently, her stomach lurching in protest. Whatever Myrim had pumped into her, it wasn't done with her yet. She managed to roll onto her side, cheek pressed against the cold stone, and took inventory.

No restraints—good. No obvious injuries beyond bruises—better. No idea where she was or how to get home—fucking perfect.

The dog stood, stretched, and padded closer. Its nose was wet against her face, breath warm and rank. She should have been disgusted. Instead, she found herself reaching out, fingers tangling in matted fur.

"You know the way to the west side?" she asked. The dog licked her hand. "Yeah, didn't think so."

She had to move. Lying here was asking to be found—by Myrim, by the watch, by any of the human vultures who picked over Lowtown's corpses. But moving meant standing, and standing meant her body had to remember how to work.

Come on, Trinelle. You've done more with less.

She pressed her palms against the ground, pushed. The world spun. She gritted her teeth, pushed harder. Made it to her knees before her body revolted, sending her scrambling for the wall. She barely made it before her stomach emptied itself—not that there was much to empty. Just bile and the chemical taste of whatever sedative was still poisoning her system.

The dog yawned, watching the performance with patient interest.

"Not my finest moment," she gasped, wiping her mouth with the back of her hand. The movement sent fresh waves of dizziness through her skull.

She used the wall to pull herself up, brick scraping against her palms. Standing was a negotiation between her will and her body's complete rejection of the concept. She won, barely.

Now what?

The alley stretched in both directions, identical in its squalor. No landmarks, no familiar graffiti, no helpful signs pointing toward home. Just gray walls and gray sky and the gray exhaustion settling over her.

Think. She'd escaped from… where? The memories were fragmenting, sliding away when she tried to grab them. Myrim's place. Somewhere in Lowtown. She'd run, but the drugs had been hitting hard. Could have gone any direction. Could be anywhere within a mile radius of where she'd started.

A mile might as well have been to Zarakar in her current state.

She picked a direction—left, because why not—and started walking. The dog fell into step beside her, a ragged shadow keeping pace with her stumbling progress.

Every step was an argument with gravity. Her legs wanted to fold, her head wanted to spin, her stomach wanted to remind her that it existed and was deeply unhappy about it. She kept one hand on the wall, leaving smears of grime and what might have been blood—when had she cut her palm?

The alley opened onto a street. Still Lowtown, judging by the boarded windows and the suspicious looks from the few people already awake. A woman pulling a cart loaded with scrap gave her a wide berth. A man huddled in a doorway tracked her movement with the calculating gaze of someone deciding if she was worth robbing.

She must have looked worse than she felt. That took some doing.

"Don't suppose you know where we are?" she asked the dog. It was sniffing at something deeply fascinating in the gutter. "Right. Helpful."

She needed landmarks. Something to orient herself. But Lowtown had a way of looking the same when you were lost—endless rows of tenements and workshops, all slowly crumbling into the same anonymous decay.

A sign caught her eye. Faded paint on rotting wood: *Estontown Tannery*. Hells, was she near Estontown? It was so far away from Azoria proper.

But it made it clear which way to go. West.

Which way was west?

The drug fog was thickening again, making thought sluggish. She'd learned to navigate by instinct, by the angle of shadows and the smell of the harbor. But the overcast sky gave no hints, and her nose was too full of alley stink to catch the salt breeze.

"Hells," she muttered, leaning heavily against a wall. The dog looked up at her, tail wagging tentatively. "Don't give me that look. Unless you've got a compass hidden in that matted fur, we're both lost."

She pushed off the wall, picked another direction. Moving was better than standing still. Standing still meant the drugs won, meant Myrim found her, meant she'd escaped for nothing.

The street opened onto another street. This one had a few more people, early workers heading to whatever miserable jobs kept them fed. She tried to blend in, to walk like she had somewhere to be. Hard to do when every third step was a stumble.

"You alright there, miss?"

She jerked away from the voice, hand going to her empty belt. No knife. Right. The speaker was an older woman, weathered face creased with what might have been concern or calculation.

"Fine," Trin managed. "Just... celebrating."

The woman's eyes took in her appearance—the bruises, the drug-dilated pupils, the way she swayed on her feet. "Celebrating hard, looks like."

"You know how it is." Trin tried for a smile. Probably looked more like a grimace.

The woman hesitated, then: "You need help getting somewhere?"

Trust no one. First rule of the streets. But she was running out of options and energy.

"West," she said. "To the sea. You know the way?"

Something shifted in the woman's expression. "West? You're going the wrong direction, dear. It's back that way, past the old brewery, then follow the cobble road."

Trin blinked, trying to process the directions through the fog. "The cobble road. Right. Thanks."

She turned to go, but the woman caught her arm. "You sure you're alright? You look like you could use—"

"I'm fine." Trin pulled free, harder than she meant to. The sudden movement sent the world spinning again. "Just need to get home."

The woman stepped back, hands raised. "Alright. Just... be careful. Streets aren't safe for a woman alone."

Tell me something I don't know.

Trin mumbled thanks and started walking again, the dog still at her heels. Back the way she'd come. Past the old brewery. She'd find it. Follow the cobble road. She'd find that too.

She had to.

Because the alternative was collapsing in some other alley, and this time maybe the dog wouldn't be the only thing that found her.

The dynamo lens was getting hot.

Too hot.

Liora shifted her grip, copper coils burning her palms. Three hours. Three bloody hours of nothing.

"Come on." She tapped the crystal housing. "Give me something."

The lens flickered. Weak pulse. Old trace. Useless.

Another crossroads. She spun in a slow circle, lens held high. North—nothing. East—maybe? No. Gone when she stepped toward it. South—same fading trail she'd been chasing. West—

A spike!

Her heart jumped. But no. Just a street lamp flickering on.

"Damn it."

She'd started near the Market District, thinking Trin might have tried to circle back to familiar territory. But the traces had led her steadily southeast, away from safety, away from anywhere that made sense. Now she was deep in the warehouse district, halfway to the slums, and the trail was growing colder with every step.

A merchant wheeled his vegetable cart past, giving her gadget a suspicious look. Right. Mad girl with weird device. Nothing to see here.

She flagged him down anyway. "Hey! You see a woman come through? Blonde hair, about this tall?" She held up her hand.

The merchant shrugged. "Lady, I see lots of people round here."

The dynamo lens heated up again. Liora took a quick look. "It might have been around dawn."

"I was in bed, like sensible folk." He wheeled on.

Liora adjusted the frequency dial. The lens whined. Too high. She dialed back. There. The sweet spot where Trin's signature *might* shine through the noise.

If it was even still active.

If she was still—

"Stop it!" She shouted it out loud. A passing woman startled.

Think. Where would Trin be? Not anywhere near their usual spots. Not anywhere Myrim might be either. Her and Shelle... well, they'd already checked those. They didn't know whether to be sad or relieved to find them empty.

The lens pulsed.

Once. Barely a hiccup.

Liora's head snapped toward it. Southeast. Deeper still, toward the border where the warehouses gave way to true Lowtown squalor.

She ran.

Dodged workers. Jumped puddles. Held the lens like a lifeline.

Another pulse. Stronger.

"That's it. That's my girl."

Down another alley. The lens flickered steadier now. Traces where Trin might have stopped. Leaned maybe. Liora could almost see it—Trin stumbling, afraid.

But she *had* been here. Where?

The alley opened onto another street. The signal scattered. Lost in morning traffic.

"No no no."

She spun. Adjusted dials. Nothing.

A doorstep. She sat. The lens rattled in her lap. Liora peered at it suspiciously.

Of course. A loose wire. No wonder it was so hot. Hells, it's a wonder it had even worked.

Had it?

Her fingers worked automatically. Tighten connections. Adjust housing. Something to do while her brain screamed.

The theory had been so elegant in her workshop. Every living thing generated a unique biodynamic field—a combination of their body's dynamo impulses, chemical signatures, and that ineffable something that made them *them*.

Just yesterday—had it only been yesterday?—Shelle had brought her Trin's green scarf, the one Lars said she was always fond of. The fabric still held traces of her biodynamic signature, and Liora had carefully extracted and stored it in a crystal matrix.

Now it was their only hope of finding her, and the technology she'd been so proud of was barely holding together.

The lens squealed. Feedback. She'd crossed wires.

"Damn it!" Hot coil burned her finger.

This was useless. She was useless.

A boy shuffled past. He couldn't have been more than ten. But he had Lowtown written all over him.

"Hey!" Liora called. "Copper for information?"

His eyes lit up. "What kind of information?"

"Woman. Blonde hair. This tall. Sick maybe. Seen anyone like that?"

The boy scratched his chin. "Sick how?"

"Stumbling. Leaning against the wall a lot. Would've been hours ago." She only knew what she thought the dynamo lens was indicating. Which wasn't much.

"Maybe." He held out his palm.

Liora dropped a coin in it. The boy pocketed it and shrugged. "Sorry. Haven't seen nothing."

"You little—"

But he was already running.

She should go back. Get Jax. Get Bunny. Search the old-fashioned way.

But going back meant failure. It meant telling Lars she couldn't find her. That all her biodynamic brilliance meant nothing.

"One more hour." She stood. The lens had cooled, glowing dim but steady. "One more hour."

Southeast. Following the ghost of a trail that might not even exist anymore. The buildings here were older, more decrepit. She was getting further into the slums, that gray area where even the watch hesitated to patrol.

An old woman sat outside a tenement, smoking a pipe.

"Morning," Liora tried. "I'm looking for someone."

The woman eyed the lens. "That thing tell fortunes?"

Liora grinned. "It finds people. Sometimes. When it works."

"Hmm." A long draw on the pipe. "Who you looking for?"

"My friend. Blonde hair. Thin and tall. She's in trouble."

"Aren't we all." But the woman's eyes softened. "Saw a girl earlier. Dawn maybe. Had a dog with her."

"A dog?" It was probably just some poor woman walking her pet for its morning relief.

The woman pointed down a street, toward Estontown proper. "Mangy thing. They went that way."

"Thank you!"

Estontown it was, then. The lens stayed quiet but Liora had something better now. Anything was worth trying.

She adjusted the lens frequency again. Too bad there wasn't a "next to a dog" setting.

The crystal flickered, then steadied into a new rhythm.

The morning sun climbed. Fog burned off. The city looked the same as always except for the Trin-shaped hole in it.

One more hour.

Even if hope was getting harder to hold.

Even if every step felt like one step further behind.

She'd find her. She had to.

The cobble road was a lie.

West to the sea, the old woman had said. Like something out of a children's story. Follow the cobble road and find your way home. Except the road kept twisting, splitting, leading her deeper into streets that all looked the same.

"This is wrong." Trin stopped at another intersection, swaying on her feet. "This is all wrong."

The dog looked up at her, waiting. Patient as always, like it had nowhere better to be than watching her fall apart.

"Don't give me that look." She wiped sweat from her forehead with a shaking hand. When had she gotten so hot? Her clothes stuck to her skin, soaked through with fever sweat. "I know what you're thinking. I shouldn't be here. I should go back."

Back to the bed. Back to the needle. Back to the restraints in that small room that smelled like antiseptic and despair.

"No." She shook her head, immediately regretting it as the world lurched sideways. She caught herself against a wall, palm scraping against rough brick. "Can't go back. Won't."

She picked a direction—left, why not—and started walking again. The dog followed, claws clicking on stone.

"You know what's stupid?" she said to the dog, needing to hear something besides her own ragged breathing and the pounding of her heart. "I used to be good at this. At finding things. I could navigate any city blindfolded. Lars said I had an internal compass."

The dog's ears perked forward, like it was actually listening.

"Now look at me. Lost. Following fairy tales about cobble roads and seas." She laughed, or tried to. It came out as more of a wheeze.

Her stomach clenched suddenly, violently. Trin fell to her knees.

"Hells," she gasped. The dog had waited, sitting a few feet away, head tilted with what looked like concern. "Thanks for not running."

She pushed off the wall, took three steps, and had to grab for support again. The drug haze was getting worse, not better. It came in waves now, each one threatening to pull her under completely. The shadows between buildings seemed to move, reaching for her with dark fingers. The walls breathed in and out like living things. The cobblestones underneath her feet shifted like water, making each step a negotiation with gravity.

"It's all a lie," she muttered, blinking hard to clear her vision. "The road. The directions. Probably even you."

The dog tilted its head the other way.

"But you're a nice lie. The nicest I've known." She tried to pet it but missed, her depth perception completely shot. "Don't want anything from me except maybe some food, and sorry, friend, but I'm fresh out."

She forced herself forward. One step. Another. The sun was fully up now, burning through the morning fog, turning the narrow streets into an oven. How long had she been walking? Hours? Days? Her legs felt like they belonged to someone else, some stranger who didn't know how to work them properly.

"You want to know a secret?" She glanced at the dog, which had taken to walking closer now, almost brushing against her leg. "I don't even remember what the sea smells like. Isn't that pathetic? I can't—"

Her knee buckled.

She went down hard, catching herself on her hands. The impact jarred through her arms, sent white spots dancing across her vision like drunken fireflies. She tried to push back up. Nothing. Her arms shook with the effort, muscles screaming, but her body was done pretending it had any strength left.

"No, no, no." Panic clawed at her throat, sharp and desperate. "Not here. Not in the middle of the street."

But her legs wouldn't listen. She was on her knees in some narrow road, buildings pressing close on either side like canyon walls, and she couldn't get up. Couldn't move. Could barely breathe through the terror of it.

She tried once more, managed to get one foot under her before the world spun viciously and dropped her back down. This time she couldn't even catch herself. Her cheek hit the cobblestones, and she tasted blood.

That's when she saw him.

Balar. Myrim.

He was on a rooftop maybe thirty feet back, silhouetted against the morning sky like something out of a nightmare. Looking right at her. Real or hallucination? She couldn't tell anymore, but the fear that shot through her felt real enough.

"No." The word came out as a whimper. "You're not real. You're not—"

He moved. Dropped from the roof to a smaller shed with casual grace, landed silent as a cat. The kind of move she used to make, back when her body obeyed her. Then to the ground. Walking toward her with that same measured pace she remembered from before, unhurried because he knew she couldn't run.

"I can't go back." She tried to crawl, made it maybe a foot before her arms gave out completely. Her fingers scraped against stone, nails breaking. "I can't, I won't—"

The dog erupted.

A snarl ripped from its throat, feral and wild. It lunged forward, placing itself between her and Myrim, teeth bared. The sound bounced off the narrow walls, multiplying into a cacophony of rage.

Through her blurring vision, she saw Myrim pause mid-step. He shifted and cocked his head—a subtle tension, like a predator catching an unexpected scent.

The dog kept snarling, snapping at the air.

Myrim took a step back. Another. His movements still fluid, controlled. But he was retreating.

"Good dog," Trin whispered, though she didn't understand.

Balar didn't retreat. Yet he was now. Maybe he didn't like dogs.

The world was graying at the edges now, darkness creeping in from all sides. She felt herself tilting, her cheek already against the stones so there was nowhere to fall but deeper into herself.

Myrim melted back into the shadows between buildings, gone as quickly as he'd appeared. Like he'd never been there at all.

But he had been. Hadn't he?

The dog's barking grew distant, muffled, as if she were hearing it from underwater.

She was going to pass out again.

The hour was up.

Liora stood at the edge of Estontown, staring at rows of tenements that seemed to stretch forever. Gray buildings under gray sky, everything coated in that particular film of hopelessness that Lowtown specialized in.

The lens in her hand had gone quiet ten minutes ago. No pulses. No flickers. Nothing but dead crystal and the weight of her own failure.

"That's it then." She lowered the device, shoulders sagging. "I tried."

The words tasted like ash. She'd tried and failed. All her brilliance, all her inventions, and she couldn't find one person in a city she'd lived in her whole life.

What good was being a genius if you couldn't use it when it mattered?

She'd been so sure the biodynamics would work. So confident when she'd explained it to Shelle, hands flying as she described the unique energy signatures, the tracking possibilities. She'd felt like a hero then. Like someone who could fix things, save people, make the world make sense through science and determination.

Now she just felt tired.

Lars would understand. He'd tell her it wasn't her fault, that she'd done everything she could. But his eyes would go a little deader, and he'd retreat further into that dark place where she couldn't reach him. He'd stop eating again. Stop talking. Stop being Lars.

And Trin would still be gone.

A few people passed her on the street, giving the girl with the strange device a wide berth. She must look half-mad—hair escaping from its pins, clothes rumpled from hours of searching, talking to herself. Her nice workshop clothes were stained with sweat and alley grime. Just another Lowtown weirdo.

She turned the lens over in her hands. The crystal had gone cloudy, either dead or damaged. The copper coils were tarnished, the connections loose despite her efforts. The whole thing had been held together by hope and wire, and now the hope was gone too.

Time to go home.

She turned west, back toward safety, back toward failure. Her feet felt like lead.

Each step away from Estontown was an admission of defeat. Trin was out here somewhere—hurt, scared, maybe dying—and Liora was giving up.

Some genius you turned out to be.

The thoughts came like a punch to the gut. All those nights in the workshop, acting like she was changing the world. All that talk about innovation and revolution and making things better.

But when it came down to it, when someone she loved needed her most, all her cleverness amounted to nothing.

She'd made it maybe twenty feet when she heard it.

A bark. Sharp, furious, echoing off the narrow walls.

Dog.

Another bark. Then another. Not playful. These barks meant business.

Dog.

It was just a dog. Lowtown was full of strays. It didn't mean anything.

But her feet were already moving.

She'd taken two steps back toward the sound when her brain caught up. *Don't be stupid. It's just a dog. You've seen lots of dogs.*

The barking continued. Frantic now. Desperate.

It's nothing. Turn around. Go home.

But what if it wasn't nothing? What if—

"Screw it."

She ran.

Around the corner towards the sound. Her workshop shoes slipped on the greasy cobblestones. She caught herself on a wall, kept going.

The street narrowed, buildings leaning in like they were sharing secrets. The barking echoed weirdly here, distorted by the architecture into something almost human in its desperation. She skidded around another corner—

And saw them.

A mangy dog, hackles raised, snarling at empty air. And beside it, crumpled on the cobblestones like discarded rags—

"TRIN!"

The name tore from her throat. She was running before she'd even finished processing what she was seeing. Blonde hair matted with sweat. Too-pale skin. The absolute stillness of someone who'd gone past exhaustion into something worse.

Liora dropped to her knees beside her friend, hands shaking as she reached for her neck. The cobblestones bit into her knees but she barely noticed. *Please, please, please*—

A pulse. Weak, thready, but there.

"Trin? Trin, can you hear me?" She brushed hair back from her friend's face, wincing at the heat radiating from her skin.

Fever. And it was a bad one.

Trin's eyes were closed, shadowed purple underneath like bruises. Her lips were cracked, bleeding at the corners. She looked smaller somehow, diminished, like whatever had happened had burned parts of her away.

The dog had stopped barking, was now whining low in its throat, pressing close to Trin's side like it could protect her even now. When Liora reached out to check Trin's breathing, the dog growled softly.

"It's okay," Liora told it, told herself. "It's going to be okay. I found her. I found you."

But looking at Trin, Liora's stomach clenched. The bruises on her wrists, dark as shackles. The needle marks on her arms, too many to count. The way her breathing came shallow and wrong, like her body was forgetting how to do it.

Whatever had been done to her, finding her was only the beginning.

She needed help. Needed to get Trin somewhere safe, somewhere clean, somewhere that wasn't a Lowtown street with who knew what kind of attention that barking had drawn.

But moving her could be dangerous. If she had internal injuries, if whatever drugs were in her system were the only things keeping her stable—

Stop. Think. You're a problem solver. Solve this.

"Right then." Liora took a shaky breath, mind already racing through options. Just like planning a heist.

First: assess.

She ran her hands carefully over Trin's body, checking for obvious injuries. No broken bones that she could feel. No wounds beyond the bruises and needle marks. But the fever, the unconsciousness, the way her muscles twitched periodically—drugs. Had to be.

Second: immediate danger.

They were exposed here, visible from three different approaches. That barking would have drawn attention. She needed to move Trin, but carefully.

Third: transport.

Maybe twenty blocks to safety. She couldn't carry Trin that far, not alone. But maybe...

"Hey." She looked at the dog, which was watching her with those amber eyes, as if measuring whether she could be trusted with its charge. "You've been protecting her, haven't you? Good dog. *Best* dog."

The dog's tail thumped once, tentatively.

"I've got her," Liora promised. "We've got her. But I need to get her out of here, and I can't do it alone."

She looked around, mind cataloging resources. Narrow alley. No carts. No convenient planks of wood. But there—a discarded canvas tarp, relatively clean, stuffed behind a drain pipe.

It would have to do.

Liora retrieved the tarp, spreading it beside Trin. Moving her onto it was harder than she'd expected. Trin was dead weight, limbs flopping uselessly, and Liora had to be careful not to jostle her too much.

"Sorry, sorry," she muttered as she rolled Trin onto the canvas. "I know. But we've got to go."

The dog watched the entire process, occasionally whining when Trin made small sounds of distress.

Finally, she had Trin on the tarp. Now for the hard part.

Twenty blocks. Through Lowtown. Dragging an unconscious woman.

But that was just another problem to solve. And Liora Banz was very, very good at solving problems.

Especially when it mattered this much.

She grabbed the corners of the tarp, tested the weight. Heavy, but manageable. Maybe.

"Alright, dog," she said. "Let's get our girl home."

Dice clattered across the scarred wooden table, but Lars didn't even look up to see how they landed. Jax's rumbling chuckle and Bunny's quiet snort of disappointment told him everything he needed to know about who was winning. Not that it mattered. Nothing much seemed to matter anymore.

Lars sat in what had become his usual spot these past two weeks—a chair by the window where he could watch the street and pretend he was doing something useful.

The box he'd nailed to the post outside was visible from here, stuffed with papers that promised everything and delivered nothing.

Saw Balar buying rope at Cadwell's. My cousin's friend knows where he sleeps. For five coppers advance, I'll tell you which sewer he hides in.

Lies. All of it lies, sold by desperate people to a desperate man.

He'd published the article about Balar two days ago. Fifty thousand coppers for information—enough money to buy a life, to buy a dozen lives. The response had been immediate and overwhelming and utterly useless.

Every shadow in Azoria had suddenly become Balar. Every woman glimpsed from behind might be Trin. Every lead had to be chased because what if this one, this time, wasn't another dead end?

But they all were.

"Your throw," Jax said, and Lars realized the big man was talking to him. When had he joined their game? He couldn't remember sitting down at the table, but here he was, dice in his hand.

"Lars?" Bunny grunted. The big Aelyndoran clutched his wooden beads in one hand. The soft click-click as he worried them between his fingers had become part of the background noise lately.

"I'm not really…" Lars set the dice down. His hand was shaking. When had that started? "You two go ahead."

They exchanged glances. Lars saw it in his peripheral vision, the way people look at each other when they're worried about someone but don't know what to say. He'd been seeing a lot of those looks lately.

The truth was a stone in his chest, heavy and cold and impossible to swallow: he had lost hope.

Two weeks. Two weeks of Trin being gone, being somewhere with that monster, being—

He couldn't finish the thought. Wouldn't. But it was there anyway, circling like a carrion bird. After two weeks, people didn't come back. Not from men like Balar. Not whole. Not themselves.

And maybe when he finally accepted that, really accepted it, he wouldn't be able to go on. He didn't know what that meant exactly. Whether he'd leave Azoria, or drink himself into oblivion, or simply… stop. Stop being Lars Harrow, gentleman thief. Stop being anything at all.

Because what was the point of any of it without—

The door exploded open.

For a heartbeat, Lars couldn't process what he was seeing. Liora stood framed in the doorway like something out of a fever dream—not the bright, bouncing genius he knew but something wild and desperate.

Tears had carved clean tracks through the dirt on her face. Her auburn hair, usually pinned back in her workshop style, hung in sweat-soaked tangles around her shoulders. Clothes torn at the knees, stained with alley muck and what looked horribly like blood. Her hands...

Lars's gaze caught on her hands. The palms were raw, bloody, wrapped in strips torn from her own sleeves. Rope burns. Deep ones.

She swayed in the doorway, and for a moment Lars thought she might collapse right there. Her chest heaved with each breath, like she'd run the whole way here. Like she'd run forever.

A dog burst through beside her—mangy, ribs showing, hackles raised like a ridge of knives along its spine. It planted itself between Liora and the room, amber eyes scanning for threats, a low growl rumbling in its chest.

And behind her...

Liora was pulling something. Her ruined hands were wrapped around the corners of what looked like an old tarp, the kind used to cover cargo. She'd fashioned it into a kind of sled, and she was pulling it through the doorway with the last of her strength, her feet slipping on the floor.

The tarp caught on the threshold. Liora made a sound—half sob, half snarl—and yanked harder. The canvas scraped forward another few inches.

"Liora?" Jax had only just processed her entrance, his chair crashing backward. "What—"

A hand slipped free from beneath the canvas, hanging over the edge. Pale as bone. Long, slim fingers that Lars recognized instantly.

Because he knew that hand like he knew his own reflection. Had held it, kissed it, watched it pick a thousand locks and steal a thousand treasures. Had seen it gentle on his face in the morning, fierce around a knife handle at night.

Trin's hand.

"I found her," Liora gasped out, and then her knees buckled.

Jax caught her before she hit the floor, his massive arms gentle as he cradled her against his chest. "You brilliant, amazing girl," he rumbled, and there were tears on his face too.

Bunny was already moving, producing a medical kit from somewhere, his movements quick and efficient despite the shock of the moment. The beads clicked against each other as he worked, a frantic percussion of prayer or worry or both.

But Lars only had eyes for the tarp. For the figure revealed as Bunny carefully pulled back the canvas.

And there she was. Bruises dark as ink on her wrists, her arms. Too thin, like something had been eating her from the inside out. But breathing. Still breathing.

The stone in his chest cracked, and everything he'd been holding back for two weeks came pouring out in a sound that was half sob, half animal howl. He dropped to his knees beside her, his hands shaking as he reached for her face.

"Trin? Hells, Trin... Can you hear me?"

Her eyelids fluttered. Opened just a sliver, revealing eyes that were Trin's but somehow not, like someone had stolen pieces of her while she was gone.

"Lars?" Her voice was barely a whisper.

"I'm here." He fumbled for the water flask Bunny pressed into his hands, carefully tipping it to her lips. "You're safe. You're home. Everything's going to be—"

She smiled then, weak but real, and his heart ached for her. Trin's hand moved slightly, found the dog's matted fur, and scratched gently behind its ears. The animal's tail thumped once against the floor.

Then her expression changed. The smile vanished like it had never been, replaced by something that made Lars's blood run cold.

Fear.

Raw, naked fear that transformed her face into something he'd never seen before.

Her lips moved. One word, barely voiced but clear as a bell in the sudden silence.

"Myrim."

And then her eyes rolled back, and she was gone again, retreating into unconsciousness like it was the only safe place left.

Lars looked up at Liora, still held in Jax's arms.

Her face had gone white beneath the dirt and tears, horror dawning in her eyes.

The horror lasted maybe three seconds.

Then Liora was struggling in Jax's arms, trying to get her feet under her, already shifting into that rapid-fire problem-solving mode that was her answer to everything.

"We need... we need to get her to a proper medic. Not just field treatment. Someone who knows about drugs, about whatever he might have—"

"Liora."

Lars's voice was quiet but it cut through her spiral. She stopped struggling, blinking at him.

"Right now," he said, still kneeling beside Trin, one hand gentle on her too-pale cheek, "all you need is rest."

"But—"

"I'll take care of getting Trin the help she needs." He looked up at her. "You brought her home. You did the impossible. Let us take it from here."

Liora's mouth opened and closed. For once, the brilliant engineer who always had an answer had nothing to say.

"Jax," Lars said, already shifting into planning mode himself, "get her some water and something to eat. Bunny, clear the sofa in the back room. And that dog—"

He looked at the mangy creature still standing guard. "The dog stays with Trin."

The crew moved into action, and they moved with purpose.

THE BREAKING POINT

16

The Jade Serpent was absolutely packed, and Darius Adalan was in his element.

"—so there I am, halfway through the vault floor, and Maren—sweet, twitchy Maren—he says 'Darius, I think I hit a sewer pipe.'"

Darius paused, letting the crowd lean in. "And I say, 'Think? Or know?' And he says—"

"'Well, there's definitely something brown coming through the hole,'" Maren called out from across the tavern, face flushed with drink and victory.

The crowd roared. Darius raised his glass to his engineer, who ducked his head but couldn't hide his grin.

This. This was what he'd been missing.

Not just the score—though pulling off the bank job had been beautiful—but the afterwards. The glory. The way every eye in the room tracked his movements, hungry for details.

"But we didn't let a little sewage stop us," Darius continued, hopping up onto his chair for better visibility. "Because we're not just thieves, my friends. We're artists. And real art requires sacrifice."

"Is that why you smell like shit?" someone yelled.

"Character building," Darius shot back as the crowd laughed. "You think Lars Harrow would crawl through sewage for a score?"

The mention of Lars got a mixed reaction—some laughs, some mutters. Darius didn't care. Tonight wasn't about old rivalries.

Tonight was about proving that Darius Adalan was back.

A young thief, maybe seventeen, pushed forward. "Is it true you caused a plague scare? That you faked the spots?"

Darius clutched his chest in mock horror. "Would I fake a deadly disease just to empty a bank?" He let the pause stretch. "Yes. Yes, I would."

More laughter. More drinks. The kid's eyes shone with something like worship.

"Show us how you did the convulsions!" another voice called.

"Ah, but that would spoil the magic." Darius winked. "Besides, Rurik's the real master. You should've seen him. Big man was thrashing around like a dying fish."

From his spot by the door, Rurik raised his drink. The tiniest of smiles crossed his face—high praise from the taciturn bruiser.

"Ah, the boss is being modest," Inora said, appearing at his elbow with her usual ability to materialize from nowhere. "His drooling technique was inspired."

"Soap shavings and egg whites," Darius confided to the crowd. "But the real secret is in the delivery. You have to believe you're dying. Method acting."

"Method stupidity," Inora corrected, but there was warmth in it.

The night spun on. More stories demanded, more drinks supplied.

Darius told them about the tunnel, the vault, the beautiful moment when Maren had appeared covered in dust and triumph. He didn't mention the crystal charges instead of money. That was a puzzle for tomorrow. Tonight was for basking.

Young thieves pressed close, drinking in every word. These kids had lost their shot at becoming big because of the ban, had never known the real Azoria. They'd heard stories, sure, but stories were just words. This—a successful heist, a master crew, money flowing like water—this was proof that the old ways were back.

"Will you take apprentices?" a girl asked, barely old enough to be out this late.

"Maybe," Darius said, though he had no such plans. "But first, you need to learn the basics. Anyone can pick a pocket. It takes an artist to pick the right pocket at the right time."

"Teach us!"

And why not? Darius launched into a demonstration, using Maren as his hapless volunteer. The engineer played along, pretending not to notice as Darius lifted his wallet, his watch, even his spectacles right off his face.

"Misdirection," Darius explained, returning the items with a flourish. "Make them look where you want them to look. The hand is quicker than the eye, but the mouth—the story—that's quicker than both."

Someone started playing a fiddle. Old songs, drinking songs, thieving songs. The crowd belted them out like war cries.

Darius found himself in the middle of it all, spinning some merchant's daughter who'd snuck out to see how the other half lived. The crowd was a living thing, pulsing with joy and relief and the bone-deep satisfaction of being themselves again.

"To the masters!" someone shouted.

"To the game!"

"To stealing every last copper from those rich bastards!"

Darius climbed onto a table, because of course he did. He stood there, coat flaring, arms spread wide like he could embrace the whole city.

"To Azoria!" he called. "Where the only crime is getting caught!"

The cheer that went up could've lifted the roof. This was it. This was everything. The year of small cons and careful moves was over. They were back, really back, and the city would learn what that meant soon enough.

He was mid-bow when the door slammed open.

A boy stood silhouetted against the gray dawn light. Couldn't be more than twelve. He clutched a newspaper like his life depended on it, chest heaving from running.

The music died. Conversations stopped. Every eye turned to the doorway.

"What is it, kid?" someone asked.

The boy raised the paper with shaking hands, the headline striking and bold.

EMERGENCY POWERS GRANTED: COUNCIL VOTES TO END THIEVING PERMANENTLY

The morning papers hit the streets, and they hit them hard.

They appeared on every corner, in every district, the ink still wet from the emergency print run. Newsboys shouted the headlines in voices that cracked with disbelief. Citizens snatched copies from stands, read the words once, twice, three times, as if repetition might change their meaning.

The lead story sprawled across the front page in bold type. The Council had voted seven to two in favor of granting emergency powers to Vivienne Dragunova, Chairwoman of the Ithris Gaming Commission.

The copper crisis, she claimed. The surge in violent thieving activities. The need for immediate action to ensure Azoria's financial stability.

What followed was a litany of reforms that read like a manifesto.

All thieving activities would be permanently banned, with mandatory sentences for violations. The right to speedy trial for crimes against property was suspended indefinitely. The City Watch would triple in size within thirty days, with a new tax on all citizens to fund the expansion.

Darius Adalan and his crew were specifically named, ordered to return the City Reserve heist proceeds immediately or face additional charges.

A citywide curfew would run from sunset to dawn, effective immediately.

At the bottom of the announcement, Vivienne's words carried the weight of a closing coffin lid. "These measures are necessary to restore order to our beloved city. I look forward to meeting with city leaders and crew representatives tomorrow evening to discuss Azoria's bright new future."

The city's reaction was immediate and visceral.

In the Market District, a fruit vendor read the news and hurled an apple at the nearest Watch patrol. Within minutes, the air was thick with produce and profanity. Merchants who'd celebrated the return of flowing money now faced the prospect of higher taxes to fund their own oppression.

In the slums, where many thieving crews made their homes, doors slammed and voices rose. Someone dragged a barrel into the street and set it ablaze. Then another. Then a dozen more, until smoke columns marked the people's fury like signal fires.

But it was at the Ithris Gaming Commission headquarters where the real storm gathered.

They came in ones and twos at first. A locksmith who'd waited a year to practice his craft again. A fence who'd just reopened her shop. Young runners who'd dreamed of joining crews. Old thieves who'd survived the ban through stubbornness alone.

Then they came in dozens. In scores. In hundreds.

By mid-morning, the plaza outside the Gaming Commission was a sea of angry faces. They pressed against the hastily erected Watch barriers, voices rising in unison.

They chanted Lars's words.

"DON'T LET FEAR BE OUR NEW CURRENCY!"

"AZORIA DESERVES BETTER!"

The phrases from his article in The Azoria Star became more than just words. They became a rallying cry for everyone who understood what made their city special. The crowd swayed with the rhythm of their chanting, a living thing united in purpose and fury.

High above, behind reinforced windows, Vivienne Dragunova watched the gathering storm with the satisfaction of a chess player whose opponent had moved exactly where expected.

The Watch response was swift and brutal.

They arrived in formation, clubs raised, faces hidden behind helmets. The new recruits—hired just that morning with promises of steady pay from the coming taxes—were eager to prove themselves. The veterans knew better than to show mercy when their jobs depended on it.

The first line of protesters crumbled under the assault. Screams mixed with chants. Blood spattered on cobblestones. But for every person who fell, two more pushed forward.

It was the math of revolution: pain multiplied by anger equals resistance.

But then, there's always the unsolved variable. In this case, fear.

"About time someone cleaned up this mess!" A shopkeeper from Merchant Row watched the Watch advance with grim satisfaction. "Thirty years of legalized theft, and for what? So Lars Harrow can throw around fifty thousand coppers like it's nothing?"

Others nodded, clustering together away from the protesters. These were the citizens who'd locked their doors during the year-long ban on thieving, who had taken the brunt of the pushback from low-level gangs and street rats.

"Fifty thousand coppers," an old woman spat. "That's more than I've seen in a lifetime. And he offers it as a reward? While we can't afford to eat?"

"The thieves brought this on themselves," a factory worker added, sporting a fresh black eye from the chaos. "All that talk about tradition and balance—where was the balance when they were bleeding us dry?"

They weren't many, these voices. But they were loud. And when the Watch pushed forward, they cheered. When protesters fell, they looked away with hard eyes that said the thieves had this coming.

Fear had done its work. Not everyone wanted the old Azoria back. Some wanted it buried so deep it would never rise again.

"HOLD THE LINE!" someone shouted. "FOR AZORIA!"

The monorail glided past on its elevated track. Liora Banz's grand achievement, symbol of Azoria's legitimate progress, hummed with prosperity as it carried morning commuters who pressed their faces to windows, watching the chaos below.

Above, the future Vivienne promised, clean and controlled and bloodless. Below, the city's true nature. Messy and violent and absolutely refusing to die.

A young thief, blood streaming from a head wound, pointed at the monorail and laughed. The sound carried across the plaza, bitter and wild. "LOOK AT IT!" he screamed. "LOOK AT THEIR BETTER TOMORROW!"

The Watch pushed them back street by street. The Gaming Commission plaza emptied, filled, emptied again as waves of protesters clashed with waves of uniformed authority. By the time the sun reached its peak, the immediate area was clear. Tomorrow evening's meeting would proceed without unseemly disruptions.

But the city seethed.

In every district, on every corner, people gathered and whispered and planned. The morning papers lay trampled in gutters, their headlines already obsolete.

Azoria had tasted freedom again. But not everyone wanted the same flavor.

Trin had slept for almost sixteen hours.

Liora sat in the corner of their hideout, watching the rise and fall of her friend's chest. Proof of life. Proof they'd actually gotten her back.

The revelation had come in fragments at first. Trin, barely conscious, whispering a name that made no sense.

Then nothing. Just exhausted sleep while the rest of them tried to process what couldn't possibly be true.

But Liora's mind wouldn't stop churning. Every memory, every moment, every hells-damned clue she'd missed. By the time Trin had finally woken, Liora had to ask. Had to be absolutely sure.

"Are you certain? About... about who he is?"

She'd hated herself for asking, for making Trin relive it. But she had to know.

And Trin had confirmed it. "I didn't know what to think," she had said. "When he took the mask off, my mind didn't want to make the connection."

Liora knew that feeling—the desperate scramble of a mind trying to reject what it already knew was true. Her hand had found the edge of the table, gripping hard enough to hurt.

"He was there," Trin had continued, each word precise despite the tremor underneath. Hells, she had sounded so distant. Numb. "In that alley. He would have gotten me if it weren't for the dog."

She paused. "And you finding me first."

Since then, they'd existed in a strange suspension. Waiting. Planning. Trying to figure out their next move while the city churned around them.

But then came the invitation.

Lars picked it up from where it had been slipped under their door. Cream paper, expensive. Vivienne's seal in burgundy wax.

"She wants to meet," he said, scanning the contents. "Tomorrow evening. The Opaline Hall. All crew leaders and city representatives."

"It's a trap," Jax said immediately.

"Of course it's a trap." Lars set the invitation down. "The question is what kind."

Liora felt the anger hit again, white-hot and blinding. How could she have been so damn stupid? All those nights Myrim came home late. When he'd ask for details on their next move.

The way he'd sometimes stare at nothing, like he was seeing through different eyes.

Her hand connected with the table before she realized she'd moved. Pain blossomed across her palm, sharp and real and somehow not enough.

The sadness came next, crushing the anger under its weight. Every kiss, every whispered promise, every morning waking up tangled together—all of it poisoned. Had any of it been real?

But she was Liora Banz. She solved problems. She fixed things that were broken. She couldn't afford to shatter, not now, not when they needed her mind working.

Not now, when Trin was finally home.

Later, she told herself firmly. *When there's time. When I can think about what this means without wanting to scream.*

"This place is out of control." Lars's voice cut through her spiral, measured and thoughtful. He'd started tapping his thigh, that thing he did when his mind was working through angles.

He stopped by the window, staring out at the smoke rising from various districts. "I write that piece about change, about what this city could be. For a moment, people listened. Then suddenly there's violence. Thefts going bloody."

"There's still plenty of good folk supporting you out there, Lars," Bunny said.

"And I'm thankful," Lars said, turning back. He picked up the invitation again. "But there are just as many and more calling for the end of thieving. And now this." He waved his hand vaguely at the letter from Vivienne.

Jax grumbled. Looked at Lars. Grumbled again.

What a diva. Liora rolled her eyes in mock exasperation. "Yes, Jax, something you'd like to say?"

"I just want to remind you that invitation is a trap."

"Yes," Lars said. "We've established that."

The big man looked uncomfortable. "It's just... we haven't done so good dealing with traps lately."

Three points for honesty. Liora couldn't find it in herself to disagree. It felt like the whole world had been squeezing them through a rusty drain pipe with nowhere to go. It seemed like Lars might have felt the same. He didn't even bother to respond. Just looked at that letter.

It was Trin who finally spoke up. "We have options."

Lars looked at her, not with curiosity but concern. Trin had been quiet, almost haunting, for most of her waking moments. Her sleeping moments... well, Liora didn't want to think about those. She shuddered.

"We have options," Trin repeated quietly. "There are plenty of other towns in Ithris."

Lars frowned. "Run? Just... leave?"

"It's not running," Trin said carefully. "It's surviving."

"No." The word came from Liora's mouth before she'd decided to speak. They all turned to look at her. "This is our city. Our home."

Trin got quiet again, staring out of the window. Hells.

"Trin," Liora said. "I'm sorry, I didn't mean to snap at you."

"It's fine."

Liora sighed. "No, really. It's just... we've done so much here. Built so much. And we already took down one tyrant, remember?"

"That was different," Jax protested. "We had Vivienne on our side then. Now—"

"Now we expose her." Liora felt something crystallizing in her chest, hard and sharp as her best tools. "Show the city who Vivienne Dragunova really is. What she's done. Who she's allied with."

"The people will choose the old ways," Lars said slowly, like he was testing the words. "Right? Why would they choose to stand behind her?"

"Don't underestimate fear," Bunny said. "But yeah, there might still be a chance."

It was probably naive. Definitely dangerous. But what else did they have? Run and let Vivienne win? Let her turn Azoria into whatever twisted vision she had planned? Let Balar—no, Myrim. Whoever he was now—keep murdering in the shadows?

Not if Liora had anything to say about it.

"So we go," she said, surprising herself with how steady her voice came out. "We go to this meeting. See what she wants. Look for weaknesses."

"And Trin?" Jax asked, protective as always.

"Stays hidden," Lars said immediately. "Vivienne doesn't know she's back, doesn't know we know who Balar is or who he's working for."

Trin nodded, something like relief flickering across her face. She wasn't ready to face that threat again. Liora didn't blame her.

"It's settled then." Lars picked up the invitation again, studying it like it might reveal its secrets. "I'll go to the Opaline Hall. Play along with whatever game she's running."

"By yourself?" Bunny asked.

"Hells no, not by himself." Liora flexed her bruised hand. "I'm going with him."

Jax, as expected, jumped up immediately. "Liora, no," he said, "there's no way you're going to—"

Liora gave him a sharp look, and his mouth clicked shut. "I'm not asking, Jax."

"I know you're trying to protect me," she added quickly. Hells, she didn't want to hurt his feelings. It was just Jax being

Jax. "But you and Bunny need to stay here. With Trin. In case... well, you know what."

Jax's face softened. "Just... be careful, yeah?"

"Always am." It was a lie and they both knew it, but sometimes lies were kinder than truth.

She looked around the room at their battered little crew. Trin, hollow but breathing. Lars, trying to hold them all together. Jax and Bunny, loyal to the end.

They weren't much against Vivienne's machine. But they were still here. Still fighting.

And tomorrow, she'd look into the eyes of the woman who'd turned her lover into a monster.

One way or another, this would end.

Myrim had wandered Lowtown through the night.

He collapsed against a warehouse wall, mask clutched in shaking hands, breath coming in ragged gasps that had nothing to do with exertion. The alley spun around him. His stomach heaved.

Liora.

She'd been right there. Close enough to see the recognition dawn in her eyes if he'd stayed a second longer. Close enough to hear her voice break when she screamed Trin's name.

He ripped the mask off, needing air, needing to breathe without leather against his face. But the air tasted like miasma. Like the look on Liora's face when she'd found her friend. When she'd found what he'd done.

Two weeks. Two weeks of keeping Trin drugged and docile, telling himself it was mercy. That killing her would be worse. That as long as she was alive, there was still a chance to fix this.

But there was no fixing this.

The dog. If it hadn't been for that hells damned dog, snarling and snapping. He could have—

What? Killed Trin in front of Liora? Added that to the list of things she'd never forgive?

Not that forgiveness was possible now. Not after this.

He pressed his palms against his eyes until he saw stars. Tried to think through the panic clawing at his throat. Trin was gone. She'd tell them everything. About the mask, about the warehouse, about—

"Myrim?"

The voice came from the alley mouth. He jerked his head up to find a Watch patrol. Three officers, clubs at their belts, surprise clear on their faces.

"Captain?" The lead officer stepped forward—Monham, Myrim remembered. They'd worked together for years. "Haven't seen you in... hells, I can't even remember. You alright?"

Myrim's hand tightened on the mask. They were looking at him. Really looking. Taking in the sweat, the shaking hands, the wild eyes.

"We heard you went private sector," another added—Morse, young but sharp. Too sharp. "Are you consulting now?"

"Yeah." His voice came out rough. "Consulting."

Monham frowned, stepping closer. "You sure you're alright? You look like hells. Maybe we should—"

They'd ask questions. Where he'd been. What he was doing in an alley looking like he'd seen a ghost. They'd want to help, want to talk, want to know why their old captain was falling apart in Lowtown.

He couldn't have that.

"I'm fine." He forced himself to stand straighter. "Just... working a case."

"A case?" Morse's eyes narrowed slightly. "What kind of—"

Myrim slipped the mask over his head.

The transformation was instant. Complete. Myrim's trembling hands became Balar's steady ones. The panic crystallized into something colder, sharper. Purpose.

The officers saw it happen. Saw the way his posture shifted, the way the air around him seemed to darken. Monham's face went white.

"B-Balar?"

Balar moved.

Three bodies hit the ground before they could scream. Precise strikes—throat, temple, solar plexus. Not dead. He wasn't killing Watch officers.

Not yet. Not yet...

Balar stood over them, breath even, mind clear.

No more running. No more hiding. No more pretending there was a way back from this.

Vivienne had made him into this. Shaped him with threats and manipulation, turned his love for Liora and Shelle into a weapon she could aim. She'd taken everything good in him and twisted it until all that was left was the mask.

This was her fault.

He moved through the city like smoke, keeping to shadows and forgotten passages. The warehouse was compromised now. Everything was compromised. But that was fine. He didn't need safe houses anymore.

He just needed to find Vivienne.

Balar turned west, toward the city center. The slums fell away behind him as he moved, not skulking now but striding with purpose. Through alleyways where garbage rotted and desperate people huddled. Over rooftops where the tiles were loose and the drop meant death. Each step carried him closer to the heart of Azoria.

The Gaming Commission headquarters rose in the distance, a monument to order and control. Vivienne's castle. Her throne.

He dropped from a warehouse roof to street level, landing in a crouch that sent puddle water splashing. When he straightened, a cluster of young toughs near a burning barrel took notice.

"Balar!" one shouted, pointing with a shaking finger.

"The bounty—" another started.

Balar turned his head toward them. Just that. A simple movement, the mask catching firelight.

They scattered like roaches, abandoning their barrel and their bravado. Fifty thousand coppers wasn't worth dying for. Not when death's mask stood there watching them with empty eyes.

He continued walking.

The river marked the boundary between Lowtown and civilization. On the far side, dynamo lamps lit clean streets and the Watch actually patrolled. Balar crossed the bridge without hesitation, boots ringing on iron and stone.

No more hiding. No more shadows.

He walked down the main thoroughfare like he belonged there. Like he was exactly what Vivienne had made him—a force of nature, inevitable as storm winds. Citizens saw him coming and pressed themselves against buildings, into doorways, anywhere but his path.

"Is that—?"

"Don't look at him."

"Someone get the Watch!"

But no one moved to stop him. How could they? He was Balar. The nightmare made flesh. The cautionary tale parents told children.

And he was done pretending otherwise.

The Gaming Commission headquarters loomed larger with each step. Guards at the main entrance, their faces going pale as they recognized the figure approaching. Not skulking in shadows or climbing through windows.

Walking up the front steps like a blade snapped in half—jagged, wrong, but twice as likely to draw blood.

Like judgment coming home.

The door opened with a whisper.

Balar stepped through. The knife was already in his hand.

Vivienne sat behind her desk, pen moving across paper in smooth strokes. She didn't look up. Didn't flinch. Just raised a single eyebrow as death walked into her office.

"Balar." She set the pen down with deliberate care. "You're late."

Something stirred in the back of his mind—*this is wrong, this is*—but he crushed it. That voice didn't matter. Only the woman across the room mattered. Only ending her mattered.

He moved deeper into the room, boots silent even on the hard floor. The mask felt like part of his face now, fused to skin and bone. Behind Vivienne, floor-to-ceiling windows framed the city in twilight. All those lights. All those lives.

None of them mattered either.

Just her. Just the knife. Just the killing that would make everything...

It didn't matter. It would simply be.

"Nothing to say?" Vivienne leaned back in her chair. "Three weeks of reports, two weeks of silence, and now you walk into my office without so much as a knock."

She studied him, fingers steepled.

"Very disappointing."

He kept moving. Closer. The knife heavy in his hand.

"I've been getting reports," she continued, voice conversational. Like they were discussing the weather. "Sloppy work at the warehouse. Letting the target escape. Allowing yourself to be seen." She clicked her tongue. "Very disappointing."

Ten feet. Eight. Six.

"Ah." Vivienne's eyes went wide in exaggerated terror. She threw up her hands. "Oh, please Balar, don't hurt me!" Her voice pitched high, simpering. "You're such a big, scary man! Have mercy!"

The knife stopped moving.

His mind reeled. She was... mocking him? Here? Now? With her death only moments away?

"What's wrong?" She dropped her hands, the fake terror vanishing. "Isn't this what you wanted? The big dramatic confrontation? The villain cowering before the hero's righteous blade?"

Something twisted in his chest. Hot. Sick.

"Oh." Her smile sharpened. "But you're not the hero, are you? Heroes don't abduct women for two weeks. Heroes don't—"

"You made me do it." The words ripped out before he could stop them, through the mask. The first Balar had ever spoken.

"Made you?" She laughed. Actually laughed. "How? Did I stab the wrong person? Did I perhaps tie Trin's restraints? Tell me, when you were standing over her unconscious body, thinking about how strong and powerful you are, where exactly was I?"

Shame burned hot. He gripped the knife tighter.

"That's what I thought." She leaned against her desk, casual as anything. "You want to kill me because you can't stand what you see in the mirror. But here's the beautiful thing—killing me won't change that. You'll still be the man who tortured Lars Harrow's lover. Who betrayed everything you claimed to stand for. Who became exactly the kind of monster you used to hunt."

"Shut up."

"Make me." She stepped closer, well within striking range. "That's what you came here for, isn't it? To shut me up permanently? To free yourself from my terrible influence?" Her voice dropped to a whisper. "To pretend that killing me will somehow undo what you've become?"

The knife trembled in his grip.

"The amusing thing," she continued, "is that you think this is about control. That I'm some puppet master pulling your strings. But the truth? You wanted this. Every time you put on that mask, every time you hurt someone in my name—that was you choosing. I just gave you permission."

"You're wrong."

"Am I?" She reached out, fingers almost touching the mask. "Then take it off. Show me Myrim. Show me the good man who would never—"

He grabbed her wrist, twisted. She gasped but didn't cry out, eyes bright with something that might have been triumph.

"See?" she breathed. "You can't. Because without the mask, you'd have to face what you've done. Who you've hurt. At least as Balar, you can pretend it's not really you."

"I said shut up."

"Poor little Myrim." Her free hand came up, traced the edge of the mask. "So desperate to be the hero. So willing to be the monster. And too stupid to realize they're the same thing."

The knife pressed against her ribs. One push. Just one push and—

"You won't do it." Her voice was certain. Calm. "You know why?"

He didn't answer. Couldn't.

"Because if you kill me, what then?" She leaned closer, completely unafraid. "You can't go back to them. Not after what you've done. Myrim is dead. Your old life is dead. Forever."

The knife wavered.

"And Balar?" She laughed softly. "Balar needs someone to hunt. Someone to blame. Without me to hate, what are you? Just a murderer in a mask with nowhere to go. No one to be."

The truth of it hit like ice water. He'd burned every bridge to get here. There was no home waiting. No forgiveness. No life beyond this moment.

"You'll wander the streets looking for someone else to blame. Someone else to punish for what you've become. But there's no one left, is there? Just you. A pointless man whose only gift is to destroy and cower behind that mask."

She cupped his leather cheek. Almost tenderly.

"You came here to kill me because you thought it would end something. But all it does is leave you exactly what you are—nothing. A ghost. A ridiculous reminder of what happens when weak men pretend to be strong."

The knife was shaking now. His whole arm trembling.

"At least as my weapon, you had purpose. Direction. Now?" She shrugged. "You're just a useless coward."

His hand dropped. The knife clattered to the floor.

A sob tore through him, muffled by the mask. Then another. His shoulders shook as something fundamental broke inside. The leather was too close, too hot, suffocating him with the smell of his own fear and shame.

His hands rose to the mask's edges.

"Don't."

Vivienne's single word stopped him cold. He froze, fingers trembling against the clasps.

She was right. He couldn't take it off. Not anymore. The mask was all he had left. All he was.

"I won't." His voice came out broken. "I... what now?"

"Now?" She straightened, brushing imaginary dust from her dress. "Now you do what you're good for. You protect me."

He looked up at her through the mask's eyeholes, lost.

"Tomorrow evening. The Opaline Hall. I'll be meeting with the city leaders and crew representatives." She moved back to her desk, already returning to her papers. "You'll be there. Hidden. Watching. Taking in everything. Ready to act if things turn... unpleasant."

"Yes." The word came out hollow.

Vivienne paused, then walked back to him. Her hand rose to his cheek, fingers gentle against the leather. He gasped at the touch—when had anyone last touched him with anything but fear?

"My poor, broken man," she murmured.

Then her hand slid down to his throat. Slim fingers wrapped around his neck, not squeezing but present. A reminder.

"And Myrim..." she said. "If you ever threaten me again, I'll make what happened to Trin look like mercy. I'll destroy Liora and Shelle so thoroughly that even their memories will taste like ash. Do you understand?"

The fingers tightened just slightly. Just enough.

"Yes, mistress."

The Opaline Hall lived up to its name.

From his position behind an ornate folding screen, Balar watched light fracture through crystal chandeliers, casting rainbow patterns across marble floors. The Gaming Commission's premier meeting space—neutral ground for the city's power brokers to pretend at civility while sharpening their knives.

He'd been in position for an hour, watching servants arrange chairs around the massive oak table. Watching Vivienne direct the placement of documents with surgical precision. Watching

Diligence take her position at Vivienne's right hand, elegant in midnight blue.

Blade and shield. The metaphor crystallized as he observed them. Diligence, sharp and ready to cut. Himself, hidden but present, ready to deflect any threat. And Vivienne at the center, calm as a general surveying a battlefield she'd already won.

The doors opened. He catalogued each arrival with the cold efficiency of his former life.

Councilman Breslin—nervous, sweating despite the cool evening. Already compromised.

Councilwoman Belmani. Sharp-eyed, wary. Still thinking she had choices.

Markus entered with ledgers under his arm, Vivienne's head of finance. The man who knew where every copper flowed and why.

Garrett Stenhouse of the Foundryworkers Union. Big man, bigger voice. He might need careful handling.

Lord Ashford, who owned half of Brighthaven and looked like he'd rather be anywhere else.

Two more entered—thieving crew leaders he recognized but who'd never achieved the fame of the main players. Old guard. Survivors who'd learned when to bend.

Then Lars Harrow walked in.

Even from behind the screen, Balar could see the changes. The hollow cheeks were filling out. The tremor in his hands was gone. He moved with purpose again. The gentleman thief, playing his role to perfection.

Darius followed, all theatrical disdain and barely leashed energy. The showman to Lars's sophisticate. Between them, they commanded the room's attention without saying a word.

"Gentlemen." Vivienne's voice cut through the murmurs. "Ladies. Thank you for accepting my invitation."

"Invitation?" Darius dropped into a chair with deliberate casualness. "That's what we're calling it?"

Vivienne's smile didn't waver. "Would you prefer 'summons'? I find civility costs nothing."

"Unlike crystal charges," Lars said quietly, taking his own seat. "Those cost quite a bit, I hear."

The temperature in the room dropped a degree. Vivienne's fingers drummed once on the table—the only sign she'd heard the barb.

"Before we begin," she said, "I wondered if there had been any word about our missing friend? Trinelle, wasn't it?"

Lars's jaw tightened. He looked away, cleared his throat. When he spoke, his voice was carefully neutral. "No. No word."

"Pity." Vivienne's sympathy was perfectly pitched. "Such a talented woman. But that's not why we're here, is it?"

"No," Lars said, meeting her eyes. "It's not."

"Good. Then let's discuss the future." She gestured to Markus, who began distributing documents.

Straight to business. No pleasantries, no dancing around the edges. Vivienne knew her battlefield and wanted to control the engagement from the first moment. Classic tactics.

But Balar found his attention pulling toward Lars. The man he'd beaten bloody in a heist that felt like a lifetime ago. The man whose lover he'd kept drugged for two weeks. Lars, who'd just lied with such perfect composure.

Because it had to be a lie. Trin was gone. Liora had found her, had dragged her away on that tarp. He'd seen it happen, had retreated rather than—

No. Lars was too calm. Too controlled. A man whose lover was still missing would show cracks, however small. A tremor in the voice. A tell in the hands. Something.

"As you all know," Vivienne continued, pulling his attention back, "the copper crisis threatens everything we've built. Trade routes disrupted. Manufacturing at a standstill. The very foundation of our economy crumbling."

The words washed over the room. Balar watched faces tighten, saw Lord Ashford's hands clench on the table. Everyone here had stakes in copper. Everyone here was bleeding money.

Except Vivienne. "The copper crisis is destroying Azoria."

"A CRISIS YOU CREATED!" Lord Ashford's face had gone purple. "When you cut off trade with Zarakar! When you—"

"That Lars Harrow created," Vivienne corrected smoothly, "when he exposed Thume's operations. Cause and effect, Lord Ashford. Actions have consequences."

"But you didn't have to cut off trade entirely! You didn't have to—"

"Enough." The word cracked like a whip. "As I said, we're not here to argue the past. I'm here to offer a solution."

She stood, moving to the window that overlooked the city. Calculated. Every gesture designed for maximum impact.

From a velvet-lined box on the sideboard, she lifted a crystal charge. The thing caught the light like captured fire—smooth, vibrant, pulsing with inner radiance. She held it up, letting everyone see the future in her palm.

"Crystal charges. Clean. Renewable. Already integrated into our infrastructure thanks to brilliant minds like Liora Banz." She turned back to them, the crystal casting prismatic patterns across her face. "Imagine a city that runs entirely on crystal power. No more dependence on copper. No more bowing to Zarakar's demands."

The crystal hummed faintly, a sound felt more than heard. Power contained. Power controlled.

"It all sounds expensive," Garrett rumbled. "My workers can barely afford food, and you want them to buy crystals?"

"Not buy. Lease." Vivienne's smile was radiant. "Recharging stations throughout the city. Citizens pay a small fee to power their devices, their homes, their lives. Predictable. Sustainable. Fair."

"Fair?" Darius laughed. "You mean controlled. By you."

"By us." She spread her hands. "Everyone in this room stands to benefit. Infrastructure contracts. Distribution rights. A percentage of every charge."

"So that's it." Lars's voice cut through the murmurs. "You're not trying to save the city. You're trying to corner the market on its lifeblood."

"I'm trying to create stability from chaos. Order from disorder."

She looked directly at Darius. "For example, Mr. Adalan—you may keep the crystal charges you... acquired. Consider it an investment in our mutual future."

Darius's eyes narrowed, calculating.

"Think of it," Vivienne continued. "No more scrambling for copper. No more watching our economy hemorrhage. Just clean, controlled power. All we need is unity. Leadership. The people look to those in this room for direction."

"And if we refuse?" Councilwoman Belmani asked.

"Then you're betting against the future. Against progress. Against—"

"Lars is right."

Everyone turned. Diligence had spoken, her cultured voice cutting through the tension.

"About what?" Vivienne said, eyes wide.

"Everything." Diligence stepped forward, addressing the room. "This isn't about saving Azoria. It's about control. About turning every citizen into a customer who can't survive without what you're selling."

The silence was deafening. From his hiding spot, Balar watched Vivienne go absolutely still. Not frozen—coiled. Like a snake before it strikes.

Vivienne's mask slipped back into place with visible effort. When she spoke, her voice was dangerously soft.

"Explain yourself."

Diligence moved to the center of the room with languid grace, as if she had all the time in the world. As if she hadn't just driven a knife between her employer's ribs.

"I've stood by your side, Vivienne. Watched you scheme. Watched you maneuver. Watched your greed slowly strangle this city." She paused, letting the words sink in. "I've been your shadow, your confidante, your blade when you needed one. I've been your lover."

She moved toward Lars's chair. "You had me tail Lars Harrow. Follow his every move, report his every weakness." Her hand came to rest on Lars's shoulder with casual familiarity. "And you know what I found? A man trying to save his city from you."

Balar saw it—the way Vivienne's fingers curled against the table. The slight tremor in her jaw. Cracks in the perfect facade.

"How dare you." The words came out low, venomous. The composure Vivienne always wore was crumbling.

"How dare I?" Diligence laughed, the sound bright and cutting. "That's rich, coming from the woman who made Balar. Who set him loose on our streets like a rabid dog. Who—"

"ENOUGH!" Vivienne surged to her feet.

The room erupted. Chairs scraped back. Voices rose in a cacophony of accusation.

"Is this true?" someone shouted. "You created that monster?"

"The blood on our streets—"

"Our children afraid to leave their homes—"

"All for your power games!"

From behind the screen, Balar watched his mistress unravel. Her perfect control shattered. This was what betrayal looked like from the outside. This was what it did to someone who'd never expected it.

Just as she had done to him.

"Enough." Vivienne's voice cut through the chaos, but it was different now. Raw. Dangerous.

Diligence turned her back on Vivienne, addressing the crowd. "She is a poison. This city deserves better leadership." She spread her arms wide, playing to her audience. "This city deserves—"

The movement was so fast Balar almost missed it.

Vivienne stepped forward. Her hand swept from her sleeve, a blade arcing toward Diligence in one fluid motion. Silver flashed in the chandelier light.

Diligence's words died in a wet gurgle. Her hands flew to her throat, but the blood was already spraying between her fingers. She turned, eyes wide with shock, mouth working soundlessly.

She took one stumbling step. Then another. Her midnight blue shirt was turning black with blood.

Then she fell.

The sound of her body hitting marble echoed through the hall. Blood spread across the pristine floor in a widening pool, reflecting the chandelier light like spilled wine.

The silence lasted a heartbeat.

Then screams. Chairs crashing over. Bodies scrambling for the door.

Balar's heart hammered against his ribs. This wasn't the plan. This wasn't—

Vivienne stood there, knife dripping, watching her former lover crumple to the marble floor. The mask was gone now. All that remained was the fury of a woman who'd been betrayed by the one person she'd trusted.

The doors burst open as the first wave of panicked bodies reached them. But instead of escape, they met resistance—a crowd of servants and attendants trying to push inside, drawn by the screams.

The collision was chaos. Bodies pressed against bodies. Someone fell. Someone else trampled them. The doorway became a writhing mass of limbs and terror.

And in the center of it all, Vivienne stood perfectly still. The knife dripped steady beats onto marble. Her face had twisted into something that wasn't quite a smile—a rictus grin of pure, unhinged fury.

Balar saw it happening. The crowd crushing itself. The panic spreading like wildfire. His mistress standing there like she wanted to watch the world burn.

He shoved the screen aside and leaped into the room.

The screams changed pitch. Not just panic now. Terror.

"BALAR!"

He moved to Vivienne's side, drawing twin knives, falling into a defensive stance. Protecting her even now. Even after everything.

Through the chaos at the door, he saw Lars go white as bone. Recognition dawned in those eyes, followed by something darker. A scowl that transformed his entire face.

"Myrim."

The name hit like a physical blow. Not Balar. Myrim. Lars knew.

Movement at the door. The crowd had thinned enough for someone to push through. Liora. She stood beside Lars, taking in the scene with quick, intelligent eyes. The blood. Diligence's twitching form. Vivienne with her dripping blade.

And him. Balar. Myrim. The man who'd—

Their eyes met.

The anger on her face was absolute. But worse was what came after. Disgust, pure and sickening.

She started forward, and for one wild moment he thought—hoped—she might be coming to him. To save him. To forgive—

Darius grabbed both her and Lars, physically hauling them backward. "We need to get out of here!"

Lars resisted for a heartbeat, still staring at Balar with that terrible understanding. Then he let himself be pulled away.

They vanished into the crowd. Into the night. Into a life he could never have again.

The hall fell silent. Diligence's corpse, twitching in her spreading pool of blood.

Just him. Vivienne. And the consequences of what they'd become.

Part 4

Summer Home
City of Whispers
The Reckoning
Losing Ground
Gaining Purpose
A Bridge Too Far
Epilogue

SUMMER HOME

17

The sound of Diligence's body hitting marble would haunt Darius for weeks. That wet, final thud of meat slapping stone, and then the slow spread of blood across the Opaline Hall's pristine floor like spilled wine at a party gone wrong.

Darius Adalan had been mid-anecdote when it happened, regaling Councilwoman Belmani with a heavily embellished tale about a mishap with a peacock and three bottles of imported champagne.

He'd had her eating out of his hand, that particular combination of scandalized and delighted that made marks so easy to fleece. The punchline was right there, perfectly timed, when Vivienne Dragunova decided to slit her lover's throat in front of a dozen witnesses.

The words died in his mouth. His carefully crafted persona—the roguish thief with a heart of gold and a wit sharp enough to cut glass—evaporated like morning mist.

All that remained was a man watching civilization bleed out on polished marble.

This wasn't in the script.

His mind, trained by years of reading rooms and playing angles, catalogued the scene with horrified precision. Vivienne standing there with the knife still dripping. Like she'd crossed out a line in a ledger. Diligence at her feet, twitching in a widening pool of her own blood.

No buildup. No dramatic confrontation. No stylish exchange of threats and counter-threats. Just crude butchery in the middle of what should have been civilized theater.

It offended him on a level deeper than morality. Darius had stolen, cheated, and lied his way across half of Azoria, but he'd done it with style.

Every con was a performance, every heist a carefully choreographed dance. Even violence, when absolutely necessary, had its own aesthetic—quick, clean, purposeful. A means to an end, not the end itself.

This was artless. It was cold.

The screams had already started. Raw, panicked sounds as chairs crashed over and bodies scrambled for the doors.

And then the screen crashed aside, and a real monster entered stage left.

He moved like violence given form, twin knives already drawn, positioning himself between Vivienne and the world like a leather-clad nightmare.

That's when the real chaos began. Chairs toppled. Bodies scrambled. The cream of Azoria's society transformed into panicked cattle, all rushing for the same door.

Through the chaos, Darius caught the moment of recognition. Saw Lars Harrow go white as fresh parchment, saw his lips form a single word: "Myrim."

Oh. The pieces clicked into place with an almost audible snap. *Oh, that's so much worse.*

He spotted Inora through the door as the crowd inside loudly met the crowd outside. Their eyes met across the carnage. Darius made the gesture—subtle, practiced, invisible to anyone not looking for it. Just a brush of fingers across his jacket, a tilt of his head.

Summer Home.

She nodded once, already moving. Good old Inora. While everyone else was losing their minds, she'd make sure the right people got the right message. The show might be over, but the troupe still needed somewhere to regroup.

Time to make his exit.

The crowd at the door had become a writhing mass of silk and terror. Councilmen who'd spent years practicing dignity were now clawing at each other like dock workers fighting over scraps.

Darius slipped sideways, using the confusion as cover. There was always more than one exit if you knew where to look.

"Coming through, lovely party, shame about the murder—"

Even now, even with blood on the floor and chaos in the air, he couldn't quite drop the performer's patter. It was his lifeline, that need to make light of the darkness. But underneath, something cold and hard had settled in his chest.

The servant's corridor was mercifully empty. His footsteps echoed off bare stone, a percussion accompaniment to the muffled screams behind him. Darius moved fast but not frantically, maintaining that crucial balance between speed and control.

Never run unless you're being chased. Running people look guilty.

He burst out into the cool night air through a delivery entrance, filling his lungs with the freshest air Azoria could offer. The sounds from inside were muffled but still audible—cries, crashes, the particular pitch of hysteria that meant society was eating itself alive.

For a moment, he just stood there in the alley, looking back at the Opaline Hall. From outside, it still looked magnificent. Columns of white marble reached toward the stars, windows glowed with warm light, pure class on a street corner.

What a sick joke.

Inside that monument to entertainment, Vivienne Dragunova had just murdered her closest ally in front of the city's elite. Not in the shadows, not with poison or a convenient accident, but with a knife across the throat in full view of everyone who mattered.

And her pet monster—Myrim, apparently, though Darius was still processing that particular revelation—had leaped to her defense like a well-trained attack dog.

The game was over. Darius could feel it in his lodes. The careful dance of sanctioned thievery, the unspoken rules that kept violence at bay, the gentleman's agreement that made their whole world possible—Vivienne had just burned it all down. And she'd done it with all the grace of a back-alley throat-slitter.

No style at all.

The thought should have been petty. People were probably dying in there, trampled in the panic or cut down by Balar's knives if they got too close. He should be thinking about the political ramifications, the power vacuum, the chaos that would follow. But all Darius could focus on was the sheer crudeness of it all.

They were supposed to be better than common thugs. They were artists, performers, practitioners of a higher form of crime. Even their rivalries had been theatrical—Lars and his crew on one side, Darius and his on the other, playing out their conflicts with style and wit and the occasional bruised ego.

Darius started walking, letting his feet carry him through familiar streets while his mind raced. The Summer Home. The abandoned warehouse he'd bought, one of those just-in-case investments that suddenly seemed prescient.

His crew knew about it—they'd used it as a backup spot more than once when heat got too high. Inora would get word to everyone who mattered. She had a gift for that sort of thing.

But who was "everyone" now? His own crew, certainly. Maren and Rurik would need to know the score had changed. But Lars's people too? After what just happened, rivalries and grudges just didn't seem to matter anymore.

And their base sure as hells wouldn't be safe for them.

The streets grew grittier as he moved east, elaborate facades giving way to brick, smoke, and suspicious shadows.

Hells, maybe that's what they'd all been fooling themselves about. Maybe Vivienne had just shown them what they really were—not celebrities or artists, but just crooks scrambling for a piece of the pie.

No. Darius rejected the thought with a flash of familiar anger. We were something more. We made ourselves something more.

The Summer Home materialized out of the darkness, all broken windows and rust-eaten metal. One of a dozen boltholes scattered across the city, each one known to the crew, each one stocked with the essentials.

He slipped inside through the loading dock, muscle memory guiding him through the darkness. Somewhere in the darkness, a rat scurried away from his footsteps.

The main floor stretched out before him, empty except for a few pieces of salvaged furniture and the ghosts of better times. They'd pulled three major scores from this place back when the world still made sense. Back when the game had rules and the players all understood their parts.

Darius found himself laughing—a short, bitter sound that echoed off the rafters. All those elaborate plans, all those carefully crafted personas, all that style.

And for what? So Vivienne could render it all meaningless with one crude stroke of a blade?

He moved to the old office that overlooked the main floor, climbing stairs that groaned under his weight. From here, he could see the whole space, could watch the entrances, could plan the next move.

Last year, when they took down Thume together, had they really messed up this bad? Dancing to Vivienne's tune while she prepared to flip the table?

The thought burned, but not as much as the memory of that artless kill. At least if she'd orchestrated some elaborate scheme, he could respect the craft. But this?

Footsteps echoed from below. Darius tensed, hand moving to the knife at his belt, then relaxed as he recognized the gait.

Inora appeared at the top of the stairs, dark clothes blending with the shadows. There was blood on her sleeve—not hers, from the way she moved. Someone else's misfortune then, likely collected in the crush.

"How bad?" he asked.

"Three dead that I saw. Maybe more in the stampede." Her raspy voice was flat, professional. Inora had always been good at compartmentalizing. "Vivienne's locked down the hall. No one in or out until her people are done 'investigating.'"

"Investigating." Darius laughed again, that same bitter sound. "All we saw was a madwoman slit her lover's throat, and a monster from a kids' story jump out of the wall to defend her. What's to investigate?"

Inora didn't answer.

Darius cleared his throat. "The others?"

"Coming. I made sure word got out before…" She paused, and for the first time since he'd known her, Darius saw something like emotion crack her professional facade. "Boss, what the hells was that?"

"That," Darius said, sinking into a moth-eaten chair that had seen better decades, "was the end of the world as we know it."

"Bit dramatic."

"Am I wrong?" He gestured at the empty space below them and his bitter thoughts came out in a rush. "The game's over, Inora. The rules are dead. Vivienne just showed everyone that power comes from the edge of a blade, not the clever hand or the silver tongue. Everything we built, everything we were—she just reduced it to common murder."

Inora was quiet for a moment. "So what do we do?"

That was the question, wasn't it? What did artists do when their medium was declared obsolete? What did performers do when someone burned down the theater?

"We survive," Darius said finally. "We adapt. And maybe, if we're very lucky and very clever, we find a way to make her pay for taking away the only thing that made any of this worth doing."

"The money?"

"The style." He stood, moving to join her at the window.

Outside, the city went about its business, unaware that the careful balance that kept it from tearing itself apart had just been shattered.

"No sign of Harrow," Inora said. "Think they'll even show? After that?"

Darius paused. Good question. Would Lars trust anyone enough to come right now?

"They'll come," he said finally. "Where else is there to go?"

The city they'd all danced through, played in, stolen from—it had just shown its teeth. And none of them were safe alone anymore.

He descended into the gloom, already hearing new footsteps echoing through the loading dock. Time to see who was left standing after Vivienne decided to flip the board.

The Summer Home squatted in the foundry district on the northeast end of the river. Lars pushed through the loading dock entrance, his people trailing behind him like shadows.

Two days. Two days since Liora had found Trin, half-mad with drugs and terror. Two days of watching her flinch at sudden movements, of seeing her stare at the door with wide, expectant eyes. Two days of pretending things might go back to normal.

Then Vivienne slit Diligence's throat in front of everyone, and normal became just another word for naive.

Lars couldn't stop glancing back at Trin as they entered the warehouse. She moved differently now. Still graceful, but careful.

The guilt sat in his chest like a stone. His games with Thume and Vivienne, his need to be the clever one, the one who always won—it had all led to this. Trin in a cellar. Myrim in a mask. Blood on marble floors.

Hells, did that just happen?

"Cozy," Bunny said, but even his attempt at levity fell flat in the dead air. The big man's usual grin was nowhere to be found, replaced by something harder. They'd all seen and heard too much tonight.

The main floor opened up before them, empty except for salvaged furniture and memories of better cons.

Nice hiding spot, Lars thought. Decent distance from anything resembling law enforcement.

"Lars."

Darius's voice from above. The man stood on the office landing with Inora, who had squawked Jax back at their base to let him know what happened and where to meet up.

Normally Lars would have come straight here—and probably beaten Darius, who liked to stop and smell the roses on the way—but there was no way he was running for safety until he knew Trin was safe. He and Liora had met up with Jax, Bunny, and Trin halfway and they all came together.

The night was still far too dangerous.

"Darius," Lars acknowledged, moving deeper into the space. Their theatrical rivalry felt like a costume from another life. One where the biggest worry was who'd pull the flashier heist, not whether they'd survive in their own city.

Trin found a crate to sit on, folding in on herself in a way that made Lars's chest tight. The stray dog that had found her during her escape settled at her feet.

She'd been the bright one, the sharp one. And, truth be told, Lars had taken that—taken her—for granted. She was the one who kept him sane, and honed him into the role of leader.

Now she sat small and quiet, one hand occasionally dropping to touch the dog's head, eyes tracking every movement in the warehouse like she was cataloguing threats.

Two days, and he still didn't know how to fix this. How to restore the partner who'd saved his ass more times than he could count with a smile and a perfectly timed distraction. The woman who he loved.

"How many dead?" Lars asked, not really wanting the answer.

"Three that Inora saw," Darius called down. "Probably more in the stampede."

Stampede. Like they were cattle. Which maybe they were now. Just animals running from a predator with sharper teeth than they'd ever imagined.

Liora stood near the cold forges, one hand pressed against the brick like she needed something solid to anchor her. Shell-shocked was too mild a word for what Lars saw in her face. The man she'd loved alongside Shelle, built a life with, had become the monster who'd tortured Trin and protected Vivienne.

How did you process that? How did you reconcile the person who'd shared your bed with a murderer in leather?

"Boss," Jax said. "What the hells do we do now?"

The question hung in the air like smoke. Such a simple question, one that Jax might have asked him a hundred times on heists or even just after breakfast. But this was different. What the hells do we do now? We regroup.

Lars felt something crystallize in his chest. All the games, all the clever schemes, all the rivalry and reputation—none of it mattered now. What mattered was the woman sitting small and quiet on that crate. What mattered was his people looking to him not for brilliance, but for direction.

"We protect each other," he said, and his voice came out steadier than he'd expected. "We gather everyone we can. And we figure out how to fight back."

It wasn't resignation in his tone. If anything it was clarity.

For years he'd been playing at being a crew leader, dancing around the edges of real danger. But seeing Trin broken, seeing Vivienne's true face, seeing what Myrim had become... it had burned away all the unnecessary parts.

What remained was simple: his people needed him to be more than clever. They needed him to be what came next.

More footsteps echoed from the loading dock. Lars tensed, then relaxed as familiar faces appeared. Rurik, Maren. Leaders from other crews. The Gimble Brothers, still in their fancy clothes from whatever job got interrupted. Serine Conwen, who ran solo operations out of the market district. Even old Creet Daws, who claimed he'd retired last year.

They all shared the same look—stunned, scared, trying to figure out what came next. Yesterday they'd been competitors, each running their own games, their own territories. Now they were just survivors of Vivienne's declaration of war.

The warehouse was filling up faster than Lars had expected. A dozen thieves, then twenty, then more. Enough, apparently, to satisfy whatever Darius had been waiting for. He descended the stairs with Inora, that casual grace intact despite everything.

"Hells of a thing," Darius said as he reached the main floor, which was about the biggest understatement Lars had heard all year.

"That's one way to put it," Lars replied. How had word spread so fast? But then, that's what thieves did. They talked, they whispered, they shared information like currency.

Darius stopped a few feet away. "Every crew in the city needs to be looking over their shoulders now. Every independent operator, every small-timer who ever lifted a purse."

Lars nodded. The old distinctions—his crew, Darius's crew, the independents—none of it mattered anymore. Vivienne had just declared war on their entire way of life.

"We're all in the same boat now," Lars said.

"One crew," Darius agreed, and the words carried weight. Not just an alliance, but something bigger. Every thief in Azoria against whatever Vivienne was becoming.

The gathered thieving crews all nodded at that. "One crew," a few of them repeated.

"One crew," Lars agreed.

Trin shifted on her crate, and Lars caught her watching him. For just a moment, something flickered in her eyes—not the old sharpness, not yet, but something. Maybe approval. Maybe just recognition that he was finally catching up to what she'd already learned in that cellar.

The world had teeth. Time to grow some of their own.

Jax moved closer to Trin, still in protection mode. The big man had taken her trauma personally, appointed himself her guardian.

"We'll need everyone," Lars continued, raising his voice so the crowd could hear. "Every set of skills, every contact, every safe house. This isn't about territory anymore. It's about survival."

"Survival's not a plan," someone called out—one of the Gimble Brothers, Lars thought. "What do we do when she comes for us?"

Lars looked at Trin again. At what they'd done to her. At what she'd survived.

"We learn," he said. "We adapt. It's what we're best at."

The gentleman thief was dead—Vivienne had killed him as surely as she'd killed Diligence. But Lars Harrow wasn't done yet. He had people to protect, a city to reclaim, and a woman to make pay for what she'd done to his family.

Darius sighed dramatically, a hint of his usual self. "Ah damn," he said. "Does this mean you're all staying?"

"Anyone who wants to, I'd say," Lars said, though most of the thieves started mumbling to each other and eyeballing the door.

He couldn't blame them. Old habits died hard, and thinking about a big bunkhouse of career burglars, conmen, and heist aficionados didn't exactly appeal to him either.

But this was war.

"Let's at least figure out watches for tonight," he said, more suggestion than order. "And check if anyone needs patching up. We can sort the rest in the morning."

The thieves began organizing themselves. They all knew how to be practical when survival was on the line.

Lars caught Darius's eye. They'd work out the details later, figure out how to coordinate without stepping on each other's toes. For now, it was enough that people weren't scattering to the winds.

That had to be Vivienne's plan. Create chaos, then step in to restore order. Paint them all as the villains while she played savior.

Well. She'd made one mistake.

She'd left them alive.

Lars moved to Trin's side, not touching—she wasn't ready for that—but close enough to be there. "We'll get through this," he said quietly.

Trin looked up at him, and for the first time since they'd found her, she spoke more than fragments. "I know," she whispered.

She shifted slightly, making room on the crate. Lars sat beside her, careful to leave space between them. Then, so gently it almost surprised him, Trin leaned over and rested her head on his shoulder. The dog, ever present, pressed against her other side, tail tucked but alert.

His heart swelled so strongly he feared it might burst. Together they watched their strange new alliance take shape. It wasn't much. But it was a start.

The warehouse had transformed in the hour since they'd arrived. What started as a collection of shocked thieves had become something almost... domestic. Liora watched from her spot near the cold forges as Azoria's criminal element settled in for what might be a long stay.

Thirty thieves trying to make a place to call home for the night. Wild. Like someone had thrown a "bring your lockpicks" party complete with a murder mystery dinner.

A few crews had slipped away once the initial shock wore off—smart, probably. Get out before Vivienne decided to go for a massacre. But more had stayed than she'd expected. Someone had gotten a barrel fire going in the corner, and the smell of cooking meat drifted through the space.

Still, it was a weird energy. Welcome to the Summer Home, folks. Watch out for psychotic rulers with pet monsters.

"Liora!"

She turned to find Maren approaching, all gangly limbs and barely contained excitement. Even the night's horror hadn't dimmed his particular brand of chaos energy.

As she'd expect from a fellow dynamo head. It was good to see someone else whose brain went sideways when stressed.

"So the bank job," he said without preamble, hands already sketching shapes in the air. "I need another engineer's opinion. The resonance locks on that vault. Impossible from the outside, right? The harmonic frequency shifts every twelve seconds, all that. So instead, calculating the tunnel trajectory while accounting for the foundation's vibration—"

"Wait, you tunneled under?" Liora's brain immediately started running calculations. "The bedrock there is—"

"Granite composite, I know!" His eyes were practically glowing. "But here's the genius part—I didn't go through it. I went around it. Used the old sewer maintenance shaft, reinforced the walls with an iron crystalline—"

"The Kellerman equation? But the variables would be—"

"Exactly! That's what was so hard to calculate. But once I had the resonance pattern mapped..." He made a victorious gesture with his hands.

"Beautiful." And it was. The kind of elegant solution that made her brain happy. It was nice to think about something that wasn't betrayal and blood. "The frequency modulation alone must have been—"

"Later, you two," Darius called from across the warehouse. "Save the technical symposium for when we're not in crisis mode."

Right. Crisis. Murder. Monster boyfriend. Her brain snapped back to the present, but she still stuck her tongue out at Darius for ruining her good time.

"Got anywhere for us engineers to work?" she asked. Because if she was expected to spiral, she might as well spiral productively.

Darius raised an eyebrow at her. "In the back. Maren knows where."

"Come on," she told Maren. "Let's see what kind of tools we're working with. Maybe we can build something that—"

The loading dock door opened.

Liora turned, and her eyes widened in shock.

Shelle stood in the doorway like she'd stepped out of one of those paintings in the museum district. Dark hair in waves, red lips, that dress that hugged curves in ways that made people stupid.

She was beautiful. She was here. She was alive.

The tears hit without warning. Zero to sobbing in half a second. Liora was moving before her brain caught up, stumbling across the warehouse floor. She didn't care who saw. Couldn't care.

Shelle caught her as she collapsed into her arms, both of them sinking to their knees on the dirty floor.

"I've got you," Shelle murmured, stroking her hair. "I've got you, darling."

Liora sobbed into her shoulder. Ugly crying. The kind that involved snot. All the horror and betrayal and confusion pouring out in gross, wrenching sounds.

Around them, the warehouse had gone quiet. Even criminals knew when to look away.

Eventually the storm passed. Shelle helped her to her feet, guiding her to a quieter corner where some old crates created privacy.

"You know what happened?" Liora asked.

"Information broker, love." Shelle's smile was sad. "My informants were tripping over each other to tell me about Vivienne's grand finale. And about who jumped out to protect her."

"Balar." The name tasted like ash.

"Myrim." Shelle's correction was gentle but firm. "That's who Lars saw. That's who you saw."

Right. That moment. Looking across the chaos and seeing those leather-wrapped hands holding knives. The mask turning toward her. Those eyes—she couldn't see them through the mask's holes, but Liora knew he was looking right at her.

The disgust on her face must have been visible even across the room. Had he seen it? Did he care?

"How did we not see it?" Liora's voice came out rough. "We shared everything with him. Our bed. Our lives. Our—"

Her brain skittered sideways. "The bruises. He always had bruises."

"Said he got them breaking up fights." Shelle's jaw was tight. "And we believed him."

Stupid. That was the only excuse. "Because we're idiots."

"Because we're in love. Were. Were in love." Shelle pulled her knees up. "People in love don't look for monsters under the mask."

They sat in silence. Liora's brain kept jumping tracks. The way he'd kiss them goodbye in the morning. How he'd come home wound tight like a spring. Late nights. Always late nights. How many people had he hurt before crawling into their bed?

"He tortured Trin," Liora said finally. "She said his name when I brought her home. Just "Myrim." Like it explained everything."

"It does explain everything." Shelle's hand found hers. "He chose to become this. Whatever Vivienne offered him, he took it."

"Power? Money?" Liora's laugh came out broken. "What makes someone decide to be a monster?"

"Maybe he always was one." Shelle's voice was bitter. "Maybe we just saw what we wanted to see. The protective captain. The one who made us feel safe."

Safe. What a joke. They'd been sleeping with the thing that went bump in the night.

"I keep thinking I should hate him," Liora admitted. "But mostly my brain just... fizzles out. Like trying to divide by zero."

Shelle shifted closer, but didn't say anything.

Liora curled up into a ball. "Are we enough?" The question jumped out before she could stop it. "You and me? Without him?"

She felt tears welling in her eyes and demanded that they stop. But Shelle cupped her face gently. "Do you still love me?"

"Always. You're my favorite person."

"And you're mine." She stroked Liora's cheek. "We were friends before we were three, remember? Dynamo girls, even then."

Back then it had been Shelle-and-Myrim, with Liora on the outside looking in. Flirting, sure. But not together. Not yet.

"Just the dynamo girls." Liora tested the formula. "I can be happy with that."

Shelle nodded. Then with that mischief that made Liora's heart skip, she added, "And who knows? Maybe one day we'll find another man worth our time."

The absurdity—relationship planning during a crisis—made Liora laugh.

"Sure," she said, leaning into Shelle's warmth. "If we need one."

Shelle kissed her forehead. "Right now, I just need you. My brilliant, chaotic, perfect disaster of a girlfriend."

"I need you too." Liora closed her eyes. Safe. Actually safe. "Love you."

"Love you too." Shelle pulled her closer. "We'll figure this out. Together."

Together. New equation, same solution: them.

The math worked.

Lars needed to move. To act. To do something other than sit in this warehouse waiting for Vivienne to find them.

The loading dock offered an illusion of space, but even out here, the walls pressed in. Thirty-odd thieves crammed inside, their nervous energy seeping through cracks in the door— bottles clinking, voices low and uncertain. His people. His responsibility.

He couldn't just sit this one out.

After squawking three former associates, he'd gotten nothing but dead air. Either they'd ditched their boxes entirely or they were listening but refusing to answer. The silence told him everything he needed to know. But there had to be others. People who remembered what Azoria used to be, who might still—

"Brought you something."

Lars turned to find Darius in the doorway, bottle in hand.

"Where'd you find that?" Lars asked, recognizing quality when he saw it.

"Always keep a bottle stashed in the office." Darius settled onto an adjacent crate with theatrical precision. "For emergencies, celebrations, war councils, that sort of thing."

Darius worked the cork free and took a long pull before passing it over. Lars accepted it, the whiskey burning away the taste of bile in the back of his throat.

"So, which one is this?" Lars asked, gesturing vaguely at their situation.

"Which what?"

Lars lifted the bottle. "Emergency, celebration, or war council?"

"Oh," Darius said. "All three, I'd say."

They fell into a rhythm after that—drink, pass, watch the city lights. Lars's mind churned through possibilities. Which merchants might still deal with them, which Watch officers remembered the old ways, which noble families had benefited from the thieving economy. There had to be something. A way to stay in the city without painting targets on their backs.

"How's Trin?" Darius's question cut through his planning.

"Alive. Safe."

"That's not what I asked."

Lars took another pull from the bottle, buying time. How did you explain what Vivienne had broken? "She flinches when people move too fast. Checks every exit. Sometimes she's just... gone. Back in that cellar with him."

Him. Myrim. Another problem that needed solving.

"Two days," Lars continued, the words bitter. "Not even two days I had her back before Vivienne—" He gestured at the warehouse, the night, everything. "It wasn't enough time to even start healing."

"You can't fix everything, you know."

Watch me. But Lars just said, "I know."

Deep down he knew it was true. But it didn't mean he had to accept it. If he accepted that this was beyond his control—then what? Let Vivienne win? Let his people scatter to the winds? Run?

No. There was always another angle. Another play. And this was *their* city.

The irony wasn't lost on him. They'd brought down Thume because he'd gotten too heavy-handed, too controlling. And yes, if Lars was honest, they'd done it because it was the score of a lifetime—the kind of heist that would be talked about for generations. Taking down Azoria's leader?

That was art. That was legend.

Except what rushed in to fill the vacuum was so much worse. Vivienne with her year-long ban, her assassin, her vision of a "clean" Azoria that had no room for people like them.

And so they'd tried to break Thume out. Another backwards step, another attempt to restore the old balance.

For the life of him, Lars couldn't figure out why. To make things like they were before? To admit they'd been wrong? Either way, it had blown up in their faces.

Now here they sat, the legendary thieves of Azoria, reduced to refugees in their own city. Hiding in warehouses. Jumping at shadows. Debating whether to run or fight when they used to own these streets. Lars had tried to play puppet master with the city's fate and discovered too late that they were the ones dancing on strings.

The worst part was that it wasn't even him that had paid the price for his mistakes.

"She took a knife for me," Lars said quietly. "Jumped right in front of Balar's blade. Then he took her, and I couldn't—"

"From a moving monorail?" Darius shook his head. "What were you supposed to do, splatter yourself all over Lowtown?"

Be faster. Be smarter. Be the Lars Harrow who never lost.

But that Lars was gone, wasn't he? Killed somewhere between Trin being taken and Diligence getting murdered right in front of their eyes. What remained was someone harder.

"I was thinking earlier," Darius said eventually. "You know what bothers me most? It's not even the killing. It's the artlessness of it all. No style, no finesse. Just... butchery."

Lars snorted. "That's what bothers you most?"

"I'm a performer, Lars. Always have been. You know that. And she just..." He made a slashing motion. "Cut through all of it. Made us all common criminals with one ugly murder."

"We were always criminals, Darius."

Darius frowned at him. "No. We were artists. There's a difference."

"Is there?" Lars asked. "When Trin was screaming in that cellar, do you think she cared about the artistry?"

The question hung between them. Lars watched understanding dawn on Darius's face—the realization that their old world, with its rules and style and elaborate games, was truly dead.

"I suppose not," Darius admitted. "So what does this make us now?"

"Whatever we need to be."

Lars heard the flatness in his own voice. He barely recognized himself.

That was what Diligence's death had shown him. Not some grand revelation about good and evil, but something simpler: hesitation killed. While they'd been planning the perfect angle, Vivienne had put a knife in her lover's throat.

If they wanted to survive, they'd all have to learn that lesson.

"She had Trin tortured," Lars said quietly. "Then murdered her own ally just to make a point. What response is proportional to that?"

He'd been turning it over in his mind. Every scenario, every approach. Hells, he'd already tried the noble route. That stirring article in the Azoria Star, calling on citizens to rise up against tyranny. Fat lot of good that had done. Fifty thousand copper reward, and all he'd gotten were con artists and desperate fools chasing shadows.

The old Lars would have kept trying, kept believing that exposing Vivienne's crimes would turn the city against her. That truth and evidence still mattered.

They didn't.

"Just remember," Darius said, interrupting his thoughts, "once you cross certain lines, you can't cross back."

"Maybe that's the point."

Tomorrow, he'd try more allies. Push harder. Find the leverage they needed to stay in Azoria without running or hiding. But if that failed...

"We'll need to be smart about this," Darius said. "Whatever we do."

"I know," Lars said.

Smart, yes. But also willing to get their hands dirty.

"And Lars? We need to remember why we're fighting."

How could he forget? "The city. Our people." Lars stood, brushing off his pants. "I should check on Trin."

"Lars." Darius caught his arm. "I'm sorry. About all of it. If there's anything my crew can do..."

"We're one crew now, remember?" The words tasted like a blend of surrender and necessity. "Your people are my people."

He understood how Darius felt. He wanted to believe in a common cause and the one clever plan that would turn everything around. Wanted to see the artistry in motion.

But in this insanity, the only art that really mattered was survival.

Maybe that had always been Vivienne's plan. Take what they all loved and twist it into something ugly, something that would break them or force them to break themselves.

She'd certainly succeeded at the first part. The second remained to be seen.

Lars headed inside, ready to face whatever came next. The show, after all, must go on.

CITY OF WHISPERS

18

The morning sun sliced through Vivienne's office windows. Her arm itched beneath fresh bandages—a shallow cut from the chaos, nothing more, but useful for what came next.

"Madam Dragunova, I came as quickly as I could."

Oyken Pellerian, editor of The Azorian Herald, stood in her doorway wringing his hands like wet laundry. Good. Nervous men were pliable men, and pliable men printed what they were told.

"Sit." She didn't look up from the papers on her desk, letting him stew in the silence. The longer he waited, the more grateful he'd be when she finally acknowledged him.

She counted to thirty, then raised her eyes. "Tell me, Oyken. What did you hear about last night?"

"I... that is..." He swallowed, throat bobbing like a fishing lure. "Chaos, Madam. Absolute chaos. Poor Miss Blythe—"

"Was murdered." Vivienne's voice cut through his stammering. Like the knife that had opened Diligence's throat. The knife she wielded. When she...

No. Stop. That story would not do.

"She was assassinated by violent criminals who have grown too bold, too comfortable in our city," she continued.

"Yes, of course. Assassinated." He pulled out a small notebook, pencil already moving. "Should I mention the, ah, the gentleman who—"

"Balar acted to protect me after the cowardly attack." She touched her bandaged arm. "He deserves commendation, not suspicion."

"Of course, of course." Scribble, scribble went the pencil. "And the perpetrators?"

This was the delicate part.

"We believe that Lars Harrow and Darius Adalan conspired together," she said, watching his face carefully. "Two rival crews united. They've been planning this for weeks, and robbed the City Reserve as a precursor to violence."

"Ah, so the Gaming Commission ruling—"

"Very good, Oyken. Yes. That's why thieving is suspended during this emergency." She leaned forward, letting him see the steel beneath the silk. "We believe these men are terrorists. They've been wantonly wasting copper, causing an economic crisis, and now they have murdered a member of the city government in cold blood. They must be stopped."

He nodded so hard she thought his neck might snap. "The headline—'Thieves Turn Violent,' perhaps? Or 'Assassination at Opaline Hall'?"

"Both. Run a special edition." She slid a paper across the desk—names, descriptions, last known locations. "These are the primary conspirators. Make sure their faces are on every street corner by noon."

"It will be done." He rose to leave, then paused. "Madam, about Diligence. Should I mention your… relationship?"

Their relationship. Vivienne looked to the chair at her desk, the one Diligence would always be sitting in. Grinning, rapier at her hip, with those eyes that always knew how to set her alight.

"She was…" Vivienne's voice caught. She may as well make it known. "She was everything to me. My advisor, my confidante, my lover." She paused. "Put that in, Oyken. Let them know what these monsters took from me."

He practically flew from the room, eager to spread her grief across every breakfast table in Azoria.

Vivienne waited until his footsteps faded, then rang for her next appointment. The tears dried instantly. But the ghost of Diligence remained. *Hells, those eyes…*

A knock at the door. This one knew better than to simply enter.

Suddenly, she couldn't breathe. Couldn't think.

Oh hells, oh Diligence, what have I—

The fury of the thought felt as though it might crush her heart. Vivienne squeezed her eyes shut, taking one breath, two…

Her eyes popped open. Her mind cleared.

She was back in control.

"Come."

The man who walked in looked like violence given a suit and a smile. Donovan Plesk, former sergeant of the City Watch, drummed out for excessive force. A fine commendation for what she needed.

"You've heard about last night," she said.

"Whole city's heard by now." His smile widened. "Shame about Diligence. She was a real beauty."

The casual disrespect set Vivienne's teeth on edge, but she needed him. For now.

"I want you to lead a new organization," she said. "The Eyes of Azoria. Citizens dedicated to protecting our city from the criminal element that's grown too bold."

"Like Balar, eh?" he smirked. "What are we, then? Vigilantes?"

"Patriots." She stood, moving to the window. The city spread below her, an overgrown field ready for reaping. "The City Watch is bound by procedures, bureaucracy. The Eyes will have more flexibility."

"How much flexibility we talking?"

Vivienne turned back to him, sneering at his crudeness. "Whatever is necessary to restore order."

Donovan's grin turned predatory. "I've got some boys who'd be interested. Good, loyal bruisers who know how to handle themselves."

"How many?"

"Fifty to start. Could have two hundred by week's end if the pay's right."

"The pay will be generous. But I need results immediately." She returned to her desk, pulling out another list. "These businesses have been suspected of harboring criminal sympathizers. Start there."

He scanned the list, eyebrows rising. "Some of these places are pretty established. Hells, this is my favorite tavern right here."

"Sadly, they'll have to learn the price of associating with violent thugs." She drummed her fingers on the desk. "Make examples, Donovan. But be smart about it. We're restoring order, not creating chaos."

"Understood." He folded the list, tucking it into his jacket.

"Remember," she continued, "resistance should be considered evidence of guilt. Document everything. We'll need it for the trials."

"Trials?" He laughed. "You planning to throw them all before a judge?"

"Of course." She pulled out a leather-bound folder, heavy with official seals. "I'm establishing emergency procedures. Special courts to handle the extraordinary circumstances we find ourselves in."

"And I'm sure you've got some great judges lined up."

"But of course." She slid the folder across. "The first appointments are already made. Loyal politicians who understand that desperate times require decisive action."

Another knock interrupted them. Softer than Donovan's had been, almost hesitant.

"Enter."

One of Vivienne's regular guards stepped inside, his face pale. "Madam, urgent news from Wending Street."

"Go on."

"There's been an incident. Some of the citizens who've been spreading the news about the thieves' actions. They cornered a shopkeeper they suspected of harboring criminals."

Vivienne's eyes flicked to Donovan, then back to the guard. "And?"

"The shopkeeper resisted. Said they had no authority to search his store. It escalated and..." The guard swallowed. "He's dead, Madam. One of the rabble struck him too hard."

Sad. But perfect timing. Vivienne kept her face carefully neutral.

"That's horrible," she said slowly. "But understandable. When citizens are forced to protect themselves because our institutions have failed them, such accidents happen."

Donovan was watching her with interest.

"The patriots who accosted him," Vivienne continued. "Do we know who they are?"

"Yes, Madam. They're... quite shaken by what happened."

"Have them report to the Third District Court at noon. Judge Matthias will review the incident."

She turned to Donovan. "It seems some citizens are already taking initiative. Perhaps your recruitment will be easier than expected."

"Nothing like a little sanctioned violence to bring out the best in us," Donovan said.

The guard shifted uncomfortably. "Should I have the attackers arrested?"

"Arrested?" Vivienne asked mildly. "For defending their community against criminal elements? Absolutely not. Make sure they report to the appropriate court. Now go."

The guard nodded and left, still looking troubled.

"Well," Donovan said once they were alone. "This is shaping up to be one fine day."

"Indeed. But there is a huge amount of work to be done." She smiled. "So will you do it?"

"Give me a day or two and I'll give you an army."

He left with that same predatory smile. Repulsive thug.

Hinde Portlun had opened her provisions shop at sunrise for twenty years. The sun had risen this morning like any other, so she'd risen with it. The brass key turned in the lock with its familiar click, the door swung open on well-oiled hinges, and the smell of dried herbs and preserved meats welcomed her like an old friend.

Same routine. Same street. Same neighbors preparing for the same day.

Except for the newsboy on the corner, screaming himself hoarse.

"SPECIAL EDITION! THIEVES TURN VIOLENT! ASSASSINATION AT OPALINE HALL!"

Now that was different. Hinde fished out a gold and took a paper, scanning the headlines as she propped her door open with the wooden stop.

DILIGENCE BLYTHE MURDERED BY THIEF CONSPIRACY

Lars Harrow and Darius Adalan Named as Primary Conspirators

She read it twice, then a third time, waiting for the words to make sense. Lars Harrow, as in the celebrity? A murderer?

Hinde folded the paper, a strange flutter in her chest. Her daughter had prints of him on her wall—the dark haired, daring rogue in his fancy coat, smiling like he owned the world. Marla would be devastated.

"Mad times," she muttered, arranging the morning's produce. Still, she couldn't quite shake that flutter. Like when the Cooper boy got caught cheating at cards after winning for months. Sometimes people needed taking down a peg.

She noticed more foot traffic than usual. Good for business, one could hope. She straightened her display of preserves, ready for the morning rush.

But as a group walked closer, something felt off. These weren't shoppers. Another group clustered on a corner across the way, voices low but animated. All riled up about something.

Maybe they're Lars Harrow fans.

Then she saw the patches.

Crude things, obviously homemade. Simple eyes stitched onto hips or sleeves, some just drawn on with charcoal. But the ones wearing them moved with purpose, putting up posters on walls, stopping passersby to ask questions.

"You seen any suspicious activity?" one asked Hinde as she watched from her doorway. She recognized him—Tomás something, he ran a small moneylending operation two streets over. His brother had lost a fortune to a thieving crew last year. "Anyone buying supplies in bulk? Anyone who might be harboring criminals?"

"Haven't seen anything," Hinde said carefully. Seeing high society rightly humbled a bit was one thing. This felt like something else.

Tomás nodded, but his gaze lingered on her shop. "You'll let us know if you do. Good citizens need to stand together."

He moved on, but more were coming. The patches seemed to multiply as she watched. There was Hendel the baker's assistant, normally so quiet. Marcon from the wine shop, chest puffed out like a strutting pigeon. Even young Felise who usually spent her mornings sleeping off the night before.

They moved in packs now, voices getting louder with each block.

And then they converged on Kellar's shop three doors down.

Everyone knew Kellar bought from fences. Hells, half the merchants in the district did—it was how the city worked. Nobody cared as long as prices stayed fair and the goods kept flowing.

Well, yesterday no one cared. Today seemed to be a different matter.

"Open up, Kellar!" Tomás banged on the door. A dozen men with patches crowded behind him. "We need to check your stock. Make sure you're not hiding stolen goods."

Kellar opened his door, face already pale. He was a thin man, nervous on his best days. Today he looked ready to bolt. "What authority do you have—"

"The authority of concerned citizens," someone called out. Hinde recognized him too—Brix, who ran a spice stall. "Unless you've got something to hide?"

"I've got nothing to hide!" Kellar's voice cracked. "I run an honest business!"

"Honest?" Tomás stepped closer. "Everyone knows you buy from thieves."

"We all buy from thieves!" He pointed at Brix. "You bought a whole shipment of smuggled Zarakaran chilies just last week!"

The accusation hung in the air like a lit fuse. Brix reached up, grabbed Kellar's business sign—hand-painted wood that had hung there for five years—and yanked it down with a crack of splintering timber.

"You lying piece of shit!" Brix threw the sign into the street. It clattered on the cobblestones, the painted letters face-down in the muck.

"You have no right!" Kellar wailed, and swung his fist at Brix.

That was the spark that lit the powder.

They grabbed Kellar by his collar and surged at the shop. The door gave way with a crash that echoed down the street.

Hinde pressed back against her own doorframe, heart hammering, as the mob poured into Kellar's shop like water through a broken dam.

The sounds that followed turned her stomach. Breaking glass. Splintering wood. And underneath it all, Kellar's voice, high and desperate: "Please! I don't have anything! Please!"

They dragged him out five minutes later.

"Criminal sympathizer," someone spat.

"Thief enabler!"

"Part of the conspiracy!"

The accusations flew like stones. More shops were opening now, people drawn by the commotion. Some looked horrified.

Others... Others were asking where they could get one of them patches, looking at their neighbors with new suspicion.

The City Watch arrived as the crowd was debating what to do with Kellar. Two officers, looking deeply uncomfortable as they surveyed the scene. The older one—Sergeant something, Hinde couldn't remember—cleared his throat.

"What's all this then?"

"Citizen's arrest," Tomás said proudly. "Found this thief sympathizer hiding stolen goods. We're doing our civic duty."

The sergeant looked at Kellar, bloody and barely standing. Then at the mob, righteous and ready for more. Hinde could see the calculation in his eyes. Two of them. Dozens of angry citizens. And somewhere above them all, Vivienne Dragunova had already declared which side was right.

"We could always deputize them," the younger watchman said quietly. "They're doing our jobs for us."

The sergeant's jaw tightened, but he didn't argue. "Take him to the station," he said finally, pointing at Kellar. "We'll process him there."

"What about his shop?" Brix asked. "Can't leave stolen goods lying around."

"Secure it," the sergeant said. Secure. Not protect. "Make sure nothing goes missing."

Permission granted. The mob flowed back into Kellar's shop like hungry animals. Hinde could hear them "securing" everything of value. For evidence, of course. For justice.

Hinde backed into her own shop, hands shaking as she turned the lock.

The morning sun climbed higher, illuminating a city learning to devour itself. On the corner, the newsboy had given up shouting. He didn't need to. The headline was writing itself on every street corner, in broken glass and fear.

She watched Tomás organize another group, pointing at the tack shop across the way.

Wonder what evidence they plan to find there?

She thought about her own dealings over the years. The Aelyndoran silk she'd bought from a crew down Tavern Row. The silverware from some fence or another... lovely pieces, good markup. Everyone did it. Everyone.

Through her window, she saw young Karine from the bakery attaching a crude patch to her hip. She was sixteen, full of fire and looking for excitement. Yesterday she'd been a counter girl. Today she was a "patriot."

Tomorrow she might be at Hinde's door.

Hinde pulled her curtains closed, blocking out the scene. But she could still hear it—the shouting, the righteousness, the sound of her community eating itself alive.

In the darkness of her shop, surrounded by goods that likely had dubious origins if anyone looked too closely, Hinde Portlun finally understood. The mighty hadn't just fallen. They'd pulled everyone down with them.

Outside, someone screamed. Breaking glass followed. Another shop being "secured," another neighbor becoming an enemy. All because some fancy thieves had pushed too far.

Hinde moved to her counter, found a piece of board and her charcoal. Her hand was steady as she drew.

She sighed and headed towards the door. The brass key turned in the lock again, opening up again. Hinde stepped out into the morning air, hung the board on the hook where her shop hours usually went.

An eye.

Better to choose your side before it was chosen for you.

The Summer Home was suffocating.

Trin sat on her crate in the corner, the dog pressed against her leg, watching thirty-odd thieves organize themselves into something resembling order. Lars was deep in discussion with Darius about safe houses. Jax hovered nearby, pretending to sharpen a knife but really just keeping watch over her. Liora and Maren had claimed a workbench, already twisting wires on something that involved a lot of noise.

The walls pressed in. The air felt thick, recycled, tasting of too many bodies and not enough hope. Every concerned glance in her direction made it worse. Every careful word, every gentle tone, every instance of people treating her like she might shatter if they spoke too loud.

She couldn't breathe.

Her fingers found the dog's fur, gripping perhaps too tight. It whined softly but didn't pull away. Smart animal. It understood about needing something solid to hold onto when the world went sideways.

"Lars."

Shelle's voice cut through the fog. The information broker moved with her usual grace, dark hair catching the light from the high windows. She'd changed from last night's outfit into practical clothes—leather pants, fitted jacket, boots made for running. Ready for business.

"I need to go see Marinda Kelway at The Azoria Star," Shelle said, but she wasn't looking at Trin. Her eyes found Lars first, then Liora. "You know she's the only editor who hasn't been bought or intimidated yet. If we're going to counter Vivienne's narrative, we need her."

Lars looked up from his discussion. The concerned leader expression slid onto his face like a mask. "You shouldn't go alone. The streets—"

"I'll go." The words came out of Trin's mouth before she'd fully formed the thought. Everyone turned to stare. She stood, leaving the dog looking confused at her sudden movement.

"Trin..." Lars started, in a careful voice she was learning to hate.

"Maybe Jax should—" Liora began.

"Look at me." Trin's voice cracked like a whip. "Not at Shelle. Not at each other. Look at ME."

They did, finally. Really looked. And maybe they saw what she felt... the walls closing in, the air getting thinner, the absolute need to be anywhere but here.

"I can't stay locked up in a room." The words tumbled out, raw and desperate. "I can't—"

She couldn't finish. Couldn't explain how the warehouse felt too much like the cellar, how every protective gesture felt like another restraint. How she needed to move, to act, to remember she was more than what had been done to her.

Understanding dawned on Lars's face. He nodded once. "Be careful."

"I'll keep her safe," Shelle promised.

Trin grinned, grabbing her jacket from a nearby barrel. "Try and keep up."

They left the building through a side door. She inhaled deeply, tasting the foundry district's particular mix of coal smoke and metal. Even that industrial stink was better than the warehouse's recycled desperation.

Her body trembled. Not from fear, but from the sheer relief of being outside again.

"Better?" Shelle asked, falling into step beside her.

Trin didn't answer. The city stretched around them, familiar and foreign all at once. She knew the time spent as a captive had changed her.

Or maybe it was the two days since, watching everyone walk on eggshells, that had done the real damage.

They moved through the morning streets, Shelle keeping up a light chatter about nothing important. The weather. The price of bread. Which merchants were reliable and which would sell their own mothers for a copper. Normal things. Trin let the words wash over her, using them as anchor points while her senses catalogued everything else.

The city had changed fast.

Wanted posters plastered every corner. Lars's face stared down from walls, labeled MURDERER in bold type. Darius got equal billing. Groups of Azorians with crude patches on their hips and sleeves clustered at intersections, watching everyone who passed.

"The Eyes of Azoria," Shelle murmured. "Vivienne's new muscle. They formed up just this morning, from what my sources say."

Trin studied them as they passed. Regular Azorians playing at being dangerous. The way they held themselves, the way they watched—amateurs. Bullies with permission.

They'd made it six blocks when Shelle's pace shifted. Just slightly, but Trin caught it.

"We've got company," Shelle said, voice still light. "Young man, brown coat. Been following since we left the foundry district. Want to lose him?"

Trin glanced back. There—trying to look casual as he studied a shop window that sold nothing he'd ever need. Twenty-something, soft face, nervous energy. One of those patches sewn crooked on his arm.

"No."

The word came out hard and certain. She remembered the needle, shrinking back as her captor brought it to her thigh.

Trin was done shrinking. She stared the boy down and advanced on him.

The boy's eyes widened. He tried to turn, to run, but she was already there. All those years of reading marks, predicting their movements—her body remembered even if her mind was still catching up.

She caught his collar as he tried to bolt, used his own momentum to slam him against the nearest wall.

"Following us?" Her voice didn't sound like her own. Harder. Colder.

"I—no—I mean—" He stammered, trying to pull free. "Civic duty! We're supposed to watch for suspicious—"

"Suspicious." She leaned in close enough to smell his breakfast. Porridge and honey. "Two women walking. Very suspicious."

"You came out of a warehouse! I saw you leave—"

So they were watching the Summer Home already. Good to know.

"And you thought what? You'd follow us? Report back to your new friends?" Her grip tightened. "Play at being important?"

"Let go!" He tried to sound commanding and failed. "I'll call the Watch!"

"Will you?"

She saw the moment he realized how empty that threat was. They stood near the bridge over the river. Morning foot traffic flowed around them, people carefully not seeing what they didn't want to get involved in. No Watch in sight. No help coming.

Just her, him, and the water below.

"Here's what's going to happen," Trin said. "You're going to stop following us. You're going to forget you saw us. And you're going to think very carefully about whether playing dress-up with that patch is worth drowning for."

"You can't—you wouldn't—"

She moved before the thought fully formed. Grabbed him properly, pivoted, and shoved with every ounce of strength and fury she'd been holding inside.

He hit the water with a splash that echoed off the bridge supports.

The current wasn't strong here. He'd be fine. Wet, humiliated, but fine. He surfaced, sputtering and flailing.

Shelle's laugh rang out bright and delighted. "Oh, that was delightful!"

Trin stared down at him as he struggled toward the bank. Her hands were steady. Her breathing even. For the first time in weeks, she felt like herself.

Whole.

"Feel better?" Shelle asked as they resumed walking.

"Yes." The admission surprised her. But it was true. The helplessness that had been choking her since taking a knife on that train had loosened its grip.

She'd done something. Chosen something. Even if it was just shoving an idiot into a river.

"Good. Because we still have three blocks to go, and I doubt he was the only one watching."

They moved faster now, Trin's senses sharp and focused. The city felt different when you were being hunted. Every shadow could hide an enemy. Every face could be marking their passage.

But that was fine. That was familiar.

That was what she'd been before Myrim had taken her. And what she'd be again.

The Azoria Star building rose before them, all red brick and tall windows. One of the few independent voices they could count on.

"Marinda's expecting me," Shelle said as they approached the entrance. "She doesn't know about you."

"She'll adjust."

"That's what I'm counting on." Shelle paused at the door. "Trin? Thank you. For coming with me."

"I needed to get out."

"I know. But still." Shelle's smile held understanding. "Sometimes the best medicine is shoving someone in a river."

Despite everything, Trin felt her lips twitch toward a smile. "Sometimes it is."

They entered the newspaper office together. Behind them, the city went about its business of tearing itself apart. But for now, for this moment, Trin had remembered something important.

She wasn't what had been done to her.

She was what she chose to do next.

And right now, she chose to fight back.

The Azoria Star building stood empty as a tomb.

Trin pushed through the door that Shelle had just picked, her boots crunching on broken glass. Someone had done a thorough job—presses smashed, type scattered like metal rain across the floor. The smell of spilled ink hung thick in the air.

"Marinda?" Shelle called out, though they both knew it was pointless.

The silence that answered told its own story.

Trin moved deeper into the wreckage, cataloging the damage with professional interest. This wasn't mob violence. It was too organized, too complete. The destruction had method to it. The presses hadn't just been damaged; they'd been systematically dismantled. The type cases lay scattered in a way that would make reconstruction impossible.

"She did this herself," Trin said, running her fingers along a bent printing plate. "Probably just after the news broke."

Shelle kicked at a pile of shredded papers. "Smart woman. She saw which way the wind was blowing and made sure no one could use her tools against her will."

They'd been too late. The last independent voice in Azoria had chosen silence over collaboration. Trin couldn't blame her. When the choice was print lies or be branded a traitor, sometimes the only winning move was to not make the choice.

"Come on," Shelle said after a moment. "There's nothing left here."

They made their way back outside, the afternoon sun harsh after the darkness of the ruined newspaper office. With no particular destination in mind, they walked west toward the sea.

The docks stretched before them, busy with the usual chaos of loading and unloading. Life going on, even as the city ate itself alive downtown.

Trin spotted some empty crates near a quiet stretch of wharf and headed for them. Her body was starting to complain about the morning's activities—apparently shoving people into rivers used muscles that had gone soft in captivity.

Shelle settled beside her with a sigh that seemed to come from her bones. "If they've driven out Marinda already, how much worse will it get?"

The rambunctious information broker looked older in the bright sunlight. Tired. Her network—carefully built over years—was probably fragmenting by the hour. People would go to ground, contacts would refuse to meet, and that would be that.

"Is there even a way back from this?" Shelle continued, watching a group of dock workers argue over cargo manifests.

"Once the mob tastes blood, once they realize they can take what they want with just an accusation..."

She trailed off, but Trin could finish the thought. How did you rebuild trust in a city where your neighbor might denounce you for a perceived slight? How did you restore order when the new order rewarded chaos?

"The mob is loud," Trin said, surprising herself with how calm she sounded. "That doesn't make them everyone."

Shelle turned to look at her, skepticism clear on her face.

"Think about it," Trin continued. "How many people put on those eyes today? A hundred? Maybe two if we're generous?"

"More than enough to terrorize the whole district."

"In a city of tens of thousands." Trin pulled her knees up, wrapping her arms around them. The position made her feel smaller, but also more contained. Safer. "The rest are just keeping their heads down, waiting to see how this plays out."

"You think they're secretly on our side?"

"I think they're on their own side. Always have been." Trin watched a seagull dive for scraps, coming up with something that might have been bread. "There are still people who believe in the old Azoria. The game, the balance, the way things worked. They're just not stupid enough to say it out loud right now."

A cart rumbled past, loaded with imported silks. The merchant kept his head down, but Trin caught him glancing nervously at a group of roughs lounging near a tavern. Not guilty of anything except existing with property someone might want.

"Fear makes people quiet," she said. "It doesn't change what they believe. Not deep down. Vivienne's betting on the mob staying louder than everyone else. But mobs burn out. They always do."

"How can you be so sure?" Shelle's voice held genuine curiosity now.

Trin found herself thinking about dinners she'd tried very hard to forget. Her father's political gatherings, back when she was Lady Trinelle Meridia, noble's daughter, being groomed for a life she'd eventually run from. The memory tasted bitter, but maybe that bitterness had aged into something useful.

"My father used to hold these dinners," she said slowly. "Politicians, merchants, anyone with influence. I was supposed to sit quietly and learn."

"Did you?"

"Sit quietly? Never." That drew a small smile from Shelle. "But I did learn. Father explained it once, after some crisis or other. 'Fear is a currency. But like any currency, it can be devalued.'"

She could still see him, wine glass in hand, treating civil unrest like an academic exercise. He'd been a cold bastard, but he'd understood power.

"Vivienne's strategy is textbook," Trin continued. "Create a crisis, provide the solution, become indispensable. My father would have admired the execution. But he also would have called it 'spending capital you can't replenish.'"

"Meaning?"

"She can't keep them terrified forever. Eventually, people want their normal lives back. They want to open their shops without worrying about mobs. They want to buy from whoever has the best prices, not whoever has the right politics." Trin gestured at the busy docks. "Look around. Commerce doesn't stop just because someone declared a war on thieves. It adapts, finds new channels, but it doesn't stop."

Shelle was quiet for a moment, processing. "So what do we do? Wait for the mob to get tired?"

"No." Trin felt herself shifting, the analyst she'd become taking over from the girl who'd once fled her father's world.

This voice was harder than before, but clearer too. Like breaking a bone and having it heal stronger.

"The Eyes are amateurs drunk on power. You can see it in how they swagger, how they cluster together for courage. They'll overreach."

"And the quiet citizens are waiting to see who wins."

"Exactly. They'll keep their heads down and wait for the dust to settle." Trin picked at a splinter in the crate. "But here's what Vivienne doesn't understand... she's given everyone a common enemy."

"The thieves? I think she understands that just fine," Shelle grinned.

"Chaos." The word came out flat. "When everyone's guilty, guilt stops mattering. When everyone's afraid, they start looking for stability. Any stability."

Shelle shifted beside her. "Have you thought of leaving? I hear you got a deal for safe harbor from Mhalendra Thume herself."

"We thought about it. But this is our city," Trin said, sharper than she intended. "They don't get to take it."

"I just hope there's something left to save."

"There's always something left." Trin thought about Lars at the warehouse, trying to hold his crew together. About Liora and Shelle finding each other in the wreckage. About her own choice to shove that Eye into the river instead of curling up in a corner.

"You can only terrorize people so long before they go numb. Then you need something else. A new threat, a new promise, a new—"

She stopped. Shelle had gone rigid beside her, staring at something out on the water.

"Trin," Shelle said.

"I see them."

Ships on the horizon. Not the usual merchant vessels that dotted Azoria's harbor. There were too many, too organized. They moved in formation, cutting through the waves with military precision. As they drew closer, Trin could make out the flags. Zarakaran colors snapping in the wind.

"That's not a trade fleet," Shelle said unnecessarily.

More ships became visible as they watched. A dozen. Two dozen. More. An armada by any definition, sailing toward Azoria's harbor like they had every right to be there.

Trin laughed.

She couldn't help it. The sound bubbled up from somewhere deep, surprising her as much as Shelle. Not hysteria—she knew what that felt like. This was something else. An appreciation for irony.

"There's Vivienne's something else," she managed between laughs.

"What do you mean?"

"Don't you see?" She turned to Shelle, still feeling that strange lightness. "She thinks she's won. The city's hers, the mob's doing her work, the thieves are scattered. But she's just opened the door for another player."

The lead ship was close enough now to make out details. Sleek lines, wood so dark it almost looked black, brass fittings that caught the sun. Gun ports closed but visible. This wasn't a conquest fleet—not yet. This was a statement.

"Thume," Shelle breathed.

"Right." Trin's mind was already racing, the spymaster in her calculating angles and possibilities. "Vivienne creates chaos, Thume offers order. The hero returning to save his city from itself."

"Damn."

"Eloquent as always." But Trin agreed with the sentiment. One tyrant was bad enough.

Two meant the city would be carved up between them, with everyone else caught in the middle.

"We need to get back," Shelle said, already standing. "Warn the others."

"Wait." Trin caught her arm. "This changes everything."

"I noticed."

"No, think about it." She stood too, but kept her eyes on the approaching fleet. "Three forces now. Vivienne's tyranny, Thume's armada, and us."

"Us?" Shelle's laugh held no humor. "A handful of thieves hiding in a warehouse."

"The quiet citizens are going to have to choose," Trin continued, ignoring the interruption. "Not between order and chaos anymore. Between Vivienne's order and Thume's. Both come with a price. Both mean the end of the Azoria they knew."

She could see it playing out. Vivienne's mobs versus Thume's soldiers. The Eyes of Azoria against whatever force he'd brought. Two versions of control battling for dominance while the city bled.

"Maybe that's where we come in," she said slowly. "Maybe we remind them there's a third option."

"Which is?"

Trin turned away from the harbor, from the approaching storm. "The Azoria that was. The game that worked. The balance that let everyone prosper." She paused. "Not perfect, but better than what's coming."

Shelle studied her for a long moment. "You're not the same woman who left the warehouse this morning."

"No." Trin thought about the needle again, about shrinking back, about choosing to push forward instead. "I'm not."

They started back toward the Summer Home, walking quickly but not running. Running attracted attention, and attention was the last thing they needed.

Around them, the docks transformed into a frenzy of shouts and fingers pointed out to sea. Soon enough, someone would sound the alarm. Set off whatever chain of events Thume had planned.

"You really think we can be a third option?" Shelle asked as they turned onto a side street. "Thieves and outcasts against two armies?"

"Not against." Trin stepped around a puddle that reflected the afternoon sky. "Outside of. Let them exhaust themselves fighting for control. We'll be the ones who remember what the city should be."

"Let's just hope they exhaust themselves," Shelle said, "because if one of them wins..."

Trin thought about her father's lessons again. About power and currency and the long game that most people were too impatient to play.

"I suppose we'll adapt," she said. "Keep the idea alive until the next chance comes." She glanced at Shelle. "Isn't that what thieves do? Find the gaps, exploit the weaknesses, take what others overlook?"

"Usually that's about stealing silverware, not cities."

"Maybe it's time to think bigger."

They passed a group of Eyes harassing a merchant about his inventory. The man was trying to explain that everything was legally purchased. The Eyes didn't seem to care.

Soon enough, Vivienne would have those same Eyes facing Zarakaran soldiers. What would their patches mean then?

"The mob thinks they've won," Trin said quietly as they passed. "Vivienne thinks she's won. Thume thinks he's already won just by showing up." She felt that strange smile tugging at her lips again. "They're all wrong."

"Because?"

"Because winning means getting people to choose your side. And right now, everyone's just trying not to get chosen by anyone."

The Summer Home was just ahead, its rusted walls and broken windows a monument to better times. Or maybe worse times. Hard to tell anymore. Time had a way of polishing memories until even the rough spots looked smooth.

Shelle looped her arm around Trin's. "I'm glad you came along with me."

"So am I," Trin smiled. "Thank you, Shelle. I needed that."

They stepped inside, back into the familiar chaos of thieves trying to organize a resistance. Conversations died as they entered, everyone hoping for good news. The dog let out an excited bark and ran to greet her.

I really should give him a name.

Trin sought out Lars in the crowd, finding him in conference with Darius and the Gimble Brothers. Both men looked up as she approached.

"Glad to see you back," Lars said with a smile. "How's Marinda?"

"Marinda's gone. The newspaper's destroyed." She kept her voice steady, matter-of-fact. "But that's not the real news."

Lars frowned. "Which is?"

"Thume's here. Or will be soon. There's an armada in the harbor, flying Zarakaran colors."

The warehouse erupted in voices, everyone talking at once. Questions, curses, declarations of doom. Trin let it wash over her, already thinking three moves ahead. The game had changed, but games were what she knew. What they all knew.

Vivienne had her mobs. Thume had his ships.

But they had something else.

They had the memory of what Azoria could be. And sometimes, in the right hands, memory was the most dangerous weapon of all.

"So what do we do?" someone called out.

Trin looked at Lars, at Darius, at all the faces turned toward them seeking answers. The old Trin would have stayed quiet, let others lead. The broken Trin would have hidden.

But she wasn't either of those anymore.

"We remind the city it has a choice," she said. "And then we show them we're willing to fight for it."

It wasn't much of a plan. But it was a start.

Outside, somewhere in the distance, bells began to ring. The armada announcing its arrival, or the Azorian navy sounding the alarm. Neither brought much comfort.

THE RECKONING

19

The "war table" was a joke.

Lars stared at the maps spread across the salvaged door they'd propped on crates, trying to find some angle they'd missed. Harbor District, marked with Shelle's notes about ship positions. Market District, covered in red marks where the Eyes had been most active.

The foundry district around them, their supposed safe haven that felt more like a trap with each passing hour.

"Thume's got forty ships out there," Darius said, tapping the harbor. "The Azorian navy's got maybe twenty, and half of those are converted merchant vessels."

"So why aren't they fighting?" Rurik asked. "Just sitting there, staring at each other."

"Because Thume's waiting," Lars said. "Letting the city tear itself apart first."

"Brilliant strategy," Serine Conwen cut in from across the room. "You and him should compare notes."

She wasn't wrong. They'd been at this all night, moving pieces around a board where they controlled none of the squares. Shelle's informants brought updates every few hours—ship movements, Eye patrols, which districts were locked down. But information without options was just a way to catalog their grievances.

"All this planning," someone muttered from the back. "For what? We can't fight an armada. Can't fight the whole city gone mad."

"We plan because it's better than giving up, shithead," Darius shot back, but even he sounded tired.

The bickering started again. Same arguments they'd been having since yesterday. Fight or flee. Strike first or wait it out. Every option equally impossible.

"Where's Creet?" Lars asked suddenly. The old thief had left before dawn, promising to scout the western district.

Shelle cleared her throat.

"They found Creet," she said quietly. "Now he's hanging from a lamppost outside the Gaming Commission headquarters. The sign around his neck said 'Thief.'"

The warehouse went silent. Creet Daws had been a player from the beginning. Thirty years in the game only to die strung up by ignorant thugs.

"That's it," someone said. "I'm done. Rather take my chances running than wait here to die."

"Running where?" Darius demanded. "You think the roads are safe? Think the Eyes don't have the whole city watched?"

More voices joined in. Fear making everyone loud, making them stupid. These weren't soldiers—they were thieves, con artists, people who survived by being clever and quick. Trapped in one place with death closing in, they were coming apart.

Lars felt his jaw tighten. They needed unity, needed purpose, and all they had was panic.

"We could raid for supplies," someone suggested. "Hit the markets before—"

"Like we're common looters now?" another voice snapped. "Might as well just join the Eyes ourselves."

"Better than starving!"

"Enough!" Lars's voice cut through the noise. "We'll figure it out."

But the words rang hollow. Figure what out? How to fight two armies with twenty—no, fifteen now—scared thieves? How to win a war when they couldn't even agree on breakfast?

He needed Trin. Needed her sharp mind, her ability to see angles others missed. She'd know what to do, or at least make him believe there was something to do.

He found her in the corner they'd claimed, sitting on a crate with the dog pressed against her leg. She was sorting through their supplies with mechanical precision—counting bolts, checking rope, tasks that didn't need doing but kept her hands busy.

"Any thoughts on our situation?" he asked, settling beside her.

She didn't look up. "About what Shelle said? Creet was careless. He shouldn't have gone alone."

"I meant about what we do next."

"Whatever you decide." Her voice was steady, professional. Like he was any crew leader asking for a report.

"I'm asking what you think, Trin."

She finally looked at him, and the distance in her eyes made his chest tight. She was right there, close enough to touch, but might as well have been across the city.

"I think we're outnumbered, outgunned, and half our people want to run." She turned back to her supplies. "But you knew that already."

He watched her hands move—the same hands that used to trace patterns on his back, that could pick any lock in the city, that had held his when everything seemed impossible. Now they just sorted bolts into neat piles.

"Trin—"

"These need organizing," she said. "In case we have to move fast."

Another argument erupted behind them. Someone wanted to try negotiating with Thume. Someone else called them an idiot. Voices rising, fear spreading like smoke.

Lars's frustration boiled over even as his heart ached. They were falling apart, and he couldn't even reach the one person who might help him hold it together.

People were suffering, the city wanted them dead, and he couldn't even figure out how to be there for Trin. For the woman he loved.

"I need some air," he announced to no one in particular.

A few people looked up. Jax started to rise, probably to offer protection, but Lars waved him off.

"I just need to walk. Clear my head. I'll stay close."

He headed for the door, and heard the click of claws on concrete behind him. The dog had left Trin's side to follow. Truth be told, he was glad for the silent company.

"At least you're still talking to me," he muttered as they stepped into the morning light.

The dog wagged its tail, tongue lolling out in what might have been agreement.

The foundry district stretched before them, all rust and shadow in the early sun. Somewhere out there, Creet's body was probably still swinging. The new rules were hard, but they were simple.

Submit or die.

Lars started walking, no destination in mind. Just away from the bickering, away from the useless plans, away from Trin's polite distance that hurt worse than anger would have.

The dog trotted beside him, occasionally stopping to sniff at something interesting. Normal dog things in a city gone mad. There was something almost comforting about it.

"She won't even look at me properly," Lars found himself saying. The dog's ears perked up. "I know she's been through hells. I know she needs time. But hells, I need her."

They turned a corner, heading deeper into the industrial maze. The morning was quiet here, most people either fled or hiding. Just empty streets and the distant sound of ships' bells from the harbor.

"Maybe I'm being selfish," he continued. "Wanting her to be herself after what she's been through. I just... I miss my partner."

The dog paused to mark a wall, then looked back at him expectantly.

"You're right," Lars said. "I'm talking to a dog about my relationship problems while the city burns. Perfect leadership right there."

But somehow it helped, putting words to the frustration. He couldn't fix the strategic situation. Couldn't make the armada disappear or the Eyes see reason. Couldn't even keep his own people from fragmenting.

And he couldn't reach Trin, couldn't breach whatever walls she'd built to survive.

All he could do was walk through empty streets with a stray dog, pretending tomorrow might be different than today.

The morning air helped, even if it tasted of coal smoke. Lars walked without direction, letting his feet choose the path while the dog investigated every corner and doorway with dedicated interest.

"I promised I'd protect her," he said, watching the dog nose through a pile of discarded crates. "Made a big show of it, too. Lars Harrow, always there to keep his crew safe."

The dog looked back at him, head tilted.

"But I didn't protect her, did I? She protected me. Jumped in front of a thrown knife for hells' sake." His hands clenched at the memory. "And Balar took her right off that train while I watched."

They turned down an unknown street, where the smaller foundries banged out dynamo parts. They were silent today, doors chained shut.

Across the way, a general store. Someone had painted "THIEF LOVER" across the doors. Another business destroyed for the crime of participating in Azoria's economy.

"Always trying to shield her," Lars continued. "Like she was something fragile that needed wrapping in cotton. I didn't respect the strength in her. Not enough. Not until it was too late."

The dog had found something interesting in an alley— probably goose droppings—and Lars waited while it conducted its important investigation.

They passed the Crooked Anchor, one of the only taverns in the foundry district. Lars could see a couple old timers nursing drinks inside. And yet, someone had nailed a crude eye symbol to the door. A warning or a claim, hard to tell.

"Ah hells," Lars said. "You almost done, boy?"

The dog finished its business and trotted back to his side, tail wagging despite the gloom. Dogs were good that way. The world could be ending and they'd still find joy in an interesting smell.

They turned onto Forge Street, making the loop back.

The dog stopped dead, a low growl building in its throat.

Ahead, a group of children had strung a rope over a broken lamp post. One boy stood on a crate with the noose around his neck while others jeered and threw pebbles. Playing at execution.

"Death to all thieves!" one of them shouted, voice high and gleeful.

The boy on the crate clutched his throat, making choking sounds. Then he "died" dramatically, tongue lolling out, and the others cheered.

"My turn! I wanna be the thief!"

"No, you were the thief last time. It's Tam's turn."

They were already switching places when one of them—a scrawny kid with dirt-smeared cheeks—glanced over and saw Lars. The child's eyes went wide. Recognition flickered there, quick and sharp.

"Hey," one of the others said, following his gaze. "Is that one of them? A thief?"

The group turned as one. Eight years old, maybe nine, armed with sticks and wearing crude Eye armbands. The game suddenly wasn't a game.

"Could be," another said, hefting his stick. "They said to watch for anyone suspicious."

"Fifty coppers if we catch a real one."

The dog's growl deepened, positioning itself between Lars and the children. The first kid—the one who'd recognized him—stood frozen.

"Well?" The biggest boy stepped forward, stick raised. "What d'you think? He look like a thief to you?"

The scrawny kid's mouth worked silently. Lars could see the calculation happening—fifty coppers split eight ways was still more than most of these kids saw in a month.

"Nah," the kid said finally, voice barely a whisper. Then more strongly, "Nah, he's nobody. Just some drunk."

"You sure? He's got that look—"

"I said he's nobody!" The words came out sharp. "Come on, let's check the warehouses. Real thieves hide in warehouses."

They moved off reluctantly, game abandoned, hunting instead. The scrawny one glanced back once, and Lars saw it all in that look—fear, hunger, shame. A child who'd chosen mercy but might not next time.

The makeshift gallows swayed in the morning breeze.

Lars stood there staring at it. At the rope. At the crate they'd used as a scaffold. Children playing at execution because that's what their world had become.

Today it was a game. Tomorrow?

Tomorrow one of them might loop that rope around a real neck.

The dog whined, pressing against his leg. It could sense the change in him, the way something fundamental had shifted. Dogs knew when the pack dynamics changed, when play turned to hunt.

"It's alright," Lars said, but his voice came out wrong. Too flat. Too calm.

He turned back toward the Summer Home, and the dog followed with its tail low. No more sniffing at interesting corners. It stayed close, confused by the transformation of its walking companion.

Lars moved with purpose now, unhurried yet deliberate. Each step calculated, each turn chosen. His mind wasn't racing anymore.

Everything was remarkably simple.

Vivienne wasn't just taking out the thieves. She was poisoning the city, to the point of turning children's games into rehearsals for murder. Making brutality into entertainment, until kids couldn't tell the difference between play and horror.

He'd been trying to play by rules. Even after Diligence, even after Balar, some part of him had clung to the old ways. The crew leader who won with style, not blood. Who believed there were lines you didn't cross.

But they'd crossed every line. And now they were using *kids* to do it.

Lars made it back to the Summer Home. From outside, he could hear voices—still arguing, still fracturing. Still pretending there was a decision to make.

There wasn't. Not anymore.

The dog hesitated at the entrance, whining softly.

"Go on," Lars said gently. "Find Trin."

The dog slipped inside, and Lars followed. The argument was still going. Something about supply raids, something about negotiation. Background noise now. Nothing that mattered.

He moved through the warehouse with singular purpose. Past the useless war table. Past the frightened thieves planning their retreat. Past everything that had seemed important an hour ago.

The crate of muskets sat in the back corner, "liberated" from a Watch shipment weeks ago. They'd talked about using them, decided against it. Not their style. Not the thief way.

Jax saw him first. "Lars? What are you—"

Lars shoved past him, hands already working the crate's latches.

"Lars, wait!" Liora now, moving to intercept. "What happened? What's wrong?"

He pulled out a musket, checking its action with jerky movements. But the weight felt right. The purpose felt right.

"Lars, stop." Trin's voice, cutting through the noise. She stood in front of him, no longer distant but sharp with understanding. "Whatever you're thinking, don't."

"I saw children playing at hanging." The words came out flat, empty. "Eight or nine years old. They had armbands on, Trin. And a rope. They were taking turns being the thief who dies."

Trin's face went still.

"One of them recognized me. Could have turned me in for fifty coppers. But he didn't." Lars selected ammunition for the musket with mechanical precision. "This time."

"I know what you're thinking," Trin said, voice steady but urgent. "But if you kill her, you make her a martyr. You validate everything she's been saying about us."

"She's turning children into hunters. Making them rehearse murder for fun."

The words hung between them. He finished loading the musket and slung it over his shoulder.

He was dimly aware of others gathering—Darius appearing at the edge of his vision, others pressing closer. But his focus stayed on Trin, on the understanding dawning in her eyes.

"Don't do this," she said. "This isn't you."

"They were laughing," he said quietly. "Playing at execution and laughing. I can't stand by anymore."

He turned to go, and found Darius in his path. His rival-turned-ally blocked him, studied him with a calculating look.

Then Darius stepped aside. "Make it count."

Lars moved toward the door, musket in hand, purpose crystallized into something harder than fear or rage or hope. Behind him, voices rose in alarm, in protest, in confusion.

None of it mattered.

Vivienne made new rules. It was time he played by them.

The silk sling was perfect. Just tight enough to suggest pain, loose enough to allow movement when needed.

Vivienne adjusted it one final time before her mirror, watching how the black silk caught the light. The wound beneath had already healed. A scrape from the Opaline Hall, just a consequence of being in the middle of carnage.

"The speech," she murmured, running through the key points. Economic terrorism. Foreign invasion. The martyred Diligence. Each word chosen to twist emotion into action, fear into fury.

Behind her, reflected in the mirror's edge, Balar stood motionless. He'd taken his position by the door an hour ago and hadn't moved since. Sometimes she forgot he was there until she turned and found those leather-wrapped hands exactly where she'd left them.

She didn't look at him directly. Couldn't, not today. Not with the memory of Diligence's blood still so fresh. Her own hand drawing the knife across that perfect throat, those eyes widening in shock...

No. Focus.

"Ready?" she asked, ostensibly to him but really to herself. The reflection that answered looked every inch the wounded leader Azoria needed.

He didn't respond. He rarely did anymore unless directly ordered. The perfect soldier she'd created, all traces of Myrim burned away.

The carriage ride to Prosperity Square passed in calculated silence. Through the windows, she watched her city transform. Signs bearing the Eye on every corner, citizens moving with the quick steps of the properly afraid. Good. Fear was easier to direct than contentment.

Prosperity Square sprawled before the Gaming Commission headquarters, all clean lines and old money. The platform they'd erected dominated the center, draped in black cloth that rippled in the afternoon breeze. Mourning colors for her murdered advisor. Lover.

The crowd was already gathering—Eyes of Azoria in prominent positions, regular citizens filling in the gaps.

Some came willingly, drawn by curiosity or conviction. Others had been "encouraged" by visits from patriots who suggested attendance was civic duty. The distinction didn't matter. Bodies were bodies, and she needed them all to hear this.

"Wait here," she told Balar as they stopped behind the platform. "Watch the crowd. Watch everything."

He melted into position without acknowledgment, another shadow among shadows.

Donovan appeared at her carriage door, grinning his predator's grin. "Good crowd, Madam. The boys made sure of it."

She let him help her down, adding a slight stumble on the steps. Quick recovery, hand to her wounded arm, brave smile through the pain. Already the nearest Eyes were murmuring, concern mixing with admiration.

"Give me five minutes," she told Donovan. "Then have someone start a chant. Nothing too orchestrated."

She climbed the platform slowly, each step measured for maximum visual impact. Let them see the effort it cost. Let them see her fighting through pain to address them. By the time she reached the podium, the square had fallen silent.

The late afternoon sun cast long shadows across the crowd. Hundreds of faces turned up toward her, waiting.

It was time to begin.

"My fellow Azorians..."

She let her voice catch, hand moving to her throat as if overwhelmed. The pause stretched just long enough for discomfort before she continued.

"Forgive me. It's still difficult to stand here, to look out at you, knowing that just days ago my dearest companion stood beside me. Diligence Blythe was more than my advisor. She was my conscience, my sword arm, my..." Another calculated pause. "My heart."

Murmurs of sympathy rippled through the crowd. Someone called out "Justice for Diligence!" Others took up the cry until she raised her good hand for silence.

"Justice. Yes. That's why I'm here, despite my physician's protests." She touched the sling gingerly. "Because you deserve to know the truth about what's happening to our city."

She had them now. The Eyes leaning forward, the regular citizens drawn despite themselves into the performance.

"For weeks, a conspiracy has festered in our midst. You know the conspirators. Lars Harrow, Darius Adalan. Thieves who grew too bold, too greedy. Copper. Banks—*your* bank."

She let that sink in, watching faces harden with understanding.

"Economic terrorism," she continued. "Designed to weaken us, to make us vulnerable. And when Diligence discovered their plans, when she came close to exposing the full extent of their conspiracy..."

The sentence hung unfinished. Let them complete it in their minds, make the conclusion their own.

"They did it in cold blood, in front of witnesses, in the very heart of our government." Her voice rose with each phrase. "They showed us what they truly are. Not romantic celebrities or clever entrepreneurs. Terrorists. Killers. Enemies of everything we've built."

The crowd stirred, anger replacing sympathy. Good. She pressed on.

"But their conspiracy runs deeper. Even now, as we mourn, a new threat sits in our harbor." She gestured toward the distant masts. "The Zarakaran pretender, Cecil Thume. The man who abandoned this city, who fled rather than face justice for his crimes, now returns with warships."

Someone in the crowd spat. Others muttered curses.

"Is it coincidence that he arrives just as the thieves sow chaos? The very thieves who broke him out of prison?" She let scorn drip from every word. "They are allied, my friends. United in their desire to tear down what we've built and replace it with their own corruption."

The Eyes were chanting now, something low and rhythmic. The regular citizens caught between them took up the sound, swept along by the current of directed rage.

"But we are not helpless." Vivienne straightened, good hand gripping the podium. "We have patriots among us. Brave citizens who refuse to let our city fall. The Eyes of Azoria grow stronger each day, protecting what the old systems failed to preserve."

Cheers from the Eyes, fists raised in salute. She acknowledged them with a grateful nod.

"Today, I announce the expansion of their authority. New courts to process the enemies among us. New powers to root out conspiracy wherever it hides. We will not wait for the criminals to strike again. We will find them, judge them, and end them."

The square erupted. Chants of her name mixed with calls for blood. She raised her hand again, letting the fever build before calling for quiet.

"I know these are frightening times. I know the path ahead seems dark. But together—together we are stronger than any conspiracy. Together we will weather this storm and emerge strong. Richer."

She leaned forward, voice dropping to force them to strain to hear.

"They took my love. They tried to take my life. But they will not take our city." Building again, crescendo approaching. "For Diligence! For order! For Azoria!"

The crowd roared back, a wall of sound that shook the platform. She raised her good arm in triumph, silk sling dark against the dying light. This was power. This was control. This was—

Movement.

The abyss had a leather mask, and it stood guard in Prosperity Square.

Myrim—no, Balar—kept his position below the platform's eastern edge, scanning the crowd with mechanical precision. No one in the windows. Side streets were clear. The crowd was angry but controlled. No threats to concern him.

She is safe. She is the mission. Protect her.

Vivienne's voice rolled over the square like honey over broken glass. Each word calculated, each pause perfect. The crowd bleated back their approval, ready to follow wherever she led them. Even to slaughter.

Protect her. It is your purpose.

His hands rested on his knife hilts, the leather of his gloves creaking slightly. When had he last removed them? Days? Weeks? Time meant nothing in the abyss. Only the mission mattered.

"For weeks, a conspiracy has festered in our midst..."

Lars Harrow. The name sparked something deep, something that shouldn't exist anymore. A friend of the people he loved. Lover to the woman he—

No. That wasn't his thought. Was it? The voices blurred together sometimes, Balar's purpose mixing with Myrim's memories until he couldn't tell which was which. Easier not to try. Easier to just watch. Just protect.

"They showed us what they truly are. Not romantic celebrities or clever entrepreneurs. Terrorists. Killers."

Like me.

The thought came unbidden, sharp as the knives at his belt. He was a killer. What he used to call justice... what he called honor... none of it mattered anymore.

Now he killed for her. Because she owned him. Because he'd sold himself for the price of becoming someone else.

Protect her. She is order. She is purpose.

The crowd was chanting now, ugly sounds from ugly mouths. The Eyes of Azoria with their crude patches, thinking they were soldiers. Children playing at war, not knowing what real violence looked like. What it did to you. What it made you.

Movement on the western rooftop.

His body reacted before conscious thought, weight shifting, hand moving toward his knives. Just a bird. A gull looking for scraps. Nothing to worry about.

"The man who abandoned this city, who fled rather than face justice for his crimes..."

Thume. Another name that sparked echoes. His former boss, who'd promised order and delivered chaos. Just like everyone else. Just like—

Stop thinking. Watch. Protect.

But the thoughts kept coming, Myrim's voice growing stronger as Vivienne reached her crescendo. This was wrong. All of it. The mob she was creating, the fear she was spreading, the city tearing itself apart while she played conductor.

She murdered Diligence.

The image flashed unbidden: knife across throat, blood on marble, eyes going dim. Not an assassination. Not justice. Just murder, crude and personal.

Like you murdered for her.

How many now? He'd stopped counting. Faces blurred together, names forgotten as soon as the blood dried. All for her. All to protect the mission that was protecting her that was the mission that was—

Movement on the eastern rooftop.

Bird?

Not a bird.

A figure prone against the tiles, afternoon sun glinting off metal. The shape was unmistakable to someone who'd spent years studying threats. Long barrel. Stock pressed to shoulder. Musket.

Time slowed.

Balar tracked the angle, found the target. Not the crowd. Not the Eyes.

Her.

PROTECT HER.

His body was already moving, hands reaching for a weapon. Take out the shooter. Eliminate the threat. Save her because she is the mission she is order she is—

Lars.

The recognition hit like cold water. It was Lars Harrow with a musket, about to become something he'd never been before.

He's going to kill her.

Good. Let him try. I'll stop him. Protect her. It's what I do.

He was about to become a murderer.

So? We're all murderers here.

Lars was going to become like him.

The internal war exploded, two voices screaming different truths. This wasn't death. This was ruin of the soul.

Vivienne's voice rose toward climax: "They took my love. They tried to take my life. But they will not take our city."

The musket barrel steadied.

MOVE. NOW. SAVE HER.

"For Diligence! For order! For Azoria!"

The crowd's roar shook the square. Vivienne raised her arm in triumph, a perfect target outlined against the dying light. On the rooftop, Lars's finger moved toward the trigger.

Protect her—let him fire. Save her—save him. The mission—the man. Order—chaos. Everything he was against everything he'd been, tearing him apart from inside.

Choose.

He couldn't. Not between duty and conscience, not between Balar and Myrim, not between the abyss and the light.

His body chose for him. He moved. Toward her.

The musket cracked.

Sound split the world. The crowd's roar cut off like a severed throat. Time crystallized into this single moment: Vivienne triumphant. Lars on the rooftop, musket smoking. The ball spinning through air, trajectory true.

And Balar, Myrim... the thing he'd become. He was shoving her aside.

The musket ball found its target.

Not the killing shot Lars intended. Not the heart or head that would have ended everything. It found her arm, the ball tearing through silk and flesh as she spun from Balar's push. Blood spray painted the platform.

She screamed. From rage or pain, impossible to tell.

The crowd erupted. Not cheers now but panic, bodies crushing toward exits, Eyes reaching for weapons, chaos spreading like fire through dry grass.

On the rooftop, Lars was already moving, disappearing into shadow.

You saved him, Myrim whispered in the quiet center of his mind.

You saved HER, Balar snarled. *The mission continues. She lives. We succeeded.*

Both voices were right. Both were wrong. He'd saved everyone and no one, preserved both the tyrant and the thief's soul, changed everything and nothing.

Vivienne clutched her bleeding arm, face twisted in fury and shock. Her mask of calm was shattered.

"Find them!" she choked.

Balar stood in the center of the chaos, Vivienne's blood on his hands, watching Lars's escape route.

The square emptied in a flurry of screaming, running, and bleeding. An aide pressed cloth to Vivienne's wound.

Out there, Donovan organized the hunt, Eyes spreading through the streets like infection.

In the center of it all, a man in a mask who'd saved everyone and no one, standing still as stone while the world burned around him.

We should do something, he thought, and wasn't sure which voice said it.

Maybe both.

Maybe neither.

Maybe it didn't matter anymore.

LOSING GROUND

20

The musket crack split the air like the world tearing in half.

Trin's body moved before thought—dropping low, hand finding the knife at her hip, eyes already tracking angles and exits. The crowd's roar transformed in an instant, fervor becoming panic, bodies crashing together in waves of terror.

She, Jax, and Liora had tried to come after Lars, of course. The moment he had stormed out with that musket, they had rushed into the streets, desperate to stop him before he did something that couldn't be undone. But he'd vanished into the city like smoke, and by the time they'd reached Prosperity Square, Vivienne was already speaking and Lars was nowhere to be found.

In her heart, she had hoped the shot would never come. That Vivienne's speech would end with nothing more than poisoned words, and they'd all walk back to the Summer Home to find Lars there with the musket, filled with regret but safe. Unbloodied. Still himself.

But no. That's not what happened.

Beside her, Jax's massive frame turned toward the sound, one hand reaching protectively for Liora. The engineer was already in motion, her sharp eyes cataloging everything with that manic energy that emerged in crisis.

"There! Smoke," Liora said, voice clipped and certain. "Rooftop, northwest corner."

Trin turned towards the building and looked up.

Lars. He had thrown the musket aside and was running.

The dog pressed against her leg, hackles raised but silent. That dog was becoming her most important anchor to the world. He really deserved a name.

"Get the assassin!" The cry rose from somewhere in the square, picked up and echoed by a dozen throats.

But it was the next shout that made her blood run cold. "There! They're with Harrow! Get them!"

The Eyes of Azoria. Those crude patches that had seemed almost laughable an hour ago suddenly meant something terrible. They weren't fleeing like the rest of the crowd. They were organizing, moving with purpose through the panic, and their purpose was revenge.

Her mind flickered to what Lars had told them. Children playing at execution, rehearsing murder.

When had their city become a place where children gathered around makeshift gallows for fun? Where eight-year-olds wore Eye armbands and hunted people for bounty money?

She thought of all the street kids she'd known over the years. The ones who'd carried messages, picked pockets, dreamed of joining crews when they grew up.

What were they dreaming of now? Their first execution? Their first bounty?

"Trin?" Liora's voice cut through her thoughts, high and rapid. "They're coming this way. Why do they have clubs? Who brings clubs to a speech?"

"Move," Trin commanded, her instincts taking control.

They had to get away from Prosperity Square. West was the market, clogged with fleeing civilians. Those Eyes were coming fast from the center of the square. And she sure as hells didn't want to lead them back to the Summer Home.

She ran along a sidewalk on the perimeter of the square. The buildings were close together there, with a cramped alleyway in between. A fruit cart, abandoned in the panic, sat next to it.

"This way," she whispered, grabbing Liora's arm while Jax cleared a path with his bulk. As they passed the stall, she hooked her foot around its leg and sent it crashing down. Oranges and apples scattered across the cobblestones like marbles, and she heard the satisfying crashes and curses as the pursuing Eyes hit the obstacle.

Harold? she thought absently as they ran. *Is that a dog's name? No, my uncle was a Harold.*

"They're flanking," Jax rumbled, and she saw. More Eyes emerged from a side street, trying to cut off their escape. The big man was doing his best to look intimidating, shoulders squared and fists ready, but she caught the way his chest heaved. He was doing better, but the big man was still not at his peak.

"Not flanking," she corrected, pulling them further down the alley. "Herding. They want us to—"

A figure dropped from above like judgment itself.

Trin's mind reeled, bile rising in her throat and she sought to shield herself, her mind screaming that it was Balar. Come to take her back, come to put her back in that hole and lock her away forever.

But Trin's heart leapt when she saw it was Lars.

He landed in a crouch. "Run."

Lars didn't wait for questions, just turned and slammed his boot into a section of wall where the boards looked weathered and dark with rot.

The wood splintered on the first kick. On the second, it gave way entirely, planks cracking inward to reveal a narrow alley she hadn't noticed before.

"Lars, you absolute—" Trin started, anger flashing hot.

"Later," he cut her off, already squeezing through the gap. "Let's go."

They dove through the gap, splinters catching at their clothes. The narrow alley beyond stank of piss and rotting garbage, barely wide enough for Jax's shoulders. But it was empty, and more importantly, it led away from Prosperity Square.

Reacher! she thought as they ran, the dog's claws clicking on stone beside her. *I like that. Here, Reacher—*

No. That didn't feel right either.

"Are we heading toward the slums?" Liora asked. "I wonder if we can take the monorail line."

They burst out onto a wider street, and Trin's mental map of the city spun like a compass finding north. The old Bellway Theater, boarded up since the fire. The Drowned Cat tavern, which would be packed with day drinkers.

"No," Trin panted, "the monorail would be a very bad idea."

She'd never ride a train again.

Lars led them across the street at an angle that would make them harder to track. Behind them, she could hear shouts and the drum of boots on stone. The mob was gaining coherence, transforming from angry individuals into something more dangerous.

Lars kicked in the door of a house that had probably been beautiful once. Now it was all broken windows and water-stained walls, furniture covered in dust sheets like funeral shrouds. They piled inside.

"Get down," Jax ordered, moving to the window to watch the street. Everyone crouched below the sill. Through the grimy glass, she watched the Eyes stream past. Dozens of them now, ordinary citizens transformed into hunters by nothing more than cloth patches and Vivienne's words.

The dog pressed against her side, warm and solid and real. She scratched him behind the ears and hoped beyond anything that he didn't bark and give them away.

"I almost had her."

Lars's voice came out cracked, hollow. He sat with his back against the wall, staring at nothing.

"She's not dead," he said. He dragged a hand through his hair. "Hells, what have I done?"

Trin looked at him. Really looked. Saw the cage he'd been building around himself with every day of inaction, every moment of letting Vivienne write the rules.

And when he finally did make a choice, it was the wrong one. But she understood it.

The problem was that actions had consequences. She had escaped Myrim, and was labeled a conspirator.

Lars tried to take out Vivienne. The consequence would be like striking flint to a powderkeg.

"Flint," she said out loud.

Lars turned towards her, brow furrowed. "What?"

"The dog's name is Flint."

Liora's face split in two with a grin. "Flint!" she cooed, reaching out to pet him. He rolled over and showed her his belly, which she scratched obligingly. "I love it!"

"You missed," Trin said quietly to Lars.

Lars's laugh was bitter. "Barely. Balar pushed her. Saved her life."

"He might have saved ours too," Trin said. "Martyrs are harder to fight than tyrants."

Through the walls, they could hear the city screaming. Voices raised in anger and fear, the crash of breaking glass, the sharp whistle of the City Watch trying to restore order. Azoria was tearing itself apart, and they were huddled in an abandoned house like children hiding from thunder.

"We can't stay here," Lars said, looking at the street nervously. "They'll do a door-to-door search eventually."

He was right. Trin's mind spun through options, calculating routes and safe houses and—

A new sound blasted through the chaos. Deep and resonant, it rolled across the city like thunder from the sea.

"What is that?" Jax yelled, covering his ears.

Liora jumped up and looked out the window. "Dynamo amplification!" she said. "It has to be! Listen, you can hear the static in… in… well, in whatever that sound is."

"It sounds like a ship's horn."

Lars's head snapped up. "Thume."

Of course. Of course he'd choose this moment, when the city was wounded and bleeding. When Vivienne was vulnerable and the people were afraid. Cecil Thume always did have a talent for reading the board.

The horns sounded again, and this time they could hear something else beneath them. A voice, amplified to reach the people of Azoria.

Flint whined softly, and Trin rested her hand on his head. Whatever came next, at least she'd given him a name.

Blood poured between Vivienne's fingers, hot and pulsing with each heartbeat.

"Move! Clear the way!" Guards surrounded her, half-carrying, half-dragging her through the Gaming Commission's marble hallways. Her legs kept buckling—shock, her mind noted distantly. Their boots thundered on polished floors as the world tilted sickeningly.

This wasn't supposed to happen. The sling, the victim act—that was theater. Politics. This agony radiating from her arm was not.

"In here, quickly."

Someone kicked open a door. They lowered her into a chair and she nearly bit through her lip to keep from screaming. Blood was everywhere—her dress, the floor, dripping between her fingers despite the pressure.

A medic appeared, already cutting away her sleeve with scissors. "The ball's still in there," he muttered, probing the wound. White-hot pain shot through her arm and she couldn't stop the gasp that escaped.

The black silk of her fake sling was soaked red now. Where her carefully fabricated injury had been, a musket ball had torn through muscle and lodged against bone. She could feel it grinding with every movement.

"Hold her," the medic ordered. Strong hands gripped her shoulders as he poured alcohol into the wound. This time she did scream—a short, sharp sound she cut off with her teeth.

Years of practice had taught her to swallow pain, but this was beyond anything she'd trained for. Still, beneath the agony, fury built like pressure in a boiler.

Someone had dared. Someone had actually dared to—

"It was Lars Harrow."

Balar's voice came quiet from his position by the door. He stood perfectly still in that unnatural way of his, leather-wrapped hands clasped before him.

Lars.

The name crystallized her rage into something pure and cutting. Of course. Of course it was him.

The first time he'd hurt her had been last year—that elegant con, making her believe they were partners while he played her for a fool.

She'd felt something then, watching him work. Admiration. Perhaps even... but no. He'd chosen his little street rat over everything she'd offered.

But now this. A bullet in her arm, her blood on Gaming Commission marble.

"I need to extract the ball," the medic said, producing a terrifying set of forceps. "This will—"

"Do it."

What followed was the longest minute of her life. The medic dug into the wound while guards held her down. She felt the metal scraping against bone, felt the ball tear free from muscle, tasted blood from where she'd bitten through her cheek. When he finally held up the deformed lead ball, slick with her blood, her vision was swimming with black spots.

"Bone's cracked but not shattered," he muttered, packing the wound. "You're lucky—another inch and it would have destroyed the joint. But there's muscle damage. Significant."

He wrapped her arm in layers of bandages, then fashioned a proper sling—not silk this time, but practical canvas.

The irony wasn't lost on her. Her theatrical prop had become medical necessity.

"You need rest," the medic insisted. "The shock alone—"

"Help me stand."

Two guards lifted her to her feet. The room spun, and she tasted bile, but she forced her legs to hold.

One step. Then another.

By the time she reached the tall windows overlooking Prosperity Square, she'd found her center again, even as pain pulsed with every heartbeat.

Below, her city burned.

The riot had spread like spilled oil. She could see the Eyes of Azoria moving in packs, their crude patches making them easy to track. They dragged people from shops, overturned carts, set fires. The thieves had given them an excuse, and they were taking it.

Good. This was what she needed. Chaos that proved her point, violence that validated every—

She gripped the windowsill as the room tilted. Balar ran to her side.

A deep breath and her mind was clear again. The people would beg for order now. They would welcome whatever measures she deemed necessary.

Lars had shot at a leader and created a symbol.

He'd made it personal. Again.

Through the window's reflection, she caught Balar shifting his weight. Such a useful tool, even with his fractured mind. He'd saved her life with that push, turned a kill shot into a wound. A horrific wound, but she was still here.

Perhaps she'd reward him, somehow.

The city's screams rose like a wail of terror. Glass breaking. Wood splintering. The city watch yelling and blowing whistles. All of it serving her purpose, even as it spiraled beyond her immediate control.

Then—a sound that didn't belong.

It hit the Gaming Commission building like a thunderclap. Not from the streets but from the harbor. Ships' horns, but amplified beyond anything natural.

Her blood turned to ice.

Another blast, and with it now, a voice. Magnified by dynamo to reach far into her city. Words she couldn't quite make out yet, but the voice itself...

She knew that voice.

It was the voice of the man who had abandoned both her and her mother. Who deserved to rot in a prison cell. Who she despised with all her being.

Her reflection in the window showed something she rarely allowed anyone to see—her face twisting into pure, undiluted hatred. Not the bitter fury she'd felt for Lars. This was older, deeper, carved into her bones by years of abandonment and grief.

He'd chosen his moment perfectly, of course. The city in chaos, her control momentarily shaken, the people desperate for any alternative to the violence in their streets.

She turned from the window, the sling holding her wounded arm tight against her body. Pain pulsed with every heartbeat, but she transformed it into clarity.

"I want Harrow's head," she said. "And I want those ships at the bottom of the Azure Sea."

The guards nodded, already moving to relay orders. Balar remained still by the door, waiting.

Let them come. Let Lars think he'd wounded her. Let Thume believe he could reclaim what he'd thrown away.

She'd show them both what happened to those who stood against Vivienne Dragunova.

They couldn't stay hidden forever.

Trin led them out the back of the abandoned house, Flint padding silently at her heels. The riots had spread through the northern slums like a plague, turning familiar streets into war zones.

Smoke drifted from a burning shop two blocks over, the acrid smell mixing with something worse—fear, thick enough to taste.

"We need to get back," she said quietly. "If we can reach the foundries, we should be good."

Lars nodded and looked down the street. "So what's the play?"

They moved in formation—Jax leading, his bulk clearing a path, Liora in the middle with her sharp eyes tracking every movement, Lars and Trin bringing up the rear. It should have been a twenty-minute walk. Should have been simple.

Nothing was simple anymore.

They'd made it only three blocks when Trin heard it. Organized footsteps. Not the chaotic stampede of rioters, but the measured pace of hunters.

She grabbed Jax's arm, and all four of them squeezed into an alcove just as a group walked past. Ten people at least, armed with clubs and kitchen knives.

"—sweep every street between here and the east end," someone was saying. "Donovan wants them found."

Donovan? Not Vivienne or Balar. Trin didn't know who this new player might be, but she definitely didn't want to find out.

Flint barked at the men as they passed by. One of them sneered at the dog, but they kept moving.

"Go," she breathed once they were out of sight.

The crew slipped out of the alcove, heading toward the foundries.

But the streets were wrong now—every corner could hide an ambush, every shadow might hold someone who'd decided that crude patch made them a soldier.

They were still far from safety when their luck ran out.

"There!" The shout came from behind. "I see them! That's Harrow!"

Trin spun to see more thugs pouring from a side street. And at their head, a man wearing a military-style uniform, complete with a band around his arm bearing the Eye.

"Yeah," Liora squeaked behind her. "He looks like a Donovan."

"Run!" Lars shouted, unnecessary but urgent.

They bolted down an alley, feet slapping on wet cobblestones. Behind them, the mob roared like a beast scenting blood. Flint ran beside her, ears flat against his head but keeping pace. Her mind raced through escape routes but found none.

They turned down an alley.

It ended in a solid brick wall.

"Shit," Jax growled, spinning to face their pursuers.

Donovan and his mob filled the alley entrance, blocking any retreat. The man's smile was calm and satisfied.

"Nowhere left to run, you filth," he said, tapping a cudgel against his palm. Not like the crude weapons the rest of his gang carried. "Did you think you could commit treason and walk away? Did you think—"

The sound that erupted into the air was like nothing Trin had ever heard. Deeper than the last horn blast, loud as the end of the world, it rolled across the city with physical force. Windows rattled. Flint howled.

And then, impossible but undeniable, words followed the horn blast. A voice amplified beyond human limits, carrying clear across the city:

"Citizens of Azoria! I see your city burning…"

Donovan's speech cut off, his head turning toward the harbor. For a moment, hunter and hunted stood frozen, united in confusion. But only for a moment.

Jax moved first.

The big man grabbed the nearest Eye and slammed him into the alley wall with a crunch that made Trin wince. The impact broke the spell, violence erupting as the mob surged forward. But something else had caught Trin's eye—a ladder, rusted and forgotten, hanging from the building's side. It ended eight feet above the ground, but if they could reach it—

"The ladder!" she shouted.

But Donovan was already moving, cudgel swinging for her head. She ducked, felt it whistle past her ear, and then—

CLANG.

Liora stood behind Donovan, a length of pipe in her hands and fury in her eyes. The man crumpled, clutching his head.

"That's for calling us filth, you self-righteous prick," Liora snarled.

Hells, when had their engineer become so fierce?

"...dismantled by a tyrant and her pet assassin."

The voice boomed again, drowning out the mob's shouts. The deep and thunderous voice of Cecil Thume.

"Jax, the ladder!" she ordered.

The big man understood immediately. He reached up, grabbed the bottom rung, and hauled himself up with a grunt of effort. Three months ago, he would have made it look easy. Now, Trin could see the strain in his shoulders, the way his breathing came hard. But he made it, pulling himself up until he could brace against the wall.

"Come on!" He reached down.

Liora went first, Jax catching her hands and pulling her up like she weighed nothing. Trin followed, light on her feet as always.

The Eyes were recovering now, Donovan groaning on the ground while others pushed past him.

"Lars!" Trin shouted.

He stood at the ladder's base. "The dog!" he cried up at them. "We can't—"

"You're mine, Harrow!" Donovan slurred as he got to his feet. "Mine."

"I offer you a choice, friends, to bring down this vile usurper..."

Thume's voice filled the alleyway. Flint barked, the hair on his back standing straight up. He stood protectively in front of Lars, growling at Donovan.

But that didn't stop the mob. They closed in around their leader, advancing towards the protective dog. Trin's breath caught. "No..." she whispered.

Suddenly, the sharp crack of a musket filled the air.

Donovan dropped to the ground, a hole in his chest.

Trin looked towards the source of the sound, and found Darius. Standing on a nearby rooftop, coat whipping behind him, hand musket smoking as he aimed it at the other attackers.

What a showoff.

Still, it worked. The cowards ran, faced with someone they couldn't strike out at. And their leader was dead. Very dead.

"Darius, I love you," Liora squealed. "That was awesome."

The man grinned. "I was aiming for Harrow."

Lars barked a laugh as Flint jumped nimbly up some stacked crates and piles of trash, landing next to Darius on the squat rooftop.

Jumping up, Lars caught the bottom rung of the ladder. Jax grabbed his wrists and pulled, muscles straining.

And then they ran.

Across the connected rooftops of the old district, leaping narrow alleys and scrambling over dormers, they ran.

Below them, the mobs milled in confusion. Trin led the way, her mental map extending upward now—which buildings touched, where the gaps were too wide, how to angle toward the foundries without dropping back to street level.

The city spread beneath them like a wound. Fires dotted the landscape, orange flowers blooming in the growing dusk. She could see the Gaming Commission building rising above it like a white tooth, and beyond it, the harbor where dark shapes sat on the water. Ships. A fleet of them, bristling with purpose.

They paused on a flat roof to catch their breath, the foundry district finally visible ahead. Not safety, not by a long shot. But getting close. Almost there. Almost—

"Azoria will be mine again."

The final words from the harbor amplifiers hit like a physical blow.

Hells. Trin looked at Lars. There it was. The ultimatum. They knew when they sprung Thume that he'd be back. They didn't know he'd bring a damn armada.

"Two tyrants," she said quietly.

Lars's laugh was bitter. "And us caught in the middle."

"The story of our lives," Jax growled.

Liora still clutched the metal pipe, knuckles white. "I miss Keer," she said. "Maybe we should name the dog Keer."

Trin couldn't help but grin. She looked at her crew. Her family. Battered, exhausted, hunted by half the city. But together.

Flint pressed against her leg, tail wagging.

"No," she said. "He's Flint."

"Listen," Darius barked nearby, "this is sweet and all, but can we get back to the Summer Home? I'd rather not wait for Balar to show up."

Shit. Him. Donovan might have died easy, but Balar would not. And apparently, neither would Vivienne. They still had a whole city against them.

How the hells were they going to survive this? Could they?

"Come on," she said, standing despite her exhaustion. "Let's get home while we still have one."

GAINING PURPOSE

21

Two days. Two hells damned days of this madness, and Darius was ready to call it.

He stood at the window of the Summer Home's main room, watching smoke rise from yet another fire in the distance. The city was eating itself alive out there, and they were stuck in the middle of the feast.

Not that they'd been sitting on their asses.

His crew had been out just this morning, roughing up a pack of Eyes who'd gotten too close to the foundry district. Rurik didn't like being told what to do, especially not by amateur thugs with patches sewn on their sleeves. The big bastard had left three of them groaning in an alley, questioning their life choices.

And Inora. Well, she was Inora. She'd been coordinating with the other crews, setting up ambushes and false trails. She'd always been good at that sort of thing, thinking three steps ahead while everyone else was still trying to figure out step one.

Under her direction, they'd bloodied plenty of noses, made the Eyes think twice about pushing too deep into thief territory.

But it wasn't enough. Not even close.

"They're getting organized," Inora said from behind him, as if reading his thoughts.

She had a map spread on the table, marked with their skirmishes and the Eyes' movements. "Look at this pattern. This isn't just mob violence anymore. Someone's directing them."

Darius turned from the window. The main room was still lively—his crew, Lars's people, half a dozen others who'd stuck around.

They all looked like shit. Exhausted, bloodied, running on anger and stubbornness alone.

"Vivienne?" Lars asked from his corner. He'd been quiet these two days, brooding over his failed assassination attempt.

"Has to be," Shelle answered. She sat with Liora, their hands intertwined. "Though my network can't confirm anything. She hasn't made a public appearance since..." She gestured vaguely at Lars.

"Since I shot her," Lars finished flatly.

"You winged her," Darius corrected. "If you'd shot her proper, we wouldn't be having this conversation."

The room fell quiet at that. Until another one of Thume's horn blasts rolled across the city. The bastard had been doing it at random—middle of the night, dawn, whenever.

It kept everyone on edge. No more speeches though. Just those deep, threatening sounds reminding everyone he was out there with his fleet.

"Boss." Rurik's voice came from the doorway. The mountain of a man had fresh bruises on his knuckles. "Just came from the river. Eyes are massing near the old copper works. Dozens of them."

"Damn," someone muttered.

Darius looked around the room. At the tired faces, the wounded, the desperate. They were thieves, not soldiers. Good at getting in and getting out, maybe knocking a head or two along the way. But not prolonged warfare.

Time to say what everyone was thinking.

"We need to leave."

The words dropped like a stone into still water. Everyone turned to stare at him.

"Leave? And go where?" Lars asked. "The Summer Home is the best hideout we've got."

"No, I mean leave Azoria. Strategic retreat," Darius corrected, meeting his gaze steady. "There ain't nothing here for us, Lars. Can't you see that? We've got Vivienne's psychos hunting us, Thume's fleet blocking the harbor, and a city tearing itself apart. What exactly are we fighting for?"

"Our home," Shelle said firmly. "This is our city."

"Was," Darius shot back. "Was our city. Now it's a battlefield, and we're losing."

He moved to the map, pointing at Inora's careful markings. "Look at this. Really look. We can win fights here and there, bloody some noses, but then what? We're outnumbered a hundred to one. Maybe more. And that's just the Eyes. What happens when Thume makes his move? Or when Vivienne comes out of whatever hole she's hiding in?"

"So we just give up?" Trin asked. She stood near Lars, that new dog of hers—Flick or Fleek or Flint or whatever—at her feet. "Let them have Azoria?"

"They already have Azoria!" Darius shouted, startling everyone, including himself. The dog barked once at him then settled down again.

He sighed. "Look," Darius continued, "I love this city too. It's my home. But it ain't anymore, is it? We can't steal. Can't get out. We're gonna run out of food soon."

"I'm not running," Shelle said, chin raised. "They're not after me. I'm not a known thief. I've got businesses here, a life, a network—"

"A network that can't even find out what's going on with Vivienne," Darius pointed out.

"That's temporary. Once things calm down—"

"Things ain't calming down, Shelle." He softened his voice. She was a good woman, smart and tough. But sometimes smart meant knowing when to fold. "What exactly are we waiting for? If Vivienne wins, we're good and screwed. If Thume wins, we're most likely still screwed. All I'm saying is, let's wait it out somewhere we're not in constant danger of death."

"I'm staying with Shelle," Liora said immediately. "And they *are* after me. I'm on their lists. But if she's staying, so am I."

Darius wanted to grab them both and shake sense into them. Love was all well and good, but it didn't stop musket balls or lynch mobs. At this point, he'd seen enough good people die for bad causes to know the difference between bravery and stupidity.

"This is insane," he said. "We're talking about survival here. About living to see next week."

"Some things are worth more than survival," Lars said quietly.

"Pretty words," Darius snapped. "You planning to engrave them on our tombstones?"

The room erupted in arguments. Some sided with him—the pragmatists who'd survived this long by knowing when to cut and run.

Others wanted to fight, to defend what they'd built.

Through it all, Darius kept his eyes on Lars. The man looked... broken wasn't the right word. Bent, maybe. Like metal that had been heated and hammered too many times. The failed assassination had cost him something, some essential belief in his own judgment.

Another horn blast shook the windows, and the arguments died for a moment. As did some of their resolve.

"Two days," Darius said into the silence. "Two days we've been hitting back, and what do we have to show for it? Some bruised Eyes? Meanwhile, they're massing by the hundreds. Vivienne's planning something. Thume's waiting for his moment. And we're sitting here arguing about whether to die in here or die out there."

"You've made your point," Lars said.

"Have I? Because from where I'm standing, it looks like half this room still thinks we can win this. Like we're going to suddenly develop an army, or the people are going to rise up and join us, or some other fairy tale ending."

He turned to address everyone. "I'm not saying it doesn't hurt. I'm not saying it's fair. But sometimes the best heist is knowing when not to pull the job. Sometimes the smartest thing is to walk away with what you've got instead of losing everything trying for more."

"And what have we got?" Trin asked. "If we run now, what are we taking with us?"

"Our lives," Darius said simply. "Our skills. Each other. That's more than we'll have if we stay."

The room fell quiet again. He could see it in their faces—the recognition of truth, even if they didn't want to accept it. They were thieves, not revolutionaries.

Hells, they'd already toppled one tyrant, last year. And now he was back. Being asked to do it again, against two at once, with the whole city turned against them... it was too much.

"Where would we even go?" someone asked. "How would we get out? The harbor's blocked, the roads are watched—"

"We'll figure it out," Darius said. "That's what we do, isn't it? Find the impossible path? Pull off the unpullable heist? Well, here's our last job in Azoria. We break ourselves out of here before the hammer falls."

Shelle stood abruptly. "I'm not listening to this."

Liora followed her out, shooting Darius a look that could have melted steel. He didn't blame her. He was asking them to give up everything they'd built, everything they'd fought for. But sometimes that was what survival demanded.

"Well?" he asked. "Anyone else need to storm out dramatically, or can we start actually planning how to keep breathing?"

"You're a cold bastard," someone muttered.

"Cold bastard who's still alive," he replied. "Which is more than I can say for the warm-hearted heroes I've known."

Lars stood slowly, and for a moment Darius thought he was going to leave too. Instead, he moved to the map, studying Inora's markings.

"Give me one more chance to find another way. If I can't..." He met Darius's intense stare. "Then we run. Strategic retreat, like you said."

It wasn't agreement, but it was progress. Darius nodded. "Fine. But I'm gonna start planning the escape now. Not that I don't believe in you, but after this my crew is leaving whether everyone's ready or not."

"Fair enough," Lars said.

The meeting broke up after that, people drifting off in small groups to argue or plan or drink away their sorrows. Darius stayed by the window, watching the city burn.

He'd been called worse things than a cold bastard. Coward, pragmatist, survivor. All true, in their way. But he'd also been called smart, and right now, smart meant getting the hells out of Azoria before it became their tomb.

One more chance. Lars could try to redeem his blunder. But when the time came, Darius would be ready to run.

Because that's what survivors did.

The arguments had died down to murmurs and the clink of bottles. Bunny sat in his usual spot, a worn armchair that gave him a view of the room. Everything had gone crazy. Everything.

He still didn't regret joining the crew. Not for a minute.

That said, he'd been listening to them go round and round for hours. Windale this, Riverton that. All Ithrisian cities. All still within reach of whoever won the battle for Azoria. They were thinking too small, these people.

Lars and Jax had retreated to a corner, heads bent together. The boss looked hollow-eyed, while his big buddy seemed to be holding everyone up through sheer will. A couple other thieves sat nearby.

Bunny rose, joints protesting—too much sitting, not enough moving lately. He made his way over, noting how both men tensed before recognizing him. Everyone was jumpy these days.

"Hello, boys," he said, settling onto a crate across from them. "Jax."

"Bunny." Lars's smile was tired. "Come to tell me I'm an idiot too?"

"Nah." Bunny scratched his beard, considering his words. "Though that stunt with the musket was pretty foolish. Good thing I stayed back to keep the others from following your example."

Lars winced. "Following my example?"

"Yeah," Bunny said mildly, "half the youngins were ready to grab weapons and storm the Gaming Commission. I had to remind them that assassination ain't exactly our style."

"Apparently it's mine now," Lars muttered into a mug of ale.

"Once," Bunny corrected. "And you botched that. So it ain't who you are."

Lars only snorted in response. They sat in silence for a moment.

From across the room, someone laughed—a bitter sound with no joy in it. Another of Thume's horn blasts echoed across the city, rattling windows.

"Darius is right, isn't he?" Jax said finally. "We can't win this."

"Not here," Bunny agreed. "Not now. But that doesn't mean it's over."

Lars looked up at that. "So you want to run too, huh?"

Bunny leaned back, choosing his words carefully. He knew Lars was *really* gonna hate this idea. "Maybe. But everyone's talking about picking a city. But that's like jumping from one frying pan to another that ain't quite as hot yet."

"What do you mean?" Jax asked.

"I mean Vivienne's got reach. Thume too. Either one wins here, they'll end up with all of Ithris. Azoria's just the capital."

"So what do you suggest?" Lars asked. "We can't exactly sail off to Zarakar or Drakoria with Thume's fleet blocking the harbor."

"Don't need to sail." Bunny kept his voice casual, like he was discussing the weather. "There's always the mountains."

Both men stared at him.

"The mountains," Jax said slowly. "You mean..."

"Aelyndor." Bunny nodded. "My homeland."

Lars set down his mug with a soft thunk. "Bunny, no offense, but isn't Aelyndor full of—"

"Weird mountain people?" Bunny smiled. "Yeah, you've told me. But maybe we just prefer bastards who can mind their own business."

"But why would we—" Jax stopped, understanding dawning on his face. "They can't reach us there."

"Exactly." Bunny leaned forward now, warming to his topic. "Vivienne's got no influence in the highlands. Neither does Thume. To them, Aelyndor might as well be the moon. Or further. It might as well not exist."

"We've got the same issue though," Lars sighed. "I get it, but the only way there is by sea anyway. And again, an armada's in the way."

"For merchants, yes. Easier to sail than climb. But there's passes through the mountains. Secret tunnels. Not all easy ones, mind. South of Stoneford, where the peaks look like a wall." He grinned. "How do you think I got here in the first place? I sure as hells didn't swim."

The two men exchanged glances. Bunny could see them thinking it through, weighing options.

"I know it feels like running," he continued. "But it's just finding the right place to regroup. Think about it—clean mountain air, good food, people who won't sell you out for a few coppers. Time to plan properly instead of just reacting."

"Plan what?" Lars asked. "We can't stay in your highlands forever."

"You don't need to. Just long enough to figure out our next move. My folks, they travel down to Stoneford regular for trade. They could bring back news, keep us informed. We'd know when it's safe to return, or if it's better to move on elsewhere."

Jax was nodding slowly. "Food wouldn't be a problem?"

"Highland hospitality," Bunny said. "You'd be guests. We've got sheep, goats, grain stores. Might not be fancy city food, but it'll keep you strong. And the mountain air..."

He breathed deep, remembering. "It does wonders for clearing your head."

"How many could make the journey?" Lars asked, practical now.

"Depends. We're all young and strong. It's not easy—couple days through rough terrain, cold nights, thin air. But doable."

"When?"

"When you're ready." He paused. "But I'm not saying we should go. Just that we could. Options, chief. Good to have them."

Lars stood, pacing to the small window. Outside, another fire glowed in the distance. "I still have one more ace up my sleeve. And Darius agreed to give me a chance."

"And if it doesn't work?"

"Then maybe we take a trip to the highlands." Lars turned back. "You really think your people would welcome a bunch of Ithris thieves?"

Bunny chuckled. "Hey, you made me family. Might as well take a visit to meet mine."

"A visit," Jax murmured. "That's one way to put it."

"That's the only way to put it," Bunny said firmly. "We're not running. We're visiting. And when we're ready—refreshed, supplied, informed—we come back. Vivienne and Thume, they'll think we're gone for good. They won't expect us to return."

"The element of surprise," Lars said, something sparking in his eyes that had been missing since the assassination attempt.

"Exactly. Let them fight over Azoria. Let them think they've won. Meanwhile, we're in the mountains, getting stronger, making plans. And when the time's right..." Bunny grinned. "Well, highland fighters have been surprising you lot for centuries. No reason to break tradition."

Another horn blast, but this time it didn't seem quite so oppressive. They had an option now. A real one, not just running from one danger to another.

"And you know the way," Lars said.

"Like the back of my hand. Made the trip dozen times before I settled here." His voice went soft. "Always figured I'd go back someday. Just didn't think it'd be like this."

"Nothing's decided," Lars reminded him.

"Of course," Bunny agreed. "But might be wise to start gathering supplies anyway. Just in case."

Lars nodded slowly. "Thank you, Bunny. For..." He gestured vaguely. "Options."

"What's family for?" Bunny stood, stretching. "I'll let you two get back to your planning. But think about it. Really think. Sometimes the best way forward is up."

He left them there, already deep in discussion. The room around him was still full of arguments and despair, but now there was something else. A possibility. A path through the mountains that no tyrant could follow.

It wasn't much. But it was more than they'd had an hour ago.

And sometimes, that was enough to keep hope alive.

The morning sun shed distorted splotches of light through the Summer Home's dusty windows. Lars methodically sorted through supplies—rope, food, crystal charges. The kind of things you'd need for a mountain crossing. Or a last stand. Might as well be ready for both.

Darius had been right. Of course he'd been right. The cheeky bastard usually was.

Bunny too. His mountain pass was honestly the only move that made sense. Stay in Azoria and be constantly hunted, or leave and live to fight another day.

It really wasn't much of a choice when you laid it out plain.

They should have left two days ago. Right after his monumentally stupid attempt to put a musket ball in Vivienne.

The moment still played in his mind—the weight of the gun, the smoke, her scream. He'd tried to become something he wasn't. A killer. An assassin. As if doing it would somehow make him stronger.

Instead, it had just made him a fool with a gun.

Lars wrapped another coil of rope, checking for frays. The work helped keep his hands busy while his mind sorted through the wreckage.

This was a shit situation, no denying it. Their city was burning, their people scattered, their whole way of life dismantled by tyrants and mobs.

But they'd survived a lot over the years. Maybe not quite this bad, but...

They could make it work. They always had.

"Planning another assassination?"

He turned to find Trin in the doorway, arms crossed, studying his preparations. Flint padded in beside her, tail wagging when he saw Lars.

"Just the opposite," Lars said, gesturing to the supplies. "Getting ready to go. Being practical for once."

She moved closer, examining his work. "Mountain gear. So we're taking Bunny's route?"

"Unless you've got a better idea." He resumed packing, keeping his voice steady. "I told Darius I had one more move. I just don't have a lot of confidence in it." He held up a water skin. "So I'm packing what I can."

Trin picked up a coil of rope, testing its strength. "Very practical. Like the old Lars."

"Yeah, well." He set down the pack, finally meeting her eyes. "Seems I've been pretty bad at being myself lately too. Trying to be something I'm not instead of just..." He gestured vaguely. "Being better at what I really ought to be."

"A thief?"

"A man who deserves you." The words came out flat, matter-of-fact. "When thieving was banned for a year. When you were taken. When you came back. I was too busy feeling sorry for myself to see what you needed."

Trin set down the rope. "Lars—"

"You survived Balar. Survived torture. Came back stronger." He returned to his packing, needing something to do with his hands. "And what did I do? Moped around, then grabbed a gun and made everything worse."

"Are you finished?"

He looked up. "Hells, see?" he said. "I'm doing it again."

Trin stood there, not angry or sad, just... focused. Like she was looking straight through him to something deeper.

"Well, if you're done listing your failures," she continued, "I'd like to point out a few things. Starting with the fact that I'm not the same woman who got captured on that train."

"I know. That's what I'm saying—"

"Right, you're saying. You should try listening."

She stepped closer. "That woman was careful. Strategic. Quiet even. This woman?" She gestured to herself. "This one got taken, broken, and put back together wrong. Or maybe right. I'm still figuring it out."

Lars stopped packing, giving her his full attention.

"But here's what I do know," she continued. "You're a man of principles. Sometimes stupid principles, like thinking you could fix everything with a musket, but principles nonetheless. You care about everyone—sometimes too much. You've got grit when it counts and kindness when it matters."

"Trin—"

"And maybe you don't think you deserve me. Maybe you're right." Her voice dropped lower, fiercer. "But damn it, you're gonna try."

He opened his mouth to argue.

She grabbed his collar and pulled him into a kiss.

It wasn't gentle. It was fierce and claiming and absolutely certain. Her fingers tangled in his hair, holding him like she was afraid he might disappear. Or like she was making sure he couldn't.

He wrapped his arms around her tight, losing himself in her embrace. Losing himself in the taste of her lips. When she finally pulled back, they were both breathing hard.

"We're doing this together," she said, still gripping his collar. "The mountains, Aelyndor, whatever comes after. Together. Clear?"

Lars found himself smiling despite everything. "Clear."

"Good." She released him but didn't step back, studying his face with those sharp eyes that missed nothing. "Now tell me what your 'last chance' plan is."

He hesitated. "What makes you think I have a plan?"

"Because I know you, Lars Harrow. You've got that look. The one that used to mean you were about to do something clever and dangerous." She tilted her head. "So what's this play of yours?"

She had him there. "Thume."

The name hung between them like a dynamo spark. Trin's eyes narrowed.

"Thume," she repeated flatly. "The man whose armada is currently blockading our harbor."

Lars shrugged. "He offered us safe passage, remember?"

"Did he?"

He grinned sheepishly. "Well, not exactly," he admitted. "But Keer said that Mhalendra did."

"Lars..." She sighed, running a hand through her hair. "You want to sneak past a frenzied mob so you can board a ship and ask the man you sent to prison for a favor since his sister said he might grant it? That's your plan?"

"Yes."

She was quiet for a moment, then shook her head. "Okay. Why not. How would you even get to his ship?"

"Same way we always do," Lars said with a grin. "Carefully."

Despite everything, she smiled. "And if it doesn't work?"

"If Thume says no, we're off to Aelyndor. I promise."

"Together," she reminded him. "If you're boarding that ship, I'm coming with you. No arguments."

He knew better than to try. "Together."

Outside, another horn blast echoed across the city. But in this room, with one last card to play and the woman who'd chosen to stand by him, it didn't seem quite so final.

They had one more chance. One more angle.

The Summer Home's side door opened without a sound. Lars slipped out first, hood pulled low, scanning the alley. Empty. He motioned for Trin to follow.

They moved like ghosts through their own city. Two shapes among shadows, keeping to the narrow spaces between foundries where the moonlight couldn't reach. Their boots whispered against cobblestones slick with industrial runoff.

"Patrol," Trin breathed, pressing them both against a wall.

A dynamo lamp bobbed past the alley mouth. Eyes, from the sound of their rough laughter. Lars counted heartbeats until the light faded, then they moved again.

The foundry district gave way to broader streets as they headed north. Here they had to be more careful—fewer shadows, more lampposts. Lars's stolen factory worker's coat felt too thin, but it changed his silhouette enough. Trin had bound her hair and dirtied her face, becoming anonymous.

Gaming Commission headquarters was on their left, windows blazing with light even at this hour. They gave it a wide berth, cutting through a demolished lot that was soon to become a monorail station.

"Remember when we robbed the dynamo plant up here?" Trin whispered as they picked their way through rubble.

"Which time?"

That earned him an elbow to the ribs, but he knew she was smiling.

The northern slums pressed close—narrow buildings leaning against each other like drunks at last call. Perfect for disappearing, dangerous for the same reason. They stuck to the edges, two more poor souls heading nowhere in particular.

A shout echoed from deeper in the slums. Then another. Then silence.

They kept walking.

The air changed as they descended toward the Azure Sea— salt and tar replacing smoke and metal. Lars could hear waves now, the frantic squawks of gulls. His pulse quickened.

"There," Trin pointed to where rocks tumbled down to meet the water.

A small canoe rested against the stones, probably abandoned by some fisherman when the blockade started. Lars checked it over—solid enough, two paddles tucked beneath the seats.

"White flag?" Trin asked.

He produced a torn piece of sheet from his coat. Trin tied it to one paddle while Lars pushed the canoe into the shallows.

The water was cold, black as ink. They paddled in rhythm, not speaking now. Ahead, the sparse line of Azoria's defenders bobbed in the harbor—fishing vessels and merchant ships hastily mounted with cannons, their crews probably wondering what they'd gotten themselves into.

Lars adjusted their course, threading between two converted cargo haulers. A watchman's lantern swept across the water, missing them by yards. They held still, letting the current drift them past.

Beyond the makeshift navy, Thume's armada waited in perfect formation.

The lead ship grew larger with each stroke. Three-masted, built for war, not commerce. Its hull black as the water beneath them. Lars could see the banners now—at the mainmast, the mountain and lightning bolt of Zarakar, proud and foreign. But below it, catching the moonlight, hung another sigil.

The serpent-twined, golden scales of the Ithris Gaming Commission.

Figures moved on deck, watching their approach. This close, Lars could see the ship's guns—not converted merchant cannons but proper naval artillery. Thume was ready for war.

"Steady," Trin murmured. "Nice and easy."

A harsh light hit them when they were ten yards out. Lars raised the white flag higher, squinting against the glare.

"State your names and business!" The deep Zarakaran voice carried across the water with authority.

"Lars Harrow and Trinelle Meridia," Lars called back. "Requesting permission to come aboard. We need to speak with Cecil Thume."

Silence. The spotlight held them pinned like insects.

The voice returned. "Approach slowly. Any sudden moves and we open fire."

They paddled to the ship's side where a rope ladder hung. Lars went first, the ladder swaying with each movement. Hands hauled him over the rail, none too gently. Trin followed, graceful even climbing rope.

They stood on the deck surrounded by hard men with harder eyes. Swords and short muskets gleamed in the lamplight.

"Well," Lars said, attempting his old smile. "Is Thume aboard?"

"Lars Harrow." The voice came from the shadows near the quarterdeck—smooth, cultured, amused. "Still making dramatic entrances, I see."

Mhalendra Thume stepped into the light, and Lars was reminded why she'd been called the Jewel of Zarakar. Silk robes that caught the wind like water, dark hair pinned with gold, movements that turned walking into art. Even on a warship, she looked like she'd stepped from a palace.

"Lady Thume." He inclined his head. "Thank you for not shooting us on sight."

"The night is young." But she smiled as she said it, descending the steps with a particular grace that made everyone else look clumsy. "Miss Meridia. I'm glad to see you survived your ordeal."

Trin nodded, wary but respectful. "Lady."

Mhalendra studied them both.

"You paddle into a war fleet with a torn bedsheet for a flag," she said finally. "Either you're desperate or confident. Knowing your reputation, Lars, probably both."

"I prefer 'optimistically practical.'"

That earned him a laugh, bright and sharp. "Come. My brother will want to hear whatever brought you here."

She turned without waiting for a response, silk swirling. The sailors parted before her like water before a ship's prow.

Lars caught Trin's eye as they followed. She gave the slightest nod—still with him, still ready.

They made their way into the ship's hold, arm in arm.

A BRIDGE TOO FAR

22

Lars found himself, once again, face to face with ex-Lord Cecil Thume.

The man certainly looked more regal now, situated behind his mahogany desk in an opulent captain's quarters. Last time Lars had seen Thume, he was wearing prison garb.

Thume's desk was covered in maps and correspondence. His fingers steepled as he studied his visitors. "Lars Harrow. So good to see you again."

"Lord Th—" Lars began, but Thume raised a hand.

"I hear Balar still breathes." His gaze shifted to Trin. "Yet you escaped him. Impressive. Perhaps you have what it takes after all."

Back to Lars. "Unlike some."

Lars pushed past the insult. "We need your help."

"Obviously." Thume leaned back. "The Opaline Hall massacre. Vivienne declaring herself untouchable. The so-called

'Eyes of Azoria' running wild." He tilted his head. "And now you're all holed up... where exactly?"

"Doesn't matter."

"My bet is on the foundry district." Thume's smile widened at Lars's flinch. "Please. Give me some credit."

Hells, was it possible to have a simple conversation with this man? Why did everything have to be a hells damned game?

"Your sister promised us safe passage," Lars pressed on. "If we needed it. Well, we need it."

Thume's gaze flicked to Mhalendra, who sat near the door. She inclined her head slightly.

"I see." Thume drummed his fingers on the table, considering. The silence stretched until Lars wanted to scream. But finally, he answered. "I'll offer you protection."

Suspicion and relief warred within Lars. "Protection?"

"But."

Of course there was a but.

"You'll remain in Azoria," Thume continued. "You'll challenge Vivienne on my behalf. Rally support. Undermine her authority. Make it clear that the rightful order must be restored."

Lars felt his jaw tighten. "On your behalf?"

"Is there a problem with that arrangement?"

"We broke you out of prison." The words came out harder than intended. "That was supposed to earn us safe passage. Not conscription into your army."

"You also put me in that prison." Thume's voice remained pleasant, but steel lurked beneath. "Or have you forgotten that detail? You're fortunate I'm offering anything at all."

Lars forced himself to consider it. They wanted to stay in Azoria anyway. They were planning to fight Vivienne regardless. But doing it as Thume's puppet...

"Let's say we do this," Lars said carefully. "We bring down Vivienne and Balar, with your protection. You get your office back. What then?"

"Then you'll have your safe harbor. Copper. A ship. A new life in Zarakar."

Zarakar? What the hells was there for him in Zarakar?

"Why Zarakar?" Trin asked. "Azoria is our home. We wouldn't want to leave."

Thume didn't blink. "It *was* your home," he said. "And you'll help me win it back. But after that, Azoria will no longer require your presence."

"So wait a minute," Lars said, "you're just going to ship all of us across the Azure Sea?"

"No."

The word dropped like a stone.

"This offer is for you and your immediate crew only," Thume said. "The others must make their own arrangements."

Lars felt his hands clench. "That's a lot of people you're condemning—"

"Those people aren't my concern." Thume's voice remained mild, reasonable. "I'm offering to save you, Lars. You and yours. Because Mhalendra made a promise, and I honor my family's word. But I'm not running a charity."

"You're asking us to abandon our family." Trin's voice cut through the cabin. "To save ourselves and let them pay the price."

Thume's golden eyes shifted to her. "I'm offering you survival. Most would call that generous."

"Most aren't thieves of Azoria." Trin stepped forward, and Lars saw the steel in her that had survived Balar's cellar. "We don't leave our crews behind. That's not how we work."

"Touching. And where has that loyalty gotten you?" Thume gestured vaguely. "Hiding in warehouses? Watching your people hang from lampposts?"

"It's gotten us here," Trin said. "Still breathing. Still together. Still fighting."

Thume's smile was thin. "Fighting. Is that what you call it?"

Lars found his voice. "She's right. Whatever else we've lost, we haven't lost each other. I won't be the one to change that."

"No?" Thume looked between them. "Not even to save Trinelle's life? You'd rather watch her die for your principles?"

"Don't." Trin's voice went dangerously quiet. "Don't you dare use me as leverage. I make my own choices."

"And what's your choice, Miss Meridia?"

Trin didn't hesitate. "I choose to stand with all of them."

Lars felt a surge of pride and love so fierce it almost hurt. This woman who'd been broken and reformed, who had every reason to take the selfish path, had just told convenience to piss off.

Thume studied them both for a long moment. "How predictable. Choosing death over pragmatism."

"We're choosing life," Lars said. "Just not the kind you're offering."

"So be it." Thume turned back to his maps, dismissing them entirely. "Mhalendra will see you get back to shore safely. After that, you're on your own."

"Thume—" Lars started.

"We're done here, Harrow." Thume didn't look up. "You've both made your choice. Now live with it. Or die with it. Either way, it's no longer my concern."

Mhalendra rose from her seat, silk whispering. "This way."

As they followed her from the cabin, Trin's hand found Lars's. Not seeking comfort, but offering strength. They were in this together, or not at all.

The cabin door clicked shut behind Mhalendra. Cecil Thume didn't look up from his maps, but he could feel her studying him.

"You could have given them all passage," she said finally. "It would have cost us nothing."

"I could have." He traced a finger along the Azorian coastline. "But then Lars Harrow might start thinking too highly of himself."

"Brother—"

"He's already proven he can topple a ruler when properly motivated." Thume glanced up at her. "I have no interest in becoming his next target once the dust settles."

Mhalendra moved closer, silk rustling. "You see him as a rival?"

"I see him as a potential one. Him and the woman both." He leaned back, considering. "Did you know she comes from nobility? Her family is old blood here in Ithris."

"I wasn't aware."

"Most aren't. She's hidden it well." He returned to his maps. "Between his reputation and her lineage, they could prove... complicated. Better to remove them entirely."

"By sending them to their deaths?"

"By letting them choose their own fate." A slight smile. "If they had taken my offer, they'd have proven they're not the people I worried they were."

He picked up his pen, making a notation. "Have them followed. Discreetly. Find out exactly where they're hiding."

"And then?"

"Make sure the Eyes find out too."

Mhalendra stood there a moment longer, then moved toward the door. "I'll see to it."

The door closed, leaving him alone with his maps and plans. Lars Harrow and Trinelle Meridia. In another life, they might have been valuable allies. But in this one, they were far more valuable removed from the board.

The Summer Home loomed before them in the pre-dawn gloom, and Lars felt the weight of failure settling into his bones. Every step closer felt like admitting defeat. Beside him, Trin moved with the same exhausted determination that had carried them back through the city's hostile streets.

They'd played their last card and lost. Thume had shown his hand—not an ally, not even neutral, but another player in the game who wanted them gone.

Two enemies instead of one. The thought should have crushed him. Instead, it crystallized something. At least now they knew where everyone stood.

The door opened before they reached it. Jax filled the doorway, eyes wild with relief and fury.

"Where the hells were you?" He grabbed Lars by the shoulders, somewhere between a hug and a shake. "We thought—"

"Lars!" Liora came running around the corner, eyes red and glasses hanging precariously on the tip of her nose. "You jerk, we thought you were dead!"

Within moments, they were surrounded. Jax and Liora, Bunny grinning despite the tension, Darius trying to look annoyed but failing, Shelle and Inora pressing close. Their people. One crew. The ones Thume would have had them abandon.

Lars looked at each face and knew he'd made the right choice.

"What happened?" Darius demanded. "Where'd you go?"

Lars glanced at Trin, who nodded.

Together, they told their story. The desperate plan, the paddle through hostile waters, Thume's offer and its impossible conditions.

"He wanted us to abandon you," Trin said flatly. "Save ourselves, let the rest burn."

"Bastard," Jax growled.

"Maybe we could negotiate—" Liora began.

"No." Lars cut her off, gentle but firm. "He's shown his true self, like he always does. He's every bit as dangerous as Vivienne. Maybe more."

Silence settled over the group. Lars watched them absorb it—another door closing, another option gone. But instead of despair, he saw something else forming on their faces. Determination. Acceptance.

"So, Aelyndor then?" Darius said finally.

Bunny clapped him on the back hard enough to stagger him. "A climb through the mountains will put some meat on those scrawny bones of yours."

"Scrawny?" Darius protested. "This is called 'lean muscle,' you oversized—"

"Children," Inora said mildly, but she was almost smiling.

Lars felt something ease in his chest. They could do this. Not the way he'd wanted, not the solution he'd imagined, but a way forward. Sometimes that was victory enough.

"Final preparations, everyone," he said, falling back into the crew leader role. "We should head out tonight. After dark, when the patrols thin out."

They dispersed slowly, everyone understanding what came next. Packing what could be carried, destroying what couldn't, saying goodbye to the city that had made them.

Lars watched them go, these people who'd chosen each other over easy salvation.

Who knew what kind of nightmares they'd be facing in mountains and forests? It was a world as alien to Lars as the life of a noble. No cobblestones to know by feel, no rooftops to leap between, no locks to pick. Just rocks and trees and whatever else mountains had.

But damn it, they were going to make it work.

And they'd be back. However long it took, whatever they had to become to survive out there—they'd be back.

Azoria could count on it.

The crash came after midday from the main foundry door. Then shouting. Then the sound every thief knew in their bones—the synchronized stomp of City Watch boots.

Trin dropped the pack she'd been checking and ran to the window. Her stomach plummeted.

They were everywhere. A sea of blue uniforms and crude Eye patches, surrounding the Summer Home like water around a sinking ship.

"They're here!" someone screamed from below.

The room erupted. Thieves grabbed weapons, supplies, whatever they could carry. At least she and Lars had packed early—she snatched her ready bag and slung it over her shoulder. Flint pressed against her leg, growling low.

"Back stairs," she commanded. "Loading dock. Move!"

Lars appeared at her side, his own pack secured. "How many?"

"Too many." She did a quick headcount. Twelve of them in this room—Lars, Jax, Liora, Bunny, Darius and his crew, a scattering of others.

Where were the rest? Had some crews already run off?

No time to wonder. She led them to the back stairs through a wide passage meant for loading bulk goods. They descended a short set of stairs, the sounds of invasion echoing down the hall. Doors crashing open. Voices shouting orders. The whistle signals of a coordinated raid.

At the ground floor, she held up a hand. Through the door crack, she could see Watch officers flooding the main hall. Professional. Ready.

"Office exit," she whispered.

They crept through dusty administrative rooms, past empty desks and filing cabinets that had once tracked ore shipments. The old foundry bones of the building worked in their favor—multiple exits, loading bays, worker passages.

Another crash ahead. Three thieves from another crew came sprinting around the corner, eyes wide with panic.

"East bay's blocked!" one gasped. "Twenty Watch at least!"

Hells, Trin thought. Twenty at a single exit? This was madness.

"This way," Lars growled, diverting down another corridor.

They burst through a side door into the main smelting floor. The massive space still smelled of coal and iron, though the furnaces had been cold for years. More thieves scattered across the floor, all running for different exits.

"The crane doors!" someone shouted.

Bad idea. Trin could already see uniforms moving outside those massive openings.

"Waste chute," Darius barked, already moving. "Where they dump the slag."

Jax reached the rusted grate first, wrenching it open with a squeal of metal. The chute angled down into darkness, just wide enough for a person.

"You first," Lars said to Liora, who looked at the hole with wide eyes.

"Oh, you've got to be—" She didn't finish, just grabbed the edge and dropped. Her cursing echoed up the chute.

Bunny went next, then Maren clutching a satchel of charges. Trin scooped up Flint—the dog was brave but not stupid enough to jump into that darkness alone.

"Move!" Rurik bellowed from behind. The big man had positioned himself by the door, watching for pursuit.

Trin jumped.

The chute was slick with decades of industrial grime. She slid faster than expected, clutching Flint tight as he whimpered against her chest. They shot out the bottom into a pile of ancient ash and debris—Liora was already rolling aside, coughing and spitting.

"That was disgusting," the engineer gasped.

More bodies came tumbling down. Jax barely fit, his shoulders scraping the sides. Finally Rurik, who hit the ash pile like a meteor.

They were in the slag yard—mountains of industrial waste that had never been cleared. Trin scrambled to her feet, and started climbing the nearest mound. The stuff shifted under their weight, decades-old cinders cascading down.

"There! I see movement!" came a shout from nearby. Too close.

CRACK. CRACK.

Musket balls flew past, punching into the slag heap with puffs of black dust.

"Since when do they pack muskets?" Maren yelped, ducking low.

"Since now," Darius growled. "Keep moving!"

They half-ran, half-slid down the far side of the heap. The perimeter fence was just ahead—fifteen feet of rusted chain link.

Jax didn't slow down. The big man hit the fence at full speed, grabbed the bottom, and heaved. Metal groaned and bent, peeling up from the ground.

"Not enough," Inora said, dropping to her belly. She went first, squirming under the gap.

Trin shoved Flint through and then followed, gravel tearing at her clothes. Liora got stuck halfway, pack caught on a metal spur.

"Leave it!" Lars said.

"Like hell!" She twisted, yanked, and came free with a rip of fabric.

The industrial district opened up around them, filled with working foundries belching smoke. Workers stopped to stare as the pack of thieves ran past.

"Which way?" Bunny called.

Trin was at a loss. No way, it seemed. They had waited too damn long.

"Split up!" Darius barked. "Meet at—"

"No," Lars cut him off. "They're coordinated. They'll pick us off in small groups."

More thieves were spilling from the Summer Home now, using windows, maintenance hatches, any gap they could find. Some made it. Others ran straight into waiting arms.

A familiar figure caught Trin's eye—one of the Gimble brothers, cornered against a wall by six Eyes. He swung a crowbar desperately before being buried under bodies.

Nothing she could do. They ran.

Through the steam and smoke of working foundries, the pursuit wasn't just behind now. Whistles answered from the sides. They were the big prize, and both the Watch and the Eyes were coming to collect.

"East," Inora gasped. "Smuggler's Bridge. We need to cross the river. Lose them in the slums."

They turned south, feet pounding on cobblestones slick with industrial runoff. More thieves joined them as they ran—survivors from other crews, all fleeing the same direction. Safety in numbers, even if those numbers made them a bigger target.

Just past the corner was the old market square. Normally packed with workers buying lunch, now it was full of Eyes and Watch officers. A solid wall of bodies and weapons.

"Back," Trin said, but more whistles shrieked behind them.

"The loading alleys," Bunny said. "Between the warehouses."

They ducked hard left into a narrow passage meant for cargo carts. Industrial debris littered the ground—broken pallets, rusted barrel hoops. Behind them, boots thundered on cobblestones.

The alley forked. Trin went right on instinct, the others following. A dead end—except for a drainage tunnel barely three feet high, grated over but the bars were bent from years of local kids sneaking through.

"You're joking," Darius said.

"Crawl or die," Inora replied, already on her knees.

They crawled. Stagnant water soaked through their clothes, the smell making Trin gag. Flint splashed ahead, surprisingly eager. Maybe the dog had been a sewer rat in a past life.

They emerged in another alley, filthy and dripping. More thieves here—she recognized faces from other crews, all running the same direction. The Smuggler's Bridge, everyone's last hope to get out of the north end.

"Through here!" someone called.

An abandoned building's doors hung open. They rushed through, past vats of chemicals that made their eyes water.

Out the back, across a courtyard where laundry lines created a maze of sheets and work clothes.

Trin caught glimpses through gaps in the fabric—uniforms converging from north and east. They were being driven into a smaller and smaller space.

The bridge was visible now when they burst onto River Street. Old wood and rope swaying in the morning wind, the Ithris rushing gray far beneath it.

Very far beneath it. Trin shuddered.

But between them and salvation stood a grim line of Eyes, clubs raised. And from behind, the pursuit closing fast.

"Trapped," Rurik growled.

Not quite. Other fleeing thieves were hitting the same bottleneck, creating a desperate mass of bodies. The Eyes' line was thin—meant to delay, not stop entirely.

"Together," Lars shouted. "All of us! Break through!"

The mass of thieves hit the line of Eyes like a hammer against glass.

Lars threw his shoulder into the nearest guard, felt the man go down under the combined weight of desperate bodies. Clubs swung wildly but there were too many thieves, too much momentum. The line shattered.

"Go! GO!" someone screamed.

They poured through the gap toward the bridge. The old structure groaned as the first runners hit the planks—Trin in the lead with Flint, then Liora, Jax, Darius, and others. The wood sagged under their weight, rope railings straining.

Lars was in the second wave, Shelle beside him, Inora and Rurik just ahead. More thieves pressed from behind, everyone trying to funnel onto the narrow crossing at once. The bridge swung sickeningly.

"One at a time!" Bunny shouted from the middle of the span. "It won't hold—"

A musket cracked. A thief near Lars spun and fell, clutching his shoulder. More shots followed, the air filling with lead and splinters.

Lars looked back. The Eyes they'd broken through were regrouping, and behind them came more. So many more. At least two dozen Watch officers in neat ranks behind Eyes with their crude weapons. An army bearing down on a single narrow bridge.

They'd never make it. Not all of them.

He rushed past Inora. She looked at the offensive line, then back at her crew nearing the other side of the span.

Drawing a long knife from her belt, she stopped at the entrance where wooden planks met stone.

She turned to Rurik. "We hold them here."

The big man didn't hesitate. He nodded, like she'd just asked him to carry her pack. No questions, just action when action was needed.

Lars was acting on pure adrenaline. He was three steps onto the bridge when he understood. He looked back at them. Calm Inora, squat but brawny Rurik, positioning themselves at the bottleneck.

Two against dozens. Against muskets.

His feet stopped moving.

Don't be stupid, the rational part of his mind said. *You've got Trin. You've got a way out. Take it.*

But he'd been stupid so many times lately. What was once more?

"Lars!" Trin's voice carried from the far side. She'd made it across, was looking back. "Come on!"

He met her eyes across the swaying span. Saw Jax and Liora and Bunny safe on the far bank. Saw Darius organizing the scattered thieves, an unlikely leader in the chaos.

"Get them out of here!" Lars heard himself shout.

Then he turned and ran back toward Inora and Rurik.

"Shelle, go!" he barked as he passed her.

She'd been right behind him on the bridge. Should have kept running. Instead, she followed him back too.

"What the hells—" he began.

"I'm doing the same thing you are," Shelle said, drawing a hand musket from her coat. "Protecting the woman I love."

Four of them now. Lars and Shelle, Inora and Rurik, standing at the mouth of the bridge as death approached in a sea of patches and uniforms.

The first wave of street thugs hit them like a tide.

Lars had never been much of a brawler. That was Jax's domain as the company bruiser.

But desperation was a quick teacher. He grabbed a club from a fallen Eye, swung it in wide arcs to keep them back. The bridge entrance was narrow—only three could come at them at once.

Rurik was a wall of meat and fury, his massive fists dropping anyone who got close. Inora danced between attackers, her knife finding gaps in their guard. Shelle's pistol cracked once, twice, before she reversed it to use as a club.

They held.

For thirty seconds, a minute, they held.

Bodies piled at the entrance, making it harder for fresh attackers to reach them. Lars's arms burned from swinging the club. Blood ran from a cut above his eye where someone's fist had connected.

"Lars, you idiot!" Darius's voice boomed from across the river. "Get over here!"

A musket ball took Rurik in the shoulder. The big man staggered but didn't fall, grabbed an attacker and threw him bodily over the edge. It took a sickeningly long time to hear the splash from the river below.

Lars risked a glance back. Most of the thieves had made it across. The bridge was clearer now, just a few stragglers. They could run—

"We go together or not at all," Inora said, as if reading his thought.

More muskets were being brought up. Officers shouting orders, another layer of the firing line. Once that happened, once more volleys started, they were done.

Lars's blood went cold. He looked back and saw Maren on the far side, fumbling with something at the bridge's anchor point. A dynamo device that looked suspiciously like a—

"Maren!" Darius's voice again, urgent now. "Do it!"

No. No no no.

They were going to blow the bridge.

"Run!" Lars screamed, shoving Shelle toward the span. "NOW!"

But the Eyes pressed forward, emboldened by reinforcements. A club caught him in the ribs, driving the air from his lungs. He went to one knee, gasping.

Inora hauled him up. "Together or not at all," she repeated.

Through the mass of bodies, Lars caught sight of Trin on the far bank. Her face was a mask of anguish, hands gripping the rope railing like she might tear it apart. Flint barked frantically beside her.

I'm sorry, he thought. *I'm so sorry.*

A musket line was forming. Eight men raising weapons in unison. An officer with his sword raised, ready to give the command.

"Down!" Inora barked.

They dove as one, behind bodies, behind scraps. Lars hit the ground hard, scuffing his arm up on cobblestone and wood.

"FIRE!"

The world exploded in smoke and lead. Musket balls slammed into fallen Eyes, whined overhead, splintered the wooden bridge supports. A chunk of wood the size of Lars's fist exploded near his face, sharp fragments cutting his thigh.

Shelle cried out—not hit, but a shot had passed close enough to singe her sleeve. Rurik grunted as one caught him in the calf, punching through meat but missing bone.

Only Inora seemed untouched, already rolling to her feet as the smoke cleared.

"RELOAD!"

Moments away from the next volley. And more Watch with muskets joining the line.

"Maren, damnit! Now!" Darius commanded.

Lars heard it then—the telltale squeal of a dynamo charge building power. He'd heard it before, in heists, in desperate escapes.

Not his own escape, this time.

"The bridge!" someone in the mob screamed. "They're destroying the bridge!"

The Eyes surged forward, trying to cross before it was too late. Lars and his three companions were driven back onto the wooden planks by sheer weight of numbers. The structure groaned and swayed.

Ten feet onto the bridge. Twenty. Fighting every step, the churning void beneath them, enemies ahead and behind.

The whine reached a crescendo.

Lars looked back one last time.

He saw Trin screaming something he couldn't hear over the chaos.

He saw tears on Liora's face.

And he saw Darius, stone-faced, looking on.

The explosion started at the far anchor point.

It wasn't huge. Dynamo charges didn't make much of a bang. But any bang was enough. The old supports, already stressed by age and weight, snapped like kindling.

The bridge lurched. Tilted. Began its death fall toward the rushing water.

Lars felt the planks drop away beneath his feet. Saw Inora reaching for Rurik as gravity claimed them. Felt Shelle's hand grab his as they fell together toward the gray and turbulent embrace of the Ithris.

His last coherent sight was Trin's face across the widening gap.

At least they're safe, he thought. *I wish—*

Then the river took him, cold as winter's bite, and the world went dark.

The first wave was across. Darius counted heads as they stumbled onto solid ground. Trin with that dog, Liora white-faced and panting, Jax already turning back to help stragglers. Bunny. Maren clutching his satchel like a lifeline. Others from various crews, maybe thirty in total.

Not enough. Not nearly enough.

"Lars, you idiot!" Darius shouted across the span. "Get over here!"

But Lars wasn't listening. The fool had turned back, running toward where Inora and Rurik had set themselves at the bridge entrance. A bottleneck defense. Classic Inora, always thinking tactically even when it meant—

Darius's stomach dropped as he understood. They were buying time.

Dying to buy time.

More thieves were still trying to cross. The bridge swayed dangerously under the weight, wood groaning. On the far side, the mass of Eyes and Watch pressed forward, eager for blood. Cudgels, blades, and muskets gleamed in the afternoon light.

Darius saw Lars reach Inora and Rurik. Watched Shelle follow him back instead of crossing to safety. Four of them now, holding the entrance against dozens.

The tactical part of his brain—the cold part that had kept him alive through years of thievery—was already doing the math. Four defenders. Maybe twenty attackers visible, more coming. The bridge could collapse any moment under this strain. Even if it held, those muskets would—

A shot cracked out. Rurik staggered as the ball took him in the shoulder, but the big man didn't fall. Instead, he grabbed an attacker and hurled him bodily into the river below.

They couldn't hold the bridge. There was no way.

Darius looked at Maren. "Can you drop it?" he asked quietly.

Maren's eyes went wide. "Drop—but there's still—"

"Can you?"

The boy swallowed. Nodded. "The supports are already stressed. Wouldn't take much. But Darius, our people—"

"I know."

He did know. Knew exactly what he was about to do. The weight of it sat in his chest like lead, but the choice was clear. Save four and lose everyone, or lose four and save thirty.

"Get it ready," he said.

Maren pulled a device from his bag, hands already working at the components.

"No!"

Liora's comprehension was instant. She lunged at Darius, hands reaching for his throat. "Shelle's still there! You can't—"

Jax caught her, wrapped his massive arms around her as she fought like a wildcat. But even as he held her back, the big man looked at Darius with something like horror.

"You can't do this," Jax said.

Darius didn't answer. He couldn't. If he spoke, if he let himself think too hard about what he was ordering, he might hesitate.

And hesitation would kill them all.

On the far side, a proper firing line was forming. Eight muskets raising in unison. An officer with his sword raised, ready to give the command.

"Maren!" Darius yelled. "Do it!"

But Maren hesitated, the device trembling in his hands as he looked at the four defenders.

"Down!" He heard Inora's shout even across the distance.

The defenders dove. Musket balls slammed into bodies and wood, sending splinters flying. When the smoke cleared, all four were still moving—injured but alive.

For now.

"RELOAD!" The shout from across the river. Twenty seconds until the next volley. And he could see more Watch joining the line, more muskets being brought to bear.

The four defenders were being driven back onto the bridge itself, the mob pressing forward. The structure groaned ominously.

"Maren, damnit! Now!"

Tears streamed down the boy's face as he connected the final wire. The charge began its telltale whine, building power.

"The bridge!" Someone in the mob screamed the warning. "They're destroying the bridge!"

The Eyes surged forward desperately. Lars and the others were driven further onto the span, fighting every step. Ten feet out. Twenty. The wood sagging under the weight of combat.

So close. But not close enough. Darius made himself watch. Made himself see what his choice meant.

He saw Lars look back one last time, saw him spot Trin on their side. Saw understanding dawn on his face.

He saw Shelle reaching for one more shot with her hand musket.

He saw Rurik, blood streaming from multiple wounds, still swinging those massive fists.

He saw Inora, calm as always, fighting like she'd already accepted what was coming.

The whine reached its peak.

"Trin," Darius said quietly. "You might want to—"

She wasn't listening. Her knuckles were white on the rope railing, her whole body straining forward like she might will Lars across through sheer desire. The dog leaned against her leg, whining.

The explosion was smaller than Darius expected. Just a sharp crack, like a tree branch breaking. But the weak supports, already pushed beyond their limits, gave way instantly.

The bridge lurched and began its final fall.

Darius saw Lars's face in that last moment, looking not at the river below but at Trin. Saw him mouth something that might have been her name.

Then they were falling. All of them—Lars and Shelle, Inora and Rurik, the Eyes who'd gone too far onto the bridge. The whole span collapsed into the Ithris, bodies and wood tumbling into the gray water.

The silence after was deafening.

Then Liora screamed. Not a word, just pure anguish as she watched the spot where Shelle had vanished. Jax still held her, but gently now, like she might shatter.

Trin hadn't made a sound. She stood frozen at the river's edge, staring at the churning water where the bridge had been. Flint pawed at her leg, whimpering.

On the far bank, the remaining Eyes and Watch milled in confusion. Some took potshots across the water, but the thieves were already out of the line of fire.

"We need to move," Darius said. His voice came out steady, which surprised him. "They'll send runners to circle around."

No one moved.

"I said—"

The slap caught him completely off-guard. Trin's palm cracked across his face hard enough to snap his head sideways. He tasted blood where his teeth cut his cheek.

He turned back to face her, didn't raise a hand to defend himself. Her eyes were wild, tears streaming down her face. She'd lost that careful control she always maintained.

She slapped him again. Harder.

His ears rang. Still he just looked at her, waiting.

"Trin—" he started.

She went for a third strike. This time he caught her wrist, gentle but firm.

"I think that's good for now."

Flint snarled, lunging forward with teeth bared. At the same moment, Jax's hand clamped on Darius's arm.

"Enough," the big man said, yanking Darius's hand away from Trin.

Darius let go immediately. Looked from Trin's devastated face to the gray water where four of their people had vanished. His eyes burned, and he realized with distant surprise that they were wet.

"Yeah," he said quietly. "Enough."

Trin turned away from him, walked to the river's edge. She stood there, scanning the water desperately. Looking for heads breaking the surface, for survivors clinging to debris.

Nothing. The Ithris had taken them all.

"You can hate me later," Darius said to the group. "All of you can hate me for the rest of your lives if you want. But right now, we need to move. Would be a real waste if they caught us after... this."

"Bastard," someone muttered.

He didn't argue. Just started walking south, into the relative safety of the alleyways. After a moment, the others followed. What choice did they have?

Lowtown opened up before them—narrow streets and cramped buildings, washing lines strung between windows, the smell of poverty and desperation. But also anonymity. The Eyes wouldn't find them easily here. Too many alleys, too many people who minded their own business.

Why hadn't they come here in the first place? Set up in some forgotten Lowtown warehouse instead of the Summer Home?

Because they'd thought Azoria belonged to them. Still theirs despite everything—the ban, Vivienne's rise, Thume's return. They'd held on to that belief right up until the city proved them wrong.

Stupid. Stupid and proud and now four of their best were gone because of it.

They moved in silence through Lowtown's maze. Darius led from instinct, taking turns that would confuse any pursuit. The locals watched them pass, but not a one came after them. Lowtown had its own relationship with authority, and it didn't include cooperation.

Trin walked like a ghost, Flint pressed close to her side. She hadn't spoken since the river. Liora stumbled along in Jax's protective shadow, her face blank with shock. The others spread out behind, a ragged parade of survivors.

They reached the eastern walls as the sun moved toward the horizon. Here, where Lowtown petered out into open plains, an old man kept a stable and rented carriages to those making the trip east.

"How many?" the stableman asked, eyeing their group.

"Three carriages," Darius said, pulling out his purse. "Your best horses."

"Going far?"

"Far enough."

The old man looked Darius up and down. "I need to know where, son. Can't rent you a carriage I can't get back, can I?"

Hells sake. Okay. "Stoneford," he grumbled.

"Weren't so hard, were it? That'll be twenty copper."

Darius counted out coins with steady hands. Twenty copper—a fortune by Lowtown standards, but the man just nodded and led them to the carriages.

"They'll get you to Stoneford," the stableman said. "Turn 'em in with Lou's Mercantile once you get there."

They divided up without discussion. Trin climbed into the first carriage, Flint jumping up beside her. Bunny followed— quiet support without words.

Jax helped Liora into the second carriage, her movements mechanical with grief. Maren climbed in after them, still clutching his satchel, tears dried but eyes haunted.

That left Darius with the third carriage and the remaining thieves who didn't split off somewhere in Lowtown. Maybe eight survivors from various crews, all looking lost.

"Look," Darius said to them. "You can join us to Stoneford. After that, who knows."

They piled into the carriages without argument, grateful for any direction.

Some he recognized, others were just faces in the crowd of people he'd saved at such horrible cost.

He climbed into the last carriage alone, flicked the reins. The wheels began to turn, carrying them away from Azoria.

Away from the river. Away from home.

The carriages rolled east toward Stoneford, and Darius sat alone on the driver's bench, reins steady in his hands. Behind him, the city's smoke still rose in columns, but from here it looked almost peaceful.

But in his mind, he could still see Lars's face. Still hear the bridge cracking. Still feel Trin's palm across his cheek.

Some things you carried with you no matter how far you ran. The weight of necessary choices. The faces of the people you couldn't save.

The knowledge that being right didn't make you any less of a bastard.

He clicked his tongue at the horses, urging them faster, and didn't look back again.

EPILOGUE

23

The city burned.

From Vivienne's office windows, Balar watched the orange glow paint patterns across Azoria's skyline. Some fires were dying now, others just catching. The mob had exhausted itself hours ago, but the embers of their rage still smoldered in a dozen different districts.

This new Azoria. Vivienne's Azoria.

He catalogued the changes. Gaming Commission checkpoints at every major intersection. Eyes of Azoria patrolling in units instead of random mobs. The harbor locked down tight, Thume's ships dark shadows on the water. That standoff was still to come.

The thieves were gone. Scattered like roaches. It's something he'd always wanted to see when he was still Myrim.

He'd watched it happen from his post at Vivienne's side. The raids. The chases. But his sight only went so far.

Balar had no idea what had happened to Harrow. To Liora.

Liora...

Stop.

He stopped. Always stopped when that command came, whether from Vivienne's lips or his own fractured mind.

The name tried to worm its way back into his brain. Liora with her bright eyes and clever hands. Who had looked at him with such horror at the Opaline Hall, seeing what he'd become.

He had a new mission now. Protect Vivienne. Protect order. Protect Azoria.

The door opened behind him. He didn't turn. But he listened to the footsteps, noted the gait. One of Vivienne's coordinators, nervous.

"Madam," the man said. "We have confirmation from the river."

Vivienne sat at her desk, arm still in its sling. She was fine right now, with work to keep her occupied. But she moaned at night. A musket wound had to heal from the inside out, and it had to hurt.

Balar worried about his mistress.

"Report," Vivienne said without looking up.

"The bridge was destroyed. By the thieves. We're planning an operation to pull bodies from the water."

Something cold settled in Myrim's chest. He kept staring out the window, watching the fires.

"Lars Harrow is dead," the coordinator continued. "Positive identification from multiple witnesses who saw him fall."

The cold spread. Lars, who'd tried to kill Vivienne. Who'd failed, but tried.

What about Liora?

What? It didn't matter—

But Balar found himself jumping up and stalking toward the man. "And Liora? Is Liora dead?" he growled, his voice muffled through the mask.

"Stop." Vivienne said it firmly, raising her head.

He stopped instantly.

Vivienne gave him a stern look, but turned to the coordinator. "Who else do we know is dead? In Harrow or Adalan's crews."

"Well, Lars, as I said. Um. Two from Adalan's crew. Inora Wolten and Rurik Abarca. And an independent. Shelina Halmuth. A spymaster."

Oh hells. Oh hells. Shelle.

The name hit Myrim like a physical blow. Shelle, who sang off-key in the mornings. Shelle, who kissed like she was drowning. Shelle, who'd loved him...

"That will be all," Vivienne said.

The coordinator fled, casting one terrified glance back at Balar.

Vivienne returned to her desk, but her eyes stayed on him. "Interesting," she said.

Balar said nothing, stood silent. But inside, Myrim wept. Shelle was dead. Fallen into the river because he'd helped create this world where thieves were hunted like animals. Because he'd chosen to become Vivienne's weapon instead of staying with the people who loved him.

"You may return to your post," Vivienne said finally.

He moved back to the window, resuming his vigil. Outside, Azoria continued its transformation into something harder, colder, more controlled. The fires were dying now, leaving only darkness behind.

Shelle. Liora.

No, they were gone. One way or the other.

The city settled into uneasy sleep, and Balar stood watch while Myrim mourned. Two souls in one body, both trapped by choices they couldn't unmake.

The morning mist hung low over the water, turning the world soft and gray.

Edmund liked these early mornings best, when the estate was still sleeping and he could pretend he was an explorer discovering new lands. The grass was wet with dew, soaking through his fine leather shoes, but Mother wasn't awake yet to scold him for ruining them.

He was hunting for ghost crabs today. They came out when the tide was low, scuttling sideways across the mudflats where the Ithris widened into the Azure Sea. If you were quick—really quick—you could catch one before it disappeared into its hole.

There! A flash of pale shell near the reeds. Edmund crept forward, hands cupped and ready. The crab sensed him, freezing for a moment before darting toward the water. He lunged, missed, and landed on his knees in the mud.

"Oh hells," he muttered, then giggled. Mother would wash his mouth out if she heard him cursing like that.

He was about to chase after another crab when he heard it— a soft splashing from deeper in the reeds. Too big for a crab. Maybe a river otter? Or one of those huge carp Cook was always hoping to catch for dinner?

Edmund pushed through the tall grass, following the sound. The reeds were thicker here, taller than his head. They whispered as he moved through them, like they were telling secrets.

The splashing came again, closer now. He parted the last curtain of reeds.

Fabric. Waterlogged and dark, caught on a fallen branch.

Well that was boring. Someone must have lost their coat in the river. But maybe there'd be coins in the pockets, or—

The fabric moved, and he saw the hand.

Pale. Still. The fingers slightly curled like they were holding something invisible.

Edmund's chest went tight. This wasn't a ghost crab. This was a dead person.

He saw the others then. Four shapes twisted together by the river's current and caught in the reeds like driftwood. Their clothes were fine—or had been, before the water. One of the men had dark hair plastered to his head. One of the women had her arm stretched out like she'd been reaching for something.

Edmund stumbled backward, a sound coming from his throat that wasn't quite a scream. His heel caught on a root and he fell, scrambling in the mud, never taking his eyes off those still, pale faces.

"Dad!" The word tore out of him. "Dad, come quick! DAD!"

He ran. Slipping in the mud, crashing through the reeds, leaving one shoe behind and not caring. Up the lawn toward the big house where windows were just starting to show lamplight.

"DAD!"

The patio door opened. Father stood there in his burgundy silk robe, hair still mussed from sleep.

"Edmund? What in the—boy, you're filthy! What are you doing?"

"By the water," Edmund gasped, pointing back toward the reeds. "There's—there's people. They're not moving. They're just—"

Father's expression shifted from annoyance to concern. "Show me."

Edmund didn't want to go back. But Father's hand was on his shoulder, firm and guiding, and somehow his legs carried him down the lawn again. The mist was lifting now, the world gaining hard edges.

"This isn't a joke, is it? Because—"

But then Father saw them. His words died, his face draining of color like water from a cup. He stood frozen for a moment, then walked slowly to the riverbank. His expensive slippers squelched in the mud, but he didn't seem to notice.

Edmund watched his father kneel by the bodies, studying the face of the dark-haired man. Father's hands hovered over the still form but didn't quite touch, like he was afraid of what he might find.

"Oh my…" Father's voice was strange. Hushed. "It's him. It's really him."

His head snapped up, looking around frantically. The estate was isolated, no neighbors for miles, but still he checked.

"Who is it, Dad? Who are they?"

Father didn't answer. He was staring at the bodies like they were a puzzle he couldn't solve.

"Are they dead?" Edmund whispered.

Father stood abruptly, mud on the knees of his fine robe. He grabbed Edmund's shoulders, turned him away from the water.

"Later," he said, his voice low and urgent. "Let's get them inside."

"Inside?" Edmund didn't understand. "But shouldn't we—"

"Now, Edmund."

There was something in Father's voice that killed all argument. Edmund had heard that tone exactly twice before—once when thieves were raiding the vault room, and once when Mother had taken fever and the physician had been whispering in the halls.

Father was already moving, calling for the servants in a voice that carried command. "Hake! Clara! Bring canvas and rope. Quickly now. And send someone for Doc Farrow. Tell him it's urgent. Tell him…" He paused, glanced back at the reeds. "Tell him to come alone and use the back entrance."

Edmund stood shivering in his wet clothes, watching the house come alive with urgent activity. He didn't understand what was happening. Didn't understand why Father looked excited and terrified at the same time. Didn't understand why they were bringing those still, pale people into their home instead of calling for the City Watch.

But he understood one thing, from the way Father kept glancing at the road, from the way he made the servants swear to silence.

Whatever Edmund had found in the reeds, it was Serious Business.

The mist cleared completely as they carried the bodies up the lawn, revealing a perfect morning. It would have been a great day for playing outside, all day. But now there was something far more interesting—

Edmund's thoughts came to a halt as he saw one of them move. Just slightly, just an arm twitching.

But that was impossible.

Wasn't it?

From the Archives of The Azoria Star

This article was published on the front page three days after the apprehension of Lord Cecil Thume and the subsequent appointment of Vivienne Dragunova as Interim Chairwoman of the Ithris Gaming Commission.

COMMISSION ISSUES UNPRECEDENTED ONE-YEAR MORATORIUM ON SANCTIONED THIEVING

Interim Chairwoman Dragunova Cites "Critical Need for Stability" in Wake of Recent Upheaval

By Marinda Kelway

AZORIA—In a sweeping and decisive first act, the Ithris Gaming Commission, under the new leadership of Interim Chairwoman Vivienne Dragunova, has issued an immediate, city-wide moratorium on all sanctioned thieving activities. The decree, effective at sunrise this morning, suspends the core tenets of the Sanctioned Heists Act for a period of no less than one year.

The move comes amidst a period of profound uncertainty for Azoria, following the shocking revelation of former Chairman Cecil Thume's criminal enterprises and his subsequent arrest. While the city has largely praised the efforts of those who brought Thume's corruption to light, the resulting power vacuum has left many citizens and business owners concerned about the potential for escalating chaos.

"Azoria needs a moment to breathe," Chairwoman Dragunova stated in an exclusive address from the Commission headquarters. "The events of the past weeks have shaken the very foundations of our city. The laws that were meant to provide structure and balance were exploited from the very top. We cannot simply continue with business as usual while the rulebook is so fundamentally broken."

The Chairwoman framed the ban not as a punishment, but as a necessary "civic pause" to allow for recovery and reform.

"Our city's greatest strength is its ingenuity and ambition," she continued, her tone calm and reassuring. "For too long, that energy has been focused on a cycle of taking. For the next year, let us refocus that energy on building. Let us channel our ambition into projects that will move Azoria forward for everyone. Projects like the proposed monorail, which promises a new era of connectivity and commerce, an era of uninterrupted progress."

The moratorium has been met with a mixture of reactions. Hinde Portlun, a provisions merchant in the northern districts, expressed a sentiment of cautious relief. "Things have felt... unsteady," she said. "If this gives the Watch a chance to get its footing and ensures things don't fly off the rails, then it's a price worth paying."

Leaders of the major thieving crews, including the recently prominent Lars Harrow and Darius Adalan, have thus far remained silent on the edict. A source within the City Watch suggested the crews are "disorganized and in disarray," lending credence to the Commission's position that the system is currently too volatile to sustain.

Chairwoman Dragunova was clear that the ban is a temporary, restorative measure. "This is not the end of the game," she assured the public. "It is an intermission. A time to repair the stage, rewrite the rules for fairness and transparency, and ensure that when the curtain rises again, it rises on an Azoria that is stronger, more stable, and more prosperous than ever before."

For now, the city will need to wait to see what this means for the common welfare. Azoria's celebrity thieves have retreated to the shadows, and for the first time in more than thirty years, the news cycle of heists has come to a halt. All eyes are on the Commission and its new, determined leader to see what kind of Azoria will emerge from the silence.